Mandy Magro lives in Cairns, Far North Queensland, with her husband, Billy, and her daughter, Chloe Rose. With pristine aqua-blue coastline in one direction and sweeping rural landscapes in the other, she describes her home as heaven on earth. A passionate woman and a romantic at heart, she loves writing about soul-deep love, the Australian rural way of life and all the wonderful characters who live there.

www.facebook.com/mandymagroauthor

www.mandymagro.com

Also by Mandy Magro

Driftwood
Country at Heart
The Wildwood Sisters
Bluegrass Bend
Walking the Line
Along Country Roads
Moment of Truth
A Country Mile
Rosalee Station
Return to Rosalee Station
Jacaranda
Flame Tree Hill

MANDY MAGRO

Secrets of Silvergum

★ mira

First Published 2019
First Australian Paperback Edition 2019
ISBN 9781489252722

Published by
Mira
An imprint of Harlequin Enterprises (Australia) Pty Limited
(ABN 47 001 180 918), a subsidiary of HarperCollins Publishers
Australia Pty Limited (ABN 36 009 913 517)
Level 13, 201 Elizabeth St
SYDNEY NSW 2000
AUSTRALIA

A catalogue record for this book is available from the National Library of Australia
www.librariesaustralia.nla.gov.au

Printed and bound in Australia by McPherson's Printing Group

MIX
Paper from
responsible sources
FSC® C001695

For my amazing husband, Billy Anderson – you rock my world, in so many breathtaking ways! Xx

No matter how far or fast you run,
your past will always catch up to you …

PROLOGUE

With Emma Kensington cradled in his arms, Zane Wolfe stared in shock and horror at the blood pooling by his bare feet. He'd been sleeping soundly until he'd heard Emma's screams, and now there was a dead man on the kitchen floor. He just thanked god she'd been able to defend herself – he couldn't stand to think of anything terrible happening to her. Ever.

He looked to where Peter and Michael were huddled, whispering between themselves. *What in the hell was going on?* 'What are you two doing? We have to call the police,' he growled, as he snatched the phone off the kitchen bench. 'Right now!'

'No, Zane, you don't want to go and do that,' Peter boomed, waving his hands about, trying to stop him from dialling 000.

Incredulously, Zane shook his head. 'Why?' Emma was shaking like a leaf, and he pulled her in tighter, wishing he could ease her anguish.

'Because, if you do …' Peter rubbed his face, huffed, stepped over the crumpled body, and came to rest his hands on Zane's shoulder and Emma's back. 'Emma might find herself on the Mafia's hit list.'

Zane dropped the phone as if it were fiery hot. It crashed to the floor. 'What in the hell are you on about?'

Emma stood back from him and lifted her cheek from his chest, her face ghostly pale. 'I only came out to get a drink of water. I didn't mean to hurt him, it's just, he came for me and I reacted to save myself.' She shuddered and her sobs rose harder.

Michael stepped in beside her, and after flashing Zane a stern look, took his girlfriend into his arms. 'It'll be okay, Em, we just have to do this right or, like Dad said, you might get hurt.' He tucked wayward strands of hair behind her ears. 'I'd never forgive myself if something happened to you, baby.'

Peter nodded as he heaved a sigh. 'Yes, you were undoubtedly defending yourself, Emma, I believe you, but Mario Zaffaro isn't going to give a shit about that. All he'll want is revenge for whoever took his cousin's life.'

'Why the hell would the Mafia want to break into our home?' His instincts telling him it would have something to do with Peter's work, Zane looked down at the tattooed thug. He'd never seen a dead body before, and nausea swirled in his stomach at the gruesome sight.

Strangely unperturbed, Peter followed his gaze. 'I'm building a case against one of Mario's boys at the moment, and I suppose he thought he might find something in the house to discredit me, or ... maybe, god forbid, he sent this thug to threaten me, or possibly even to kill me.' He cleared his throat and seemed to ponder this for a few moments. 'Whatever the case, thank goodness Emma stopped him.'

Zane found himself lost for words. Emma, too distraught to take anything more in, huddled against Michael. Zane felt a pang of jealousy that he wasn't the one soothing her, but he swallowed it down. Now wasn't the time for his hidden feelings to come into play. Hands laced behind his head, he paced, and finally found his voice. 'So what do you suggest we do, Peter?'

'I don't want you and Emma to do anything. The less you know now, the better. I'll take care of it. Okay?'

Wide eyed, Zane turned to him. 'How do you intend to do that?'

'Like I said, the less you know, the better.' He gestured to Emma. 'Take her and calm her down, will you? Michael and I will clean up this mess. And then tomorrow, for the sake of Emma's life, and ours, I want us all to get on with our routine like this never happened. You're not to speak of it, to anyone. Ever. Do you understand?' His face was a picture of caution.

Zane was reluctant but because he cared more about Emma than some thug he didn't know, he did as Peter had demanded. If only this were a nightmare they'd all wake up from tomorrow. But it was terrifyingly real, and something told him, as horrifying as it was, there was a hell of a lot more to the story.

CHAPTER
1

Silvergum, North Queensland

Shattered after two weeks with virtually no sleep, Zane dared a glance in Emma's direction and then heaved a weary sigh. Although the classic Cold Chisel tune playing from the radio was a welcome distraction, what remained silent between them was resounding off every inch of the sun-speckled windscreen. He and Emma had talked about it all until they were blue in the face, and there was nothing to be gained from going over it with her for the hundredth time. As much as they both wanted to go to the cops, risking her safety just wasn't an option. There was no way in hell he was going to endanger her life, or Michael and Peter's, all because of his yearning to do the right thing.

Staring out the passenger window, he tried to pretend it had never happened, tried not to imagine the dead man, who he'd last seen slumped on the kitchen floor, now at the bottom of

Campfire River, with bricks tied to his feet, or buried somewhere deep in the middle of Silvergum's national park. Not that he knew what had transpired once he'd dragged a very distraught Emma back to his bedroom and locked the door. Nor did he know what it had to do with the Mafia, and he didn't want to know. All that mattered was that Emma was alive, and unharmed. He wouldn't put it past Peter to do whatever it took to cover up the evidence – the lengths his adoptive father would go to preserve his reputation as a cutthroat criminal defence lawyer were beyond Zane's comprehension. It came with the territory of representing the bad guys, the delinquents who deserved to be locked away for life that the state felt deserved a fair trial – that's where Peter came in to save the day. In Zane's opinion, Peter manipulated the justice system so criminals could walk free while their victims and their families suffered. The under-the-table payoffs and the who-knew-who in the land of the Law was a goddamn joke.

A smashing headache behind his eyes, he closed them and squeezed the bridge of his nose. No matter how hard he tried, and regardless of whether the thug was a part of a cartel that harmed and hurt for money, the dead man's face continued to haunt him. He just hoped that by leaving Aussie shores, he could put it all behind him. He craved a distraction from his relentless thoughts, wanting to think of anything but that shocking night. If only it were that easy.

After an hour of driving in virtual silence, thankfully, they were almost at Cairns International Airport. Other than the odd comment here and there as they'd wound down the Kuranda Range at a snail's pace, the evasiveness between them was killing him. But what was he meant to say to fill the agonising gaps?

Don't worry about killing a man, she'll be right? Or, *I'm sorry about making such sweet love to you when you're already dating Michael?* There was nothing he could say that would make their situation any better or less painful.

Grabbing his wide-brimmed hat from the dash, he did his best to keep his turbulent emotions at bay. A true-blue cowboy never broke down. He'd never done it to this day, and he wasn't about to do it now, even though he felt as if his entire world was crumbling around him. The most frustrating thing was that he was helpless to stop it. As he caught her eye, the exquisite brunette behind the wheel offered him a brusque smile before focusing again on the long line of traffic in front of them. The tremble in her soft, sweet, kissable lips was ever so slight and the quickened pulse in her chest was obvious to him only because he knew her so well. Angry for giving in to the desires he'd kept under lock and key for years, he wanted to give himself a good slap around the ears. Emma Kensington deserved so much better, better than him, better than Michael, better than *this*.

Michael had wooed her from the get-go, pulled the wool over her eyes in his most charming of ways, but soon enough, he'd go and hurt her. It wasn't in Michael's nature to remain committed, to anyone. But try as Zane might to warn Emma of this, she refused to see it. Her dream of the whole white picket fence lifestyle, to be happily married with three kids by the time she was twenty-five, seemed to overshadow her voice of reason. It was an idea that terrified Zane, but it was the life Emma was looking for.

Worried out of his mind and nervous as all hell about what lay in front of him with the American professional bull-riding circuit, and also the dark past that incessantly shadowed him, and Emma, his stomach twisted into an even tighter knot. He hated leaving her to deal with all this on her own, but not wanting to make a scene at the airport, he had to pull himself together. Squeezing the bridge of his nose again, he heaved another weary sigh, adjusted his sunnies and then gave a few short, sharp tugs on his seatbelt to loosen it, wishing he could unbuckle the damn thing altogether. He hated feeling confined, constricted, loathed anything to do with rules and regulations. Telling him he couldn't do something was like waving a red cape at a charging bull.

He was a self-confessed wild child, although his wayward acts had all been quite harmless. He'd lived seventeen long years without getting into too much trouble with the law. Having a renowned defence lawyer for an adoptive father might have had something to do with that. But this, being a witness to homicide, as accidental as it was, was immeasurably worse than the times he'd driven a car unlicensed, dashed down the main street of Silvergum butt naked for a dare, and failed to pay a couple of speeding fines. No amount of prayer would ever get them out of this mess – not that he'd ever drop to his knees to try. Even though he'd been raised by his god-fearing adoptive mother, Kay, since he was three months old, he was no longer a religious man. He had all but turned his back on the Church the day she'd died of cancer almost a year ago. What kind of god took such a kind and loving soul in such a horrendous way, especially after all the years of verbal and emotional abuse she'd endured from Peter's acid tongue?

Looking out the window at the rows of seemingly identical houses becoming claustrophobically closer together – a country-blooded man through and through, suburban living wasn't for him – he tried to rid himself of his disturbing thoughts. They had kept him pacing the darkened hallway of the Kensingtons' old workers' cottage these past two weeks. Staying at Wattle Acres just hadn't been an option after what had happened. Peter and Michael's increasing animosity towards him, combined with the eeriness of the kitchen had him packing his bags and taking up Emma's offer to stay at her family's property, Serendipity, until he left for America. And it let him keep an eye out for her, just in case she had a mark on her back. How Peter and Michael could keep going as if nothing had happened, how they could go to sleep at night and wake refreshed and ready for the day ahead at their prestigious law firm was beyond him. He'd told them so, and they hadn't liked it, reminding him to keep his mouth shut or Emma might end up dead. Their words were as harsh and as blunt as that.

Branded as the black sheep of the family by many Silvergum locals, unlike Michael – who was his father's blood and bone – Zane had proved time and time again he wasn't Peter's progeny. Professional bull riding was a far cry from the world of Law Peter and Michael immersed themselves in. But Zane was proud that his passion lay in something so completely different. He didn't care that he was a disappointment to Peter; he'd never wanted to be anything like the arrogant, ruthless, selfish bastard. Growing up feeling as if he were nothing but a thorn in their sides, and even more so now Kay was gone, he was relieved to be leaving this life behind, and hopefully, for good. Apart from this captivatingly spirited woman beside him, who he'd known since kindergarten, there was no one he'd miss. Fighting to divert his thoughts from the heartache he was going to feel saying goodbye to her, he watched a flock of seagulls soar through the sky, the seemingly endless blue a sharp contrast to the darkness he was feeling deep down in his soul.

Nearing the airport, he stole another glance at the only woman he'd ever truly made love to, not just slept with for the fun of it. The tension in her glossy lips and the whites of her knuckles as she gripped the steering wheel unnecessarily tight told him her mind was tormented by the same images and thoughts as his. While his pounding concern for her safety was almost too much to cope with, he knew for sure that she was carrying so much on her petite shoulders. He couldn't even begin to imagine how she was feeling, knowing she'd been the cause of the intruder's death, despite the fact she was only defending herself. Zane knew that Emma desperately wanted to go to the police, but she feared for her life if she did. It was almost too much for one person to handle, he thought, glancing at her. He ached to reach out and soothe her worries away, but that wasn't his place. He'd tried to do just that last night, to comfort her when she'd come to him in tears, and look where that had led them … even deeper into unbearable secrecy. If only Michael was there more for her, it might never have happened.

Slowing, Emma indicated and pulled into the drop-off zone out the front of International Departures. Without allowing himself time for any hesitation, Zane jumped out and shut the ute's door behind him. Grabbing his suitcase from the back while avoiding slobbery licks from her Great Dane, Bo, he paused to drink Emma in one more time. He knew not to let her innocent appearance fool him – she was like him, as wild as they came.

Resting his forearm on the open passenger window, he feigned a nonchalance he was far from feeling. 'You sure you're going to be okay, Em?' Man, his heart was aching.

Tucking wisps of wind-tousled hair from her lightly freckled cheeks, she offered a sad smile and shrugged. 'If I say no, are you going to stay?'

Wishing he could say yes, he found himself at a loss for words.

'Thought as much.' She blinked her dazzling, gold-speckled green eyes, wet with tears. 'Then I suppose I'm just going to have to be, aren't I, Casanova?'

He flinched at hearing his nickname. 'Yeah, I suppose. I'm so sorry, Em, about everything.' He didn't feel the need to elaborate.

She laughed softly as she picked at the grease beneath her short fingernails – she'd been under the bonnet when he'd found her this morning. 'Even though I should be, I'm not sorry about what happened last night, Zane. It felt so right, and sooo good.' She looked at him. 'I know you felt whatever it was, too. I could see it in your eyes.'

So many emotion-fuelled words tumbled to his lips, but he fought them back. Now wasn't the time to tell her how he really felt about her – not when he was leaving for good. Unable to hold her intense gaze any longer, for fear of jumping back into the ute and throwing his dreams away, he looked down at his boots. Drawing in a breath, he shook his head. 'I don't know what to say, Em, but if I don't go now—'

She cut him off. 'I know, Zane, it's okay. If I were in your shoes, after everything that's happened, I'd be running like a bat out of hell and never looking back.' She sighed. 'I'm so happy for you, finally getting the break you deserve.'

He dared a glance back at her and his heart tumbled. 'I wish you could come with me.'

'Me too ... but then I'd probably cramp your style, Casanova.' She tried to flash her knee-buckling smile, but failed, miserably.

Once he could cop it, but not twice in a matter of minutes. 'Please, Em, don't call me that, not after last night ...' He shook his head, his heart feeling like a lead weight.

She unbuckled her seatbelt and slid across the seat, her fierce gaze daring the mean-looking parking inspector heading towards them to try to tell her to move on. 'I'm going to miss you, Zane Wolfe.' She brushed a kiss over his lips, igniting the blazing fire in his heart all over again. 'Take care, won't you?'

'I will, you too.' He cleared his throat. Damn this was even harder than he'd expected.

Ever so gently, she placed a trembling hand against his cheek. 'Please don't ever forget me.'

'How could I ever forget you?' Desperate to lighten the mood, he tried to laugh it off. 'I'm not going away forever, you know. I'll be back sometime.'

She offered him a smile that showed how much she doubted that. She knew him all too well. 'Remember to keep our secrets under lock and key, okay?' She eyed him carefully.

He shrugged and forced a smile he was far from feeling. 'What are these secrets you speak of, Miss Kensington?'

'That's the way.' Nodding, she sniffled and wiped at her eyes. 'Bye, Zane.'

'Yup, catch ya round like a rissole, Em.'

'Gravy and all,' she said. Then buckling herself back in, she revved the Holden V8 to life and pulled out and away, taking a huge piece of Zane's heart with her.

It was a fight not to look back when he stepped through the sliding doors, the coolness of the air-conditioning like a sharp slap to the face. Finally taking his sunnies off, he groaned and cursed beneath his breath. The airport was jam-packed with travellers, the line to the check-in counter a mile long. He joined the queue, and the nerves and doubts multiplied. Checking his phone almost every five seconds, just in case Emma texted or rang him, he had to fight the urge to look over his shoulder, as he had done for the past two weeks. Having witnessed the unthinkable, and knowing it had something to do with the Mafia, he found it incredibly hard to stand still. He wanted to stay and play Emma's bodyguard, to make sure no harm came to her, but they had to get on with their lives. Besides, she had Michael there to do that for her.

Finally, he was standing at the check-in counter. The impeccably dressed woman with lips painted bright red offered a smile, revealing lipstick-smudged teeth, as she handed back his passport. Zane shoved it in his top pocket, wished her a good day, and then made his way down the corridor leading to airport security. Emptying his pockets, cursing when he pulled out his favourite pocketknife that would be confiscated for sure, he tried to shake the unease from the pit of his stomach. The terror of that night had a grip on him so damn tight he was powerless to be free of it. It had all happened so fast – Emma's panicked cries, him running from his bedroom still half asleep, the thug tumbling backwards and smashing his head on the granite bench, the pool of blood beneath his motionless body spreading further by the second. He'd never forget the strange expression shared between Peter and Michael as they raced into the kitchen to find the intruder on the floor. Peter's explanation of exactly who the dead man was was believable, but it hadn't excused the way he and Michael had reacted.

Through the metal detector, and with his pocketknife frustratingly taken from him, Zane slung his backpack over his shoulder. Every step he took towards the waiting plane was a step away from the life he loathed, and the family he despised. As he stood a head above the rest, and with shoulders as wide as a professional footy player, gazes followed him down the aisle of the Boeing 747 – some subtle, some not so much. His country get-up of cowboy boots, faded jeans and his trusty Akubra (there was no way he was risking it getting squashed in his luggage), and the tattoos that were visible, drew all sorts of attention. A few passengers looked cautious, others were curious. Zane took it all in his stride, offering a courteous smile whenever his eyes met those of a gushing woman. In his line of work, female admiration came with the territory, and like his mum had always said – God rest her soul – it cost nothing to be a gentleman. Opening a door for a woman, young or old, was a given in his world, as too was standing whenever a lady walked into a room.

Hopeful the seat beside him was going to remain unoccupied, so he could unravel his six-foot-three frame, he sat down and latched his damn seatbelt. He couldn't get away from constraints today. The only place he truly felt free was on the back of a one-tonne bucking bull – at least then he could get off whenever he wanted. At last, right where he needed to be, and with the dreaded goodbye with Emma done and dusted, he released a pent-up breath. This journey was going to bring a whole new meaning to a long-haul flight – an entire eighteen or so hours, to think about the horror of the last two weeks and the mind-blowing pleasures of last night. Damn his lack of willpower. And even though he'd gone and stuffed everything up, just as he always did when it came to women, not that Emma was just *any* woman, she'd still insisted on dropping him off as planned. In the throes of passion, she'd also promised not to hold it against him, because it took two to tango. Her determination to shoulder her share of the blame made him fall for her even harder. The tears that had been building in her hazel eyes, and the quiver in her lips as she'd unravelled from his arms and crawled from his bed at some ungodly hour, so she could sneak home before her parents got up, had almost broken him.

While the plane taxied and lifted off, his eyes darted around as he familiarised himself with his surroundings. Staring at the seatbelt sign, keen for it to be switched off, he clenched his clammy hands together and cursed himself for the hundredth time that day. He wasn't afraid of flying, but having never passed over the oceans, this was all new to him. He trusted in the pilot to get him to Dallas safe and sound, but if it were possible, he'd prefer the feel of a well-worn saddle beneath him, and the sound of pounding hooves as he voyaged to his new home.

He fought to focus on the here and now. This was meant to be a magical moment – leaving Australia to chase his bull-riding dreams. It was one he'd counted down to for what felt like forever and worked damn hard to achieve. He should be elated he'd made the cut, but he was finding it near impossible to be anything but anxious. As the plane rose higher and higher, the sun shone from behind the cottony clouds and sparkled on the turquoise water far below – it was a sight to behold. After years of his mother encouraging him to become a world-champion bull rider, as fearful as she was for his safety, he'd finally taken the first step in making his lifelong dream a reality. It broke his heart she wasn't around any longer to witness it.

His face pressed up against the window, he watched the scenic coastline of Far North Queensland fade away. His heart ached as it reached back for Emma's. Memories of last night came thick and fast – the fresh scent of her hair, the silkiness of her skin, the sharp intake of her breath as he'd become one with her, the feeling of her fingernails scraping down his back, and the look in her eyes as she'd tumbled over the edge with him. When her lips had first touched his, while they'd ripped at each other's clothes, as if trying to tear away the layers that were stopping their hearts caressing one another's, something deep inside his soul had slipped into place. In that lust-filled moment, they'd been stripped of pretence, and all their worries had faded away in an instant. It was as if they'd been skin on skin a thousand times over, a thousand years ago. Emma was spot on when she'd said it had felt so right, so damn good, even though it had been so very wrong of them. As difficult as it had been in the heat of the moment, he'd made sure to not make promises to her he couldn't keep – he didn't have the nickname of 'Casanova' around Silvergum for no good reason. Commitment terrified him, and Emma knew that so well.

The *what ifs* slogged him – what if he stayed instead of chasing his dreams? What if he gave in to how he really felt about her, what if they ran away together, what if she wasn't so tied to her family property, with a dream to make it her own one day, what if she wasn't in a relationship with Michael? Trust his luck, he'd gone and found the girl of his dreams, but only realised it when it was way too late. But if given the freedom, would he have jumped at the chance to make her his? If he thought about it rationally, Emma's dreams of picket fences and having an army of children had never been his thing, and if he were being honest with himself, he wasn't sure it ever would be.

Shaken from his deep thoughts by a wave of bone-shuddering turbulence, his hands clenched the armrests. If this giant tin can dived and crashed, he'd have no hope of survival. It was completely out of his control – and he didn't like that. One. Little. Bit. He squeezed his eyes shut, desperately trying to block out images of Emma as the sounds of rattling bags and nervous passengers heightened his panic. His mind tumbled and twisted, filled with thoughts of surviving a plane crash and not seeing her again. Flashes of them skin on skin came into his head – the desperate crash of their lips, the scent of whisky on her breath, and her whispers, her sweet rasping voice telling him how she wished he wasn't so scared of commitment, squeezed his already pain-filled heart tighter. Goddamn it, this was the hardest thing he'd ever had to do, other than watching his mum wasting away from cancer.

Knowing he needed to get a grip, Zane fought off the memories. Even though he worshipped the ground Emma Kensington walked on in her sexy cowgirl boots, in his soul he knew he could never have her without the big possibility of letting her down, of somehow breaking her beautiful heart because he was so scared of tying himself down, of laying down roots. That meant they were never possible. They could never be. Would never be. He had to keep telling himself that, and he needed to let the thought go of there ever being a *them*. He just had to. He wasn't good for her. He wasn't the one for her. He was doing her a favour, leaving her behind. And one day, she would thank him for it.

As the turbulence cleared and the nervous excitement of the crowded plane settled, he allowed his heart to calm too. When he stepped from this plane and strode into Dallas International Airport, there was going to be no looking back, no longing for what could never be with her. Ever.

CHAPTER
2

Serendipity Farm, Silvergum
Nine years later

Wiping her hands on the tea towel slung over her shoulder, June Kensington cupped her daughter's cheeks, the compassion in her eyes almost sending Emma into a flood of tears. 'I know it hurts, love, him not being here, but try to focus on the positives, okay.'

Placing her hands over her mother's, Emma smiled sadly. 'And what might they be, Mum?'

'Well, let's see …' June rolled her eyes skywards, as if asking the good lord for silent answers. 'Michael does love you, very much. He's a hard worker, and on a good day, when he forgets about work for a while, he's still that carefree larrikin you fell for.'

Emma bit her lip to stop from crying. 'I still see glimpses, Mum, but they're becoming few and far between, these days.'

'I know, love.' June kissed her on the forehead. 'Marriage isn't easy, by a long shot. Trust me, there were times when your father and I weren't very keen on one another, but we pushed through them, and I'm glad we did, because I love him more than ever now. As annoying as the old codger can be at times.' She chuckled softly, shaking her head.

Emma couldn't help but smile when she came to meet her mother's gaze. 'That's all I want – a happy marriage like yours and Dad's. Is that too much to ask?'

'It takes a hell of a lot of work, and tonnes of grit and determination.' June sighed. 'And that's from both sides, mind you. Michael needs to take more responsibility and be there for you.'

'I wish he would, I really do.'

'Your father and I do, too, love. We know how much it would mean to you, and Riley, if he was home more.' She stepped back and drew in a breath. 'Just know we're here for you, anytime, okay. I hate seeing you so torn.'

'I know, Mum, thank you. I love you, so much.'

'Love you too, Em.' She clapped her hands together and flashed a broad smile. 'Now, before we get all soppy and sentimental, let's get back out there and celebrate with Riley.'

'Yes. I'll be back out soon. Just need to visit the little girls' room.'

Striding down the hallway after her quick trip to the loo, Emma stopped off at the bathroom to wash her hands. She wished her best mate, Renee, could have made it to her godchild's eighth birthday party, but she understood the shortage of nurses at the local hospital had Renee shouldering a double shift. The same couldn't be said about Michael. Try as she might to understand it, his absence was just plain selfish. It broke her heart to see how far they'd slipped from each other's lives over the years, but she was determined to try to make it work, to stick with it through the bad times, desperate to believe there would once again be good days ahead for them, as a family.

Pulling open the flyscreen door, she padded out onto the wide verandah of the renovated cottage, next door to her parents' homestead, and with a sweeping view of the family property, Serendipity. Sidestepping battered cane chairs and thriving potted ferns, she made her way towards the back steps. Her ten-month-old Great Dane, Tiny, leapt from his hammock bed and stumbled over his massive feet to get to her, keen for some loving. Pausing to give him a scratch on his massive noggin, she sighed wearily – thoughts of climbing into her bed tonight the only thing keeping one foot in front of the other. Last night had been a restless one, her tossing and turning brought on by a myriad of scenarios, none of them ideal.

Her gaze found Zane, the mere sight of him arousing feelings she shouldn't have as a married woman. Tangles of childhood adventures, secrets and lies, had bound them all those years ago. She closed her eyes, willing her anxiety away by counting her blessings. Although her life was often challenging, she also had so much to be thankful for.

She still couldn't believe he was here after all those years of avoiding Aussie shores. The ten-year anniversary of his mother's death had lured him back to pay his respects at the memorial held by the local CWA women. And by god, other than maturing into one hell of a man, he hadn't changed a bit. Watching him out of the corner of her eye, Emma took a moment to re-group. She was struggling, slipping, drowning in apprehension as she pictured ripping open the envelope that could change everyone's lives. But if it were so, would Zane want to step up to the plate? Fear gripped her heart. Squeezed it so tight she could barely draw a breath. Was she ready to face this? Her entire world might be turned upside down and inside out.

Guaranteed a seven-day turn-around, the results of the test would be here any day. And they couldn't come quickly enough. It had been the longest week of her life, her nights spent wide awake as she worried herself sick, and her days besieged with mental and emotional exhaustion. She took a deep, calming breath, followed by another. She couldn't crumble today, not in front of everyone. Nobody could know what she was going through, not even her parents or her best mate. What good would it do, letting the cat out of the bag? It would tear their lives apart, and for what? A hunch? She'd never forgive herself.

As terrified as she was about finally knowing, at the very least there'd be no more guessing, no more wondering. One outcome and she could go on with her life as though nothing had changed; another and she'd have to do the only thing she could – tell the truth. Tomorrow, she'd drive into town to check if it was at the post office, where she would have to personally sign for it. She'd made sure to have it posted as securely as possible. She had to be the first one to open the envelope.

Wandering across her backyard with Tiny close beside her, she looked at her watch. There was less than an hour of bedlam to go, thank god. As much fun as she'd had, making sure her little girl had a ripper of an eighth birthday party, the thought of all the kids going home was comforting. She'd made it through having seventeen of Riley's classmates there; all of them still alive and mostly unscathed, not a small feat. As if on cue, three boys, clearly high on sugar, tore past in a fit of chuckles, a football passing between them, almost knocking her over. She swayed out of their way, and felt a strong hand on her arm, steadying her. Looking into eyes the colour of the spectacular sky they'd been blessed with today, she was transported to another time, another place – one she'd tried to force herself over the years to believe she'd left behind, but possibly never could. They shared an enchanting, private moment, before laughing it off and going their separate ways. Zane saying something first about her ability to trip over air, and her telling him, playfully, to go and get stuffed.

Completely exhausted, and with everyone now in a food stupor, she stretched out in the hammock that hung in the shade of a big old red gum. It was the same tree she'd fallen out of and broken her arm as a twelve-year-old – so much for trying to keep up with the Wolfe boys and their antics. With a bit of enticement from Zane, they'd had a bet on who could climb the highest and the fastest, the winner gaining both bragging rights and a milkshake and burger at the local fish and chippy. Of course, she'd risen to the challenge with enthusiasm. Halfway to the top, and with the two boys hot on her heels, she'd missed her mark and tumbled, hitting the ground so hard it had knocked the wind right out of her and bent her arm into a very unnatural angle. Zane had been beside himself with concern; Michael, on the other hand, had laughed his arse off. Looking back, it had been two very painful lessons learnt. First, that a girl couldn't always outdo the boys. Although that hadn't stopped her trying – coming from a long line of strong country women, giving in or giving up just wasn't an option. And secondly, the cocky, confident and very popular older brother of her best guy-friend at high school wasn't necessarily the one to go for, as much as her friends at the time had made her think Michael was an absolute catch. Hindsight was a bitch, but she took her vows seriously – for better or worse, she had to believe she and Michael would make it through, just like her mum and dad had. There was no going back, no option to rewind and redo the past – no matter what she found out tomorrow.

As always, her heart swelled with the vision of this majestic land she called home, the hundred-acre property nestled nicely between the Great Barrier Reef, the lush tropical rainforests of the Daintree and the fringes of the outback. Rich and fertile, Serendipity was strikingly green for the majority of the year. The dry season never lasted long before the monsoonal weather would swoop in, enticing new growth from the depths of Mother Nature's heart. It was the perfect spot for the grass-fed cattle her father raised and sold to gourmet butchers, and also for her side of the business, the highly sought-after horse agistment paddocks she rented out for a pretty penny.

As arduous and unforgiving as living off the land could sometimes be, she wouldn't want to do anything else, anywhere else – a sharp contrast to Michael's ambitions. Recently appointed a partner in the new office of his father's prestigious law firm, a good hour's drive away, representing a very shady bunch was his idea of making it. Long gone was the easy-going country boy she'd fallen for. She couldn't even remember the last time he'd got in the saddle or spent time in the paddocks. With all the late nights at the office, he spent the majority of the week holed up in one of his father's seafront apartments on the Cairns Esplanade, and he was hinting more and more about moving there. But Emma didn't know how he could suggest such a thing.

Wild horses wouldn't drag her from Silvergum. She'd worked so hard to build her business here, and Riley loved her country lifestyle – the paddocks of Serendipity, Silvergum primary school, her friends and her horse. Michael must have realised that it was Riley's whole world. He was becoming more like his cunning, egotistical father every day, and less of the man she'd fallen for as a teenage girl. The rose-coloured glasses were now well and truly off and she could see all too clearly.

Turning her attention back to the present, Emma followed the flight of a magnificent Ulysses butterfly, its vibrant blue wings spellbinding. Afternoon sunshine filtered through the canopy of leaves and touched her face. The rolling land that stretched out to meet with the bluest of skies dusted with the occasional wisp of cloud, was bathed in warm golden light. Her two beloved cows, Gertrude and Helga, old dairy girls she'd saved from a distant cousin the morning before they were destined for the meatworks, grazed lazily, their days certainly not numbered here. Along the rustic timber fence that separated the backyard from the neatly arranged agistment paddocks, the brilliant yellow sunflowers she and Riley had planted a few months ago stood tall, their petals reaching for the sunshine. The scene truly was worthy to be on a postcard. Her eyelids heavy, she allowed them to shut as she drifted with the sway of the hammock, suspended in the blissful land between consciousness and daydreams.

A delighted squeal woke her with a start. Flicking her eyes open, she was briefly met with a cobalt-blue gaze and a delighted Twistie-stained grin as Riley raced past with three of her friends and Tiny hurtling behind them – the mammoth puppy all legs and paws, and no sense. She missed her old doggy mate Bo like mad, losing him to old age a year ago, but Tiny had certainly helped fill the void in both her and Riley's hearts. All four girls giggled madly as Tiny finally caught up, bowled them over, and then licked them excitedly. Their laughter was heart-warming, and Emma sighed, deeply satisfied with her role as a mother. Her life might not always be a bed of roses, but what more could she ask for than a happy, healthy child, with a heart so big it sometimes brought her to tears.

Looking to where her dad snoozed in his newly purchased, you-beaut fold-out camp chair, his tattered, wide-brimmed hat pulled down and snoring for all of Australia, she chuckled to herself. How her mother got any sleep beside him was beyond her. As a child she could hear him from her room – he used to almost suck the walls in with his relentless snorts. Her uncle and a few of his mates mulled about, beers in hand, beside the barbeque as men do, and a few of the teenagers were sprawled out on the grass staring at their phones like their lives depended on it. Her nanna and mum, god bless their country-loving souls, were in deep conversation with the rest of their CWA crew about how good the sponge cake had been. Emma had to agree; the fresh strawberries and cream had been finger-lickingly decadent amongst the layers of soft, fluffy cake.

If only she'd spent more time indoors with her mum and nanna, learning the art of baking, instead of outside with her cattleman father, learning the ways of the land and the art of horsemanship, she may have shared their passion. When she was little, she thought her nanna had an apron permanently tied around her waist and a wooden spoon constantly in hand for both cooking and for occasionally tapping very naughty bums when the need arose. For her part, Emma wouldn't be happy stuck inside. A tomboy through and through, the only time she'd stayed indoors was when she'd been grounded, which had happened quite often in her teenage years. Give her a view of wide-open fields from up high in a saddle over cooking any day. It was a side of her that Michael had increasingly struggled with, but had known and liked when he'd first met her. Emma had discovered that things could gradually change once a wedding ring was slid on a finger.

From her comfy spot in the hammock, she couldn't help but admire the way Zane's jeans fit so snugly around his butt, or how his t-shirt stretched across his deliciously wide chest, six-packed abs and brawny tattooed arms, or his messy yet somehow perfect dark hair that fell across his forehead; she knew all too well what it felt like to press her lips against his body. A quiver ran through her with the memory, and she mentally slapped herself for her wayward thoughts. Even though she hadn't felt the intimate touch of a man for months – Michael seemingly uninterested in being affectionate because he was always too tired – she was a married woman. It was wrong of her to look at Zane in such a way, but she'd also come to accept that the chemistry they'd shared as teenagers was never going away. They just had to keep it at bay, and keep pretending their one night of unadulterated, toe-curling passion never happened, unless the paternity test she'd secretly done with Michael and Riley's samples came back confirming what she felt in her bones was true.

Breaking away from the huddle of men, Zane met her eyes and smiled charmingly, right before being tackled to the ground by Riley and her friends. Tiny made sure to include himself in the fun. The four girls giggled and begged Zane to start the pony rides he'd promised. Trying unsuccessfully to avoid slobbery doggy kisses, he quickly succumbed to their demands, the huge grin on his rugged face enhancing his dimples. Emma smiled from the heart. Zane was still the life of any party – even for these demanding whippersnappers. The piñata he'd brought along had been a hit; the lollies that had rained down as he'd helped the kids slog the thing to smithereens had sent them into an absolute feeding frenzy. If only Michael could be more like him, then her life and Riley's would be filled with all the enjoyment that came with being a family, and hers would be filled with the passion, excitement and contentment she craved every day. Occasionally, she fantasied that she'd married Zane and not his brother. She would imagine his hands sliding around her waist and his lips trailing down her neck as she stood at the kitchen sink, the tower of a manly man taking her then and there with the kind of fervent desire she'd only ever felt with him.

Oh, a sex-deprived woman could dream …

But the voice of reason would always remind her that the chivalrous and ever-so-charming Zane Wolfe had never been one to take commitment seriously, his gypsy soul giving him itchy feet as soon as anything in life got too serious. Knowing that Zane left a trail of broken hearts wherever he went, Emma had never let herself become another notch on his bedpost. She was well aware his blazing fire would only consume her, leaving the charred ashes of her heart behind. Nonetheless, it was a romp between the sheets she'd never, ever forget.

The erotic memories searing her thoughts and making her ache with longing in places she shouldn't, Emma suddenly needed to move. So up she got, quick smart, almost upending the hammock and landing on the ground as she did. With Zane and Riley's retired trail-riding horse keeping the partygoers busy, she grabbed the opportunity to tidy up. Rearranging what was left of the fairy bread, sausage rolls, chips, lollies and birthday cake, and then gathering the empty plates and cups, she made her way towards the back stairs of the cottage. She graciously declined help along the way from Renee's granny, May, and the beer-wielding blokes.

As the afternoon breeze picked up, the bamboo wind chimes she'd bought in Thailand last year played melodious tunes as she climbed the back steps. As beautiful as they were, and as much as she loved the tinkles and jingles, they did tend to remind her of Michael's absence, both then and now. It was a family trip only she and Riley had gone on, after Michael told her at the last minute that he couldn't go. Her heart pinched. When had they fallen out of love and out of sync with each other?

Reaching the back door, it was a feat to flick off her thongs, kick Riley's muddy gumboots out of the way, and then open the flyscreen door with the tip of her toe while balancing an armful of plates and cups. But as her mother always said, where there's a will, there's a way – a motto Emma liked to live by. Stepping inside, her eyes took a few seconds to adjust as the screen door groaned shut behind her. The scent of incense lingered and mingled with what she could only describe as home, the Cat Stevens' tune playing from the radio tempting her into singing the lyrics softly. As she carefully manoeuvred around the couch and coffee table, a distinguishable pitter-pattering caught her attention. It only took her a second to figure out what was going on.

'Peking, you little bugger,' she grumbled. 'How many times do I have to tell you that you're not allowed in the house?' The insubordinate duck had obviously come in through the cat door. Again. Locking it didn't help one little bit now he'd figured out how to unlock it with his beak.

The timber floorboards cool against her bare feet, and her paisley-patterned boho skirt swishing around her ankles, she hightailed it down the hallway and into the kitchen, barely avoiding falling flat on her face as her Russian Blue kitten darted in front of her. 'Oh dear, Kat, are you okay, love?' she cooed, smiling.

Peking was in hot pursuit; the web-footed brute was hell bent on tormenting Kat whenever he had the chance. It was all in good fun for Peking, but certainly not for the frightened feline. Emma watched Kat hightail it into the open pantry cupboard just in time, before Peking could get a hold of her tail. When a box of fruit loops came crashing to the floor, spilling half the contents, Peking lost interest in the chase and eagerly helped himself to the sugary morsels.

'The way to your heart is through your stomach, hey, Peking,' she said, chuckling to herself.

Now safe and sound, and feeling like the queen of the castle, Kat snarled a low warning meow for the duck to back off. Emma rolled her eyes at the mayhem. If only she'd had her phone handy, it would have made for the perfect entry for *Australia's Funniest Home Videos*.

Dumping her armful of crockery on the bench, she checked that Kat was all right. Then, after picking up the box and what was left of the fruit loops, she ushered a quacking Peking out of the kitchen, down the hallway and back out the way he'd come – through the cat door. He looked her fair in the eyes and shat on the verandah, twice, as if to say *Stuff you*, before waddling off.

She guffawed. 'You little shit … literally!' Funny but not funny at the same time; she shook her head, groaning. She'd clean it up when she'd finished with the dishes.

Wandering back to the kitchen she made a mental note to *not* shut Kat in the pantry, as she had accidentally done a few times before. It was her kitten's go-to place when life became too hectic – and with fifteen-odd kids squealing and running about, it was certainly one of those days.

Filling the sink with hot soapy water, putting the pile of plates into it, then tossing the disposable cups into the recycling bin she paused, mesmerised by the view out the window. She and Michael had called the cottage home for eight and a half years now, and although it was a bit on the small side, she loved the rustic charm of the place. The fact she was right next door to her parents was a bonus, although Michael didn't see it that way. He was never backwards in coming forwards about how much he wanted to move from here. A big flash apartment in Cairns was high on his agenda, but certainly not on hers. Silvergum was her home and always would be.

She looked past the old jacaranda tree that had covered the grass beneath in a blanket of purple flowers, and to the place where Michael's flash four-wheel drive, which would never see a true-bush track in its life, should be parked. Anger simmered, and her heart squeezed. How he thought missing Riley's birthday party was acceptable was beyond her comprehension, and the fact he wasn't answering her calls to explain why was even more infuriating. But with his track record of late, why had she expected anything more from him? School plays, parent–teacher interviews, daddy–daughter days at school, even Christmas – work came before anything and everything these past couple of years. Then again, maybe he wasn't at work but was having an affair? The scenario had crossed her mind more and more of late, and had kept her awake at night. It would explain his lack of affection. Her irritation rising to a whole new level, she decided to leave the dishes and head outside again.

Perching on the back steps alongside an exhausted Tiny, she watched Zane swoop Riley up and into the saddle of her pony, her pretty dress now covered in god only knew what. While giving her pooch a preoccupied scratch behind the ears, his tail smacking the verandah floorboards in pleasure, she couldn't help the warm smile that claimed her lips. The bond Zane and Riley shared was unique, immeasurable – the pair's love of horses and anything to do with getting muddy or dirty was always high on their agendas. With the past week spent doing exactly that, while Zane crashed in the guest room at her parents' place, he and Riley were now best buddies. Or was it more than that? Matching crooked little toes, comparable hands, and the same little curl at the corners of their lips when they smiled, could he be Riley's father? And if he were, would he run for the hills and never come back, his commitment phobia going into overdrive, if she told him? She honestly had no idea. Feeling someone standing beside her, she tensed – the chinking of ice and the smell of whisky told her that Peter had chosen to show his face.

'Emma.' His tone was, as always, terse.

'Peter.' She matched his coolness, the cold-hearted man the only person who could get beneath her skin within seconds.

He looked to the sky. 'Nice day for it.' Groaning as he tried to bend over his plump belly, he placed a huge wrapped box down on the ground. Then shoving Tiny aside with his Louis Vuitton shoes, he sat; his strong cologne was overpowering – just like him. Tiny growled, and even though Emma almost wished her dog would give Peter Wolfe a damn good bite to the rump, she told him to behave. Tiny obliged and came to her other side, well away from Peter – a testament to the fact that dogs were great judges of character.

Peter took a swig from the glass of whisky he'd helped himself to inside. 'Michael's been waylaid with a client. From the list of the charges, I think it may be another late night.'

'I gathered that.' Emma bit back the swearwords vying to roll off her tongue as she looked to the gift, recalling how last year Peter had turned up with a guinea pig, wrapped in a very similar box. The poor thing was almost dead from lack of oxygen. 'So, do I need to know if something is alive in there?'

'Don't worry, after seeing how distraught Riley was when her guinea pig was taken by a snake because *you* weren't keeping an eye on it, I've decided not to give her any more pets.'

'That's a bit harsh, Peter.'

He smirked. 'Is it?'

'Yes, it is. I can't be expected to watch a guinea pig twenty-four-seven with the workload I've got here, and it's not like I can rely on Michael to help me.' Her blood reaching boiling point, she couldn't help but snap.

Peter tutted. 'That subject is getting old, Emma. Michael is where he should be, beside me at the firm … not gallivanting around the countryside like some hillbilly cowboy with no purpose.'

Emma bit her tongue so hard she almost expected to taste blood. Now wasn't the time to get into an explosive argument.

'I hope Riley likes it.' He tipped his head towards the box. 'It's a cubby house.'

'Bit small for a cubby house, isn't it?'

'It's one of those pop-up thingamajigs, you know, like a tepee – my secretary picked it out because her granddaughter has one, and apparently loves it.'

Couldn't even take the time to go and get your own granddaughter a gift? Emma wanted to say but chose to remain silent.

'Before I forget …' Reaching inside his jacket, he pulled out a wad of mail bound by a rubber band. 'Janine asked me to give these to you. She said you were meant to sign for one of them, but seeing as we're family she didn't think you'd mind her giving them to me to pass on.' His gaze darkened. 'So thoughtful of her, wasn't it, Emma?'

Emma's heart skidded to a stop as she took them from him. She peered down at the torn top of one envelope. Despite the warmth, she was suddenly chilled to the bone. The ground beneath her spun so wildly, her belly pitched and rolled. Peter leant into her space, chilling her with the look in his eyes. It took a few seconds for Emma to register what he murmured into her ear, and once she did, his words smashed her hard. Blood drained from her head in a dizzying rush. Her throat was tight as she struggled to draw a breath. Stumbling to her feet, she took a few steps back from him, almost tripping over Tiny as she did. He was the last person on earth she wanted to know what was inside that envelope.

His gaze never leaving hers, Peter pushed himself to standing and then straightened his tie; the knowing smirk plastered on his thin lips was sickening. She remained staring at him for a long moment, and all the while his sneer widened. Livid he'd invaded her privacy, and then that he'd threatened her, she finally found her nerve. 'Who the hell do you think you are?' Although surprisingly steady, her voice didn't sound like her own.

'Let's not play games, Emma. We both know who the father is … I've had my suspicions for a long time and this has only confirmed it.' Peter shook his head, his huff one of utter impatience. 'If I were you, I'd keep your mouth firmly shut about the results, or I will do as just I promised.'

'You mean threatened?'

Peter shrugged. 'Take it however you wish.'

She felt as if she'd just been king hit in the chest, and struggled to draw in a breath. 'I don't believe you'd go to the police about that night, not when you'd be an accessory, along with Michael, I might add.'

'I'm at the top of the courtroom food chain now, Emma, and I have my ways and means – it's not necessarily what you know, but who.' He rolled his eyes as if she were a pathetic annoyance. 'Don't doubt for a second I'll swear under oath that Michael and I weren't even home that night, and that I've only been made privy to what went down now because you came to me out of fear for your life, asking for my professional help. I'll walk away from it all, as will Michael, whereas you'll go to prison for a very long time, along with Zane when I drop his name into the mix.' His face glowing a bright shade of red, he flashed her a shrewd smile that spoke of just how much he wasn't going to give an inch.

'You might not care if the Mafia go after me, even if I'm in prison …' Emma stood her ground, as hard as that was. 'But you wouldn't do that to Zane, surely?'

'Zane's nothing to me.'

'But Kay raised him as her own … doesn't that count for anything?'

'He's no family of mine.' Peter snorted. 'He's a bastard child Kay felt the need to adopt when her deadbeat brother went to prison for murdering Zane's mother in a drug-infused rage.' He smiled at her shocked expression. 'You can pick your friends but you can't pick your family … it's no wonder Zane's the way he is, with genetics like that. The runt of the bloody litter, if you ask me.'

It was said nonchalantly, yet packed such a brutal punch, Emma had to grab hold of the bannister to remain standing. 'Zane is your nephew?' Her words were choked.

'By marriage, yes, but not by blood.' He leant in and prodded Emma in the chest. 'Ironic, really, that the man you're in love with has you to thank for killing his father.'

Emma felt the world vanish from beneath her feet and she grabbed the bannister to stop from falling. 'What did you just say?'

Peter smiled gratifyingly. 'Yes, that's right, Emma, the man you killed was Zane's father, Martin Turner.'

Hearing his name made it all the more real. Emma fought off an overwhelming wave of nausea. 'Zane's father was part of the Mafia?' Her head spinning, every word was a struggle to get out.

'No, you stupid girl. He was just some deadbeat who wanted to cause trouble, and thanks to you, he couldn't.'

Bile rose in her throat and she fought the urge to slap him hard across the face. 'Go to hell, you bastard.' She spat it through clenched teeth as she bit back hot tears. Over the years, she'd tried to piece together the fragments of those fateful minutes, but this was way worse than she ever could have imagined.

'I'm sure I will go to hell one day, but not for now.' He sneered. 'Only the good die young.'

'Tell me this much, what was Martin doing breaking into the homestead that night?'

'Your guess is as good as mine.' Peter tried to act indifferent but Emma could see right through his lie. 'Maybe looking for his son, or something to steal to feed his drug habit.'

Emma folded her arms in a bid to hold herself together. 'So why didn't you just let Zane call the police that night, so I could tell them it was self-defence? What was in it for you?'

'I was merely doing a good deed and helping you out by getting rid of the body, so you didn't end up in jail.'

'Yeah, right, pull the other leg.'

Peter's smirk broadened. 'Think what you wish.'

'So what's stopping me going to the police now and telling them everything?'

Peter shook his head, tutting. 'You really think they're going to let you off with just a slap to the wrist, after hiding it all these years? Come on, Emma, think rationally.'

Emma's head was spinning, to the point she felt as if she were about to heave her lunch back up. There was much more to the shocking story, she just knew it. She wanted to scream at him, wanted to slap the truth right out of his deceitful mouth, but she drew in a deep breath and spoke low and slow. 'You're even more vile than I thought you were, Peter. I honestly don't know how you sleep at night.'

'Easy peasy, lemon squeezy … I just lie down and sleep like a baby, knowing everything in my world is exactly how it should be.' He sighed at her exasperated expression. 'You see, Emma, I do the things that most can't, simple as that.' Staring into his glass, he swirled the last of the whisky, a sly expression plastered on his chubby face.

'How can you be so sure I'm not going to tell Zane it was his father I accidentally killed that night?'

His beady eyes narrowed to slits. 'Because if you do, I swear to God I'll ruin your life, and Zane's for that matter, and Riley will have to visit her mother in prison for the rest of your days.'

Emma felt the weight of the world land on her chest as a deadening terror gripped her. Zane deserved to know the truth, and she desperately wanted to make things right, but her baby girl was her world, her everything – she wouldn't risk putting Riley through something as horrific as seeing her behind bars. She had no doubt Peter would stick to his word and put her there, and get the key thrown away. She heaved in a tortured breath, frantically trying to get a grip on the slippery slope she was fast sliding down. 'Surely you wouldn't do such a thing to Riley?' Playing his bluff, she did her very best to remain calm, composed. 'You know how close she and I are.'

'Exactly, Emma. She is your Achilles heel, and I will use every means possible if you make me. Trust me when I say, I've done much worse.' His grey eyes narrowed even further and if looks could kill, she would have been dead on the spot.

'I wouldn't doubt that for a second.' Emma backed up until she was pressed against the wall. 'Does Michael know about all of this?'

Peter shrugged, but the look on his face told her everything she needed to know. If she'd thought she was falling out of love with her husband, she now hated him with a vengeance. Michael had watched her go through hell after that night – all those years of bashing herself up for killing a man, and not being able to go to the police about it. What were he and Peter getting out of all of this? She was sure it had something to do with money. The man was as loathsome as his goddamn father.

Peter closed the distance between them and put his lips so close to her ear it made her shudder in disgust. 'I'm warning you, don't underestimate me, girly. I've never liked you; you're not good enough for my Michael. So you'll pay if you speak a word of this, or the results of your test, to anyone. Ever. Do. You. Understand. Me?'

Her blood froze solid in her veins as she nodded.

'Clever girl.' He stepped away and smoothed his business shirt over his stomach. 'You really should have gone with your heart, instead of your head. Zane is more your calibre.' He chuckled mockingly. 'As much as he tends to think otherwise, a bull rider will never get anywhere and will never amount to anything. He's a lost bloody cause, if I've ever seen one, just like his father was. You two would make a wonderful couple.'

'I'm so glad Zane is nothing like you,' she said, her voice a low growl. 'You oxygen thief ... I hope you rot in hell, and while you're at it, take Michael with you.'

'Never speak about Michael like that in front of me again.' The veins in Peter's forehead looked as though they were about to pop. Whisky sloshed over the glass as he waved his hand at her. 'Just keep your damn mouth shut or you'll be sorry. Got it?' One hand now shoved in his pocket and the other wrapped tightly around the glass, he sculled the last of his drink.

'You're one selfish son of a bitch, you know that?'

'Yup, I'm as selfish as they come, and I bloody well own my shit, unlike some.' He eyed her up and down. 'You should be ashamed of yourself, sleeping with Zane when you were meant to be with Michael.'

She matched his fierce gaze. 'That's the pot calling the kettle black, don't you think? After what you did to Kay when she was on her death bed, sleeping with that fly-by-night hussy from the pub.'

'A man has to get it somewhere, my dear.' He smiled like the cat that had got the cream.

'You're one hell of a sick man, Peter Wolfe.' Unable to look him in the eyes any longer, for fear of gouging them out, she turned so she was shoulder to shoulder, her arms now folded even tighter across her chest. 'I knew you were callous, but I can't believe you're going to blackmail me over this. You clearly have a motive in keeping me quiet about the results, whatever that might be.'

'Oh, come on now, Emma, you've never liked me and I've never liked you, so it's no love lost.' He shrugged, his tone too casual for the seriousness of the situation. 'I'm just looking out for the ones I love, and to be fair, you should be doing the same. Riley needs her mother, but she won't have one around if you go and do something stupid.'

She shot him a sideways glance, the urge to scratch his eyeballs out growing by the second. 'Get the hell out of my house.'

'When I'm good and ready, I'll leave. I've come to see my granddaughter for her birthday, and that's exactly what I'm going to do.'

'You're a bastard, Peter.'

'If that's what you think, fair enough.' Peter offered an amused smirk.

Fighting off tears, all Emma could do was glare at him. She swallowed hard, trying to rid her throat of the lump of emotion lodged there. Janine had a lot to answer for, giving her private mail to Peter, but that was a battle she would fight once the shock of all this had waned. 'Get the hell away from me,' she said through gritted teeth. 'I honestly can't stand the sight of you.'

'Likewise, so it would be my absolute pleasure.' He plonked his empty glass down beside where her hands still gripped the railing. 'I warn you not to start a fire you can't control, because if you flick the match, there'll be no going back. So be very, *very* careful.' He turned on his heel and walked away from her, his double chin jutted out and his chest puffed like an ape needing to assert his manhood.

Spotting her grandfather trudging across the back lawn, Riley's face lit up like a Christmas tree. With Zane's help, she jumped down from her pony and ran for him, arms outstretched. Peter picked her up and spun her around, showering her cheeks with kisses and deliberately ignoring Zane in the process. Emma wanted to scream at the godawful man, tell him to keep his filthy hands off her daughter and to have the common decency to acknowledge Zane. Little did Riley know how much of a detestable man her grandfather was. Emma hoped that when Riley was old enough, she would see for herself – she wasn't about to try to ruin their relationship for her own selfish reasons.

Out of Riley's line of sight, Zane gave Emma a glance as he pulled his wide-brimmed hat down, turned, and headed in the opposite direction, pony in tow, away from Peter. The hurt and rejection written across his face tore at her already shattered heart. How was she meant to keep something like this from him? And here she'd been, worried about possibly having to break the news that he was Riley's father. It just went to show that things could always get worse. What a goddamn mess, and she was helpless to fix it. As much as she wanted to stand up to Peter and do the right thing by Zane and Zane's father, Emma knew her father-in-law was not a man to cross.

A sudden wave of nausea overwhelmed her. She quickly ducked inside, her hands covering her mouth as she ran for the bathroom, barely making it to the toilet before her lunch came up. Her back against the wall, she slid down to the floor and wrapped her arms around her knees, her gaze glued to the envelope she'd thrown to the floor – whatever it said, didn't change a thing. Regardless of what the results proved, her past was going to have to stay where it was, no matter how much it hounded her, or how much she ached to tell the truth. What Peter had just told her would have to be buried deep down in her soul, and she would have to learn to live with that torment, because as long as the vile man was alive, the truth could never be set free. And if that meant she had to cut ties with Zane to be able to deal with the secrets she was keeping from him, as much as that was going to tear her to shreds, that's what she would have to do. Riley needed her – she wasn't about to risk not being here for her daughter because she was thrown behind bars.

CHAPTER

3

Kissimmee, Florida, United States
Present day

Zane looked down at his World Champion belt buckle and was filled with a familiar sense of pride that he'd done it. Five years ago, he'd achieved his bull-riding dream. Nevertheless, that hadn't stopped his drive to win, to keep setting new goals in the toughest sport on dirt. Although surrounded by other bull riders, from all four corners of the globe, he still felt a sense of loneliness, of somehow not belonging. Shrugging the thought aside, he put it down to being the oldest of the group. At thirty-four, he was well aware he was reaching the end of his bull-riding career, but with nothing or nobody else to switch his focus to, he was hesitant to throw in the towel.

Groaning, he pushed his gear bag under the wooden bench. For some damn reason, before every ride, Emma was the one he thought of – maybe thinking of her gave him strength, maybe the heartache of their last encounter gave him all the more reason to not care if he lost his life in the arena. Either way, he wished he could just forget about her, as she had him. But after years of trying, he knew that wasn't possible. It was seven years since he'd seen her and heard her sweet voice, and to this day, he could still picture every freckle dusted upon her cheeks, and the fierceness in her hazel eyes as he'd stupidly tried to kiss her on the night of Riley's birthday party. Her slap had stung, as had her words when she'd told him enough was enough, and that they needed to put a stop to whatever it was between them.

And so he had.

His chaps buckled on, he straightened and rolled his left shoulder, tensing against the pain that knifed through it – a souvenir from a rank bull he'd got hooked up on last month. The first and only steadfast rule for a bull rider was to stay alive, and so far he'd done a good job of it … as much as he could; it was also up to fate, or God, or whomever a man put his faith in. Zane put his faith in himself, because he'd learnt over the years that no amount of prayers worked – he had to put the hard yards in himself. Effort equalled rewards. It was as simple as that – he didn't need complications. That was the main reason why he'd walked away from his wife of four years.

Climbing the steps, Zane headed behind the chutes and hoisted himself up on the railings. With blue sky as far as the eye could see, and only the occasional cloud drifting about, it was a spectacular winter's day. The rough-stock events were in full swing and the crowd was amped up. Having grown from the humble beginnings of a gathering of ranchers in 1941, Silver Spurs Rodeo was now the largest rodeo east of Mississippi – cowgirls, cowboys, cowpokes and broncobusters had descended in their masses to the legendary bull bash, keen either to win a piece of the prize money or to watch from the state-of-the-art grandstands. Stock contractors were busy tending to their prized bucking bulls roaming the holding yards, the one-tonne brutes clearly eager to do what they were bred for, and the lip-smacking scent of briskets and ribs cooking low and slow on smokehouse barbeques drifted on the gentle, late-afternoon breeze.

From his steel perch, sitting between other jean-clad, adrenaline-fuelled cowboys, Zane's mouth watered as he thought about tucking into a rack of sauce-covered ribs later, along with a charred corn cob and coleslaw, followed by a couple of beers at the after-party down at the local honky tonk. Having skipped breakfast, and lunch, his stomach growled in protest, the anticipation of his imminent feast spurring him on and making him downright ravenous. But first things first, he needed to buck it out in the arena one more time. It was the final round, and with his recent divorce costing an arm and a leg, he was banking on walking out a winner.

Scanning the crowded Silver Spur grandstands, filled to the brim with over eight thousand spectators, he smiled to himself. As always, the atmosphere of the rodeo grounds was beyond electric, the adrenaline almost dripping from the railings of the stadium. Speaking in his southern drawl, the compere built the hype and urged on the crowds, their collective roar virtually lifting the roof. In between rides the speakers blared overhead; the combination of seventies rock and good old-fashioned country tunes set the tone for a bucking good time. The music muting, the next rider would be announced, the compere calling out the rider's name, hometown and place on the leader board.

Like Zane, every bull rider here was ready to risk it all – life and limb – to climb up the leader board. Preparation and fitness were on every serious cowboy's agenda leading up to each event, but as soon as that gate flung open, fate and chance came into play. The bulls couldn't be choreographed, rider injuries were frighteningly real, and the shadow of death was always lurking. But Zane knew that fear of a bad injury, or worse, always took a back seat as instinct and groundwork took over. It was what a bull rider had to do to survive yet another round on the back of that mass of muscle. Fear wasn't part of a successful bull rider's equation.

The mammoth bull in the centre ring was bucking like the pro it was; the young rider's form was okay but needed some work. Zane gave the kid kudos for hanging in there. The buzzer rang out, and the stocky nineteen-year-old leapt from the back of his bucking brute, his smile from ear to ear. With the bull hot on his trail, he scooted for the railing and hightailed it over, grinning cheekily as he barely avoided a horn to the rear end. Out of harm's way, he then gave the bull the finger. The crowd loved the shenanigans. Zane chuckled. What a way to spend a Sunday. A shiver of exhilaration sent a flood of goosebumps all over him. This, right here, was his idea of living the high life. He'd never tire of the charged atmosphere that came with a good old-fashioned country rodeo. He didn't need to be rubbing shoulders with the elite to feel worthy – unlike his father and brother back in Australia, who he'd tried to forget. He had his adoptive mother to thank for his love of anything country. Kay had been a champion barrel racer, and Zane had spent what years he'd had with her, before her cancer, at events just like this. Lured by the bigger pay cheques of the professional bull-riding world, which comprised of bull riding alone – events such as this one that encompassed team roping, steer wrestling, barrel racing, bareback riding and bull riding – was where he felt more at home. He enjoyed watching the other events while he waited for his time to buck it out atop a one-tonne bull in the arena. Having spent the last sixteen years driving the US rodeo circuit, this wasn't his first time here.

Comfortable amongst the sea of wide-brimmed hats, sparkling rhinestones, cotton candy, and gleaming belt buckles, Zane sucked in a lungful of salty Florida air. Something about it always made him homesick. Although he wasn't thinking about going back to the golden shores of Australia anytime in the near future, or the far one for that matter, even though his marriage to a sweet, all-American girl had failed. Miserably. As much as he'd wanted to, he hadn't been able to live up to the expectations of a husband as well as continuing to be a bull rider, and she, keen for a man to keep her bed warm each and every night, had done the dirty on him with their neighbour – and was now eight months' pregnant with the bloke's baby.

Watching the next bull ride, the heavy sensation of homesickness lingered in his stomach. Was it really his home among the gum trees that he missed, or was he wistful for the feisty woman behind those delicious lips, the ones that had trailed across his seventeen-year-old stubbled cheek before kissing him like he'd never been kissed before, or again? If he were to stand in front of her now that she was divorced from Michael, and show how he *really* felt for her, how would she respond? Hot and hungry, or would she recoil and slap him across the face, like the last time? She'd always had a fire in her belly, and a bite to her tongue if she was pissed off, and he'd loved that about her. Emma

Kensington was the epitome of an alpha female, with the heart of an angel – she was his perfect woman.

If only things had been different …

Smiling, he couldn't help but wonder how her luscious mouth would feel now, after all these years, if he could do what he craved and seize her lips with his own. Would he like it just as much as he had way back then? The furious heat sparking through his veins and burning in his stomach was his answer. If only it were that simple, but it wasn't, never was and never would be. Listening to the voice of reason, he turned his attention outward. The Brazilian bull rider beside him was up next. The five-foot-nothing guy jumped down, his spurs clanking, giving Zane more space on the railing. Zane tipped his hat to wish him good luck. The bloke gave him the thumbs up – a gesture Zane had taught him and the rest of the Brazilian crew a couple of rodeos ago.

Glancing to his right, he watched his steely eyed, four-legged opponents pacing the holding yards, and smirked – unlike the last time he rode, he was hell bent on not letting any of his blood be spilt tonight. Instinctively, he touched the place the bull had horned him in the side two weeks ago. It had meant a trip to the ER and fifty stitches – the three nights spent in hospital had almost sent him batty. But it was all part of the job. It was never if, but when, an injury would happen.

Needing to get away from the chaos before his ride so he could clear his head and steady the nerves, Zane jumped down and walked around the side of the arena. Time out among the rodeo-loving spectators always did him a world of good. Resting the heel of his timeworn cowboy boot on the bottom rung of the steel railings, he watched his Brazilian buddy get tossed like a rag doll from the bucking brute he'd drawn, and then basically cartwheel across the dusty ground. His wide-brimmed black hat followed, tumbling through the air and landing at Zane's feet. With the chaos in full swing, it would have to stay there for the time being. The Brazilian went to get up but stumbled back into a heap – the bull now on a snorting warpath. The fans were on their feet, some cheering, some with hands over their mouths.

Determined to horn his adversary, the bull charged while the three bullfighters worked like magnets, seamlessly pulling together and distracting the beast – fearlessly putting themselves in the firing line; their job was to get the bull riders home safe and sound. Zane grimaced and held his breath. It didn't help that he knew exactly how it felt to hit the ground so hard you lost your bearings, or how challenging it was to roll out of the way and somehow get to your feet when a beast of that size was just about to crush the air right out of you. Seconds later, and thankfully out of harm's way, the Brazilian rider hobbled out the side gate, unhurt except for his wounded pride. Zane knew so well what that felt like too. And it sucked. Unravelling his clenched fists from the railings, he leant through to retrieve the dusty hat, his muscular bulk stretching his blue shirt and snug jeans. He tossed it to one of the bullfighters to give back to its owner and resumed his position against the railings. As dangerous as bull riding was, this was the life he lived for, the life he loved – being a cowboy was in his blood.

As his mobile started to vibrate, he yanked it out of the back pocket of his jeans. Noting the caller's identity, his smile all but disappeared – five calls in a matter of days was beyond a joke. His curiosity almost getting the better of him, he debated answering, but didn't feel like being reminded of his apparent shortcomings right now. Gritting his teeth, he ended the call with a stab of his finger – he didn't have message bank, so he wouldn't have to hear his voice. After not bothering to contact him for many years, what in hell did Peter want? It would be close to ten on a Friday night back in the land down under and Zane could picture him sitting in his leather chair, Mister High-and-Mighty, with a glass of whisky in hand, ready to drink to his pathetic existence.

Needing a distraction before he tumbled into a world of melancholy, Zane looked to the grandstands. The woman he'd fallen into bed with last night, after the rodeo ball, smiled sassily back at him. Not interested in it going any further, and he'd told her as much before they'd ravished each other, he graced her with a polite smile and then quickly shifted his gaze. As beautiful as she was, there was nothing there for him. He wasn't interested in commitment – that was his way of avoiding screwing everything up and getting hurt in the process. Other than his unwavering dedication to bull riding, galloping away from anything that required promises was the motto he now lived by. His favourite country music legend, Waylon Jennings, sung it well. Cowboys weren't that easy to love, and were, without a doubt, even harder to hold. Was he destined to grow old alone? With the way he was going, quite possibly. And he'd just have to learn to live with that, if it were the case.

Zane openly admitted, to others and himself, that his wife had deserved the picket fence and the chance to start a family – the happily ever after they'd spoken of whilst wrapped up in the honeymoon phase. But the life of a travelling bull rider didn't easily allow for such a life of normalcy, and she'd resented him for that. Big time. Although, it took two to tango; he couldn't blame her for falling out of love with him. So, for now, there was always another town, another woman. But the problem was, he no longer enjoyed the chase like he used to – his Casanova persona had just about left him. Shallow and meaningless romps in the hay no longer gave him satisfaction, but instead left him feeling emptier than ever. For years he'd thought it safer to be *that* guy, the one not worth crying over, but that approach was losing its shine, real fast. As much as he tried to fight the need for something more gratifying, there was an unfamiliar niggle deep down inside him, as if something was scratching at his soul.

Annoyed by his lack of control over his mindset right now, he groaned and rubbed his face. If he didn't get his shit together, it was going to cost him, in his performance and possibly even his life. While he watched one bull rider after the other buck it out in the arena – some triumphant, some not so much – he skated over his career thus far, recalling the bigger moments that had landed him where he was today. A lot had happened, good and bad – he'd achieved everything he'd wanted to, and more. But times were changing, and so was he – he just wasn't ready to accept it. After years of pushing himself beyond his limits, of enduring countless concussions and hospital stays, he'd finally reached the pinnacle of his career. So now what? Where did he go from here?

It was almost his time to shine out in the arena. Thank Christ – he needed to get away from his thoughts. Pushing off the railings, he made his way back to the prep area. The buckle-bunnies gave him their best come-hither eyes as he sauntered past them. Tipping his hat, he graced them with his trademark dimpled grin, sending them into an excited tither. It was all for show – he knew it, and so did they. Heading behind the chutes, he wandered over to his gear bag and slumped down beside his

Australian comrade and best mate – a long lanky guy who went by the nickname of Shorty. Go figure. The place was a hive of activity where spurs chinked, heartbeats slammed, and prayers were silently uttered as each seemingly fearless cowboy who had made it into the finals readied himself for the ride of his life.

Covered in sweat after his unsuccessful ride, Shorty wiped blood from his lip. 'Well that was a major fail. I won't be telling the folks back in Aussieland about that one.'

Quietly envious of Shorty's unwavering support from his family, Zane gave him a slap on the back. 'You tried, and that's all that matters, bud. Onwards and upwards, hey?'

'Yeah, true … thanks.' Shorty flashed a lopsided grin, his lip swelling bigger by the second. 'Make sure you stay focused out there, buddy, that bastard you've drawn has some spring in his buck.'

'I bloody well hope so, Shorty, the meaner the better.'

Shorty shook his head, grinning. 'You've always been a crazy bastard, Wolfe.'

'Touché, old mate.' Zane smirked as he strapped on his spurs. A tough bull meant more bang for his buck, literally, because the harder they bucked, spun and kicked, the more points he had the possibility of getting – which meant a bigger pay cheque if he made it to the top of the leader board. He'd had his fair share of Sunday bulls, ones that would take a stroll out of the chutes instead of blasting out like a bullet fired, and that guaranteed nothing but a mundane ride, and score.

Shorty stood like an eighty-year-old, his hand going to his lower back. 'I'm busting for the pisser, and hanging for a beer to wash down the tonne of dirt I inhaled when I landed on me face. Catch ya on the flip side.'

'Righto, mate.' Watching Shorty limp away, Zane stood and did his final stretches. It was his turn to step up and show the crowd exactly how it was done, as he had countless times before.

Climbing the rails, he threw a leg over the chute and looked down at the one-tonne monster. The animal slammed his horns through the rails and sprung up. Zane grinned. This bull was living up to his reputation of being feisty as all hell. He shoved in his mouthguard, grabbed the opposite rail, and climbed aboard, straddling the snorting beast. The rich scent of musky hide sparked his senses into overdrive. Tightening his grip, he hammered his gloved hand in hard against the rope, strapped in and braced for lift-off.

Satisfied with his hold, time slowed.

He took a deep, steadying breath and nodded.

The gate flew open. The bull blasted out of the chutes like a train off the tracks, bucking, twisting and snorting. Faking a twist to the left, he then spun right, his back-end lifting and turning, sometimes with all four hooves off the ground. Silence reigned. Breaths were held. One arm held high, Zane kept his seat, but the muscles in his arm seized with the tight grip he had on the rope. As if pirouetting, the bull's haunches rose and met with Zane's shoulder blades, its tail whipping over his shoulder and slapping him in the face. Gravity snatched them back down with a shuddering thud, followed by another, and another. Zane's head jerked forwards, his cheek barely missing the deadly tip of the bull's horns. Clenching his thighs even tighter, he held on for dear life as the seconds ticked by like minutes. The world faded away, leaving just him and this brute, battling it out on the dirt. Soaring, spinning, thudding, and repeating, this was the dance of the hard-core cowboy.

The buzzer sounded and reality struck, ripping his instincts from the battle of the fittest to one of survival. He'd made the eight seconds. The roar of the crowd once again deafening, he wrestled his hand free of the rope and then leapt from the bull. Tumbling across the dirt, he sprang to his feet, ran for the railings and hoisted himself up. The bull followed, charging, horns positioned to strike. The bullfighters distracted him, skilfully directing the beast back towards the gate that led out to the holding pens. Now safe, Zane leapt down, scooped up his wide-brimmed hat, waved it to the crowd, tugged it back on and then swaggered out of the arena to raucous cheers and wolf whistles.

One of the other riders met him at the gate. 'Good job, Wolfe, I don't reckon anyone's gonna beat that score tonight.'

'Cheers, bud, I hope you're right.' Zane was breathing hard, his hand resting on his back where it had taken a beating.

Hobbling towards his gear bag, he heard his mobile's distinctive ringtone, 'Ain't Goin' Down Til the Sun Comes Up'. Slumping down, he grabbed it out. It was Peter's office number. Again. Why the hell couldn't he just leave him alone? Groaning as though the weight of the world had landed on his broad shoulders, he rolled his eyes – answering would be the only way to stop the incessant calls.

'Hey.' As he held it tight to his ear to try to hear over the noise, the voice of his father's long-time personal assistant greeted him.

'Zane, is that you?'

His defensive tone softened. 'Mary, it's been a long time. How are you?'

Silence hung heavy at the other end. 'I have some bad news, Zane.' A swift intake of air resounded. 'Peter …' her voice cracked, 'has passed away.'

Zane froze, his breath held. It wasn't so. Couldn't be. The man was immortal. He found his voice. 'How, when?'

'Three days ago. He was on a business trip in Germany and suffered a fatal heart attack.' She sighed. 'His body is being flown back to Australia tomorrow night.'

Peter was dead. Just like that. Gone. Forever. He shook his head. This had to be a cruel joke, an evil conspiracy for some godforsaken reason to try to haul him back to Australia.

'Zane, are you there?'

He squeezed his eyes shut. His throat tightened, strangling his reply. 'Uh-huh. Yup.' Pacing now, he tried to clear his throat while the world around him seemed to flicker and distort.

'I know this must be a terrible shock, and I'm so sorry to do it over the phone – but there was no other way. You and Peter may not have seen eye to eye, but he was still a part of your family.' She sniffled and then blew her nose.

'Thanks for calling and letting me know, I really appreciate it.'

'I've been trying to get hold of you since it happened, so if you want to be back in time for the funeral, you'll have to think about catching the next flight out.' Mary's tone carried with it a slight air of annoyance. 'You are going to be coming back for it, aren't you?'

'Of course I am,' he spluttered out.

'Good, I'm glad.' The phone muffled, as if Mary had put her hand over the receiver.

Zane pictured Michael standing beside her, giving her instructions on what to tell him and what not to.

Following a short conversation, Mary came back on the line. 'Oh, another thing ... there's also the matter of the will being read. They have been holding off making a time for that until we knew what you decided to do.'

'Right.' Zane's stomach heaved and he ran for the bin, dry retching. He hadn't even come to grips with the news, let alone thought about his gain from Peter's death, if any. Not that he expected anything or wanted it.

'Zane, are you okay?' Mary's voice was shrill.

Wiping his lips, he placed the phone back against his ear, ignoring the strange looks from some of the riders. 'Yeah, all good.' Feeling as though his legs were going to buckle, he wandered out of the prep area and leant against the back trailer of the stock truck. 'When's the funeral?'

'On Thursday, at 11 am.'

'Okay.' Zane was having a tough time stringing any words together.

'So we'll see you when you get here.'

'Yup, okay, Mary, and thanks for letting me know.'

'Of course, bye, Zane, travel safe.' And the line went dead.

In a daze, his phone tumbled from his hand. Staring into space, a tidal wave of dizziness surged over him. His vision clouded as he tried to draw in a breath. Sinking to his knees, his entire world felt as if it were crumbling around him. He tried to come to grips with the fact he'd never see Peter again, or hear the apology he'd so longed for from Peter for always making Zane feel like a thorn in his side.

CHAPTER
4

Serendipity Farm

The distant drone of a tractor carried on the balmy breeze, as did the hint of seaside saltiness from nearby Crystal Beach. The rustle of the leaves in the Bangkok Rose bush was followed by a bellbird singing its one-noted tune. Momentarily distracted, Emma closed her eyes, and her book, drew in a deep breath and wished for another life, far away from all the heartache and drama of late. Then peering past the cottage she used to call home before moving into the main homestead when her parents left for their travels, she gazed towards the horizon. Although it was still stinking hot, the blazing sun had begun to slide towards the haze of the distant mountain ranges that embraced the coastal country town.

Shadows stretched along the back lawn that separated the homestead from the cottage, helping to conceal Kat's metal-grey coat. The middle-aged feline was biding her time, waiting for the perfect moment to pounce on her seemingly unsuspecting archenemy, Peking the second. Over the years Kat had learnt from the duck's father, Peking the first, that hiding was fruitless. Although they were unlikely friends, it was a game both feathered and furred revelled in. Above the pair, a flock of pink and grey galahs had landed in the branches of the towering jacaranda, their squawks loud and incessant as if each bird was trying to talk over the other. The old dairy cows, Gertrude and Daisy, hung their heads over the back fence, reaching for the grass that always appeared so much greener. At the far end of the verandah, the bamboo and copper wind chimes jingled. Tiny lay sprawled on the back lawn as if he'd melted, his relentless panting and the whirr of the ceiling fans inside the house keeping company with the call of the cicadas from the golden wattle trees that grew along the fence line.

Burying her head back into the most recent addition to her already overflowing bookshelves, Emma tried to focus on the welcome escape her romance novels always granted her. The characters seemed so real, she wished she could somehow disappear into the pages to be with them, if only for a little while. But, unlike the late nights when she would crawl into bed, aching and bone-tired, yet still keen to catch up with her latest hero and heroine, to read that little bit more of their poignant love story, today it was proving a real struggle.

After four days spent coming to terms with the shocking news of Peter's death and consoling Riley, all the while wondering if she would now have the freedom to expose what should have been revealed all those years ago, she'd hoped reading would give her the release she so desperately needed. She had to find some clear headspace to work it all out. It had helped for a little while, but with so much weighing on her mind, her thoughts were starting to overwhelm her. There was only so long she could pretend her life wouldn't be turned upside down, even more so than it already was, if she spoke about what she knew.

Pausing on a sentence after re-reading it three times, she thought about what could happen if she found the courage to tell everything. Timing would be important. It would be disrespectful and heartless of her to do it before the funeral – everyone already had enough on their plates. And then they needed time to grieve, to heal, before she upended their lives. There were so many scenarios she'd played over and over while unable to sleep, and none of them ended with happily ever afters. Zane felt like a stranger now – they hadn't spoken for the past seven years – and with Michael bitter and vindictive, even though he was the one who cheated with a woman almost half his age, there was no way he was going to take kindly to her news. There was so much to consider and torment herself with; just the thought of it all unfolding made her stomach churn. Emma knew her daughter loved her dearly, but as a teenager her darling Riley seemed to always be angry with her – for everything from Michael leaving to not having the right brand of juice in the fridge. Revealing the truth, especially after all this time, was going to make matters much worse before they had a chance to get any better.

Emotions overwhelming her, Emma blinked back tears. Her beautiful Riley had gone from a loving little girl who would wrap her arms so tightly around her neck she could barely breathe, to a fifteen-year-old, hormone-riddled time bomb in what felt like the blink of an eye. Her body tensed as she recalled the look on her strong-willed daughter's face when she'd busted

Riley sneaking back into the house at two this morning, after sneaking out to meet her unruly boyfriend. With Riley's mobile switched off, and after unsuccessfully driving the streets of town looking for her, and then anxiously pacing the hallway for hours waiting for her to return home, Emma had been both relieved and livid to see Riley when she'd climbed back through her bedroom window. Although livid had quickly won out when Riley had stormed past her as if *she* were the one having done wrong by worrying and waiting up for her. When she heard she was grounded, Riley's baby-blues had turned so fierce and full of animosity, Emma would've preferred to be stabbed in the heart right then and there. Being a mother was the hardest job she'd ever had to do, especially now she was a single parent – quite a few of her mates, both single and married, with teenage daughters, agreed.

Unable to hold back her tears any longer, they rolled down her cheeks as she recalled the argument that had ensued.

I hate you ...
Please, Riley, don't say that.
I'll say whatever I damn well like.
Not when you're under my roof you won't.
Fine then, I'll go and live with Dad.
Oh, for god's sake, Riley, not this again.
Yes, Mum, this again, but this time I damn well mean it.
Really? We both know what happened the last time you tried that.
Yeah, well, that was different.
Was it? How so?
Go to hell, Mum. I don't need to explain anything to you.
I beg your pardon, miss.
You heard me.

Heartbroken, shocked and furious, Emma had bit her tongue, for fear of saying something she'd deeply regret. Both of them with their arms crossed, tempers raging, and a stance that meant business, they'd reached a stalemate. As they'd stood staring at each other like two outlaws about to quick draw, she'd taken a deep breath and tried to play Riley's bluff, calmly telling her that if living with her father was what she wanted, then she wasn't going to stop her. It had almost blown up in her face, with Riley going as far as packing a bag this morning and calling Michael to come and get her. But, no surprise, he hadn't shown up. Instead he called three hours later to say he'd been caught up at work and would catch her over the weekend. Riley had slammed her bedroom door so hard after the phone call Emma was surprised it hadn't fallen off its hinges. She'd tried to go and comfort her, but with the door locked Riley had let her know in no uncertain terms she wanted to be left alone.

Like father like son, the apple didn't fall far from the tree when it came to Michael. Riley was very much like her – a sensitive soul, even though she came across as strong as an ox. Riley needed a father who made her feel wanted, loved, cherished; a father who showed he was proud of her many achievements at school and came to cheer her on at her horse sports. Michael was doing a shitty job of all of that, making it known that losing, at anything, was never an option. It put Riley under an immense amount of pressure. Not for lack of trying, Emma was helpless to stop the toll it was taking on her beautiful, free-spirited daughter, or the rebellion it was causing. Something had to give before it all blew up, and before Riley's broken heart was irreparable. Maybe Peter's death was a gift from the heavens, for all their sakes.

Emma's heart squeezed tight as the guilt she'd carried for years pounded her even harder. There was a possible way out of this mess, a way around it all, but it was going to take a damn truckload of courage on her behalf. And could it cause more harm than good after all this time? She often wondered if Zane would have done any better than Michael. Would he do a good job of fatherhood now Riley was older and more independent? But with Zane's nomadic lifestyle, over on the other side of the world, chasing the next rodeo and probably the next notch on his bedpost, Emma wasn't too sure he'd have been, or would be, a better father than Michael.

She heaved a weary sigh. What was she meant to do? 'Please, angels, give me some sort of sign, and show me the way …' she whispered, while blinking back more tears.

Drawing in a shaky breath, she closed her eyes while she fought off the sorrow, guilt and uncertainty. The angst of it all, as well as the thought of attending Peter's funeral and seeing Zane after all these years, had her fretting. Even though she'd secretly followed his amazing bull-riding journey on his Facebook page (she hadn't been able to help herself), how was she going to feel laying eyes on him after all this time? Would the secrets she'd kept from him be her undoing? Would she crumble the minute he was near her? Would the chasm between them be so wide, she'd not find the strength to cross it?

She rubbed her temples and heaved another unsatisfying sigh. No matter what, the truth had to be told, sometime. She knew that without a shadow of a doubt. But the thought of it pushing Riley even further away, at such an important time in her life, terrified Emma beyond words. She wished her parents were here, instead of gallivanting around Europe like the loved-up nomads they'd become, so she could draw strength from them. But after all their years of hard work at Serendipity, they were entitled to revel in their retirement and chase their travelling dreams to their hearts' content. They'd offered to come back for the funeral, but as they'd never been fans of Peter and his arrogant ways, Emma had told them not to. Why spend a fortune to attend a funeral of a man they despised? She would just have to pull on her big-girl boots to deal with the situation. Somehow. Some way.

A whinny sounded from the paddock, pulling her away from her incessant thoughts. Her buckskin, Bundy, was letting her know it was that time of the day, and he was hungry, like literally starving to death, so she'd better hurry up. He did this at the same time every day, on the dot. It was around the same time she'd usually see Riley wandering down the driveway after her Saturday shift at the local IGA, her head buried in her phone and her shoulders slumped as if the entire world rested upon them. Emma had a feeling today was going to be one of those times when Riley chose to get under her skin by not showing up at home when she should. She made a conscious effort not to rise to the bait – it wasn't worth the argument. Scraping a wisp of hair behind her ear, she smiled at Bundy's audacity while trying to ignore the relentless heat still inching its way across the verandah. It had been a scorching January so far, the temperature reaching a record forty-three degrees just after midday. Not the kind of weather to be outside unless you had to.

Her bare feet resting up on the railing of the wide, wrap-around verandah, she waved a fly from her face. Well aware she really should think about pulling her boots back on and making a move to feed the critters before the sun slunk away and Bundy starved to death, she couldn't resist the yearning to read just one more page, hoping it might help lift her mood. She smiled when she realised she'd been saying that to herself for the past couple of hours. Even though she'd initially felt guilty, sitting about doing nothing, she told herself it was what she needed after the godawful week she and Riley had endured. As her best mate, Renee, always said to her, she really needed to learn to stop and smell the roses – life was way too short not to. If only her roses weren't so thorny, she might actually try to do just that.

Squinting, she cast her gaze over Serendipity, only to be reminded of everything she had to do. Her trusty old John Deere tractor was where she'd parked it at dusk last night, beside the quad bike that was in need of a service. The slashing still had to be finished in the top paddocks; and then she'd have to go back to where she'd started and slash it all over again as the grass grew so quickly. The bonnet of her Land Rover was still up, reminding her to top it up with oil before she drove it into town again – the old girl was drinking it the way a parched person sculled water. She really needed to think about upgrading, but with the sentimental value of it being her dad's old beast, she couldn't find it in herself to part with it. Then there were her few DIY projects half finished in the shed – the stack of wooden pallets she'd scored from the stockfeed place in town that she'd eventually use to make a stand-alone bar, a coffee table, a wall-mounted wine rack and a fresh herb planter. High hopes – she had many.

Besides the upkeep and usual TLC of a farm, there were the everyday jobs of feeding and mucking out the agisted horses, as well as her own, checking on the hundred and fifty head of cattle, and keeping on top of the household and motherly duties – with an audacious teenager on her hands that was proving to be a massive feat in itself. It bloody well never ended. But where there was a will, there was a way. Her breath caught as she tried to make herself believe that. If only she had a helping hand around the place, someone who didn't cost an arm and a leg, and preferably a hunk of manly man she could occasionally perve at. Wasn't asking too much, was it? She chuckled and rolled her eyes. She had to laugh or she'd cry.

Her mind now going like a bull at a gate with everything she needed to do, guilt pounded her once more. She really shouldn't have taken time out to read; the daylight hours were precious. If only Riley were home more often to help her, instead of gallivanting around the countryside with the eighteen-year-old boyfriend she believed was the love of her life, the load would lighten a little. But not wanting to sound like a broken record, Emma had given up asking. The last time she said anything about it, they'd erupted into world war three. In a flood of tears she'd basically begged Riley to understand she wasn't nagging or being unfair. She. Just. Needed. Help. But Riley only saw it as Emma trying to keep her from the boyfriend who meant everything to her.

Groaning, she finally stopped procrastinating, gave up the idea of a little more reading, and accepted that nothing was going to get done if she didn't do it herself. Placing her bookmark between the pages, she stood and stretched her arms high, willing her body to some sort of life while the heat of the verandah suddenly burned the bare soles of her feet. Grimacing, she hopped across the scorching floorboards, and once safe on the welcome mat near the top of the steps, she grabbed her boots and socks from where she'd kicked them off and tugged them back on. Heading down the front steps, she paused to give Tiny a ruffle behind the ears – her loyal mate now greying around his muzzle.

'Come on, buddy, let's get to it, hey.'

Eager as always to be by her side, Tiny's tail spun like a chopper blade while he padded down the garden path and through the rickety little gate, licking her hand as she clipped the gate shut. As she headed towards the quad bike, the grit of the driveway crunched beneath her boots and her eyes watered from the glare of the corrugated-iron roof on the shed. Everything appeared to be simmering beneath the fierce sun; in the heat-hazed mirage, the horses looked like they were walking on water. The windmill she'd spent countless hours servicing and repairing over the years spun lazily in the distance, pumping essential water into the troughs. Grey and pink galahs squawked from their perches in the surrounding trees, their ruckus deafening. Beneath it all, Kat was still in stealth mode, her tail jiggling like a rattle snake as she lay hiding in the grass, once again ready to pounce on poor Peking the second. The jingling bell around her neck didn't help the feline's plight whatsoever, but Emma gave credit where credit was due – Kat never gave up trying, and Peking seemed to revel in the game.

Throwing her leg over the quad, Emma got settled and revved it to life. Tiny wagged his tail even faster, if that were even possible, and looked at her expectantly. Grinning, she patted the seat behind her, and he leapt to his second favourite spot, his first being in front of his food bowl. A head above her, he rested his muzzle on her shoulder as they headed towards the feed shed. Emma took the long way around, wanting to gauge the growth in the three paddocks she'd left empty to rejuvenate the past month. They were looking good.

Skidding to a stop, Emma threw her leg over the bike and Tiny bounded off. Stepping into the shadows of the feed and tack room, Tiny went to his usual corner, sniffing like a bomb dog all around the spot where the chooks sometimes laid a random egg. Laughing at his antics, Emma started scooping feed from different bins and measuring it into the line of buckets – knowing by heart what each of the twelve agisted horses needed in their diets. Some were fairly basic, while others had a gourmet regimen that was not really necessary, in her opinion. But what the customer wanted, the customer always got. Bundy, being the tough, bush-bred horse he was, got a basic feed of chaff and sometimes, for a treat, molasses, as did Riley's gelding, Boomerang.

Her Aries mind wandering as she worked methodically, Emma recalled the last time she'd seen Zane in all his handsome, manly flesh. After leaving Riley's birthday party when Peter had turned up, he'd arrived back at her door around midnight, reeking of whisky, nursing a bloodied lip and grazed knuckles, and mumbling something about having taught Michael a lesson in being a better father and husband. He'd tried to kiss her and she'd slapped him, hard, and then told him they needed to cut ties. It had been the only way to stop from giving in to his very tempting advance. She'd later found out that Michael had fared worse, with a broken nose, a hospital visit, and twelve stitches beneath his right eye. Peter had publicly and humiliatingly disowned Zane in an all-out verbal war in the hospital corridor. The next day Zane had boarded an American Airlines flight, claiming he'd never return, and he hadn't, until now. Not having to look him in the eyes for the past seven years, or hear his deep, husky voice at the end of the phone, had given her the freedom to bury all her dirty laundry deep down, and had helped her to try to ignore the anguish of keeping it to herself. But it had been a false sense of security – the day she'd have to face her fears and tell all was speeding towards her at an alarming rate.

Loading the feed buckets onto the quad bike, she rewound her mind sixteen years. Seventeen years old, fighting with Michael about not having gone to the police, terrified out of her wits that the Mafia would find out and come after her, and unable to talk to her parents about accidentally killing a man, she'd grabbed a bottle of her dad's whisky and wandered over to the cottage, desperate for a sympathetic ear and a few drinks to drown her sorrows. Zane had answered the door in his boxers, a concerned smile on his face. Two hours later, and both drunk, she gave in to the urges she'd harboured for years, and kissed Zane smack on the lips. At first, he'd hesitated, until she'd garbled something about getting whatever it was between them out of their systems before he left for god only knew how long. Not needing her to twist his arm any further, he'd tugged her to him and kissed her back, so possessively, so fiercely, it had buckled her legs beneath her. Then he'd scooped her up and carried her to his room, where they'd made love like she'd never made love before, or ever made love again.

Young, naïve, spontaneous, uninhibited – he'd known all the right places to touch, kiss and bite. Her entire body fired to life with the thought of canoodling with him again, let alone having sex with him – not that that was *ever* going to happen. She wouldn't allow it, couldn't allow it. Once was a mistake, twice would be a stupid choice. Nevertheless, heat rushed to her cheeks, and her nether regions ached to be caressed by him, and only him.

A wave of emotions – guilt, lust, longing – overcame her. She wrapped her arms around herself, quivering as if he were touching her again. This was exactly why she tried not to think about him. Ever. Because even now, the memory of being naked with him, and the look in his eyes as he'd become one with her, stole her breath. It was not only because the memory made her tingle in places she didn't want to while thinking about him, but because, if she were being completely honest with herself, she wanted more of what they'd shared that night. So. Much. More.

But neither then, nor now, would Mister Casanova ever give her the commitment she'd expect from a man she was intimate with, so it just wasn't an option. She really needed to get a grip before she saw him at the funeral. Shaking her head, she tossed her ponytail over her shoulder and got back on the quad bike, followed by Tiny. Swiftly changing gears, she headed down the long gravel drive, away from the memories of Zane, and towards the bottom paddock, keen to get everything done before sundown.

CHAPTER
5

Waking super early, with her mind troubled, experience had taught Emma that the best way to heal and deal was to go deep into nature, on the back of a horse. So, the slashing finished, the quad bike serviced, her old girl topped up with oil, the cattle checked, and all the horses fed, she felt a little more in control and had achieved a lot more than this time yesterday. Totally in the moment as she and Bundy cantered across the flats, she startled when Johnny Cash's 'I Walk the Line' rang out through the serenity of the scrub.

Giving Bundy a gentle cue to woo up, she grabbed her mobile from the saddlebag. She smiled knowing she was about to hear Renee's voice. 'Hey, my beautiful soul sister, about bloody time, I thought you'd slipped off the edge of the earth or been abducted by aliens.'

'Hey, Em, half my bloody luck. Sorry I've taken so long to call you. I've been doing back-to-back shifts and I've finally come up for some air.'

Renee groaned melodramatically and Emma could picture her rolling her big brown eyes. Two long weeks between coffee catch-ups was almost a record for them. 'No worries, hun, I know you're a busy gal. The way the hospital has to run with so little staff is a joke.'

'You're not telling me anything I don't already know. I feel like I'm one of those zombies out of *The Walking Dead* at the moment.' She chortled then snorted. 'But anyways, enough about my problems … tell me, has everything eased off a bit now?'

'Yeah, sort of. I still find it hard to believe he's gone, just like that, and as harsh as it sounds, I'm not really upset about it. More relieved in a way.' She huffed. 'I'm going to hell for saying that out loud, aren't I?'

'No way, Em, and if you do, I'll come with you.'

They both laughed.

'Why should you be grieving when the man put you through hell and back the entire time you were married to Mister Idiot Features? It's no wonder you're feeling a weight lift.'

Emma bit back a cynical laugh – little did Renee know just *how* much Peter had put her through. She'd wanted to confide in her bestie for years, but Peter's threat had stopped her. 'I just feel for Riley, especially as it seems to be the only thing people are talking about around town. She really did love the man, warts and all.'

'Understandably so; he was her grandfather. Can't pick your family.' Renee sighed. 'So how are things with her now? Have they calmed down at all?'

Cradling the phone between her shoulder and ear, Emma readjusted the reins. 'Not really, we had a doozy of an argument the other night, over her boyfriend, again – two days later and she still can't stand the sight of me.'

'Oh, Em, it will get better – just hang in there. You're a good mum and you do your best for her. Maybe not now, but one day she'll look back and be grateful for all the tough love you've had to dish out of late.'

'I hope you're right, Rennie. It breaks my heart, us being like this, but I can't let her get away with things when she's in the wrong.'

'I know, it's hard, but you're strong and you got this.'

'Thanks for the vote of confidence.'

'My pleasure, treasure … that little ratbag doesn't know how good she's got it, having a cool mum like you.' The sound of the whistling kettle Emma had bought Renee for Christmas carried down the line. 'Do you think it'd help if I tried to talk to her?'

Emma hadn't even thought about it. 'You'd do that?'

'Of course, especially seeing as she's my godchild. With Michael out of the picture, I kinda feel it's my place to step in if you need help.'

'I think it might be worth a shot.'

'Well, in that case, consider it done.'

Emma bit back a sob. 'Thanks, Rennie, I don't know where I'd be without you.'

'Probably up shit creek without a paddle.' Renee chuckled. 'I've always got your back, and anytime you have one too many, I'll hold your hair back too, if need be.'

Hazy memories of paying the price after one too many down the pub with Renee made Emma grin and grimace at the same time – those days were long gone. 'Ditto, and speaking of that …' Emma's throat closed up and it took her a moment to free her voice.

'Yeah?' It was said with concerned caution.

'I have something I really need to talk to you about.' Emma
spat the words out as if toxic.

'Shoot, hun, I'm all ears.'

Emma frowned, and even though she was in the middle of the
scrub, very much alone, she still glanced over her shoulder – a
habit she'd never been able to shake since that fateful night. 'No,
not right now … I can't talk about it on the phone.' Her heart
thumped so hard she could hear it over the clip clop of Bundy's
new shoes, ones she'd spent the good part of the morning putting
on.

'Oh shit, this sounds serious. Has Michael gone and upset you
again, because if he has, I'd be more than happy to go and kick
him in the nuts. I've wanted to do it for years …'

'There'll be no need for that, but thanks.' Smiling, Emma
sucked in a desperate breath.

'You okay, Em?'

'Yes and no.'

The line was quiet for a few moments; the ding of a teaspoon
hitting the side of a cup broke the silence. 'Right, well, now I'm
really worried about you, so let me scull a strong coffee so I can
get my wits about me and put some clothes on so I don't walk
out the front door butt naked, and I'll be there in about half an
hour.'

Renee had always been a bit of a nudist, much to Emma's
amusement, and the postman's, who had arrived at Renee's door
to find her half asleep and totally naked – it had been the talk of
the town for weeks. 'No, don't rush. How bouts you come over
around six and I'll cook us some dinner, if you like.'

'Yeah, I'd like that a lot. I'll bring the wine – sounds like we're
gonna need it.'

The memory of the last time she and Renee had caught up for a wine and had ended up drinking almost two bottles between them made Emma's stomach turn. 'It's a date.'

'You sure whatever you need to talk to me about can wait a few hours?'

She'd already waited almost half her life, so a few hours weren't going to make a world of difference. 'A hundred and ten percent positive, Rennie ... and don't drive like a maniac to get over here either; the roos have been out in force the past week.'

'Okay, I promise to drive like Granny May, minus the two phone books she sits on to see over the steering wheel. I'll see you around six.'

'Ha-ha, there's no denying you've got a groovy granny. Love ya, hun.'

'Love you too, Em. See you soon. Bye.'

'Bye, lovely.' Slipping her phone into the saddlebag, Emma dragged in a deep breath, and slowly blew it away. Just revealing to Renee she had something important to talk about with her made her feel a little lighter. She could only imagine what actually saying it out loud was going to feel like – terrifying and liberating all at once.

At this time of the day there was too much sun to see into the distance, but she could just make out the tops of the mountains that cradled the aqua-blue sea that rolled into the white-sand shoreline Silvergum was famous for. She really needed to get down to Crystal Beach more often, but the recent sighting of a massive saltwater croc had scared her, and almost every other local, off swimming there. Even wandering along the beach wasn't the safest – the joys of living in Northern Queensland where everything wanted to bite you. With the roof of the homestead coming into sight, Bundy picked up pace. His steps rhythmic, the saddle creaked beneath Emma. She looked to where her lasso hung at the ready from the saddlebag. Hopefully, she'd get one last chance to put it to work before heading home.

Spotting a large tree stump poking out of the long grass, a shiver charged through her fingertips as they coiled around the rope. To be able to lasso from a horse was a talent she'd learnt from her father many years ago, and one she found brought her clear-headedness when she needed it. Today was one of those times, which was why she'd spent the last two hours riding and lassoing everything in sight. Securing her seat in the saddle with her thighs, she twirled the rope above her head, her gaze focused on her target. Three whirls and she let it fly. Bundy didn't flinch, the horse accustomed to the movements. The rope sailed through the air and landed dead on. Hot dang, she was good. With a gentle nudge, Bundy trotted over to let her retrieve it. She gave it a tug, cursing when she saw it was hooked up. In seconds she'd swung out of the saddle and was on the ground sorting it out.

Parched, she grabbed her water bottle from the saddlebag and took a swig. Then, taking off her wide-brimmed hat and tipping some water into it, she offered it to Bundy to wet his lips – and he did, with comical vigour. Popping it back on her head, the dampness cooled her off a little. Reaching out, she wrapped her arms around his neck, inhaling his horsey scent – earthy and wholesome. If someone could come up with a way to bottle it, she was sure they'd be a squillionaire. Give her a hardworking man that smelt of horse and leather over a bottle of aftershave any day.

Strolling down to the trickling waterfall that descended to the valley behind them, she bent, washed her face and filled her water bottle. This stuff tasted like fine wine compared to the town water. Drawing in the aromas of the bush, she wandered over to Bundy and climbed back into the saddle. The scent of impending rain made her look up to the sky. Black clouds were quickly swallowing up the blue, and she worked out she had about ten minutes to get home before it bucketed down. Giving Bundy the cue to run wild and free, her horse widened his gait and within seconds they were galloping towards home.

Just as they reached the stables, a reverberating crack of thunder shook the ground beneath them, and not long after a flash of iridescent lightning zoomed across the sky. Then the heavens rained down. Emma smiled from the heart. Tonight, she would hopefully be able to sleep a little easier with the pitter-patter of raindrops on the tin roof – her definition of bliss. Dismounting under the awning, she quickly got to work unsaddling Bundy, brushing him down and then giving him a special treat of lucerne with a trickle of molasses.

Racing towards the homestead, across the back lawn, then climbing the steps two at a time, Emma paused to give Tiny a pat before kicking her boots off and making a beeline for the drinks fridge. She needed an icy cold beer to wash the dust of the day from her parched throat while watching from the verandah as the storm did the same for Mother Earth. Peering through the kitchen window, she looked for any signs of life – lights, the sounds of the telly, footsteps, anything. The homestead was as quiet and dark as she'd left it.

Glancing at the empty rack near the back door where Riley usually dropped her shoes, she then looked at her watch, shaking her head. Riley was late home. Again. A distant memory claimed her as she stared down the driveway, bringing tears to her eyes.

Year after year, she'd stood in this exact spot, her heart swelling as she'd watched Riley wander down the drive, Tiny loyally beside her, and her head buried in a book. When Riley finally did look up, a broad smile would claim her pretty little face, and she would run into Emma's arms, excited to tell her about her day. Back then, she'd thought they'd always remain so close, so tightly knit that nothing could ever come between them – if only that were so.

Grabbing her mobile from her pocket, she looked to see if there were any missed called or texts, and wasn't surprised when there weren't any. She dialled Riley's number. As usual, it went to message bank. Huffing, she hung up and dialled it again, in the desperate hope Riley simply hadn't heard the incoming call. Once again, message bank.

'Hi, Riley here, you know the drill ...'

Keeping her voice as calm as she possibly could given her rising exasperation, Emma closed her eyes and fought off the urge to explode. 'Riley, it's Mum, you were meant to come home straight after school. Can you please give me a call and let me know what you're doing? Aunty Rennie is coming for dinner and I'm sure she'd love to see you, and so would I sometimes, you know. I love you.' Hitting *end*, she tossed the phone onto the outdoor settee.

And then she paced, beer in hand, wondering if she should do the desperate-mother thing and go looking for her. Lord only knew what she could be up to, with the unruly mob she was hanging around these days, her boyfriend's mates not ones Emma liked or approved of. Making a snap decision, she stormed down the front steps and towards her Land Rover, no longer caring about the rain. Enough was enough. Still her little girl, Riley needed to learn some respect, come hell or high water, and if that meant Emma had to be the bad guy for now, then so be it.

Driving over the bridge that led into town, a known hangout for the rebellious kids of the area, she made sure to keep her eyes peeled. A glimpse of shadows beneath it had her making a quick U-turn. She parked off to the side, out of sight. The rain was easing off now to a light sprinkle, the dark clouds that had consumed the blue now thundering into the distance. As she stepped from the four-wheel drive the stench of marijuana struck her first, followed by raucous laughter. Her breath tightened even more. Would her sweet, innocent girl be here, smoking pot? She doubted it, but with everything going on right now, anything was possible. Panic fuelled the determination in her steps as she stormed down the bank. Ben Lewis's sticker-clad, aerial-overloaded ute came into her line of sight and confirmed her fears in an instant. Riley wouldn't be far from her boyfriend's side. A well-known rogue, Emma knew Ben was bad news, but she didn't even stop to think about that he might be into drugs. With the incoming adult being spotted by the group, teenagers ran left, right and centre. Riley jumped into the passenger seat as Ben revved the V8 to life.

'Riley Jane Wolfe, you get out of that ute, missy, or you can kiss next weekend's gymkhana goodbye,' Emma called out, every word choked by stormy emotions.

Her expression one of defiance, Riley completely ignored Emma's words.

'Don't you dare drive off, Ben, or I'll make damn sure the police know you've been here smoking pot.' Glaring at the copper-haired boy behind the wheel, and then to the deathly quiet teenagers now piled in the tray, Emma stormed over to them. Her hands coming down hard on the driver's window, she stuck her head through until she was only inches from Ben's face. 'You stay the hell away from my daughter, you got it?'

'Mum, please.' Riley's red-rimmed eyes were as wide as saucers.

The acne-faced eighteen-year-old flashed Emma a smartarse smile. 'Make me.'

She had to fight from grabbing him by the ear and dragging him from the car. 'Oh, trust me, Ben, I've got a really big shotgun at home that I'm not afraid to use, so don't even try me.'

He sniggered and shook his head. 'Yeah, right, pull the other one.'

With Ben getting it over her, because yes, she'd never pull a gun on anyone, let alone a teenage boy, Emma stepped back before she did something she could get charged for. 'Riley, get out of the car, right now.' If it were possible, smoke would have been billowing from her ears she was so furious.

With an almighty huff, Riley went to do as she was told, but Ben grabbed her arm, squeezing it so tight Riley winced in pain. 'If you get out, we're finished.'

'Let go, Ben, you're hurting me.'

But he squeezed even tighter. 'It's me or her.' His tone was menacing.

'Ben, please stop it, you're scaring me,' Riley cried out as she tried to yank her arm free.

Emma reached back through the window and grabbed his shirt collar. 'Let her go, you bastard.' *Who did this little shit think he was?*

The distraction had him freeing Riley from his vice-like grip, allowing her to tumble from the passenger door.

'She wouldn't give out anyway, so no loss to me,' Ben said, snarling in Emma's face. His foot slamming to the floor, the wheels spun and gravel flew out behind as the four-wheel drive fishtailed up the bank and screeched onto the bitumen of the main road into town, all the teenagers in the back hanging on for dear life.

Spinning around to face her daughter, Emma did her very best not to lose her temper – it would get them nowhere fast. 'You okay?' She rushed to Riley's side, but noting how her daughter took a step back from her, she resisted the urge to take her into her arms and comfort her.

Shaking, Riley nodded, her eyes as bloodshot as they come.

'I hope you can see how much of an arsehole he is now.'

Unmoving, Riley remained mute.

'So you're smoking pot now?' As sorry as she felt for Riley, Emma couldn't help the icy tone.

Riley's face scrunched up. 'You've just embarrassed me in front of all of my friends.'

'I don't give two hoots, Riley.' She folded her arms. 'Answer my goddamn question.'

'So what if I was smoking pot, Mum?' Her blue eyes flashing, Riley stood her ground. Although trying to look as if she were okay, her bottom lip twitched and she was clearly fighting back tears.

Emma couldn't believe what she was hearing. '*So what?* Oh my god. Are you being serious right now?'

Other than a hefty sigh – a common occurrence of late, and a habit that really got under Emma's skin almost as much as the *whatever* shoulder shrug – Riley remained silent.

'Well, let me see.' Emma rubbed her chin as though deep in thought. 'Firstly, it's illegal, and secondly, it's not good for you.

But most importantly of all, if you get caught you'll have it on your record and you can kiss any hope of having a good career goodbye.'

'How can they charge me when people use it for medicinal purposes?' With Emma at a loss for words, Riley shrugged. 'I'll just say that's what it's for, if I'm unlucky enough to get busted.'

As serious as this all was, Emma couldn't help but laugh. 'Is that what Ben told you?'

'Yes.'

'Well, you're a fool, listening to what comes out of that bully's mouth. He only cares about himself and would throw you under the bus in a heartbeat if it meant saving himself. As you just witnessed.'

Unable to fend them off any longer, heavy tears rolled down Riley's cheeks. As though the wind had been knocked right out of her, she bent and then squatted to her heels, sobbing hard.

Emma instantly felt terrible. 'Oh, love, I'm so sorry, I know you truly believe you love him. I just don't understand why.'

'You wouldn't understand if I told you.'

Emma squatted down beside her. 'Try me.'

Riley paused, as if debating whether it would be a good idea, but to Emma's relief, she began to talk. 'Because I felt like he really cared about me.' Sniffling, Riley looked to her. 'And it was nice to think there was a guy in my life who might actually love me for me.' Her voice was so small, so innocent, it was heart wrenching. 'But after what he just did, I was obviously *very* wrong.'

Her heart hurting like hell, Emma placed her hand on her chest and the other over her quivering mouth. She shook her head and blinked back tears, everything suddenly so crystal clear. 'Oh, my beautiful girl, you do know your dad loves you, right?'

'If he does, he's got a really funny way of showing it.'

'I know he can be a tough one to read sometimes, sweetheart, but there's no shadow of a doubt he loves you very much.'

'I really wish he'd tell me that, instead of constantly telling me what I'm doing wrong. I never feel good enough for him.' The sadness in Riley's voice shattered Emma's already aching heart.

Emma leapt over the imaginary barrier that had built up between them and helped Riley to stand. Then she tenderly cupped her face. 'My darling girl, you're more than good enough. You're the best daughter anyone could ever wish for.'

'You really mean that?' Hopeful eyes held Emma's.

'Of course I mean it. You sometimes make me want to pull my hair out, but you're beautiful through and through, Riley, and don't ever let anyone make you think otherwise.'

'Thanks, Mum.' A small smile flittered across Riley's tear-stained face.

Emma could feel the defences Riley had put up around herself begin to crumble and fall, leaving her daughter looking so young, so vulnerable, so broken. Her heart tumbling to the ground, she did her best to reel in her anger about the marijuana – they could deal with that later. She pulled Riley to her. 'I know you've been through so much lately, with mine and Dad's divorce, and Grandad's passing. Just please know I love you so much, and I'm sorry you're hurting so badly, but please, please let me help you. I'm not the enemy here.' She kissed the top of her daughter's head and stroked her hair. 'If you could just let me in, we could get through all of this together, I promise.'

Riley sucked in a shuddering breath. 'I promise I'll try really hard, Mum, it's just, sometimes I'm so angry with you and Dad breaking up that I can't help what I do or say.' She wrapped her arms around Emma, rested her head on her shoulder, and held her tight. 'It hurts so much that sometimes I just wish I could go to sleep and never wake up.'

'Oh, baby girl, please don't say things like that. Everything's going to work out just fine, I promise.'

Riley's chilling words like daggers to her heart, Emma cradled her daughter to her chest as her own tears gathered and fell. They'd been through so much, and Riley clearly couldn't take much more, her scars running a whole lot deeper than Emma had thought. She'd have to take her next steps slowly and carefully, or she could risk losing Riley forever, in more ways than one.

CHAPTER
6

Tiptoeing down the hallway, the two glasses of red wine she'd enjoyed over dinner now going to her legs, Emma paused by Riley's room and checked for any light filtering beneath the door. There was none, and there were no sounds either. Fingers crossed, Riley had finally been able to drift off to sleep. Slowing creaking the door open, she crept in. From the glow of the iPhone lying on the pillow Emma could see the scattering of freckles across Riley's nose and cheeks, and the tinge of red in her chestnut-coloured hair – like mother like daughter. The soft melody of music drifted from the headphones, ones that were almost permanently in Riley's ears, as Emma slowly pulled the sheet up and over her. Leaning in, she brushed a lock of hair from her daughter's forehead and gently kissed her goodnight.

'I love you so much, my beautiful girl. Dream sweet,' she whispered.

Riley's eyelids flickered. 'Love you too, Mum.' She rolled onto her side, her breathing deep and steady.

Emma stood for a few moments, her arms wrapped around herself. The love a parent felt for their child could never be measured, or surpassed. It was infinite, endless. She blinked back tears as she quietly made her way out, shut the door, and headed to where Renee was curled up on the couch, a glass of wine in her hands and a fresh bottle of pinot noir just opened.

Renee looked up. 'She asleep, hun?'

'Yeah, she is, thank god.' Emma poured herself another wine, and then taking Renee's outstretched glass, filled hers up too. 'Thanks so much for talking to her; it seems to have done the trick.'

'My pleasure, Em, I just hope it helps to bring you two back together again. I hate seeing the people I love most in the world heartbroken – you both deserve to be happy.'

'Awww, thanks, Rennie.' As the room was a little stuffy, Emma pulled the curtains open, allowing the cool night air to drift in. 'Should I dare ask what you two spoke about?' She turned the ceiling fan up. The wine must be making her feel a little flushed, or was it because she was about to divulge a colossal secret?

Renee flashed her pearly whites. 'I was sworn to secrecy, so if I tell you I'll have to kill you.'

'Righto, as much as not knowing is going to drive me nuts, you're a good godparent. I'll give you that.'

'She's such a good kid, Em, just a bit messed up after everything that's happened, and that's understandable. She genuinely wants to make things right between you and her, especially now Ben is out of the picture. I truly believe things will improve heaps with him gone.'

'I hope so, Rennie.'

'I *know* so, Em.' Renee offered a gentle smile as she watched Emma wandering around the lounge room, tidying things up. 'You're really edgy tonight.'

Emma stopped straightening the stack of CDs atop the TV cabinet. 'I am, aren't I?'

'Come, my dearest, most fabulous friend, and tell me all your dirty dark secrets.' Renee patted the couch. 'It might help to get them all off your chest.'

Sucking in a deep breath and then nodding, Emma joined her on the three-seater couch. Curling her legs up beneath her, she got as settled as she could given the circumstances. 'I honestly don't know where to begin.' She sighed, briefly closing her eyes to ward off tears.

'Oh, Em ...' Renee rubbed her back. 'How about at the beginning?'

Emma smiled through her unease. 'Yeah, I reckon that might be a good idea.' She drew in another deep breath and then slowly blew it away. 'Right, here we go.'

For the next hour, Emma felt as if she didn't draw a breath, everything she'd been dying to share with another living soul pouring from her, along with floods of tears. Other than a few questions along the way, Renee lent her non-judgemental ear, and the occasional hug, to help ease her through it. 'I wanted to go to the police, Rennie, I really truly did, but I was terrified that Mario guy would kill me. And then, even when I found out the truth, that Zane's father wasn't part of the Mafia, Peter scared me into believing that if I did go to the cops, he'd make damn sure I'd be sent to jail for life.' Emma sucked in a shaky breath. 'So no matter which way I turned, I had my back up against the wall.'

'Holy shit, Em. I'm honestly at a loss for words, which is very unlike me.' Renee offered a gentle smile before sighing and rubbing her face. 'It's like something out of a movie, what you've been through, only ten million times worse because this is so chillingly real.'

'Sure is, huh.' Emma tossed her used tissue onto the growing pile on the coffee table.

Reaching out, Renee gave her hands a squeeze. 'I'm so sorry you've had to deal with all this, Em, and for all these years too. How you're still in one piece, I do not know.' She shook her head. 'You should've told me sooner, so I could've been there for you. I feel terrible knowing you've been going through all this on your own.'

Emma placed her hand on Renee's cheek. 'I'm so sorry, Rennie, but I couldn't tell you while Peter was alive. I didn't want to put you in any danger. Who knew what the bastard would do if he found out I told you, and it's without a doubt he would've followed through with his threats to me, too. I couldn't risk it. Riley's my absolute everything.'

'I understand completely,' Renee said, and then heaved a heavy sigh. 'On a positive note, we don't need to worry about all that now he's gone.' She grimaced. 'Sorry to say this, but good riddance to bad bloody rubbish.'

'I totally agree.' Grabbing her glass from the coffee table, Emma took more of a glug than a sip, and then lowered her voice to a whisper. 'Add all of this to the fact Zane is Riley's biological father, and with Riley as fragile as she is right now, I'm in a world of trouble.'

'I know you feel like that right now, but in the grand scheme of things, I'm glad Zane is Riley's father. Although he might be a bit of a player when it comes to women, he's got a good heart.'

'Yeah, he has.' Looking down, Emma tried to fight off fresh tears. 'I just don't know what the right thing to do is. I know everyone deserves to know the truth, and I can't go on with the shadow of that night hanging over me the way it does, but I don't want to risk hurting Riley any more than she already is. I'd never forgive myself if she …' She couldn't say the words out loud. Gathering the courage to meet Renee's gaze, all Emma saw was kindness. It broke her small wall of reserve and she burst into tears.

'Riley's not going to take her own life, Emma. She's got too much fire in her belly for that.' Renee pulled her into her arms. 'That son of a bitch, no wonder you're so bloody relieved he's gone. He's made your life a living hell, and all for his benefit. The selfish prick.'

Her sobs easing, Emma sat up and tugged a handful of tissues from the box. 'That he most certainly was, Rennie, but he's gone now, and has no power over me anymore. What I choose to do from here on in is entirely up to me.' She blew her nose and wiped her eyes. 'Riley is my number one priority, and I just don't know which way to go about it so I don't hurt her.'

'I think you need to wait until after the funeral to decide which way to go, and even then, don't rush it. The universe has funny ways of showing us the right path, as long as we stand still and quiet enough to watch and listen.'

Renee's words settling deep down within her, Emma nodded. 'You know what, you're so right. I need to stop bashing myself up, and just wait for the right time, for everyone involved.'

'Yes, you do. You've waited this long, so what's a few more weeks, or months, going to hurt, huh?'

'I suppose.' Emma stared at the curtains fluttering in the breeze. 'It's just, I really wanted to look Zane in the eyes when I told him, but maybe it would be best to give him the news when he's back in America. It'll give him all the time and space he needs to come to accept it, or not.'

'When do you think you'll tell Riley? Before or after Zane?'

'Definitely after, because if Zane doesn't want to accept that he's her father, I'll never speak a word of it to her. She doesn't need to feel that another father figure has rejected her.' She looked at Renee. 'And as for Michael, I'll tell him after Zane and Riley, what do you reckon?'

'I think, whatever feels right for you, is the right way to go about it. Nobody's walking your path, Em.' She offered another sympathetic smile. 'And when you're ready to go to the police, I'll be right beside you, holding your hand and helping you through it all. You don't have to do any of this alone anymore. I got you, okay?'

Biting her lip to stop from crying again, Emma nodded. 'Thanks, hun, for everything.'

'Don't speak of it ... it's what friendship is all about, Em, being there for each other, no matter what.' Sniffling, she wiped gathering tears away with the back of her hand.

Emma reached out and gave Renee's arm a squeeze. 'I'm sorry, throwing everything on top of you in one go. I know it's a lot to take in.'

'Don't you dare apologise, Em. I'll be right, it's just going to take a little while for me to filter it all, so it doesn't feel so surreal.'

Emma smiled softly. 'That's completely understandable.'

'Oh, my beautiful, strong, brave friend, if only I can be half the woman you are, I'll be happy ...' Renee smiled through her tears, and the women hugged tightly again – it took a few long moments for them to finally untangle. 'I know you're going to want to say no, but I'm not going to hear of it – tomorrow night I'm taking you to the pub and Riley can go hang out with Granny for the night.'

As Renee suspected, Emma went to graciously decline but she shushed her. 'You need to let your hair down and try to put all of this out of your mind, if only for a few hours. As well as that, it would do Riley the world of good to spend some time with Granny May – those two love each other to absolute death.'

Emma threw her hands up in defeat. 'Okay, all right, I'll come out, but only for a few drinks.' She followed it up with a groan.

Renee edged closer and wrapped an arm around her shoulder. 'I promise it'll be just what the doctor ordered.'

'Don't you mean the nurse, seeing it's coming from you?'

'Good point, my dear friend.' Renee grabbed her glass from the table and raised it. 'To the future, filled with love, laughter, good times, and the cold hard truth.'

Emma held hers up and they chinked glasses. 'Cheers to all of that.'

'We got this, girlfriend, you and me, okay?' Renee said with utmost conviction.

Emma nodded, feeling so very blessed to have this amazingly supportive woman in her life.

CHAPTER
7

It was still pitch black outside when the alarm beeped incessantly from the bedside table. On autopilot, Emma slapped it quiet. Rolling onto her side she groaned and then peeled herself from the bed before she'd even opened her sleep-heavy eyes. It was always the way, to be dead to the world on the one morning she really needed to get a move on. Over their dinner of Riley's favourite – spaghetti bolognaise – she'd promised to take her into town to pick out a dress for her debutante ball, followed by some lunch at their favourite little cafe, The Mad Hatters. With Riley finally excited to spend time with her in god knew how long, Emma was determined to stick to the plan – which meant getting up earlier than sparrow's fart to get everything done.

Willing her body awake, while her mind still lagged behind, she tugged off her singlet and boxer shorts, then rifling through the clothes basket of unfolded laundry, she hauled on a pair of jeans and a shirt that could really benefit from an iron – not that she even knew where hers was. Anything unacceptably crinkled usually got tossed into the dryer for all of five minutes – worked wonders. Yawning, she shuffled down the hallway towards the bathroom. A splash of cold water, followed by brushing her teeth, dragging her hair into a messy bun and then hunting down a super strong coffee was the norm, before she headed out the door to start her day. Breakfast would have to be something from the fruit bowl – a sugar banana, perhaps. Riley had kindly offered to get up early and help, but Emma wanted her to have a bit of a sleep-in. It would make for a much more enjoyable day if Riley wasn't tried and grumpy.

Bathroom duties done, and now feeling alert, the scent of bacon slapped her tastebuds and stopped her in her tracks. Padding down the stairs, she walked into the cottage-style kitchen, blinking both from the brightness of the fluorescent bulb and the fact Riley was standing at the stove, tongs in hand and dressed for a morning of shovelling horse poo. Spotting his master, Tiny leapt from his rug near the back door and like a foal unstable on its long legs, scuttled to her side, clearly excited by the mouth-watering aroma of bacon filling the kitchen as he did donuts around her.

Giving him a scratch behind his floppy ears, Emma smiled from her soul. 'Morning, sweetheart.' Her heart reaching for her daughter's, she wandered over and pecked her on the cheek. 'Are you feeling okay, love?' she said with an affectionate grin. 'It's not like you to be up before the sun.'

'Morning, Mum. I woke up about an hour ago and tried to go back to sleep, but I couldn't.' She flipped the bacon just as the toaster popped up two slices. 'And then I thought about the fact I hadn't made you breakfast in like, forever, so here you go.' She spiritedly threw her hands in the air. 'I hope we've got time to enjoy it before we head off to sort out the horses and check on the cattle.'

Emma nodded. 'Yes, of course we do – four hands are going to make for half the time.' She wrapped an arm around Riley's shoulder and gave her a squeeze. 'Thanks, sweetheart, this is so lovely to wake up to ... you and bacon are my favourite things.'

'Don't thank me yet, Mum, you haven't tasted it.' She offered a playful smile.

Emma matched it. 'True that.' She winked. 'I'm sure it's going to be beautiful.'

'Let's hope.' Riley glanced towards the toaster. 'Can you do the buttering duties, I've got my hands full here.'

Emma's grin widened as the chasm between them all but disappeared. 'Yes, love, of course.' She took out two plates from the dishwasher and got down to business. 'You want me to make us both a cuppa too?'

'Yes, please. I'll have a tea though, instead of a coffee, please.' Holding the frypan, Riley glanced over her shoulder. 'One or two bum nuts, Mum?'

'Just one for me thanks, love.' She rubbed the place on her belly wishing she could scare away the carbs she loved to eat. 'I want to try and get nice and fit for your deb ball, so I can wear my favourite dress.'

'Isn't it more like your only dress, Mum?' Riley smiled cheekily.

'Yes, smarty bum, it is.' Grabbing the tea towel, Emma flicked it in Riley's direction. 'And who are you to talk, Miss I-only-wear-shorts-or-jeans? We're more alike than you care to admit.'

'Uh-huh, I can't argue with any of that.' Switching off the gas hob, Riley grabbed the oven mitt and then carried the hot cast-iron pan over to the plates. 'I didn't think I was hungry, but now I'm looking at that bacon and those perfectly cooked eggs, I'm starving!'

Emma placed a piece of toast on each of the plates just in time to be loaded up. 'Bacon and eggs are my weakness too. How anyone can become a vegetarian, or god forbid, a vegan, is beyond me.'

'Me too, I'd end up biting the butt of some poor unsuspecting cow if I even tried.'

Emma chuckled. 'I love your way with words, Riley Wolfe, always straight to the point.'

'I wonder where I get that trait from, Mum.'

Emma played dumb. 'Hmmm, I wonder.'

They sat down at the table, and Emma groaned in pleasure after the first bite. 'Holy heck, this is mighty good, Riley. You should cook brekkie more often, little Miss Masterchef.' She pointed her fork at Riley, who was busy chewing her massive mouthful. 'In fact, I think I might go on kitchen strike and leave all the cooking to you from now on.'

'Don't push your luck, Mum,' she said, grinning.

Chuckling, Emma shook her head. 'Oh well, I thought it was worth a shot.'

Clutching her cup of tea, Riley took a sip and then proceeded to dip her bacon in her runny egg yolk. 'I really want to apologise for yesterday, Mum.'

Emma almost choked on her food. 'You do?'

'Yes, shock horror ... I do.' Riley's smile faded as she chewed her bottom lip, her eyes filling with tears. Sniffling, she straightened her shoulders and blinked them away. 'I know I've been angry at the world since Dad left, and I know you're only trying to do what's best for me now you're on your own. It's just, sometimes, you have to try and give me space to make my own mistakes.' Her brows creased in thought. 'We all make them, you know.'

'Yes, we do.' Emma stared into eyes that reminded her so much of Zane's, and her heart ached. 'I know I'm over-protective at times, love. I suppose I just don't want to see you hurt or make the same mistakes that I have made in my life.'

'Isn't being hurt all part of the learning process?'

'Well, yes, it is.' Her breakfast finished, Emma sat back with her coffee cradled in her hands. 'Where's this change of heart coming from?'

Riley shrugged. 'Aunty Rennie explained things in a way that made me look at them differently, that's all.' She paused momentarily and shook her head ever so slightly, blinking fast. 'She made me see I'm pushing away the only person in my life that has ever made me feel loved unconditionally.' She blinked wet lashes. 'You, Mum.'

'Oh, sweetheart, that's a mother's job, to love no matter what.' Hot tears stung Emma's eyes. 'And trust me, you're very easy to love, even when you are being a right handful and I want to throttle you.'

Riley had a little giggle, along with Emma. 'Thanks, Mum, but shouldn't it be a father's job, too, to love unconditionally?'

'Yes, it should, but when it comes to Michael, well, he's ...' Emma ached to tell Riley about Zane, but knew it would be a huge mistake to say anything just when they were coming so close again.

'Selfish and big-headed, just like Grandad was.'

'I was trying to find a nicer way to put it, but yes.' She offered a kind smile. 'You see a lot more than you let on, don't you?'

Riley nodded gently. 'I'm a big girl now, believe it or not, and I'm beginning to see things for what they are, not how people want me to see them.'

Emma reached across the table and gave Riley's hand a squeeze, noticing how small it still felt within her own. 'It has nothing to do with you, Riley, how your dad is, and all to do with the way he was raised by your grandfather. He doesn't understand that family should come before work.'

'It's hard to make myself believe it's not my fault, even though deep down I know it's not. Sometimes …' She sat in silence for a few moments. 'Sometimes, I wish he wasn't my dad, because all he seems to do is hurt me over and over.'

'Oh, sweetheart, you don't really mean that.' Emma wondered if this was the universe's way of giving her the stage, but then quickly shrugged off the idea.

'Yes, actually, I really do mean it.' Riley sniffled.

'I'm sorry you feel like that, I truly am.' Emotion lodged in Emma's throat. 'Things will get better, I promise,' she choked out.

'I hope you're right, Mum.'

'I'll make sure of it.' Desperate to change the subject, before she blurted everything out, Emma said, 'So, tell me, are you going to stay away from Whatshisname now you've seen what a horrible person he is?'

Riley cracked a smile. 'You mean Ben?'

'Yeah, him.'

'After the way he grabbed me yesterday, I'm staying well away from him from now on.' She sighed. 'Is this where I'm meant to say you were right, Mum?'

'No, love, just take it as one of those lessons learnt.'

Riley leant forwards, her elbows resting on the table and her chin in her hands. 'Aunty Rennie helped me to see I was acting out, trying to make you and Dad pay for hurting me, by dating the rebel of the town.'

Emma owed Renee for this, big time – she'd be making sure to shout her a few drinks tonight. 'You're a clever girl, Riley, wiser than I give you credit for sometimes.'

'Yup, but I can be a silly bugger sometimes too.'

'I'm not going to argue with that.'

Riley poked her tongue out, and then giggled.

Standing, her smile now from ear to ear, Emma gathered the empty plates. 'So does this mean you're going to accept James's offer for him to escort you to the deb?'

Riley joined her in clearing the table. 'Yeah, I suppose so.'

'Good, I like James.'

'I know you do, Mum, but honestly, he's such a dork.'

Emma turned on the tap and began rinsing the dishes, piling them on the sink for later, once they'd had time to unpack the dishwasher. 'Well, a dork is much better than a dick, don't you think?'

Riley gasped. 'Mum, language.' She gave her a playful shove.

Emma flicked some water in Riley's direction. 'I'm just speaking the truth, telling it how it is.'

A pile of clean plates gathered from the dishwasher and now cradled in her arms, Riley began stacking them in the cupboard. 'Did you know that you're the bestest mum in the world?'

'Aw thanks, love, and do you know you're the bestest daughter in the whole entire universe?' Emma smiled warmly. The fact she and Riley still said this to each other, after all these years, moved her beyond words. She kissed her on the forehead. 'Right, let's get cracking, and get the jobs done, so we can head into town for some much needed girly time.'

Riley clapped her hands together. 'Sounds like a plan to me.'

* * *

It was just after eleven o'clock when Emma and Riley piled into the cab of the Land Rover, both of them now showered, dressed and smelling as fresh as daisies. Tiny danced around in the back tray, tripping over his chain. An eager beaver, as always, for the trip into town, where he would scare the bejesus out of unsuspecting passers-by if they came too close to the four-wheel drive. His bark was way worse than his bite – he was likely to lick someone to death if given half the chance.

Heading down the dirt drive, Emma caught sight of Kat in the horse paddock – one of the feline's favourite spots was on Bundy's back. Bundy loved the company and the massage Kat would sometimes give him as she pawed him. 'Thanks for helping me this morning, love, it got the jobs done so much faster.'

'You're welcome. As much as I hate picking up horse poo, it was kinda nice to hang out with you.' She offered a smile.

'Just kinda nice, huh?' Reaching over, Emma playfully poked her in the ribs.

Riley laughed and slapped her hand away. 'Yeah, kinda sorta.' She grinned again before shoving her earphones in, her face now buried in her phone as she flicked through her Spotify list.

Emma had come to accept the teenage ways, and besides, she and Riley had vastly different tastes in music. Riley loved the new-style country rock, which Emma didn't think even warranted being classed as country, whereas give her the old-style country boys like Johnny, Waylon, Willie and Hank, or good old-fashioned seventies tunes, like Led Zeppelin or Pink Floyd, any day.

Turning onto the highway, she grabbed her sunglasses from her head, rolling her eyes at the fact she'd been squinting into the blinding sun for the past five minutes. The wisps of clouds were like painter's strokes across the azure sky; it was a stunning summer's day. Plucking a CD from the binder on the dash, she popped her favourite Creedence Clearwater Revival compilation into the stereo, turned it up a little and then wound her window down. The wind whipping her loose hair into a frenzy, she sung the lyrics to 'Lookin' Out My Back Door' out loud, while getting amused sideways looks from Riley. She grinned, enjoying the light mood between them and making the most of it, never knowing how long it would last before their next heated bout.

Fifteen minutes later and they'd reached the one and only roundabout in Silvergum. As they passed the bakers, the rich buttery scent of their famous pies wafted out. Next was the newsagency, with a line out the door, followed by the chemist, doctor's surgery and the Chinese takeaway. Almost at the dress shop, Emma started looking for a spot to pull into. The main street was much busier than usual, so she ducked in behind the IGA, cheering when she nabbed the last park there.

Riley unplugged her ears and wound the earphones around her iPhone.

Pulling the keys from the ignition, Emma turned to her. 'You excited?'

Riley groaned playfully. 'Oh yeah, because you know how much I just *love* shopping for dresses.' She offered a feeble smile before climbing out.

'I'm hearing you loud and clear. But it's just gotta be done, I'm afraid.' Emma grabbed her handbag from the floor. 'You can't turn up to a ball wearing jeans and a polo top.' She gave Tiny orders to be nice to anyone who walked by, and joined Riley on the footpath.

Wandering past the only regional movie theatre left in the wider area, the slap of air-conditioning hit them as the sliding doors of IGA flung open. Janine from the post office shuffled out, grocery bags hanging from both arms. As much as Emma hadn't forgiven the woman for passing on confidential mail all those years ago, she still offered a smile and a wave. Janine wasn't to know what mayhem she'd caused that day. Her hands full, Janine smiled and said a quick hello in passing. Emma thanked the powers that be for the weight of the grocery bags in her hands, because the woman could seriously talk under water, and she didn't feel like being cornered for half an hour as she heard all about who said what to who, and oh my god have you heard about so and so.

They'd reached the front of Granny May's dress shop, which from the outside seemed no bigger than a hole in the wall. The bell dangling from the door tinkled as they stepped inside. The boutique was a hive of activity, the fifty percent off sale drawing people from far and wide, especially with the debutante ball fast approaching. With Cairns an hour's drive down the coast, Renee's granny had struck gold when she'd opened the shop's doors eight years ago. It was something to throw her heart into when her husband had passed, and she'd never missed a day in here since – the place was her pride and joy. Filled with both new and vintage clothing, unique quirky accessories, and peculiar bric-a-brac gift ideas, it was a treasure trove for young and old.

'Emma, Riley, helloooo, my darlings.' Granny May stopped what she was doing at the counter and ran to embrace the pair of them, her ankle-length boho dress making her look as if she were floating on air. 'It's so good to see you both.' She stepped back and clapped her hands, her cluster of silver bangles jingling. 'And I hear we're hanging out tonight, Riley.'

Riley's face lit up. 'We sure are, Granny May.'

'How does a pizza and movie night sound?'

'Perfect.'

Emma gave Granny May's arm a squeeze. 'Thanks so much for having her over … no matter how hard I tried to get out of it, Renee was determined to take me out.'

Granny May smiled so warmly Emma got goosebumps from the depth of love she felt from this woman, who'd known her since she was in nappies. 'It will do you good, Em, to get out for a night. Go and enjoy yourself.' She cupped Riley's cheek. 'This gorgeous girl and I will have a groovy girls' night in, with plenty of cookies and cream ice-cream.'

'Oh, yay, I'm so looking forward to it.' Riley clasped her hands together and grinned.

'Goodo …' Granny May looked over her shoulder at the two ladies now waiting at the counter. 'I best get back to it and let you two get shopping. Give me a shout if you need any help, okay?'

'Will do,' Emma said with a smile.

Sorting through the racks while pulling faces at anything Emma held up, Riley paused and held up a slinky emerald number. 'Oh my god, Mum, this would look stunning on you.'

Eyes wide, Emma pulled the hem out, revealing a low-cut back that had her wondering if her preferred comfy cotton knickers would be on show. 'Oh, I don't think so, sweetheart, I'm getting a bit old for this kind of thing.' She eyed the diamanté spaghetti straps, and as Riley spun it around, the plunging neckline. Good god, it wouldn't leave anything to the imagination. 'And besides, this trip is about finding you a dress, Riley, not me. I've already got one. Remember?'

'That dress is as old as I am, Mum.'

'Oh, it is not,' Emma said, sounding horrified.

'You wore it to my confirmation, when I was eight, Mum. Need I say more?'

Emma sucked in a sharp breath. 'Oh my god, I did too, didn't I?'

'Uh-huh.' Riley's eyes were comically wide.

Touching the soft fabric that slipped across her fingertips, Emma had to admit she loved the striking colour. 'I don't know. I don't want to look like mutton dressed up as lamb.'

'Oh, come on, Mum, you won't … just try it on.' Riley scowled playfully. 'If you don't, then I refuse to try on anything.'

Emma laughed. 'You little terror.' She took the coat hanger from Riley's outstretched hand. 'I'll try it on, but that doesn't mean I'm buying it.'

'We'll see about that.'

Half an hour later, and after being told in no uncertain terms that Riley didn't want a dress in any colour that was part of a salad – eggplant, avocado, or peach – they'd picked out four possible dresses for her. Standing in line, they waited for a change room to become available. A curtain flung open and a girl stomped out, her scowl so deep it was actually hilarious, a pile of dresses tossed over her arm. Her mother flashed Emma a lord-help-me grin. Emma smiled back. No words were needed.

Riley gestured towards the empty change room. 'Let's just share, Mum, or we'll be waiting here forever. I'm so starving I'm about to chew my own arm off.'

'Well, we don't want that.' Emma followed Riley in, and they stripped down to their underwear, the lack of room sending them into fits of giggles as they tried to pull on their dresses.

After awkwardly zipping up her dress, and then helping Riley do hers, Emma blinked back a rush of tears. She'd promised herself on the drive into town that she wasn't going to become a blubbering mess. But seeing Riley in the formal dress threw all promises aside. It hugged Riley in all the right places – this was the very first time Emma had really seen her little girl for the young woman she was becoming, way too fast for her liking. She realised she needed to accept it and embrace it. 'Oh, sweetheart, it looks absolutely amazing on you.'

Riley stared into the mirror, her expression one of utter shock. Emma stood behind her, not wanting to take this moment from Riley. 'I really don't think you need to try on the others – this is the one!'

'You think?'

Emma nodded. 'I know.'

Riley turned around and gasped. 'Holy shitballs, Mum, you look smoking hot.' She stepped aside, giving Emma full view of the mirror.

'Oh, my good lord.' Emma smoothed her hands down her hips, feeling very sexy indeed, but terrified at the same time to see her reflection. Not used to getting dolled up, this was a sight she wasn't familiar with at all. 'You don't think it's too much?' She turned from side to side, her concerns about her comfortable undies showing now very real.

Riley shook her head. 'No way, Mum, it looks amazing.' She looked down at the outline of Emma's Bridget Jones style knickers.

'But you might want to get yourself some different undies, or go commando.'

'Not sure about going knicker free, but yes, new undies are definitely on the shopping list.'

'So does that mean you're getting it?'

'No.' As much as she tried to, Emma couldn't hide her playful grin.

'Mum, you have to.' Riley folded her arms, her foot tapping.

Emma matched her stance. 'Why.'

'Because.' Riley broke into a smile.

'That's not an acceptable answer.'

'Okay then. Here's the deal.' Riley stepped in front of her, hogging the mirror and spinning from side to side. The mermaid cut swirled at her feet and the lace bodice accentuated her long, elegant neck. 'If I have to get a new dress to wear to this stupid ball, then you have to as well, so we can both suffer in femininity together.'

Emma sucked in a breath, paused, and then held out her hand. 'Deal.'

Riley shook it with vigour. 'Good, now let's go eat. I'm hanging out to tuck into a green goddess bowl topped with crispy salmon and black sesame seeds.'

'Oh, yummy, me too.'

* * *

With a watermelon, mint and apple mocktail each, they were sitting at a table on the footpath, devouring their salads. Deep in girly conversation, they looked up as a silhouette suddenly blocked out the glorious sunshine.

'Dad.' Riley leapt up and wrapped her arms around Michael's waist. 'What a surprise.'

Emma stifled a groan and forced a smile as she tilted her head to greet her ex. 'Michael.' She placed her fork down before she gave in to her urge to use it to stab him in the ribs. 'You didn't tell us you were coming to town today. I thought you were holed up in Cairns for the week.' Although a simple statement, it was laced with condemnation.

'Yeah, it was last minute. I had to drop off some paperwork to Dad's solicitor here.' He straightened his tie, something he always did when he was about to lie. 'I was going to pop out to Serendipity to surprise this one.' He gave Riley a smile, her arms still wrapped around his waist. 'But now you've saved me the trip.'

'Would you like to join us for lunch?' Only thinking of Riley, Emma forced out every single word.

'Thanks, but no thanks. I have to be back to meet with a client in just over an hour.'

Emma wondered whether he was lying about the visit to Serendipity, or the need to meet a client, because he wouldn't have had time to do them both.

Riley pouted. 'Oh, but I haven't seen you since Grandad ...' She stopped. Her smile all but faded as she sunk back into her chair.

Momentarily thrown off centre by the mention of his father, Michael cleared his throat and recomposed himself in the blink of an eye. He reached out and stroked some flyaway hair back from Riley's face. 'I know, and I'm sorry. It's been a tough week, for all of us. We'll see each other in two days, though, at the funeral.'

'That's not really quality time, Dad.' Unable to look at him any longer, Riley pushed what was left of her salad around in her bowl.

He heaved a sigh. 'I'll make sure I'm at horse sports next weekend, okay?'

Riley didn't even look up at him. 'You promise?'

'You have my word.'

Emma choked back a sarcastic laugh. She'd heard that line a million times over, and rarely did he ever follow through with his promises. For Riley's sake, she hoped to god he did this time, and she'd be making a phone call to him later, to tell him so.

'Right, well, I best be off.' He leant in and kissed Riley on the cheek that she turned to him. 'Love you, button.'

'Yup, love you.'

'Emma.' He gave her a nod.

'Michael.' She nodded back, feeling ridiculous in doing so.

His mobile ringing, he grabbed it like he was expecting the most important call in the world, and then plodded off down the footpath.

Emma's heart ached. 'I'm so sorry, Riley.'

'Don't you dare apologise for him, Mum. He's the one who should be saying sorry, not you.' She forked in a mouthful of avocado and rocket. 'It's his loss,' she garbled through her mouthful.

'It most certainly is, sweetheart.' Emma bit back tears. 'I love you.'

Riley reached across the table and gave Emma's hand a squeeze. 'I love you, too, so much.'

Her guilt almost crushing her, Emma forced a smile.

CHAPTER

8

Feeling a little out of whack driving on the opposite side of the road, Zane dug his hand into the lolly packet and grabbed another. Behind the wheel of the four-wheel drive, after almost forty-eight hours with hardly any sleep, and with the bright lights of Cairns now far behind him, he was fighting to stay awake. Tuning in the radio to the local country station, he flicked the air-conditioner off and wound the window down, the balmy breeze laced with the salty scent of the ocean helping to revitalise him.

Arriving at Cairns International Airport to no welcoming arms had been exactly how he'd wanted it. Keeping to himself would be the only way he'd get through the funeral and back on the next plane out of here, somewhat unscathed. He wondered how Emma was going to act around him – like a long-lost friend or a stranger? The latter would be the safest bet, for both of them. If he had the opportunity to revisit the past, even though it had landed him in deep water last time he was here, he wasn't sure he'd be able to stop himself trying to kiss her again. He had no self-control when it came to Emma. Like a drug, she was a sweet addiction he'd never stopped craving; one he found almost impossible to resist. He wondered if she secretly still felt the same as she had the night she'd torn his clothes from him and taken him to places he'd never been before, or again. But he doubted it. She'd made it very clear where they stood – he could still feel the sting of the slap across his face and see the look of disbelief in her striking green eyes. And rightly so, she was a married woman at the time. But now, with Michael out of the equation, would it be any different? Did he want it to be? Or did he crave her because she'd always been just out of his reach? Was it a case of wanting what he couldn't have? With his track record, that was a possibility. He was man enough to admit his faults and own them.

Angry at himself for even fantasising about going there again with Emma, he shook the images from his mind. There'd be no going back there, regardless of what he felt. It would only spell disaster. He was home for the funeral, to pay his respects to a man who never really showed him an ounce of it, and then he was out of here, never to return. If only that fateful night hadn't happened, maybe he wouldn't feel the need to keep running and would make a go of it here now Peter was gone. So many *maybes*, so many unreachable possibilities – it was the story of his goddamn life. Bull riding was the only constant he had, the only thing he was really good at. He hated to think about what he would do when he was too old to keep bucking it out in the arena. He heaved a weary sigh and shook his head. What a tangled web they'd woven that night, Emma, Michael, Peter and him.

Sighing again, he ran a hand through his hair and over his five o'clock shadow. He knew he looked like death warmed up, and he didn't give a damn. He had no one to impress. It had been three long days since the phone call and since then he'd scarcely had time to look in a mirror, let alone enjoy an unhurried hot shower with a razor in his hand. Not long now and he'd be there, back where it all began. His whole body aching from all the sitting, the endless hours on the plane making him want to climb the walls, he fidgeted in his seat and gave the seatbelt a frustrated yank. He sucked in a deep breath and forced it to the bottom of his lungs. Even with open paddocks on one side and the ocean on the other, he'd never felt so boxed in.

The radio station began playing one of his favourite songs, 'If You've Got the Money, I've Got the Time' by the late Merle Haggard. A small smile curled the corners of his lips. He'd twirled many a southern woman around the dance floors of honky tonks to it. Turning it up, he sang the lyrics out loud, his thumbs tapping in time on the steering wheel. Spotting the half-eaten bag of Reese's Peanut Butter Cups, he grabbed one and tossed it into his mouth, savouring the mixture of sweet chocolate and peanut butter. He had to give it to them, the Americans knew how to create flavour sensations from the strangest concoctions; their ribs, steaks, fried chicken, and pecan pies were to die for. Doing anything and everything to try to take his mind back to the US, he sucked in another deep breath and huffed it away. With nothing but bad memories, bar all the times he'd spent with the beautiful Miss Emma Kensington, he seriously didn't want to be here. This was going to be tough, and something was telling him there were going to be some bombshells – there always were when Peter Wolfe was involved. For everyone's sake, he hoped his instincts were wrong.

On a long, straight stretch of highway and with a lone oncoming car finally passing him, he flicked the headlights of the hire car back to high beam, keeping a keen eye out for any roos with a death wish. A colony of flying foxes soaring across the sky, illuminated for a few brief seconds, reminded him of the time Emma had lost her dearly loved horse to the Hendra virus – a deadly disease spread by the flying foxes. She had been distraught, taking almost six months before she could welcome another horse into her life, and he'd been by her side the entire way, comforting her, encouraging her and supporting her – his heart breaking every time he felt her tears on his shoulders.

He caught the scent of rain, then it started to fall on the car roof. The few drops quickly became a steady drum as the sky opened up and thunder crackled and roared in the distance. It was typical tropical weather – a monsoonal storm arriving with hardly any warning. Quickly winding his window up, and with the windscreen wipers now going like the clappers, he sat forward and strained to see a metre in front. It was usually a jaw-dropping view from this vantage point; he'd just have to jog his memory to imagine the expanse of ocean and the long jetty extending from the western rock wall, where he'd spent many hours fishing. Other than on the back of a bull, that had been his happy place, with a fishing rod in one hand and a nice cold beer in the other. And the mud crabs he used to catch in his selectively placed pots were to die for – his mouth watered with the thought of tucking into one.

He was very close now; the urge to hit the brakes, turn around and go back to what he now considered his home, the United

States of America, was strong, overwhelmingly so. But he couldn't run like he had all those years ago, at least not for now – his return flight was locked in for six days' time. Clutching the steering wheel, he sat up straighter; the confines of the seatbelt, the closed windows, and the foggy windscreen were almost suffocating. He tried to rub some life into his eyes and strained to focus on the white lines of the road, rather than the burning emotion rising in his throat the closer he got to Silvergum. Before hitting the sack in his hotel room, and after a nice long shower, he knew he'd be in desperate need of a whisky at the downstairs bar to calm him.

Reaching a T-intersection, he came to a stop and indicated to turn away from the coast. His heart took off in a wild gallop as he drove on. Now shit was getting real. Just up in front, the familiar sign announcing he'd arrived in Silvergum Shire lit up like a Christmas tree in the high beam. His stomach tumbled and backflipped. His breath quickened, and his grip on the steering wheel tightened. The headlights cut a narrow swathe through the darkness, showing nothing but open paddocks on either side. Then, in the blink of an eye, he was driving along suburban streets, towards his destination. Only minutes down the road, and after passing shopfronts so familiar he felt as if he'd never left, he'd arrived at Silvergum's oldest pub, and his old watering hole, The Railway Hotel. On many a drunken night, he'd somehow got on his horse, which he'd tethered to the hitching post hours earlier, and followed its lead back home from here. He'd probably be booked for drink driving now if he even dared it, no matter that he wasn't behind a wheel.

Seeing the car park full and cars parked the length of the street, he groaned. There must be an out-of-town band on, drawing every man, woman and their dog here. Heading around the corner, past the drive-through bottle shop and the well-lit ATM, he looked up. Other than a fresh lick of paint and new latticework railings around the verandah, the old building looked exactly the same. Parking where he always used to, away from the drunken louts who would roll out the doors at closing time – he didn't want to foot a repair bill because some idiot had sideswiped the rental – he killed the ignition and pushed his door open. Unfolding like a pocketknife, he groaned gratifyingly. It felt dang tootin' good to stand up and stretch his arms above his head.

He grabbed his wide-brimmed hat from the dash, his luggage from the back seat, blipped the LandCruiser keys to make sure it was locked, and then headed towards the back door, which he knew led straight to the check-in counter. He wasn't in the mood to run into anyone he knew just yet – and round these parts, with half the town packed inside, that was most certainly on the cards. Mumbling a g'day then holding his breath, he sidestepped a bloke sucking on a cigarette like his life depended on it. Kicking any dirt off the bottom of his boots, he pushed the door open with the toe of one and strolled in. Riotous laughter and the thump of a bass carried from the front of the historic building, while the aroma of chargrilled steak and tap beer smacked him in the face. His stomach rumbled in anticipation of a decent counter meal. Greeting the young German backpacker at the desk, her hair bright pink and her face with more piercings than he had time to count, he paid for the next five nights, accepted his keys, and headed upstairs – thank Christ he'd been lucky enough to get a room with an ensuite.

Later, after he'd dumped his bag onto the single bed, showered, shaved, eaten a mouth-watering meal of steak, chips and salad – the 500 gram slab of medium-rare rump doused in plate-licking béarnaise sauce – and washed it down with an icy cold beer, he was feeling a little more human, albeit still exhausted. Wandering out of the family-orientated dining room and into the much rowdier front bar, he scanned the sea of faces for any he wasn't keen to run into – planning to make a wide berth to avoid them. Eyes fell upon him as he made his way towards the bar. As he said his g'days in passing to the couple of blokes he'd gone to high school with, he could almost hear their whispers about the fact he was back – not that he gave a shit what any of them thought.

All four pool tables were taken, and the five-piece band was pumping out an old Midnight Oil tune to a packed, gyrating dance floor. Pulling up a stool at the end of the bar, he rested his forearms on the mahogany counter and waited his turn to be served. He needed a whisky on ice, swiftly followed by another, and another, so he could drag himself back to his room and hopefully get some sleep. He'd give almost anything to escape reality and his thoughts for just a little while. Maybe a romp between the sheets with a hot-blooded woman would help him out with that. There were plenty of them in here, but none that fitted the bill like the captivating Emma Kensington would – memories of her lingered everywhere and he couldn't think of anything but her.

Thanks to the breakneck speed of the barman, Zane sculled his first whisky and then sat with a second in hand. Taking sips while watching a couple almost undressing each other on the dance floor, he chuckled to himself. With his thoughts wavering between the pleasures of the alcohol warming his throat, to the pleasures of flesh warming his single bed upstairs, his gaze snagged on an attractive woman over the other side of the room, her long legs making her stand out above the rest of her group. She flashed him a come-hither smile and he flashed her one back. Although humouring the thought of noncommittal sex, he decided he was too tired to put the effort in tonight. So, he turned in his seat, tapping his boot in rhythm as he watched the band rocking it out on stage.

CHAPTER

9

Grinning at the way almost every bloke cocked his neck to gawk at her gorgeous friend, Emma watched Renee disappear into the thick of it all. The old Railway Pub was packed to the rafters; almost everyone, apart from a few ringers huddled around the pool tables with beers in hand, was decked out in their good, going-to-town clothes. Of the three pubs in Silvergum, this was evidently still the one to be seen at. Texting 'Goodnight and I love you' to Riley, Emma then shoved her mobile in her bag so she'd stop checking it every five minutes. She just couldn't help herself. Knowing Riley was happy and enjoying her night with Granny May, despite the fact she had a bellyache from the entire tub of ice-cream she and Granny had gorged themselves on while watching *Dirty Dancing*, made her relax a little. Sipping the last of her vodka, lime and soda, she gazed around the rowdy crowd, not seeing one bloke she would make a beeline for, that was, if she were on the prowl. Which she wasn't. Men were too much like hard work.

Waving to a familiar face, she curled her legs up beneath her in the booth. She was pleased they'd nabbed the last table in the place, in a dark corner, away from drunken louts who'd grab her butt or try to chat her up, while spilling beer down her top. From when she was a young single woman, she'd always loathed men who behaved that way. It took a lot more than an offer of a free drink, and possibly a shag in the back of someone's ute at the end of the night, to win her over. She liked her men tall, dark, witty, and handsome, a little rough around the edges but with a solid gold heart; someone who kept her on her toes but was there to catch her when she fell, and most definitely chivalrous. Not too much to ask, was it? With most of the crowd much younger than her, she felt a little like a fish out of water, but tried not to dwell on it. Tonight was all about spending time with her bestie, and to hell with the rest; as they both led hectic lives, times like these were few and far between.

Renee arrived back at their table with four shot glasses balanced between her fingers and a very mischievous grin on her face. Carefully manoeuvring into her seat, she shoved two in front of Emma. 'I give thee a Horny Southerner and a Buttery Nipple.'

'Oh, yay, just what I need after a year and a half of no sex – a horny bloke and slippery nipples.' Emma cracked a sassy smile as she held up one of the glasses, inspecting the neatly layered contents. 'What's in this one?'

'Oh, that's the horny one … Southern Comfort, Midori, Triple Sec, and a splash of orange juice.' Renee grinned and held her glass up. 'Bottoms up, my friend.' She threw it back.

Emma did the same, her expression immediately showing her immense displeasure as she forced it down. 'Oh my god, that was horrible.' She smacked her glass down on the table then wiped her lips with the back of her hand.

'Horrible, but potent.' Renee grinned wickedly.

'Oh lord, help me.' Emma chuckled. 'What is it with you nurses? You can drink any guy under the table and still stay steady on your feet.'

'We don't buckle under pressure, and we rise to the challenge.' Renee punched the air and both women laughed.

Emma held up the next shot glass. 'Should I ask what's in this one?'

'Butterscotch Schnapps, Baileys and a layer of cream.'

'Damn, Rennie, mixing stuff like this, you're going to have to hold my hair back at some point.'

Renee grinned. 'I've done it before and I'll do it again.'

'Ditto, my friend.'

They threw the shots back, smacked the glasses down and then grinned.

Needing something to wash the taste out of her mouth, Emma stood and picked up her empty glass. 'You want another vodka, lime and soda?'

'Yes, please.'

'Groovy, I'll be back as soon as I've hunted two down.' She grinned. 'Drinks, I mean, not men.'

'Oh, bugger.' Pouting playfully, Renee sat back and stretched her arms wide. 'I'll hold the fort.'

Emma weaved her way through the crowd, diverting en route for a quick pit stop at the loo. Now she'd broken the seal, she'd need to go every half an hour. Staring at her reflection under the unflattering lights, she thought about reapplying her powder foundation and lippy, but then shrugged it off. Who was she trying to impress anyway? Washing her hands, she smiled while listening to the clucking of conversations.

She reached the bar on increasingly wobbly legs. Not as much a party animal as she used to be, she really needed to slow up on the drinks after throwing back the two shooters. She was usually in bed before nine, with her knee pillow jammed between her legs, and she was suddenly finding it hard to keep her eyes open.

Waiting to be served, she leant on the bar, doing her best not to catch the eyes of the two blokes beside her. Both young enough to pass as her sons, the pimply faced of the two openly tried to look down her top while his mate egged him on. Self-conscious, she tugged it up, straightened, and heaved a sigh. What had happened to all the good ones? Men who actually behaved like men? At her age, she guessed they were all taken and at home with their wives and families.

On either side of her, every bar stool had a jeans-clad butt on it, and there wasn't a table to be begged, borrowed or stolen. Raised voices were in competition with the blare of the country band rocking it out on stage; their rendition of Jimmy Barnes's 'Rising Sun' had people grooving on the dance floor.

When it was finally her turn, Emma ordered and then handed over a twenty. Thanking the barman, she grabbed her change and the two vodka, lime and sodas. Easing back into her seat, she took a sip and leant across the table so Renee could hear her over the band. 'Thanks so much for dragging me out. You were right, after the week I've had I really need to let off some steam, and I'm actually enjoying myself.'

Reaching out and squeezing her hand, Renee offered a sympathetic smile. 'After the past few years you've had, I reckon you could use an entire month away, letting off said steam.'

'Yeah, tell me about it, but that ain't going to be happening anytime soon.'

'Bali flights are on sale, we could make it happen …'

'Afraid not, Rennie, there's no way I'll be leaving Riley for any length of time. She really needs me right now.' She looked at her friend. 'Thanks so much for talking to her last night – it made a huge difference.'

'She's a normal hormonal teenager, who has a dick for a so-called father, and her grandfather has just died. She just needed a gentle reminder of how wonderful you are to her.'

'Thanks, hun, sometimes I feel like such a failure as a mother.'

'Not everything that happens in her life is your fault, Em.'

'I know, I just want to protect her from the tough things in life, and I can't. And with everything I've told you about …' She shook her head and stared into her drink. 'I'm just so scared of losing her when the truth finally comes out.'

'And how are you going to lose her, Em? She might be angry for a while, hurt you kept it all from her, but she will eventually understand. You'll see.'

'But what if she packs her bags and goes and lives with Michael?'

'Trust me, as much as she swears black and blue she's going to, she won't. And even if she does, it will be just like the last two times, she'll be back home before you know it. She loves you, Em. You two are best friends, always have been and always will be. Nothing will ever change that.'

'I really hope you're right, Rennie.'

'I'm always right, and if I'm not, then I'm just mistaken.' Renee grinned. 'Now come on, old girl, we got ourselves some partying to do.'

'Hey, speak for yourself, you old fart.'

'I'm two months older than you ...' Renee winked cheekily and held up her glass. 'So I'll drink to that.'

Trying to swing her thoughts to the here and now, Emma eased back into her seat and tapped her foot in time to the music.

Renee's eyebrows shot up as she peered over her shoulder. 'Oh, shit, Em.'

'What?'

'Don't turn around.'

Emma spun around and the familiar bulk of manly man her gaze snagged on made her insides twist and tumble. 'Oh, shit.' She turned back to Renee, her friend's shocked expression matching her own, she was sure of it.

'Exactly what I said before I said don't turn around.'

'Well, of course I'm going to turn around when you tell me not to.' Emma rolled her eyes. 'How in the hell did I not see him when I went over to the bar?'

'I have no idea.' Renee shrugged. 'He's one hell of a hunky spunky man, Em. It's no wonder you—'

'Shhh.' Emma cut her off while trying to stop her coy smile. 'I have to go and say hello now, don't I?'

'Look at the way you're smiling, Miss Kensington.' A brow raised, Renee leant across the table. 'Anyone would think you still like the bloke.' She ignored Emma's protests. 'And yes, seeing as he's the father of your child, and your ex-brother-in-law who's here for his father's funeral, yes, you kind of do.' She sat back. 'Unless you want him to spot you first, and then come and sit with us for the rest of the night,' she said, grinning audaciously. 'I haven't got a problem if he does.'

'Well, I do.' Emma swallowed her smile and sighed. 'There's a lot of water under the bridge where he's concerned, especially after last time.'

Renee nodded. 'Have to agree there.'

Emma took a sip from her drink and then sucked in a breath. 'I'd rather go to him, and that way I can make an exit if I start feeling uncomfortable.'

'You want me to come with you?'

'Nope, you do a good job of holding the fort, so stick to that.' Emma stood. 'I won't be long.'

Renee smiled. 'Alrighty then.'

Drawing Dutch courage from the few drinks she'd had, Emma moved behind a big bloke waiting at the bar for a drink, out of Zane's line of sight. Skulking on the edge of the crowd, she stole a few moments to gather herself. She couldn't let Zane see how much she was shaking. And luckily, for both their sakes, she did hesitate, because the foxy brunette who'd just appeared at Zane's side looked mighty cosy, as did he. How damn awkward that would have been. Emma shook her head – Casanova at his finest. He knew how to draw the women to him, and always had. She groaned, her swooning heart sinking. Looks like he still hadn't got over his womanising ways, she decided. She should have known – a leopard never changed its spots.

* * *

Zane turned in his seat, a little taken aback by the brunette's audacity, as he looked into eyes the colour of dark chocolate. Her long locks were slung over one shoulder and her denim shorts were so damn short he really didn't have to use much of his imagination. The heart attack waiting to happen hadn't wasted any time closing in on him.

'Well, howdy there.' He flashed her a broad smile.

She returned it, her pearl-white teeth stark against her red lips. 'Howdy, yourself, cowboy.' She had a thick accent, one he couldn't quite put his finger on. She pointed to the group she'd just walked away from. 'My friends over there dared me to come talk to you, and me being me, I never knock back a challenge.'

'Did they now?' He took a lazy swig from his whisky while cautiously eyeing the long-legged woman.

She curled a lock of hair around her finger. 'Uh-huh, and they bet me a hundred bucks that I wouldn't be able to get you to kiss me within five minutes.'

Gobsmacked, he stared at the vivacious female, who was undressing him with her eyes like there was no tomorrow. Confidence was always sexy, but she was heading into conceited territory. Quickly pulling himself together, and not wanting to come across as arrogant, he smiled charmingly. 'And what's in it for me if I do, kiss you, that is?'

'You get the awesome experience of touching these lips.' She grinned, pointing to her glossy red smile.

'Right.' As much as he didn't find her brazenness attractive, he had to give her kudos for having the guts to do such a thing. He paused, not sure of what to do, and not wanting to give her the wrong impression. But then again, what would it hurt, to help her get the hundred bucks? It wasn't like he was going to have sex with her, and her cherry red lips *were* tempting. They might help take his mind off things, if only for a couple of seconds, maybe a little longer.

Possibly sensing his hesitancy, she put her hands on her hips, guiding his gaze down her deliciously curvy figure. He could imagine just how that body would feel if he got his hands on her, which he was mentally telling himself over and over not to even consider, as hard as that was being a hot-blooded man. Besides, it would probably only cause trouble, and he had enough trouble in his life right now.

She flashed him a coy smile. 'Do you like what you see?'

'How could any man not like what he sees when he looks at you?' He had to be honest, she was stunning.

Running a finger down his chest peeking out from his button-up shirt, she threw her head back and laughed. 'Why, thank you, cowboy.'

Feeling a little uncomfortable, he started to make conversation. 'So, I gather from your accent you're not from around these parts?'

She took another step closer to him. 'Nope, just swinging through, on my way to Port Douglas. My girlfriends and I are on a six-week holiday all the way from Russia.'

Now here was a woman who wouldn't want any form of commitment, and yet he felt no desire to give her what she so clearly fancied, which was way more than a measly kiss. 'Wow, you're a long way from home.'

'Yes, I am, and we're all loving the Aussie hospitality so far. Aussie blokes are so, how do I put it, accommodating.' Smirking, she looked back at her friends, who all gave her the thumbs up. Turning to him, she placed a hand on his bouncing knee. 'So, are you up for it, or not?'

He almost choked on his mouthful of whisky. 'A kiss?'

She placed her other hand on his other knee, steadying that one too, her ample cleavage now on show. 'Yes, a kiss.'

For god's sake, as much as he had to admit she was striking, he just wanted to get rid of her. 'Well, with so much riding on it, how could a bloke say no?'

Her brown eyes widened, as did her coquettish smile. 'That's a good man.'

Placing his empty glass down on the bar, and nodding to the barman for another, he then leant in, grabbed her around the waist, and kissed her like he meant it. Like anything in his life, if he was going to do something, he was going to do it well.

The woman wrapped her arms around his neck, possessively, lustfully. In that split-second, he couldn't help feeling the yearnings to drag her off to his room, to take pleasure in meaningless sex, but he fought them off. His gut told him it would be a really bad decision, and he'd made enough of them in his life.

Finally untangling from him, she stood back, wiping the corners of her lips as if she'd just eaten a delicious meal. Her red lipstick was smudged. 'That was good.'

'Only good, huh?' Zane flashed her a cheeky smile, then wiped where he imagined her lipstick was left around his mouth.

'Okay, cowboy, maybe a little more than good.' She purred, her smile mischievous. 'Thank you for helping me out ...' She leant in close and brought her lips to his ear. 'If you want more, we can finish what we started a little later, yes?' Stepping back, she bit her bottom lip as she waited for his agreement.

Put on the spot, and not wanting to hurt her feelings, Zane cleared his throat. 'Oh, thanks, but I've had a really long day, so I'm going to hit the sack soon.'

'That's okay, I can hit the sack with you.' She fluttered her lashes.

'Ah, I appreciate the offer, but I'm beat and would be no good to you anyway.'

Her smile all but fading, she said something to him in what he gathered to be Russian. Whatever it was, she didn't look happy. Turning on her heel, she sashayed back to her friends, giving him the finger over her shoulder.

'Charming,' he mumbled as he passed the barman ten dollars.

Grabbing his whisky on the rocks from the bar, he felt a tap on his shoulder. Far out, she was back to give him what for, or to try harder. Either way, he wasn't in the mood for it any longer. Ready to fob her off, his heart almost exploded in his chest when he spun around to come face to face with the woman of his dreams and fantasies. Age had most certainly worked in her favour – she looked even more beautiful than he remembered. He shot to his feet.

'Zane Wolfe, it feels like forever.' Her smile didn't hold its usual effervescence, and he wasn't sure if it was because of what he'd done before, or because of what she'd undoubtedly just seen him do.

His soul instantly reaching for hers, he wanted to scoop her into his arms, but refrained. He took a brief moment to catch his breath. 'More like a lifetime, Em. It's really good to see you,' he said, before clearing his throat. 'How have you been?'

'Yeah, can't complain, I suppose.' Reaching out, she touched his hand resting on the bar, sending a flood of heat through him. 'I'm so sorry about Peter. I could only imagine how much of a shock it's been for you. Of course, I'm gathering you haven't been in touch with him much over the past few years.' The gentle concern in her eyes ignited an unwelcome hunger in his chest, laced with a deep nostalgia he wasn't ready to face. Not now. Not ever.

His heart racing and at a loss for words, he looked to where her hand still rested on his, and then back at her sparkling eyes. Her mouth parted ever so slightly as she inhaled sharply. The noise of the pub faded away as something unfathomable passed between then, so fleetingly he wondered if he'd imagined it. Then her cheeks suddenly flushed, and she quickly straightened and shoved both her hands into her jeans' pockets, as if she had to hide them to stop from touching him.

He finally found his voice. 'Thanks, Em. It still feels so surreal that he's not here anymore.'

'Yeah, I bet it does. I can't believe it either.'

'I'd always thought the tough old bastard would somehow outlive me.' He forced a smile, desperate to lighten the mood.

'Yeah, well, I suppose, with bull riding, you never know if your time is going to be up way too soon.'

'Yup, it's not a case of if you get hurt … but when.' He shrugged. 'All part of the excitement, I guess, for us, and the spectators.'

'Uh-huh.' She rocked back and forth on her heels. 'Sooooo …' She drew the word out, her eyes travelling to the leggy Russian woman who was now playing pool with the bunch of wild-looking ringers. 'I see you're still up to your old tricks, Casanova.' Her mouth flattened as she dragged her gaze back to him, a fire within them that wasn't there moments ago.

The nickname she knew he hated hit him like a sucker punch to the chest, but he smiled through it. He wasn't going to let her see how much it still hurt him. Was she jealous? He liked the thought. One hell of a lot. Too bloody much, actually. She was clearly still the same, rebellious, stubborn creature – composed on the outside but with something so wild and untamed behind her stare. 'It was just a dare, Em, no biggy.'

'It looked like a hell of a lot more than that, Zane.' Her tone was curt, tense, and almost accusatory. She folded her arms defensively.

'Is that a little bit of jealousy I can hear?' He couldn't help himself, or the satisfied smirk curling his lips.

She glared at him, and then gazed over his shoulder at the band, as though not looking into his eyes any longer was the safest option.

Following her line of sight, Zane pretended to be engrossed in the band too, while stealing subtle sideways glances. She'd always been a firecracker, which is why he'd nicknamed her so. Like a provoked micky bull, her nostrils flared a little and her hands were fisted at her sides. Provoke her any more, and he knew from experience, she would give him a piece of her mind – and he liked that about her. He always knew where he stood with Em, and too bad for him if he didn't like it. Even when she was angry, she was magnificent.

Hating this uncomfortable tension between them, he itched to reach out and pull her to him, to hold her close and kiss her beautiful, glossy lips; to tell her how much she'd been on his mind over the years and reveal just how much she meant to him. But he had no right to, and he was fairly certain she wouldn't want to hear any of it anyway. He touched his cheek, remembering the harsh sting her slap had left as if it'd just happened, and then suddenly he was right back there, at her front door, his heart being smashed to smithereens as she told him the night they'd shared before he'd left Aussie shores had been a one-off, a moment in time he needed to find a way to forget. If that wasn't cutting enough, she then went on to say he was the type of man she could never see herself with … the cheating type. He may have been a bit of a womaniser, it came with the bull-riding territory, but he never, ever, would have cheated on her. Not like Michael had, many times over.

'Earth to Zane …' Emma gave him a playful shove, snapping him from the painful memories.

He shifted so he was facing her again. 'Oh, shit, sorry, I was miles away.'

'Yeah, I could see that.' She smiled so genuinely it warmed his heart. 'Do you remember this song?'

Drumming the bar with his fingertips, he took a few moments, and then it hit him. 'Oh, hell yes! We boogied our arses off to it at the Silvergum B&S ball and won the prize for best crazy dancers.'

She nodded, her smile widening. 'We sure did, not that Michael was too happy about it.'

'Michael was never happy about anything.' His brows rose.

'Oh, come on, as unlikeable as he can be these days, you have to admit he was heaps of fun back then. Before Peter had completely brainwashed him.'

Zane shrugged. 'Yeah, he was an all right bloke back in the day, I'll give him that much.' He placed his drink down and held out his hands, gesturing towards the dance floor with a tip of his head. 'Should we go and burn up the floor, for old times' sake?'

She hesitated, jiggled on the spot as though mentally reasoning with herself, and then to his surprise, accepted his offer. Her petite hand entwined in his, and he enjoyed the looks they got as he led her to the dance floor. Making sure not to overcrowd her as they eased themselves into the rhythm of the beat, he slowly closed the distance between them. She yielded to his touch, her smile soft and her eyes breathtaking. With the disco light filtering over her face, and both of them falling into the groove with the music and each other, the past sixteen years faded away, leaving just her and him, seventeen, footloose and fancy free … with their whole lives ahead of them.

CHAPTER
10

Emma had been with Zane for all of ten minutes, and yet he'd succeeded in getting her onto the dance floor and into his arms. As much as it irked her that he still had that irresistible magnetism over her, she had to smile – his charm was one of the many things she'd found attractive about him, and still did. Not that she'd let him know that. A bloke with a hell of a lot going for himself already, he didn't need any more of an ego boost, especially not from her.

From the crowded dance floor, she finally caught Renee's eyes, and gave a quick wave so her friend knew where she was. A knowing grin plastered on her pretty face, Renee gave her the thumbs up before turning back to the handsome, and unfamiliar bloke, who was now cosied up beside her. The pair were seemingly engrossed in deep conversation, and Emma couldn't help but notice the way Renee was twirling a lock of hair around her finger – a sure sign she was really into him. Glad her mate wasn't sitting alone,

she focused on Zane. Again. The expression on his gorgeous face
was one of pure joy as he bopped and grooved his way around
her. A seasoned dancer, the pair of them having done rock-n-roll
classes in preparation for their deb ball years ago, she couldn't
help but let herself flow in sync with him. She loved how he was
always able to bring out her playful side, no matter what mood
she was in. Even now, with everything that was troubling her, he
made her feel as though life couldn't be any sweeter.

His intense gaze capturing hers, she allowed him to grab her
by the hand and twirl her out, only to quickly rein her back in.
She was so close to him she could smell the hint of aftershave
on his neck and the lingering scent of leather on his shirt. Their
bodies brushing past each other's and then colliding as they rock
and rolled, she sensed old flames blazing to life, and by Christ
it felt good to feel so sensual, so sexy and so wanted. She knew
she'd have to douse them down when reality kicked back in,
but not just yet. Right at this second, she didn't care about the
consequences; this was the freest she'd felt in what seemed like
forever. As though the years had all but vanished, it was just like
the good old times, when she and Zane and all their mates would
hit the dance floors of the B&S balls they travelled to in convoys,
their utes with more stickers and aerials on them than you could
poke a stick at.

The upbeat song ending and the band announcing one for all
the star-struck lovers in the house tonight, reality finally kicked
in and she quickly made her exit, with Zane close behind her. A
slow love song wasn't a good idea, especially not when the sexual
chemistry was sizzling between them and her voice of reason
was clouded with the effects of alcohol. Although there was no
denying she had feelings for Mister Zane Wolfe, she was shocked

by just how much she was drawn to him – it was almost out of her control. *Almost* …

Hiking it from the dance floor before he could haul her back onto it, she pulled up at the bar, hot and sweaty and keen for a drink. While fanning her face, she tucked sweaty strands of hair behind her ears.

'We need something to wet our whistles after that effort, Em. My shout …' The broad smile he'd worn the entire time they were bopping away to the music still plastered to his handsome face, Zane stepped in front of her to order. 'Is vodka, lime and soda still your poison?'

'Yup, creature of habit, I'm afraid.' Sweat trickled between her breasts and down her back as she wiped beads of it from her forehead.

'There ain't nothing wrong with being a creature of habit, Firecracker.' He grinned mischievously, and she walloped his arm.

'You cheeky bugger. You know how much I hate that nickname.'

Zane playfully rubbed where her hand had connected. 'My wild guess is about as much as I hate "Casanova"?'

She grinned, enjoying their familiar banter. 'Touché, my friend.'

He grinned and she fought the urge to give him another hard shove.

The barman sprang over to them, keen as ever to take their order. Emma had to give him credit for being committed to his job. Zane leant over the bar to be heard above the music, his arse at the perfect angle for her to perve on. He'd always filled out a pair of jeans to perfection, and not only at the rear. She almost slapped herself with the wicked thought while wishing she could rein in her animalistic attraction to the macho man. But she couldn't help but drink in all six-foot-three of his unrivalled hunkiness. It was all she could do to tear her eyes from him and try to think rationally. When he turned to pass her the drink, she had a sudden urge to press her lips on that part of his chest where she knew she would feel his big, beautiful heart beating. He may have been a lady-killer, and infuriatingly stubborn at times, but she couldn't deny he had a heart of gold beneath his thick armour. Not many had witnessed his soft side, but she had, many times over.

Taking a sip from his whisky, he pointed to the jam-packed dance floor. 'Now that was good old-fashioned fun out there.'

His deep husky voice made her legs weak; weaker than they'd been already from the effects of the alcohol. She took a desperate swig from her glass while trying to get her heart rate back to normal. 'Yeah, it sure was. I've needed to let my hair down. These past few days have been super tough.'

'No doubt about that ... how's Riley handling it all?' Emma's mouth dropped open but when nothing came out, he quickly elaborated. 'You and Michael separating, I mean, and then Peter passing away?'

'It's all hit her pretty hard, the poor kid, and I ...' A surge of emotion stole her ability to speak. She offered a shaky smile.

Reaching out, Zane gave her arm a squeeze. 'Oh, Em, it's gotta be tough, being a single mum, but I know you'd be hitting goals.'

Ready to burst into tears, she laughed instead, her gaze darting this way and that so she didn't have to look into his kind eyes. Her heart was broken enough when it came to Riley, but having to talk about her daughter to a man who had no idea he was her father was beyond overwhelming. With all the strength she could muster, she bit back the guilt. 'Um, yeah, sometimes I feel like I'm getting a grip on the whole mothering thing, and then other times I feel like I'm way off the mark and have no idea what I should be doing.' Recalling how tightly Riley had wrapped her arms around her yesterday afternoon, her eyes stung with tears. She quickly blinked them away before Zane noticed.

'You've always been your toughest critic, Em. You really have to stop being so hard on yourself all the time.' His voice was filled with so much compassion it only made it harder for her to remain composed.

'It's just not that easy, Zane.' A tear escaped and she quickly wiped it away while forcing a smile. 'Being a mother is the hardest job I've ever done.' Her heart rate increased in frantic rhythm as she gazed into eyes she could so easily tumble into, if she allowed herself.

His expression one of anguish, he placed his drink down on the bar. 'Oh shit, Em, please don't cry. Me and my habit of putting my damn foot in my mouth.' Without warning, he leant in and gave her a hug so tight there wasn't an inch between them. His hand gently rubbed her back, both consoling her and unintentionally tempting her. The hustle and bustle of the pub faded away, and all she felt, heard and smelt was him – she wanted to stay in his arms forever.

'I'm sorry, I don't know what came over me,' she mumbled into his shirt as she hugged him a little awkwardly. Not about to crumble in the middle of a packed pub she tried not to let his kindness break her resolve. And besides, he'd just lost his father, no matter the fissure between the men, so she should be comforting him, not the other way around. Her guilty conscience getting the better of her, she pushed back from him and smiled. 'Thanks for caring so much.' She wiped her cheeks. 'Have I got mascara everywhere now?'

'A little bit.' His perfect set of lips curled into the most tender of smiles, and his blue eyes held her captive as he reached out and gently wiped beneath her eyes with his thumb. 'There, just like new again.' He placed both hands on her shoulders protectively. 'You sure you're okay, Em?'

'Yeah, I'll be right, just being a bit of a sook, that's all.' She pushed the words out from her tight throat. 'A decent night's sleep will make the world of difference.'

He gave her a look to say he didn't believe a word she'd just said. 'Well, I'm all ears, if you need to talk about it.' He chuckled, deep and throaty. 'And I've got plenty of shoulder for you to cry on, if you need.'

She had cried on his big broad shoulders many times, and scratched her nails on them in the throes of passion too. Her cheeks flamed with the memory. 'Thanks, I'll keep it in mind.'

Taking a sip of whisky, he stared at her over the rim of the glass. 'You sure there's nothing else bothering you?'

'No, what makes you think there is?' It was said a little too fast, and a little too defensively.

He shrugged. 'Dunno, I just feel like there's more to the story than what you're telling me.'

'Nope.' Her mouth growing drier by the second, she quickly grabbed her drink, taking big gulps as if it were water. He'd always been able to read her like a book, and she damn well didn't want him to.

'Okay, that's good then.' He gestured towards the now empty glass. 'Want another?'

She sucked in a deep breath as she placed her glass back on the bar. 'No, thanks, I better get back to Rennie before she thinks I've deserted her for the night.'

'Right, yup.' He paused, his gaze gaining intensity. 'I'm sorry.'

'What for?'

'Doing what I did last time I was here.'

'It's okay, all forgotten.'

'Just like that?' He half grinned, half frowned.

'Yup, just like that.' She lowered her eyes. She could so easily open up right now and tell him how she'd never stopped thinking about him all these years, but … mentally slapping herself, she reminded herself of all she was keeping from him. There was enough for him to possibly hate her throughout this lifetime and into the next.

'I really want you to know that I …' His hand came to rest on her.

Terrified of what she was about to hear, Emma almost covered her ears. A declaration of his feelings for her was the last thing she needed, or deserved. At least, not until she'd had a chance to tell him the truth about Riley, and about his father.

Unknowingly saving the day, Renee suddenly skidded in beside them. The handsome man she'd been chatting to had his arm coiled in hers. Renee's wayward smile spoke of everything she was hoping to get up to with him later. Emma stifled a grin; with her best friend not having bedded a bloke since she broke up with her cheating ex six months ago, lord help the poor man.

'Oh, my god, how are you, my long-lost friend?' Disentangling herself from her new date, Renee threw her arms around Zane. 'It's been way too long between visits.'

Giving her a tight hug, Zane smiled as Renee stepped back. 'Yeah, it has been … life kinda got away from me over there. How've you been?'

'Overworked, underpaid and exhausted, but other than that, I'm bloody great.' She grinned and then gestured to the man standing patiently beside her. 'I'd like to introduce you both to Silvergum's newest police recruit, Constable Jackson Hume.'

A copper? Holy shit. Not ideal, after what she'd told Renee last night. Not that she thought Renee would ever reveal her secret, but it was all just a little weird. Emma gave her mate a quick raised brow before turning and flashing him a broad smile. 'Hi, Jackson, nice to meet you. I'm Emma.'

'Nice to meet you, Emma … I've just heard lots about you.'

His handshake was firm and his smile genuine; Emma liked him instantly. 'I hope it was all good.'

'Most of it.' He grinned as he gave her a playful wink.

Zane held out his hand. 'G'day, Jackson, Zane Wolfe.' He tipped his head to Renee. 'You're keeping good company with this one.'

Reaching out, Jackson accepted the handshake with vigour. 'Oh, hey, Zane, am I? We've only just met, so I'm yet to find that out.' It was said light-heartedly.

Silence settled and they all looked to one another, smiling.

Renee jumped to action and grabbed both of Jackson's hands. 'You want to join me on the dance floor?' She began dragging him out before he could even reply.

'He seems nice,' Emma said as she watched them on the crowded dance floor.

Zane edged up beside her. 'Yeah, he does.'

Yawning, Emma looked to her watch. It was almost midnight. 'Holy crap, I'm going to turn into a pumpkin if I don't hit the sack soon.'

Zane offered her a steady sideways glance, a smile on his lips. 'Have one more dance with me, before you head off?'

'Oh, I don't know, I'm really tired.' She looked to where Renee and Jackson were now kissing beneath the glittering disco ball. 'Shit, she moves quick.'

'Yup, Rennie has never been one to beat around the bush.' Zane leant into her ear. 'And about that dance, I'm not taking no for an answer.'

Grinning, Emma tried to ignore the pleasure-filled quiver that travelled all the way from the top of her head to the tips of her toes. She light-heartedly groaned. 'Fine, but only one, and then I'm going home to bed, where I hope I'm going to sleep for all of Australia, and then some.'

'I promise, just one dance, and I'll let you go.'

'Hmm, I don't know if I've got the energy for it.' Tugging the scrunchy from her wrist, Emma pulled her hair up into a ponytail.

'Oh, come on … I'll make the decision for you.' Grabbing her around the waist, he picked her up, tossed her over his shoulder, and carried her to the dance floor without any fight from her; the crowd too busy in their own drunken dancing worlds to take much notice of them.

From her prime position atop his broad shoulders Emma couldn't help but feel his strapping back muscles clenching with her weight, her gaze fixed on his perfect arse again. Good god, this man was a package – if only he wasn't such a ladies' man, and her ex-brother-in-law, and the secret father of her beautiful child, as well as the son of the man she'd accidentally killed, life would be peachy perfect. She almost laughed at the absurdity of it all. Yup, she was officially drunk.

When he placed her down, Emma struggled to shake off all the reasons she shouldn't be standing here with him as the steel guitar came to life, along with the beat of drums. Taking her by the hand, Zane swung her out and brought her back to him, so effortlessly, so charmingly, her breath caught. The other couples moved out of their space a little, and eyes fell upon them as they tumbled into each other's arms. As soon as she was in his firm grasp, Zane picked her up and twirled her in the air. Back on her feet in seconds, Emma swayed with him to the beat of the music, their boots moving in tempo, their bodies in perfect union. His piercing gaze flirted with her the entire time and swept her up in the moment. She couldn't help but send him some sultry looks of her own.

Renee and Jackson bopped beside them, all four of them laughing and enjoying every second of the party classic. Then, before Emma knew it, the addictive tune of 'Khe Sanh' ended, and the tempo slowed as Chris Stapleton's 'More of You' rang out, the vocalist doing the song proud with his husky, honky-tonk voice. Before Emma had time to escape, Zane closed the distance, pulled her arms up and around his neck, and then dropped his hands to her lower back. The poignant country song caressed her very core, and every lyric felt as if it were written about Zane and her. From the expression in his eyes, she knew he was thinking exactly the same thing. This. Was. Dangerous. Territory.

Tearing her gaze from his, she looked down at their boots sliding across the floor as she tried to catch the breath he was stealing from her, over and over again. Possibly sensing her hesitation, he drew her even closer, until her face was pressed up against his chest, and he buried his face in her hair. He pressed his lips up against her ear, and for a delicious moment, he just inhaled, exhaled, deeply, slowly, sending shivers all over her. And then, 'I've missed you so much, Em,' he whispered.

Her heart galloping, Emma dared a glance into his eyes, and as she did his lips came hazardously close to hers. With only an inch between them, she almost allowed herself to freefall into him, as she had when they were seventeen. But then the voice of reason stepped in, stridently telling her to get the hell away from him before she made another huge mistake. She'd unintentionally broken his heart once already, when he was last here, and broken hers good and proper in the process. Neither of them needed to go through that again. Not ever.

Begrudgingly unravelling from his strong, protective arms, she pushed her way through the packed dance floor, grabbed her bag from the corner of the booth, and then bolted towards the front doors, her vision blurred by tears. Zane called her name, but she dared not turn around for fear of collapsing into his arms and giving in as he made her feel safe and loved, and the truest form of herself she'd ever experienced. If only things could be different … She needed to get outside before she did something she'd regret the next day. Zane deserved to know all the secrets she was keeping, but she wasn't about to give in to her conscience and blurt them out in the middle of a dance floor. She'd find the right time – she had no other choice. But not now. Not tonight.

Cool air slapped her wide awake as she stepped outside, her breath rasping. Moving past the glare of the overhead sign and into the comforting darkness, she stopped and stared up at the glimmering blanket of stars. Her breathing slowing, she heard the crunch of footsteps behind her. Almost too afraid to look back and see Zane, she tried to sneak a peek over her shoulder. What was she going to say to him after running out like that?

'Em, are you okay, hun?' Renee came to face her, her arms reaching for her.

She shook her head and wiped at her cheeks. 'Not really, Rennie.'

'Oh, babe, it must be so hard, seeing him after all this time, especially with everything you're keeping from him. I can't even begin to comprehend what you must be going through right now.' She pulled Emma to her.

Wrapping her arms tightly around her friend, and now unable to speak for the ball of emotion lodged in her throat, Emma nodded against Renee's shoulder.

'Even though you never talk about him anymore, I know you love him, Em … you always have, and no doubt always will.' Renee stroked her hair. 'You were never together, but he was your very first crush, and your first true love, and you were undoubtedly his. It's just that life had other plans for you both by the time you realised it.'

Emma went to deny every word, but then thought better of it. Her best mate knew her inside out and back to front, so there was nothing to be gained from being dishonest, to Renee, or herself. There were enough damn lies complicating her life right now; enough to last her a lifetime and then some. So, she remained silent, her tears falling hard and fast and her body shuddering with deep sobs.

'And just for the record, Zane did the noble thing and went to follow you, but I stopped him and told him it's secret women's business, so it'd be best if he stayed in there with Jackson.' She chuckled. 'He tried to argue with me, but you know me, Em, stubborn as an ox.'

'Yup, you're even more stubborn than me, if that's possible.' Emma loosened her hold on Renee and cracked a tiny smile. 'I thought he would've tried to follow me ... he'd be worried.'

'Yup, he is, but that's not your concern, my friend.' Renee's face was a picture of compassion. 'You just focus on yourself and that gorgeous daughter of yours. I'll sort Zane out.'

Emma sucked in a sharp breath. 'Don't tell him anything about ...'

'As if I'd go and do something as stupid as that. I'll just tell him you thought you were going to throw up and made a dash for it.'

'Yeah, sounds good.' Emma groaned. 'To be honest, I really don't feel very well.'

'Yeah, well, you hardly drink anymore, so no wonder.' Renee smiled softly. 'How bouts we get you home, huh?'

Emma cleared her throat and took Renee's hands in hers. 'No, I don't want to put a dampener on your night. You stay with your new friend and I'll catch a cab home.'

'Oh, Em, are you sure?'

'Absolutely positive. No offence, but I just want to be on my own for a while.'

'No offence taken, Em. We all need a little time by ourselves to rest and recoup.'

'Thanks, Rennie.' Emma reached into her bag and fished for her mobile phone. 'I'll give Lui a call. He'll be parked around here somewhere, listening to his Italian love songs and waiting for closing time.'

'Okay, just make sure you text me when you're tucked up in bed, so I know you're home safe and sound.'

'I will, thanks, hun.' Emma dialled Lui's number and pressed the phone to her ear. 'Hey, Rennie, Jackson seems very nice.'

'He does, doesn't he?' She beamed from ear to ear. 'And I promise, your secrets are safe with me, even though I'm about to ravish a copper.' She grinned and then mocked zipping her lips shut.

'I want all the goss in the morning,' she whispered, as the town's one and only cab driver answered.

'Deal,' Renee whispered.

Genuinely smiling now, at both the dreamy look on Renee's face and Lui's sing-song Italian voice on the other end of the phone, Emma booked her ride home. 'All I can say about Jackson, is you go, girlfriend. You deserve to be happy.'

'Thanks, Em, and trust me when I say, I'm gonna make the most of tonight. Who knows where it'll go after that?'

'Ha-ha, why the hell not test the waters?'

Lights approached and Lui pulled up beside them. They gave each other another tight hug and a kiss goodbye. 'I'll be over to pick Riley up from Granny May's around nine ... that'll give us a couple of hours to get ready for the funeral.'

'Okay, Em. I'll make sure I'm ready to come along with you to the church ... love you.'

'Love you too, Rennie.' She climbed in beside Lui. 'Night.'

Twenty-five minutes later and Emma was walking through her front door with Tiny's tail excitedly slapping her on one side and Kat meowing on the other. Tossing her bag and keys on the entrance table, she stopped to give them both a quick pat hello before climbing the stairs, both critters in tow. Kat made her exit at Emma's bedroom door to wait for her, she'd be sleeping at Emma's feet as usual, and Tiny followed her and flopped down on the tiled bathroom floor, looking up at her beneath worried brows.

Emma smiled down at her loyal companion. 'I'm okay, mate … just need some sleep.'

Stripping off, she tossed her jeans, top, knickers and bra in the general direction of the clothes basket, all but the jeans landing inside it, and then stepped under the steaming hot shower. After the water had warmed her, she lathered up her hair and then allowed the hot spray to beat down on her aching shoulders as she rested her head against the tiles. Taking slow, deep breaths, she tried to make sense of what just happened at the pub. She knew she was going to feel a connection with Zane, especially as he was Riley's father, but nothing to the extent she had, and certainly not so quickly. Time and distance had done nothing to quell their flame. If anything, it had made it more intense, and somehow more tangible. Was it because she was single now that she could acknowledge what had been there all along? Or was it because of everything she kept hidden from him, that she somehow felt indebted to him? God only knew. One thing was for certain – tomorrow was Peter's funeral, and just thinking about seeing Zane in the light of day made her stomach tumble as if she were about to take a leap out of a plane, with no parachute to save her.

CHAPTER
11

The alarm Zane had set as he'd slumped into bed echoed through the hotel room, shrill and incessant, stirring him from his fitful few hours of sleep. The curtains open, blinding sunlight had flooded the tiny space, along with the drone of traffic. Freefalling from oblivion and slamming into reality, his heart squeezed – today was the day they would bury the man who had raised him, the man he'd once looked up to. The man he'd always wished would love him for who he was and not despise him for who he'd become. Never would he get to hear the word 'sorry' he'd so longed for, for most of his life. Not that he'd held high hopes of Peter ever saying it, but there'd always been a glimmer of a chance. The shock of Peter's death was making him re-evaluate everything, especially the feelings he'd held under lock and key for all these years for Emma.

Grabbing his jeans from the floor beside him, he plucked out his phone and flicked the alarm off. His head pounding, the sudden silence was a welcome relief. Blinking hangover-heavy eyes, he groaned and rolled onto his side while readjusting his boxer shorts. After too many whiskies, enjoyed before running into the gorgeous Miss Kensington, and then sculled afterwards to curb his worry after she raced out on him, he felt like death warmed up, times a hundred. Regret hung heavy in his heart. Right back at the beginning, when he'd first felt the flutters of lust for her, she been his step-brother's girlfriend, and he still wasn't in her scope. He was batting above his weight – that thought kept circling in his head. He shouldn't have tried to kiss her. Again. But goddamn it, how was he supposed to act like just friends when he adored the woman with every inch of his being?

Easing himself up from the floor, he took a few moments to get his bearings. As the hotel bed was lumpy and uncomfortable, he'd succumbed to sleeping on the floor, the doona now bunched up underneath him and the two pillows tossed to the side. Leaning his bare back against the wall, he rubbed his throbbing temples as thoughts of Emma pounded him left, right and centre. She'd owned his every dream throughout the night, and now awake, she still possessed his thoughts. The hold she had over his heart was one he both treasured and despised. The connection between them was undeniably beautiful, but what good was it when neither of them was in a position to see where it could take them? But as much as he knew it was useless to open his heart to her, to allow her to see what she meant to him, he just couldn't seem to help himself when he was with her, especially when she was in his embrace. He'd held many women in his arms before, but Emma was so different, in so many ways. Everything he loved about her stormed to the front of his thoughts, reminding him exactly why he couldn't, and wouldn't, ever shake her from his mind or heart.

A soft smile claimed his lips as he recalled twirling her around the dance floor – no matter what was going on in their lives, they'd always fallen in perfect sync with each other while rock and rolling. Then, when the music had slowed and he'd dared to hold her close, her shallow breathing had told him all he needed to know, as had the passion in her eyes when she'd looked at him. So sexy in her jeans, skin-tight blouse and cowgirl boots, he wouldn't have been able to take his eyes off her even if he'd wanted to. And her feisty determination turned him on no end.

Watching her move her curvaceous body to the music, and to him, he'd ached to throw her over his shoulder and drag her up to his hotel room, had longed to make love to her all night long. He adored how she never covered the sexy freckles that dusted her nose with make-up, or felt the need to wear skimpy clothes to grab men's attention. She owned what she had, and she rocked every single sexy, smooth, silky inch of her five-foot-nothing killer body with class and pizzazz. And as well as all of that, she could hold her own in a bar full of tanked cattlemen, could hammer fence posts in just as fiercely as any man, could pull a motor apart and then put it back together, could tame the wildest of horses. But then get her within his arms and she'd melt into him as if they were made for each other, as if she was home, safe and sound, and could finally let go of everything around them. Their relationship had always been like a rollercoaster – complicated, frustrated, strained, beautiful, ugly and real, and sometimes all at once. But never had he thought they would still have hungered for each other the way they had last night. The smell of her coconut shampoo mixed with the scent of her had taken him away to the time and place that only they'd been privy to. What he'd give to feel that with her again.

Sighing the memories away, he looked at his watch – it was time to make a move. With a little over two hours before the service began, he needed a long hot shower to freshen up, a pit stop at the bakery to buy something for breakfast, and then on to the church – where he would see Michael again. How that was going to go down, he hadn't a damn clue, after they'd come to blows eight years ago when Zane was last in town. But he hoped, for the sake of everyone attending the funeral and out of respect for Peter, it would be uneventful. He'd do his very best to make it so, but he could only bite his tongue for so long, before Michael's arrogance and obnoxiousness would push him over the edge. To avoid that, he needed to keep his distance.

An hour later, Zane, dressed in his finest black jeans, button-up shirt and tie, hightailed it from the bakery and leapt back into his rental. His breakfast, a sausage roll smothered in tomato sauce, in hand, he winced as a sharp ray of sunshine struck the windscreen of the four-wheel drive. Eyes watering, he grabbed his sunnies from the rim of his wide-brimmed black hat and slipped them on, hoping to god no one would smell the stale whisky on his breath. The renowned prodigal son of one of the most powerful men of Silvergum, half the township would be keen to prove that Peter had been right to dismiss him as worse than useless, so the packet of mints he'd just bought would be his only saviour. Cursing beneath his breath, he wished he could rewind the clock and not have drunk so much, but it had felt damn good at the time to be able to let everything go, while also holding Emma tight. Hindsight was a bitch.

His empty stomach desperate for sustenance, he ate quickly. Licking the sauce from his fingers as he devoured the last mouthful, he then wiped the crumbs from his shirt. With the church only two streets down from the bakery, he'd be saying his final goodbyes before he knew it. Not knowing what to expect or how he was going to feel as Peter's coffin was lowered into the earth, his stomach swirled nauseatingly. And then, he thought again, there was the matter of seeing Michael. He heaved a sigh. Just like when he'd climb on the back of a snorting, belligerent bull, most of what was about to unfold was out of his hands. He'd just have to roll with the punches, hopefully not literally.

Up ahead a crowd huddled under the church's covered driveway, which also shaded the black hearse from the scorching sunshine. An old red-brick building with leadlight windows, this was the church where Zane had once been an altar boy. The parking spots few and far between, he finally found a place out the front of the police station, almost a block away from where he needed to be. Checking his reflection in the rear-view mirror, he wiped the few crumbs from around his lips, sucked in a deep, calming breath, made sure his mobile was on silent, and then stepped out of the car, confident in the man he'd become. To hell with anyone who had a different opinion.

His steps quick and determined, he ran a finger around his collar, wishing he could have worn more comfortable clothes. It didn't take him long to reach the church, just as the last few members of the congregation were making their way inside. Keen to lose himself amongst it all, so he could avoid any small talk, he made a beeline for the steps. But before he could climb them, a kindly face greeted him. His father's long-standing PA's pink-lipped smile was filled with such genuine sadness it snagged his breath. Zane forced a smile he was far from feeling.

'Hi, Mary.' Reaching out, he gave her a quick hug. 'Thanks for making such an effort to get in touch with me.' She smelt faintly of mothballs and rose oil, as she always did, and he liked the familiarity of it.

Reciprocating the embrace, Mary then took a small step back and nodded, the black netting draped from her stylish hat shading her time-weathered face. 'Of course, Zane, it's so good to see you, dear.' She paused and drew in a shuddering breath, then wiped the corners of her eyes with a floral handkerchief. 'I'm just sorry it's under such sad circumstances.'

'Me too, Mary ...' Zane placed a hand on her back, feeling her elderly fragility through her cotton blouse. 'Shall we go in?'

'Yes, I suppose we should.' She offered a quivering smile as she glanced around him. 'Have you come alone?'

'Yes.' He knew she was hoping for his sake that he'd have a wife and kids in tow.

'Would you like to sit with Frank and me then?'

'Thanks, Mary, I'd like that.'

'I'm so glad you made the trip home.' Reaching out, she gave his arm a gentle squeeze. 'Contrary to what anyone else thinks, you were always a good boy, and I knew you would make it back to pay your respects.'

Her words, although well intentioned, struck him right where it hurt. Hesitating for a moment, he then followed her up the stairs and through the wide arch of the entrance. His eyes took a few seconds to adjust to the change of light, but when they did, the first thing his gaze fell upon was the opulent coffin, and all he felt was cold detachment. It gleamed in the sunlight streaming through the stained-glass windows. Had it been chosen to soothe the living into believing there could be grandeur in death? Wreaths covered the floor all around it.

Standing at the front of the church, Michael's dark eyes shot daggers towards him. If looks could kill, he was sure he'd have been dead. A cynical smirk claiming his lips, Michael shook his head ever so slightly, suggesting disbelief that Zane had bothered to come. Not wanting to take his bait, Zane looked away, his hands now fisted at his sides and his jaw clenched. This was certainly not the time nor place to tell Michael what he thought of him. He was sure he'd have plenty of opportunity for that in the coming days – especially with the reading of the will set down for tomorrow. Why he'd been requested to be there was beyond him – but he'd go, regardless, and do the right thing.

Zane wasn't surprised to see the church was crowded; every pew was full. Fold-out chairs had been placed around the sides and still some people had to stand. Eyes followed him down the aisle, and he tried to ignore the disapproving stares and whispers. He was no longer the skinny, pimply-faced boy who had left here all those years ago; the lad who local gossips said had left and broken Peter's heart. The one who returned eight years later only to break his brother's nose in a jealous rage and leave again.

None of them knew what that fight had been about – Zane had confronted Michael for not even bothering to be at his daughter's birthday party. Nor did they know the dark secrets Peter had made him keep, to protect Emma, or so Peter had said. None of them had walked in his boots, so who were they to judge? Damn the small-town narrow-mindedness of some people, who had nothing better to do with their lives than spread lies. He had to give it to Peter, though – even in death, the man knew how to draw a crowd. He was the one man that everyone in this room, apart from Michael, at one time or another, would have been happy to see gone. But now, in the harsh reality of death, they must have felt guilty for their thoughts – himself included. Considering that Peter always commanded respect but would walk over anyone to get what he wanted, the people of Silvergum had forgiving hearts. Zane sighed. If only he could find forgiveness in his, it would make this tragedy a whole lot easier to deal with. Would he ever be able to let go of the past, so he could step out of the shadows that it cast? After the past sixteen years of his life spent trying to run from the pain, he doubted it.

Wishing he were any place but here, he shifted his gaze from the deep mahogany coffin with the large wreath and framed photo of Peter atop it, looking only for her. He needed to know if Emma was going to carry whatever it was that had made her run from his arms last night, into the events of today. Renee had tried to lay his concerns to rest when she'd walked back into the pub, saying Emma had gone home because she wasn't feeling well, but he wasn't born yesterday. Knowing Emma the way he did, he was sure there was a lot more to it. But he wasn't about to press for answers he possibly wouldn't like hearing. He had to admit, he'd overstepped the friendship line thanks to alcohol and desire-fuelled recklessness. His deep-seated feelings for her were no excuse. But even if that were the case and Emma was cranky with him for acting like a lovesick fool, he knew that by seeing her now, he would feel a certain kind of comfort that only she could give. She'd always had the knack of soothing him when he felt as if he were spiralling out of control, and right about now, he could use a good dose of soothing. As he'd always been her rock when they were growing up, she had been his soft landing; a voice of reason that always made him feel worthy of standing tall and entitled to follow his own path. She was his calm in a storm, and also the fuel to his fire. It was an intoxicating combination – one no other woman had been able to give him.

Seated in the front row, near Michael and some woman Zane gathered must be Michael's girlfriend, Emma peered over her shoulder as if sensing his eyes upon her. Liking that thought, he acknowledged her with a restrained smile. She smiled softly back at him, the compassion in her dazzling eyes letting him know it was all going to be okay between them. It was like an offering of an olive branch, and he grabbed it before she pulled it away. Flooded with relief, he finally felt like he could draw in a decent breath. The young girl beside her turned to see what Emma was looking at, and a bolt of nostalgia struck him as their eyes met, the unshed tears she was wiping away wrenching at his heartstrings. Like mother like daughter, the striking teenager sitting between Emma and Renee was undoubtedly Riley. A wave of protectiveness overcame him, and he yearned to try to shield her from the agony of her grandfather's funeral, to wipe the tears from her cheeks. He offered her a small smile, but Riley looked at him as if he were a stranger, and it cut deeper than he thought it should. How could he blame her, when he hadn't bothered to keep in touch?

Mary seemed to be heading straight for Michael and the woman half his age cosied up beside him, but thankfully she slid into a pew three rows back. Saying a quiet hello to Frank, Zane sat down beside the now seventy-something man, noticing how much thinner and greyer the ex-publican's hair had become. Sitting in silence, Zane's gaze blurred past Michael and settled on

Peter's coffin. He tried to imagine the irrepressible Peter Wolfe lying in submission in such a confined space. It was a hard image to swallow and stirred emotions he'd hidden so deeply he quickly diverted his attention to stop them rising to the surface. He'd shed his tears the day Mary had called him with the news, in truth only because of the fact he'd never hear the apology he'd so wanted to hear slip from Peter's lips.

Clearing his throat excessively, as if telling everyone to quieten down, the priest stepped out from behind the altar and nodded. Following the sudden hush, the young man, sweating in his vestments, didn't waste any time in beginning the service. After welcoming everyone, he spoke of beginnings and endings, and how the only way forward was to accept both with a wholesome heart, and how it was important to embrace grief at such a tragic time. Two people unknown to Zane went up to read scriptures from the Bible, even though Peter was never a god-fearing man. Then it was Michael's turn to stand up and make Peter into a man he wasn't, to sugar coat his life. His objective clearly was to leave a sweet memory of a man who Zane would always remember as a harsh figure in his life. As Michael's words jumbled and faded into mindless drivel, Zane shifted his gaze between Emma and Riley, the coffin, and back again, his heart vaulting from nostalgia to despair, to longing and regret. It was only when Michael spoke the words that struck his very core, did Zane turn his attention back to him once more.

'We all come from the earth, and in the end, we yield to it, free and void of pain, sins and sorrow. It is only then, once the dirt is placed over us, we are returned to Christ, our Lord, in our purest form, to be pardoned for our wrong deeds, celebrated for our good ones, and accepted into heaven unconditionally.'

Zane gritted his teeth – Michael must have copied his words from some book.

Gripping the sides of the pulpit, Michael closed his eyes and drew in a deep breath before continuing. 'This, my dear friends and family, is what I wish for, for my father, a man who deserves to be honoured for the righteousness he brought into this world, and not remembered or judged for things we may or may not agree with.'

Zane unfurled his white-knuckled hands from the pew in front of him, the proclamation so close to home the haunting memories he'd learnt to disregard stormed into his mind, and the terror and shock he'd experienced was suddenly as palpable as it had been that terrible night. Emma glanced towards him, her face as pale as what he imagined his to be. Trying to offer her comfort with his gaze, he fought not to show what he was thinking as Michael stepped down from the polished wooden pulpit, descended the steps and placed his hand on the coffin, whispering words Zane wished he could hear. Or maybe it was best he didn't.

The priest nodded solemnly and said a few final words, inviting all to the cemetery. The congregation then stood, and Zane joined them, unsure of what to do next. It was time to carry the coffin. Up until this second, he hadn't even considered if he should be one of the pallbearers. His mind tipped and swayed. Should he or shouldn't he?

Sensing his uncertainty, Mary leant into him. 'Go on, love, if you feel it's the right thing to do, you should. I'm sure Kay would have liked you to be involved, if she were here.'

Still unsure, but with no time to think, he stepped past Mary and Frank and over to help carry the coffin. With six men already on either side, he chose to go to the back.

Michael subtly elbowed him in the stomach as he passed him. 'Don't you dare …' he spat out beneath his breath.

Anger and humiliation settled in Zane's gut, cold and hateful. But not wanting to make a scene, he stepped back. This was the lowest blow, but where Michael was concerned, what had he expected? Shame washed over him, and he turned away from prying eyes.

Emma came to his side and gently placed her hand on his back. 'Don't let him get to you … you're a better man than he'll ever be,' she whispered, before stepping past him and taking a weeping Riley by the hand.

Emma's words soothing his anger and heartache, Zane waited for the church to begin to empty before following the remaining line of people outside. Keeping to himself, he stepped around the side of the church and drew in the deepest breath he could muster, while reminding himself to calm the hell down. Michael had always known just how to flick his switch, and he wasn't going to give him the satisfaction of losing it in front of everyone, especially today. It was exactly what the son of a bitch wanted, so he could prove to everyone that his and Peter's theories about Zane were right. Wandering in circles under the shade of a paperbark tree, he watched the hearse pull out and the mulling people disperse. Safe from being cornered by some well-meaning Silvergum local, he strode over to his four-wheel drive and retrieved his cowboy cover. It was well needed.

Head down, he walked to the cemetery, hands shoved in his pockets and his wide-brimmed hat pulled low. Apart from a nod of acknowledgement or a short g'day in passing, he kept to himself. A block down from the church, spiked black fencing surrounded the graveyard as if it were a prison. Stepping through the open wrought-iron gates, he made his way up the path that weaved its way through a maze of graves, both new and run-down. Although hot in his long-sleeved shirt, he shivered – the place felt so full, yet so empty at the same time. His mother having chosen a cremation, the family had followed her wishes and spread her ashes at Wattle Acres. Zane was thankful she wasn't laid to rest amongst all of this. A free spirit in life, she deserved to be so in her death.

Atop the hill, a freshly dug hole awaited its new occupant, and a portable canopy covered it. Trust Peter to buy a site at the highest point of the cemetery – he was always above everyone when he was alive, and now he would remain so in death. The black hearse was parked nearby, the pallbearers ready to carry the coffin. Successful in dropping his anger a few notches on his walk over, he avoided catching Michael's eyes. He didn't want to deal with his mean spirit right now, or the drive to knock it right out of him.

As the mourners gathered by the grave, he remained off to the side, his gaze fixed on Emma. She was, as always, a beautiful distraction. Despite her five-foot-nothing height, she was an impressive sight. Her long hair tied back in a braid accentuated her petite features and the tiny diamond stud in her nose. As she lifted her hand to push a stray tendril of hair back from Riley's face, her sleeve slipped, revealing the tattoo of an angel he remembered so well. He had given it to Emma as her sixteenth birthday present, from one mate to another, and he'd sat right beside her as she'd braved the pain of the tattoo gun. He knew she had more, too, a black rose on her exquisite hip, a Native American woman at the top of her thigh, and a lotus flower at the lower part of her back, right at the place he now longed to place his hands while he pulled her to him, just like he had last night.

He found himself mesmerised, watching how her lips moved into a soft smile while she wiped tears from Riley's cheeks, before pulling her daughter to her, protectively, lovingly. He ached to be a part of their bond, to share their sense of family. These two special souls had endured so much of late and he longed to embrace the pair of them, to protect them from any more hurt in their lives, and to shelter them from Michael's narcissism. Something he should have done a long time ago, instead of running back to the States with his tail between his legs. And so, without another thought, he closed the distance, ignoring Michael's gaze burning a hole in his back. Even though adopted, he was a Wolfe, Kay had made him so, and he deserved to be here as much as any other person – to hell with Michael and his self-righteousness.

'Hey, Em …' He kept his voice low as he watched Riley turn and snuggle into Renee, who offered him a kind smile. 'You okay?' he said to Emma.

'Yeah, you?'

'Yup, all good.'

'Uh-huh.' She didn't look convinced.

'Don't worry about me, I'm a big boy and can deal with my own shit.'

Up on her tippy toes before he realised what she was doing, Emma brushed a kiss over his cheek and gave him a tight hug. 'I'm so sorry about what happened back at the church.' She looked to where Michael was standing by the hearse, waiting to carry the coffin over. 'He's such an arsehole,' she whispered behind her hand.

'Damn straight he is.' He leant towards her. 'How's Riley doing?'

'Not great, but to be expected. She loved her grandfather.' A worried shadow lurked as she swept her eyes over him. 'How are you doing? You look beat.'

'Oh gees, thanks ... lack of sleep will do that to a person.' She looked like an angel, and he ached to tell her as much. 'It's just been a big couple of days, and last night didn't help. I should've just hit the sack as soon as I got here, but I kind of wanted to drown my sorrows. Hindsight can be a bitch, huh?'

'Yup, it bloody well can be, and a big fat ditto to drowning the sorrows.' She smiled ever so slightly as Riley wandered back to her side. 'Do you remember Zane, sweetheart?'

'Hey, Riley.' He reached out and touched her arm. 'You've shot up a fair bit since I was last here ...' He smiled. 'It was at your eighth birthday, if I remember right.'

Sniffling, Riley tipped her head to the side. 'I kinda do. You're my long-lost uncle, aren't you?'

Her honesty was confronting, but he smiled through it. 'Correctomundo.' He looked to Emma. Her face suddenly pale, something unfathomable passed in her gaze. Had he said something he shouldn't have? He went to ask but Riley continued.

'It's nice you made it all the way here, Uncle Zane. I'm sure Grandad would appreciate it, even if my father doesn't. It wasn't very nice, what he did to you at the church. I'm really sorry about that.' Riley smiled, the fragility behind it reaching right into Zane's heart and squeezing it tight.

'Thanks, Riley, and please don't apologise for him. It's not your fault.' He recognised the hollow look in his niece's eyes and understood all too well the hurt of having a father who didn't know how to show any love for his child. Unsure of what to say when silence fell, he grabbed onto his first thought and ran with it. 'You still obsessed with horses?' Stupid question, as he knew she would be with a horse-loving mother like Emma, but he wanted to divert Riley's attention to something that made her smile from the inside out – if that were possible on a day like today.

His strategy worked, and her sad smile broadened into one filled with joy and warmth and everything good in this world. 'I sure am.'

'I'll have to call around sometime before I head back to the States, maybe go for a ride with you and your mum, if that's okay with you both.'

'That'd be nice, hey, Mum?' She looked to Emma for her agreement.

'It would be lovely. How about tomorrow afternoon, and then you can stay for dinner, if you like?'

'It's a date,' he said all too quickly.

The priest's arrival meant he didn't have the chance to back-pedal and explain that wasn't exactly what he meant. They all turned to watch the coffin being carried across the picture-perfect green lawn to the tune of 'Time to Say Goodbye'. His heart heavy, more for never having experienced Peter's love or pride, as Michael had, Zane still couldn't quite come to grips with the fact this was all really happening. Emma stood so close to him now, the gentle breeze whipping the hem of her long skirt against his leg. His senses heightening, he could feel her warmth, her energy, and hear the small intake and outtake of her breath. Riley cuddled into her, her weeping becoming more of a deep sob as the coffin was lowered. In that instant, hearing Riley's raw heartbreak, something deep inside him slipped and shattered, taking him by surprise. He fought to remain composed as he longed to pull his niece into his arms, to somehow take away her pain and make it his. Clasping his hands together tightly, so he didn't do just that, he drew in a desperate breath and then another, the surge of emotions overwhelming him.

Emma gently wrapped her arm around his waist, closing the inches between them. Catching sight of them so comfortably close, Michael scowled across the grave towards them, while mumbling beneath his breath. Zane returned the look of disapproval, ten-fold. Michael was, and always would be, a selfish prick. His arm was wrapped around his expressionless girlfriend, who Zane imagined to be counting the inheritance while staring at Peter's coffin, instead of wrapped around his heartbroken daughter. Zane sucked in a desperate breath. The heartache gripping him like a vice wasn't for the loss of Peter, but for the only people other than his mother who had ever made him feel a part of a family. He felt a bond with Emma and Riley he'd never felt with another living soul. For the first time in as long as he could remember, unconditional love and a sense of belonging replaced the empty restlessness that had occupied his tortured soul.

CHAPTER
12

Wattle Acres, Silvergum, North Queensland

Not much had changed in the seven years since she'd last stepped foot in here. Emma knew her face was ashen because she'd felt the colour drain as she'd inched her way through the front doors. Memories clung to every inch of the homestead, some good, some horrific; she just had to find a way, for today, to let them all go. Never in her wildest dreams would she have believed she'd be back here. She looked at the table where she and her own mother and Kay Wolfe used to sit, drinking tea and sharing scones when they would pop in for a visit – which was quite often, given the two women were close friends and neighbours. If only she'd known then what she did now, how different their conversations would have been.

Wiping sweaty palms down her cotton skirt, she tried to rid her mind of the harrowing images of Martin Turner collapsing to the floor, blood pouring from the wound where he'd knocked his head against the marble bench top. Just what he'd been doing kneeling on the floor of the kitchen, of all places, was beyond her. Her pulse was racing and had been since stepping foot in here. She wondered if anyone could hear it thudding against her ribcage, for the sound of it filled her head. Turning her back on the busy CWA women who had gathered in the kitchen to lend helping hands, she stole a second of privacy. A tear rolled down her cheek before she even realised she was crying – if only Peter hadn't lied to them about Martin being part of the Mafia, she would have gone to the police. What had he wanted to cover up with his deceitfulness? It sure as heck wasn't to save her sorry arse. With a quivering hand she quickly wiped the tears away and drew in a steadying breath. Nobody could know what had happened in here. She needed to get a damn grip.

Placing the bowl of whipped cream in the fridge for the time being, she shuddered as if icy fingers had run up her spine. A home was meant to be full of warmth and love and security, but all she felt in this place was loathing and fear. But she could do this – she just had to. The funeral done and dusted, the wake had now begun – a few more hours and it would all be over, and she and Riley could move on with their lives. The sun-drenched kitchen was a hive of activity; too much for her quivering nerves. She excused herself, desperately needing a few moments to calm down. She forced a smile she was far from feeling as she saw Riley, pausing briefly to brush a kiss over her cheek in passing.

Touched by something far deeper than the gloomy hallway, she shivered as she made her way to the bathroom, the scorching temperatures outside doing nothing to rid the chill of the place. She didn't need directions; she'd walked the floorboards of this house a hundred times over. With tall-ceilinged hallways and rooms all leading out to the wide, wrap-around verandah, the grand Wattle Acres homestead was both striking and eerie, with the shadows of days gone by lingering in every corner.

Splashing cool water on her face and then drying her hands on the guest towel, Emma paused to stare at her reflection in the bathroom mirror. She looked tired; the haunted look in her eyes something she could do nothing to conceal. Hopefully, people would think it was because of her sadness and shock, dealing with Peter's death. Little did they know just how much she despised the man and was relieved with his passing. Taking a few minutes to calm down, she then turned on her heel and wandered back towards the kitchen. Passing through the doorway, she forced a smile in Riley's direction and got back to work, desperate to keep her trembling hands busy. Putting away some cartons of milk, she fought to steady her galloping heartbeat. Her senses on high alert, she could hear the pendulum of the grandfather clock in the nearby lounge room swinging back and forth: *tick, tock, tick, tock*. Very soon it would be chiming the hour, and she knew the sound would send her nerves firing on all cylinders. The walls of the old homestead started to feel as though they were closing in on her; she used all the strength she had to remain composed as she grabbed a cloth and wiped down the already spick and span benches. She had to hold it together for Riley's sake. On the outside she hoped she appeared unruffled, but inside it felt as if her heart had become a stone in her chest, so heavy it could almost crush her.

Desperate to get out of her head, she turned her attention to the ABC radio humming softly in the background, the announcer way too chirpy for a day like today. Staring into the sink filled with suds, she dropped the cloth and fought to stay focused on washing up, a tough ask while standing in the exact spot where she'd done something that had altered all of their lives almost sixteen years ago. For what felt like the millionth time, she wondered where they'd buried him. An outsider, he hadn't been missed from Silvergum. She wondered if he'd been reported missing wherever he was from.

Her mind zigzagging back to the day after Riley's eighth birthday party – the last time she'd stepped foot in here – she shuddered when she recalled Peter's hands locked around her throat as if it were only yesterday. Dropping off the ironing she used to do for him for a bit of extra cash – he never handed it out freely – she'd already made the decision it would be the final time she did so. With Peter's car at the mechanics, she'd mistakenly thought he wasn't home. Reeking of stale alcohol, he'd cornered her, invading her personal space until she'd had her back pressed up against the wall. She'd begged him to stop, and maybe she'd cried; she couldn't remember. Wrapping his hands around her throat, tightly enough for her to be gasping for breath, he'd reminded her of his threats the day before, had hit home the necessity for her to never speak a word of the DNA results, to anyone, ever. For a fleeting moment, she'd believed her life was about to end, but then he'd unfurled his fingers, roaring at her to get the hell out of his house and never come back.

Drawing in a shaky breath while fighting off the haunting memories, she carefully placed the bowl she'd just washed on the draining rack. Urgently needing fresh air, she leant over the sink and tried to tug the window open. It didn't budge, so she tried harder, reaching up on her toes as she rested her hips against the sink for leverage. It finally sprung free, and a breeze licked the sheer curtain upwards. She drew in a deep breath, feeling a little calmer with the cool air. As she stood back down she knocked the kickboard under the cupboard with her foot. It fell in, so, grumbling to herself, she knelt down and pushed it back into place. Even with all the money Peter had, the homestead was falling apart. Everywhere she looked, she could see timberwork that needed a lick of paint, rooms that could do with some tender loving care, something Peter knew nothing about.

Holding the edge of the sink and pulling herself to standing, she startled as Renee tossed an arm over her shoulder. 'You okay?'

'Yeah, sort of.' She nervously glanced about, making sure none of the women working in the kitchen were listening. 'I can't wait for today to be over.'

'After what you told me, that's understandable, my friend.' She gave her shoulder a squeeze. 'I'm right here beside you.'

Emma smiled appreciatively. 'Thanks, Rennie.'

Renee brushed a kiss over her cheek. 'I've finished putting the cream, strawberries and passionfruit on the pav, so I'm just going to pop to the loo before we take it all outside,' she said. 'Can you point me in the right direction? This house is like a maze and I'm bloody busting.'

'Down the hall, three doors to your left.'

'Thanks, be back in two shakes of a lamb's tail.'

'I need to go too, Aunty Rennie,' Riley called after her. 'Back in a sec, Mum.'

'Of course, no worries, love.'

Catching her eye, Granny May came over and wrapped a protective arm around her waist. 'It must be hard, being here.'

'It sure is.' Emma breathed out. Little did Granny May know just how hard it was, and why.

'Head high and shoulders back, love.' She moved closer to Emma. 'The old bastard is gone for good, so life will be a heck of a lot easier for you and Riley now he's not in Michael's ear all the time, trying to come up with ways to make you suffer,' she said quietly.

'Very true.' She patted Granny May's weathered hand. 'Thanks so much for helping out today. I couldn't have done it without you and your lovely CWA crew.'

'It's our pleasure, treasure. We women have to stick together, especially in the hard times.' She clapped her hands, her bangles jingling. 'Right then, let's get this prep finished and this show on the road ...' She looked over at her CWA friends. 'Shall we, ladies?'

There was collective agreement and the activity in the kitchen became even more hectic. Her temples throbbing, Emma turned and gazed out the window at a few kids playing on the back verandah; their laughter was uplifting. Just hearing a child's glee made her feel as though everything was going to be all right in the world. She looked at all the guests standing around in the backyard, some with beers, others with wine, and only a few with cups of tea or coffee. She wondered how many were there for the free alcohol and food. Worried that Zane might be feeling like a fish out of water amongst them all, she tried to catch sight of him, but he was still nowhere to be seen. As they'd left the cemetery, he'd said he'd be here. Maybe he'd had second thoughts, and to be honest, after the way Michael had shunned and shamed him at the funeral, she couldn't blame him one little bit. Zane had paid his respects, so in her opinion, job done.

With so many thoughts crowding her mind, she tried to ignore the profound ache in her heart and the crushing guilt sitting on her shoulders as she wiped her hands on a tea towel and hung it back on the oven door. Adding the last of the curried egg and lettuce sandwiches Granny May had just made to the sandwich platter, she covered it with some plastic wrap and placed it with the rest of the dishes to go outside just as Riley and Renee returned. Like a well-oiled machine, she, Riley and the rest of the women picked up whatever they could carry and began marching towards the back door.

Squinting into the glorious sunshine, a decent-looking chocolate mud cake balanced in one hand and a nibbles platter in the other, Emma headed to the trestle tables set up under the towering paperbark trees. Why she'd agreed to take charge of the catering for the wake was beyond her, but then again, it had been important to Riley and she hadn't been able to say no at the time. Riley's spirits had lifted since leaving the cemetery, so it had clearly been the right decision.

Emma looked around the back lawn again for Zane, while reminding herself it was purely out of concern for him. Even with over a hundred people on the lawn, and many in the cool shade of the verandah, trying to escape the soaring temperatures, she saw him almost instantly. Strikingly tall, deliciously tattooed, the epitome of dark and handsome, and with the air of a good man but bad boy, he hadn't changed much over the years, other than becoming more manly, more tempting, and all the more charming. One glimpse of him last night and it felt as if all the years had just faded away, and she was right back there, in his bedroom at the cottage, the pair of them tearing clothes from each other – a naïve, scared seventeen-year-old girl desperate for him not to go, not to leave her for his bull-riding dreams. She'd been so torn between her feelings for him and Michael, both of them dear to her in their own ways. If Zane had just once told her he would commit to her, that he wanted to be with her and make a life together, there was a huge chance she would have broken it off with Michael. She'd loved him then, just like she loved him now, but her need to be with a man who would give her the family life she'd dreamed of won over. It had been a case of letting her head rule and not her heart. Big mistake.

Leaning against the verandah railing, his attention seemed to be locked on the horizon, as though in the deepest of thoughts. She didn't need to see the sky-blue eyes, hidden with dark sunglasses, to know they would be shadowed with memories of this place. His black hat was down low, hiding his face. His shirt pulled against his muscular chest, and his black jeans hugged him in all the right places. Putting the mud cake on the table, her eyes trailed down his torso, to the silver belt buckle shining beneath his tucked-in shirt. She fought hard not to go down any further but couldn't help herself. She knew all too well the pleasures that lay beneath that taut denim. God how she wanted him to stay, to make a life back here in Silvergum, near her, and not only because he was Riley's father. She'd missed him so much over the years, although hadn't allowed herself to acknowledge it. But now he was here, she was helpless to ignore it any longer. He was the only man she'd ever truly craved with every inch of her being, the only man she'd ever truly loved. He'd finally come home, but not to stay. Maybe what she had to tell him was going to change all of that.

Too restless to sit with the other women, and with all the food out and already being devoured, she made her way towards him, feeling Michael's eyes burning a hole in her back as she did. She'd usually be more vigilant, not wanting to upset the apple cart, but after the way Michael had treated him at the church, she didn't give a damn what her ex-husband thought, or felt, about her undeniable connection with Zane.

As though sensing her, Zane turned and the warm smile that claimed his lips told her everything she needed to know. Resting his forearm on the railing, he watched her approach. Her emotions overwhelmed her as she climbed the few steps.

'You hanging in there?' she whispered, unsure of what else to say.

'Yeah, all good, Em.' Lifting his sunglasses, his eyes skidded over her. 'How 'bout you, how are you coping being back here?'

'Not great …' She shrugged. 'But I'm trying not to let it get to me.' She fell silent, her thoughts churning. There was plenty more she could add, like how she'd thought about him often, or how she had cried for weeks, months even, after he'd left the shores of Australia.

'Yeah, me too. I'm trying to focus on all the good memories here, especially the ones with Mum, and you.' He grinned and shook his head. 'Far out, we used to have some good old-fashioned country fun, didn't we? Especially in the saddle and swimming in the dam until we were a pair of prunes.'

'We sure did. Those were the days, huh.' She came in close to him and leant on the railing, leaving little space between them. 'So much has happened since then, it feels like a lifetime ago.'

'It kinda was, I suppose.' He released a long sigh. 'You know, as much as I've avoided it, I'm going to miss this place. It's the only home I've ever really known, when Mum was alive, that is, and it's where her memory lives on for me. It'll kind of be like losing her all over again, never stepping a foot back here.'

Emma's heart stopped. 'You never know what's around the corner … you might end up with Wattle Acres yet.' Even as the words left her lips, she didn't believe them. 'Stranger things have happened,' she added.

'Thanks for trying to be upbeat about it, Em, but I doubt it.' His chiselled features hardened as he shrugged. 'It's not a secret there was no love lost between Peter and me, so he sure as hell wouldn't have left much, if anything at all, to me, even though this was Mum's place to begin with. I don't even understand why I have to be at the reading of the will tomorrow to be honest, but I'll do the right thing and go along.'

Emma's heart squeezed with the sight of the shadows in his eyes. So much hurt had been caused over the years, and she'd been helpless to stop any of it. The thought that she was only going to add to it, tore her to pieces. 'I wish I could come with you tomorrow morning, for moral support.' She reached out and touched his hand, feeling as though she was touching fire. Electricity sizzled up her arm and stung her heart.

'Thanks, Em, not that I would let you be locked in the same room as Michael and me, it could get ugly knowing us two.' He chuckled. 'But seriously, it means a lot, you wanting to be here for me, especially when no other bastard is.'

'No matter what, I'll always be here for you, Zane.' She longed to wrap her arms around him but was afraid of what she might do if she was that close to him again. 'I know we'd fallen out of touch, but I'd like to change that now you've come back and we've smoothed it over.'

'You're a good woman, Em. Michael was a fool, treating you the way he did, but then again, the bastard never deserved you in the first place. I know you loved him when you married him, but I knew he would eventually let you down. You're way too good-hearted for a man like him.' Scorn bit into his harsh tone. 'He's too self-obsessed to ever give you, and Riley for that matter, the love and respect you both deserve.' He paused, looking in Riley's direction, a soft smile easing the tension in his expression. 'If I were Riley's father, I'd be loving that girl like there's no tomorrow.' He turned to Emma. 'She beautiful, inside and out, just like you are.'

Emma found herself at a complete loss for words. The shockwave Zane had innocently just shot her way almost sent her crumpling to the floor. She gripped the railing hard to stay upright, hoping to god Zane didn't notice the whites of her knuckles, or the sudden paleness of her face. She needed to change the direction of the conversation before she told him everything – now wasn't the time, or place. Her mouth felt like it was filled with cotton. Desperate for a drink, she grabbed his half empty beer from the bannister and sculled it.

His eyes widened and he laughed. 'You right there?'

She stifled a small burp and wiped her lips. 'Uh-huh. Sorry, was parched.' She held up the empty stubby. 'Want me to go and get you another from the esky?'

'Nah, thanks, I wasn't really in the mood for that one anyway.'

'After our efforts last night, I can't say I blame you for feeling a bit on the seedy side.' She offered him a wayward smile. 'So, are you going to hang around Silvergum, for a while at least?'

'I'm not planning on staying any longer than necessary. I want to be out of here before Michael puts the place on the market. I couldn't bear to watch it be sold off.' He rubbed his face, his chest rising and falling with his rough breath. 'My plane is booked for five days' time, and then I'm outta here.'

'Oh, right.' Even though she suspected as much, it was hard to hide her disappointment. 'But what if hell freezes over and you end up with this place ... would you stay then?'

'I hadn't really thought about it, because there's no way it's going to happen, but yeah, I probably would ... at the very least for Mum's sake.' He straightened up. 'But Michael's going to get it, and being the money hungry bastard he is, he'll definitely sell it. I can't even bear thinking about it, not with Mum's ashes spread here.' His voice cracked, and he looked away from her, drumming his fingers on the balustrade.

Emma regarded him thoughtfully, while choosing her next words carefully. 'I really think, regardless of what happens tomorrow, you should stick around for a while.' She picked at the corners of the soggy beer label.

'Why, what have I got to stick around for?' His hasty words hit hard and left a hollow sensation in her stomach.

She shrugged. 'Maybe you could stay at the cottage and spend some time with Riley. She could use a male around for a bit, and I could use a hand around the place.'

His expression hard to read, Zane took her by the shoulders and peered down at her. 'Thank you, Em, for caring so much. You've always had my back, and I adore you for that, more than I could ever put into words.' He paused, then said, 'I think you and I both know it would be a really bad decision for me to come and stay at your place, for any length of time.'

'Maybe you're right,' she said, ever so gently. She bit her lip in a bid to stop it quivering. 'But then again, maybe you're wrong.'

'I'm really not sure it would be wise for us to try and find out. You know what happened the last time I was here.' The tenderness in his eyes stole her breath.

'That was different, I was married to your brother, for god's sake.' A sob broke from the depths of her heart, one that had nothing to do with her loathing of being here, or what she was keeping from him, and more to do with the fact they'd just never found the right time or place to be together.

'Oh, Em, please don't cry. It tears me apart to see you upset.' He pulled her close and tucked her head beneath his chin, and she felt a warm sense of coming home after a lifetime away. 'You'll be right, and so will Riley, you'll see.'

She closed her eyes, her heart clenching with both nostalgia and heartache. She'd gone and chosen the wrong brother, and now, it seemed, there was no going back from that mistake.

'Emma?' Michael's stern tone and heavy footsteps carried from the end of the verandah.

Untangling from Zane's embrace, she quickly tried to wipe the tears from her eyes.

Michael's expression was fierce. Scotch in hand, he sculled it and then slammed the empty tumbler down on the railing, knocking the empty beer bottle to the floor.

'You've had way too much to drink,' Emma said, her angry gaze matching his.

Michael's eyebrows lifted in astonishment. 'Have I now? And just who the hell are you to decide that?' He took her by the arm and gave it a firm tug. 'Come on, it's time to leave before you make any more of a fool of yourself, or me, with the likes of him.' He eyed Zane as if he were gum beneath his shiny shoes.

'If I were you, I'd let her go, Michael.' Zane stepped forwards, but Emma blocked his path.

'Here's the thing, though, Zane, you're not me.' Michael's words were slurred.

Growling, Emma tugged her arm free. 'You have no right to tell me what to do, Michael,' she snapped.

'Haven't I, Emma?' Michael's smirk reminded her of Peter's, the day he'd wrapped his hands around her throat.

Zane's breathing was becoming more and more laboured, and his fists were clenched tightly at his sides. Emma knew she needed to get Michael away, before Zane decked him. 'Please, Michael, just leave me the hell alone.'

'You know I like it when you get all feisty on me.' Michael reached out and grabbed hold of her arm once more, but this time her pained expression gave away just how much it hurt.

Zane stepped in, and Emma was helpless to stop him this time. 'Oi, I said get your filthy hands off her.'

'Make me,' Michael snarled through clenched teeth.

The crack as Zane's fist met with Michael's face was bone crushing. Emma cried out as she grabbed his arm, desperately trying to drag him away from where Michael was now sprawled out on the verandah.

A hand cupped over his nose, Michael tried to scramble to his feet, and once he did, backed away, well out of Zane's swinging range. 'I'm going to make you pay for that, you son of a bitch.' A trickle of blood ran over his lip.

Zane's eyes burned with hatred. 'Like I said, keep your damn hands off her.'

Riley raced across the backyard and rushed to Michael's side, her steely gaze glued to Zane's. 'What in the hell are you two doing? It's Grandad's funeral, for god's sake. I know you hate each other, but can't you control yourselves, just this once?' She waved an arm towards the crowd. 'This isn't right, letting everyone see this.'

Zane shook his head, clearly disappointed with himself. 'You're right, I'm so sorry, Riley.'

Riley huffed and turned her attention to Michael. 'I watched you grabbing Mum's arm. Twice! A guy shouldn't touch a woman like that, ever! Uncle Zane was only protecting her. You need to learn how to treat women, including me.'

'I'm sorry, Riley.' Michael tried to pull her to him.

She stepped away. 'Don't you touch me.' Heavy tears now falling, she wiped at them as she stormed away, arms folded across her chest as if trying to hold herself together.

Racing after her daughter, Emma could feel the weight of Zane's stare. She ached to look back at him, to somehow, telepathically, tell him how much more she loved him for protecting her as he just had. But instead, one hurried step in front of the other, she did what she had to, sidestepping Michael with an angry glance, and went to Riley. She would call Zane and beg him not to go back to the States just yet, and also hit home that she wasn't going to take no for an answer to him staying in the workers' cottage. She needed to make things right, and come hell or high water, she was going to do just that. But to do so, she needed Zane here, and she needed a little time to gather up the courage to do it. Regardless, she would do everything in her power to stop him stepping foot on a plane out of here. She wanted him to stay, and not only for now.

CHAPTER

13

Strolling along the busy footpath, hands shoved deeply in his jeans' pockets and his hat brim pulled low, Zane tried not to let his gloomy thoughts consume him. Sitting in a room with Michael, while being told he'd been left jack shit, was not his idea of a morning well spent. He avoided looking at passers-by, knowing full well some of their gazes would be bursting with condemnation and judgement after he swung a hard-hitting punch Michael's way yesterday. No doubt he'd be the talk of the town; it came with the territory in a small place like Silvergum. With his reputation for being a bit of a hooligan in his younger years, he really couldn't blame them. But feeling like death warmed up and then some, he wasn't in the mood to hear their ignorant opinions. None of them knew the brute Michael Wolfe was behind closed doors. He was a narcissist to the very core, although he knew how to make himself appear saintlike.

Zane's boots pounding the pavement, he tried to stretch out the kinks in his neck. He'd found it impossible to sleep; he had endured another long night filled with regrets and guilt, pooled with the deep sense of not really belonging here. That is, except when he stood by Emma's side. Filled with remorse for brandishing his fist, not for Michael's sake but for Riley and Emma, he'd spent the entire night staring at the squeaky ceiling fan and checking his phone for a reply from Emma to his text apologising for his behaviour. All the while he was chastising himself for stooping to Michael's level. There was no doubt the egocentric bastard had deserved it, after grabbing Emma the way he had. How a man could lay a finger on a woman was beyond him, but he could have handled it better given the circumstances. It was always the way with him, though – his instincts were to react first and think about it later. Seeing the pain written all over Emma's face, a red rage had stolen his ability to think straight, and wild adrenaline, fiercer than what he'd ever felt on the back of a bull, had owned him.

Rounding a corner, the mouth-watering aroma of freshly baked bread snatched his attention away from his incessant thoughts and his stomach growled. Not having eaten since the sausage roll he'd inhaled on the way to the funeral yesterday morning, ravenous hunger had driven him from his hotel room early in the morning. Slowing down, he noticed the sandwich board advertising the weekly special of authentic sourdough. He walked in, pushing aside the beaded curtain designed to keep the flies out. It reminded him of happier days. His mum had thrown herself into the craze when he was a kid, and strings of colourful beads had dangled from almost every doorway in the homestead, driving them all nuts, apart from his mum. God, how he missed her and her quirky ways.

Today was one of the only days to score a loaf of the Italian head baker's ridgy-didge sourdough, and as it was also pension day, the little shop was a hive of activity. Sidestepping a kid devouring a cream bun, more of it seemingly on the little boy's face than in his mouth, Zane joined the long line to the counter. Although not in the mood to wait in a slow-moving queue, he was pleased that some of Silvergum's traditions hadn't changed over the years. Hoping it would be a good peace offering when he braved calling in to Serendipity later, he made a mental note to buy a loaf of the sourdough for Emma – it had always been her favourite. He remembered the many times they'd ridden their pushbikes all the way into town on a weekend to buy one. Then they'd race back home to devour it. Sandwiches of sourdough with his mum's legendary homemade corned beef, slices of tomato, mustard pickles and thin slices of onions, were to die for. He'd give his right arm to devour one right now.

Patiently waiting his turn to be served, he stifled a yawn, his eyes so heavy they could do with a set of toothpicks to keep them open. Nearing the counter, he admired the decadent mini lemon tarts, cream horns, oozy chocolate and walnut brownies, and mammoth lamingtons piled high in the display fridge. He added a few of the coconut and chocolate-encrusted mounds of spongy heaven and a couple of the brownies to his ever-growing wishlist. Hopefully Riley would like some treats – it was the very least he could do after the upset he'd caused her yesterday. Worried Emma hadn't replied to his text last night out of anger, he needed to see her face to face. He just hoped he was still welcome to call in on them, especially as he was meant to be going there for a ride and dinner later this arvo. He refused to leave Australian shores on bad terms with her again. Their silence had been a never-ending struggle for him last time; his heart just couldn't cope with it a second time.

A wave of longing came over him as he watched a little girl jumping up and down on the spot while her mother ordered her a pink meringue topped with hundreds and thousands. The bond between parent and child was so special. Then the phone in his top pocket vibrated. Reaching in, he plucked it out, relief flooding him when he spotted the caller ID. Gladly giving up his place in line, even though he was next to be served, he stood off to the side and pressed it to his ear. 'Morning, Em, how goes it?' He did his best to sound high-spirited, hoping it might help her to forgive him.

'Hey, Zane, I'm okay, thanks. I'm so sorry I didn't reply to your lovely text last night. My phone went flat and I plugged it in downstairs in the office, and I haven't had a chance to check it until now.'

Zane felt a massive weight lift, from both his shoulders and his heart. Even so, he tried to sound nonchalant. 'Oh, all good, Em, I thought you must've got caught up.'

'Yeah, after cleaning up after the wake, and then having to feed all the critters after dark, time kinda got away from me.' She sighed as though exhausted. 'Anyway, enough about me, how are you going?'

'I could do with a few more hours' sleep, but not too bad. How's Riley? Is she still mad with me?' Grimacing, he held his breath. Emma's quiet little chuckle soothed him.

'She's still upset, but not as bad as she was yesterday. The poor kid has had a really crappy time of late, so everything affects her much more than it usually would.'

'I'm really sorry, doing that in front of her.'

'Hmmm, it wasn't the best decision you've ever made, but she gets why you did it, and to be honest, I appreciate you standing up for me … although, just for the record, you do know I'm big enough and scary enough to have my own back, don't you?'

'Yeah, I know you got fire in your belly, little Miss Firecracker, but it doesn't stop him from being aggressive towards you, Em. If anything, it makes him worse.'

'Yeah, tell me about it. After almost seventeen years of dealing with him, I've learnt the hard way that nothing I do will change who he is. A leopard doesn't change its spots, huh?'

'And a tiger can't change its stripes … but I don't agree with any of that. We can all make choices to change, or not. Saying otherwise is just a poor excuse.'

'Gee whizz, that's pretty deep for this time of the morning, Zane.'

He chuckled. 'I'm a deep-thinking guy.'

'Yeah, you always have been.' It was said softly, and then a deep breath followed the silence. 'Anyhow, the reason I'm calling, other than to thank you for your apology text is because I've just made up the bed in the workers' cottage, and I've pulled a couple of fillet steaks out of the freezer for dinner, so you're coming to stay, whether you like it or not. And then we can maybe go for our ride tomorrow – Riley has made plans with her friend for this arvo.'

'Far out, Em, you don't beat around the bush, do ya?'

Emma laughed. 'Why waste the time and energy doing that?'

Zane stole a few brief moments, his heart aching to say yes, but his mind screaming not to do it. He couldn't go getting attached, even more than he already was, only to leave again. It wouldn't be fair to either of them. 'Thanks, Em, but I really don't reckon it's a good idea—'

She cut him off with a playful groan. 'For once in your life will you stop thinking so damn much. We're adults, with bucket-loads of willpower, so we'll be fine.'

'Uh-huh.' Maybe she would be fine, but he wasn't sure he could say the same for himself. His self-control all but vanished whenever he was around her.

'And besides, at least here, you can eat good food, have good company, and you can give me a hand around the place. It's a win–win for both of us.'

He stood in silence, not knowing what to say.

'Why's it so noisy in the background? Where are you?'

He glanced around, the line to the counter now disappearing out the beaded doorway. 'I'm just at the bakery, getting brekkie.'

'And there you have it, my point exactly. You can't live on pies and sausage rolls.'

He grinned. 'Why not? It's been done before.'

Emma huffed, and he could picture her rolling her spectacular green eyes at him, with a coy smile on her kissable lips. 'I'll see you this arvo, with your bag. I'll even make some of my famous béarnaise sauce to go with the steak, if you're lucky.'

'Well, in that case, how can I say no?'

'Eggzacory.' She sounded mightily pleased with herself. 'I'll let Riley know. She's looking forward to spending some time with her famous bull-riding ...' She stalled.

'Uncle,' Zane added as he smiled into the phone. 'Catch you and Riley sometime after lunch, Em.'

'Sounds like a plan. See ya round like a rissole, Zane.' And she was gone before he could reply, 'With "gravy and all".'

A spring in his step, he joined the line, the length of it not worrying him one bit now his anxiety had eased and his mood had lightened. By the time he bought his breakfast, along with the second last loaf of sourdough and the sweet treats for Riley, the sun was high in the bright blue sky and the air was so thick from the heat it was a job to draw a decent breath. Paper bags and can of Coke in hand, he strode back to where he'd parked in the shade of a soaring Bowen mango tree. Black spots all over the bonnet, he glanced up and shook his head, cursing as the acid stench hit him. No wonder there'd been so many parking spaces here – the hundreds of fruit bats hanging from the branches of the mango tree caused one hell of a mess. He'd been too preoccupied to notice when he'd pulled up. Before he dropped the rental back, a drive through the car wash was on the cards.

Sliding into the driver's seat, he tugged his seatbelt on, loosening it off as much as he could before turning the ignition on. Adam Harvey and Troy Cassar-Daley's twangy country voices rang out; their rendition of 'He Stopped Loving Her Today' gave him goosebumps. Tearing the little sauce sachet open with his teeth, then swirling the tomato sauce around on the top of his beef and mushroom pie, he went in for the kill. Burning his tongue on the first bite, he grabbed his can of Coke from the dash to try to ease it. Experience told him it was going to be sore later, but that wouldn't stop him tucking in.

Catching sight of the clock on the dashboard, and realising he now only had minutes to spare before he had to be at the solicitor's office, he swung into action. Time having got away from him with Emma's phone call, he needed to get a shift on. Balancing the pie on his lap, he reversed out and then headed up the main street, making sure to stick to the forty k speed limit, even though his inclination was to speed. With the kind of skill worthy of many a pie-loving Aussie eating from behind the wheel, he carefully controlled the steering with his knees and ate as quickly as the temperature of the pie would allow.

Windows down, he breathed in the town he'd once called home. Every shopfront on Silvergum's main street was different, the buildings borrowing this and that from different eras. Dusty four-wheel drives parked in between others so shiny that they looked as though they'd never seen a dirt road, let alone the bush. On the busy footpaths, mothers pushed prams and fathers carried or held the hands of distracted children; a group of hoody-wearers walked by quickly, everything about them seemed shady; old Italian men hung on the corners of the local IGA, smoking and chatting while their wives shopped. And farmers, both men and women, hurried in and out of the agricultural shed. There were busy people everywhere he looked. He couldn't help but notice the majority of them had their heads buried in a mobile phone – gone were the days when people exchanged smiles, slapped backs or shook hands in greeting.

Pulling to a stop at a pedestrian crossing, an old lady with hair so white it was almost iridescent began to hobble across, a walking frame in one hand and two bags of groceries in the other. She gave him a half-apologetic smile, her steps slow and laboured. If on foot, he would have helped her. Halfway to the other side of the street, the handle of one of the plastic bags snapped, and apples and oranges scattered everywhere. Covering her mouth, the lady watched the fruit roll away from her. Leaving the four-wheel drive running, Zane flicked his seatbelt off, made sure the handbrake was on, and jumped out, grabbing the fruit as fast as he could as he dashed towards her. By the time he'd gathered it all up, cars were lined up behind him, one dickhead even feeling the need to beep. Gritting his teeth, he fought back the urge to give the impatient bloke a mouthful.

'Thank you so very much, dear.' The old lady smiled warmly.

'No worries at all.' His arms full, he returned her smile. 'Not too sure where we're going to put these now the bag is busted.'

'Oh, I know.' She opened her handbag wide. 'How about in here?'

'That'll do.' He carefully offloaded his armful and made sure to help her to the sidewalk. Some cars were now going around where he'd left his – the world stopped for no one, not even an old lady. 'You live far from here?' he asked with a tip of his hat.

She pointed up the street, her frail hand shaking from age. 'I'm only three doors up.' She turned back to him and patted him on the arm. 'You should get moving …' She gestured towards the long line of cars now banked up. 'I don't think you're going to be too popular otherwise.'

'Let them wait, I have a fair maiden I'm saving.' He grinned gallantly. 'And besides, I'm not one for popularity.'

'Well, aren't we a charmer? It's nice to see chivalry isn't dead.' A blush rising to her cheeks, she smiled even wider. 'There should be more like you. Thanks again.'

'My pleasure.' He tipped his hat. 'You have yourself a nice day.'

'I'm going home for a nice cup of tea and some fresh scones, so I most certainly will.'

Back behind the wheel, he tried not to slam his foot to the floor in his haste. Two blocks down and he was there. 'Wolfe and Son Lawyers' was written in bold black letters across the shopfront. His guts twisted and knotted; thanks to his good deed he was late. Parked and out of the driver's seat in seconds, he took long strides towards the foyer, the corridor as cold and dark as he remembered it to be. Mary greeted him and ushered him towards a large corner office with views of the adjacent park; it had been Peter's office, where he had done all his dirty deals.

'Zane's here to see you, George.' Introduction done, Mary gave Zane a warm smile and quickly excused herself.

Zane looked to where Michael was sitting beside a vaguely familiar, grey-haired man at a dark oak table, scattered files and folders in front of them. He nodded a greeting.

''Bout time.' Michael's sneer wasn't lost on him, and neither was his belligerent glare – a warning of the storm about to come. Even with a black eye and a swollen lip, he was evidently itching for another round. But there was no point in adding fuel to the fire, so Zane zipped it.

The solicitor stood and then held out his hand. 'Zane …' His tone was as bland as his grey suit and matching tie. 'It's been a very long time. You probably don't remember me?'

Zane reached out, noting George's grasp was soft and his hand was sweaty. 'Not really, sorry I've kept you waiting,' he said flatly.

'Can't be helped, I'm sure.' Bushy grey brows shadowed narrow eyes. The man gestured towards the table. 'Have a seat and let's get started, shall we?'

Zane sat as far away from Michael as he could, just out of arm-swinging range.

George picked up a pile of papers and straightened them. 'I know it's a difficult time, but I'm afraid this has to be done, and the sooner the better as I have to fly out of the country tomorrow to finish off the business Peter was attending to in Germany.'

'Harder for some than others,' Michael said, as he leant back in his chair and folded his hands behind his head.

Zane bit his tongue even harder. Choose your battles, he thought, as his hands fisted beneath the table.

'Cat got your tongue today, Zane?' Michael looked at him with cold eyes.

Heaving in a deep breath, Zane shrugged. 'Why bother speaking when I have nothing to say to you.'

'Really, that's all you've got for me? A bit of a change from yesterday, when you were swinging your fists like some barbaric ape.' Michael straightened his tie. 'And at my father's wake, of all places.'

Zane's fists tightened even more beneath the table. 'If you'd learn to keep your dirty hands off Emma, and treat her with the respect she deserves, especially seeing as she's the mother of your child, I wouldn't have had to knock some damn sense into you.'

Michael smirked. 'After leaving me the way she did, Emma doesn't deserve my respect.'

'You were having an affair, what did you bloody expect?'

'Well, if she put out every now and again, I wouldn't have gone looking for it elsewhere.'

Zane's fury engulfed him. 'You want to go another round, do you?' He leant forwards in his chair to make his point.

Michael swivelled around and pulled something from a drawer in his father's old desk, his gaze malevolent as he placed a handgun on the table. 'Do it again and we'll see what happens.'

Shocked, Zane looked from the gun to Michael and back again. 'Are you serious?'

'Now, now, you two, enough is enough.' George's tone was brusque. 'Put that thing away, Michael, and you ...' He turned his steely gaze to Zane. 'Don't even think about raising a hand to him or I'll have you charged with assault.'

'Do what the man says, Michael,' Zane said.

'Cocky bastard, aren't you?' Snatching the gun from the table, Michael stood up and tossed it back in the drawer.

'So that's how you get business done around here, huh, with a gun?' A hard smile curled the corners of Zane's tight lips. 'Real nice that is.'

'Cut the shit, would you? The only reason you came to Australia was to find out if you've got any inheritance.' Michael's tone was arctic.

'Is that so? Well, sorry to burst your bubble, but not everything's about money, Michael,' he said dismissively.

'Maybe not to someone that's never earnt it.' He sat down heavily.

Talk about trying to rub salt into the damn wound. 'Oh, for god's sake, Michael. You have no idea what it's like to have to work to the bone to make a living. You were born into this and have had everything handed to you on a silver platter, whereas I've worked for what I have.'

Michael leant forward, his palms pressed against the table. 'Is that jealousy I hear talking?'

Over the drama, Zane huffed. 'Take it however you want, I damn well give up arguing with you over bullshit.' He shook his head. 'You've always been a bloody drama queen, and a bully. Emma's right, you're never going to change.'

'Emma's right?' He scrunched up his face. 'What the hell are you on about? Have you two been talking about me behind my back?'

Zane simply shrugged.

'Well, screw the pair of you.' Michael's face becoming redder by the second, his fists connected with the oak table, making the crystal decanter and matching glasses at the centre of it shudder. 'And why shouldn't I be handed everything on a silver platter, when I'm blood and I stuck by my father's side … unlike you, the adopted bastard who's too busy riding bulls and women to give a shit about what goes on round here.' Michael's eyes were flinting with anger as he shoved his seat back, stood up again and then stepped away from the table, his chin high and his jaw clenched.

'I followed my dreams, Michael, not the smell of Peter's money.' Zane's gut churned and his face singed hot, but he kept himself planted firmly in the seat. Standing would only spell more trouble.

'I've heard enough,' George growled. 'Now let's get this done and dusted so we can all get on with our day.' Producing a scrunched-up handkerchief, he mopped his brow and then tucked it back into his pocket. 'Can we please just try to keep this civil, for god's sake.' With his index finger, he nudged his glasses further up his nose, and then tapped the paperwork.

Michael grunted and sat.

'Yup, sorry.' Zane took a deep breath and willed himself to calm down before he leapt across the table and grabbed Michael by his ridiculous tie.

'First things first, as you both probably already have guessed, Michael is the sole beneficiary of Peter's estate.'

'Yup, no surprises there, George,' Zane said matter-of-factly.

Sitting up straighter, Michael grinned like the cat that had got the cream.

'Although, he has left one thing to you, Zane ...' Rifling through the paperwork, George found a typed sheet and handed it over to him. 'I'll let you discover for yourself what it is.'

Stunned, Zane took it from him and read through it. It appeared he was the sole heir to Kay's father's pride and joy, a beat-up old LandCruiser that would no doubt be in desperate need of repair. Nonetheless, he'd spent many happy hours in it as a kid, when he and his adoptive grandad had driven around Wattle Acres, checking the cattle and fixing fences.

'In preparation for today, I'd already organised for it to be fixed up at the mechanics, so it could be re-registered. It's being dropped off to the pub as we speak. I'd guessed Michael would be none too happy about you going to collect it from Wattle Acres.'

Michael grunted his agreement.

George cleared his throat as he looked through the pile of paperwork again. 'Oh, and can you drop this over to Emma please, Zane?' He held out a sealed yellow envelope. 'For some reason, Peter has requested you handle the delivery of it.'

Michael's grin had all but faded. 'What's this letter about, George?'

'I have no idea. I'm just following Peter's instructions.'

Zane took it and then shoved it in his back pocket before Michael had a chance to grab it and tear it open – something he wouldn't put past him. 'I'm heading over there after we're finished, so no problem.'

'You've organised to go over to Emma's?' Michael looked as if he were about to explode.

'Oh, yeah, she's offered for me to stay for a couple of days, until I go back to the States.' Zane took pleasure in the way Michael squirmed in his seat.

Sucking in a sharp breath, Michael appeared to gather himself as he blew it out. 'You've always wanted what you can't have, haven't you, Zane?'

'Are we finished here, George?' Zane asked.

George nodded.

Having heard enough of Michael's crap for one day, Zane stood. 'Is that jealousy I hear, Michael?' Grinning triumphantly, he acknowledged George with a tip of his head, turned and walked out, choosing to ignore whatever Michael was bellowing after him.

CHAPTER
14

Dangling precariously into the fourteen-litre washing machine while trying to retrieve an ankle sock from its depths, Emma cursed the day she'd thought a big machine would be the best way to go.

'Oh god, Mum,' Riley said, coming up behind her. 'You're gonna fall head first into there one of these days.' Her laughter was a beautiful sound.

'Been there, done that, love.' Sock in hand, Emma resurfaced, grinning as she waved it about. 'I got the little bugger.'

Riley punched the air. 'Good for you … now you just have to find all the other odd socks of mine that seem to disappear and mission accomplished.'

'Ha-ha, true.' Emma eyed Riley up and down, smiling. Dressed in spangled jeans and a nice blouse, Riley was no longer a little girl.

'What?' Riley eyed her curiously.

'Nothing, you just look so lovely, sweetheart.'

'Why thank ya.' Riley brushed a hand over her flat stomach. 'This shirt doesn't make me look fat, does it?'

'Oh, Riley, you haven't got an ounce of fat on you.' Playfully slapping her with the sock, she then tossed it in the overflowing basket. 'Did you grab the fifty dollars out of my wallet?'

'Yes, thanks.' Riley hugged her. 'Thanks for saying yes to me hanging out with Jasmine this arvo.'

'Of course, love.' Emma kissed her forehead. 'I'm glad you and Jasmine are hanging out again. She's a lovely girl.'

'Yeah, me too, I can't blame her for fobbing me off when I started hanging around Ben and his loser friends – they're nothing like Jasmine.' Her message tone bleeping, Riley grabbed her phone from her back pocket. 'They're almost here. I'll go wait out front for them.'

'Okay, have fun at the movies, and please make sure you're back by dark.'

'Yes, I promise – Mrs Ambles is going to drop us back once we're done. I want to make sure I'm here to have dinner with Uncle Zane.' She smiled. 'I'm glad he's staying for a few days. I only have vague memories of him, but the ones I do have make me feel happy. It'll be nice to spend some time with him, get to know him a bit before he heads off again.'

'Yeah, it sure will be.' Emma cupped Riley's cheek, the word 'uncle' circling in her brain. 'I love you so much. You know that, right?'

'Of course.' Riley placed her hand over her mother's. 'Love you too, Mum.'

Tiny's excited barking was swiftly followed by the sound of car tyres crunching on gravel.

'Right, that's my cue to move it.'

Following Riley to the front door, Emma gave Jasmine's mother a wave. 'Thank you for taking them, Jane.'

'My pleasure, Em.'

Having said his doggy hellos to their visitors, Tiny ran up to her side then followed her back to the laundry. Hauling the washing basket through the back door and out to the clothesline, Emma began pegging the clothes out while Tiny flopped at her bare feet. The scrunch of the grass underfoot felt good – as though grounding her to her roots. The air was tinged with the scent of jasmine and wild lavender, and she could just hear the bubbling of the creek up the back. Vivid pink and purple bougainvillea had grown across the back fence over the years, and butterflies flittered and danced above the flowers. The buzzing of the native bees combined with the call of cicadas and the cackle of a kookaburra to create a country symphony worthy of her applause. With a clear view of the surrounding paddocks dotted with her rotund grass-fed cows, she smiled at the exquisiteness of it all. Serendipity was her and Riley's haven, and she loved it with all her heart and soul.

Job done, she headed back towards the homestead. Hearing her mobile ringing from inside the house, she dashed for it, thinking it might have been Riley saying she'd forgotten something – which was well on the cards knowing her forgetful daughter.

She looked to the caller ID and had to draw a breath. 'Hey, Michael, to what do I owe this call?'

'What do you think you're playing at, having Zane there, Emma?'

She gritted her teeth to stop from telling him to go jump. 'He's not staying here, Michael. He's going to be camping in the cottage.' Her tone was icy and she didn't care.

'Same diff, Emma.' He grunted. 'I don't want him there.'

Every one of her muscles clenched in defence to his arrogance. 'How dare you try and tell me who I can have here. This is my home, and I'll do as I damn well please.'

'But my daughter lives there, so legally, no you can't do as you damn well please.'

'So now you're going to use the law to try and get your way?'

'Maybe I am.'

'You haven't got an ounce of goodness in your heart, have you?'

'Now that's a bit harsh, don't you think?'

'You've never been a father to Riley, but now that Zane's staying here for a few days, you want to exert your parental rights.' Furious, she didn't wait for him to respond. 'Well, Michael, do your damn best, because you don't scare me anymore, and I'm not your little puppet you get to control.'

'Who said I'm trying to scare you?'

Michael the epitome of a gas lighter, Emma knew all too well it was pointless to argue with him, because that's exactly what he wanted. So she drew in a deep breath and calmed herself. 'Thanks for the call, I have to go now.' As she stabbed the *end call* button, the crushing weight she'd been carrying for what felt like an eternity bore down even harder on her shoulders. She wondered if Michael would even give a damn that Riley wasn't his.

As she paced in circles, her mobile rang again, and of course, it was Michael. She ignored it this time – it would only end with her in tears. Fuming, she put the mobile on the bench, grabbed a bridle from where she'd left it hanging from the back of a dining chair, stormed through the house and pushed open the front screen door. The ever-increasing heat was like a furnace blast, the weeping willows lining the driveway appearing even more exhausted than they usually did. She looked at her watch. She had about an hour before Zane arrived. Enough time to go for a blast on her horse, to help rid her of this overwhelming feeling of disaster.

Her boots on in record time, she leapt down the steps and crossed the yard, whistling for her right-hand man. Tiny appeared from under the house, his face covered in dirt and his tail whipping excitedly. Life was always a wonderful adventure in his eyes, and she wished she felt the same way. She stroked his head and received a lick of comfort in return. With her loyal mate at her side, she strode towards the stables and saddled up her beautiful boy. Other than her father, the only males she'd ever been able to rely on over the years were the four-legged kind.

Twenty minutes later she and Bundy had passed over the paddocks and were heading through the scrublands that surrounded Serendipity. Usually taking great satisfaction in the magic of the Australian bushlands she called home, she was too preoccupied to find solace within Mother Nature's heart. She rode in deep thought – things were going to go from bad to worse, she could feel it in her bones. Knowing she had to take action terrified her, but it had to be done. *When?* was the question assaulting her every waking thought.

The headache she'd awoken with at five this morning was still hammering relentlessly, Michael's phone call only adding to its intensity. Her compassionate nature left her wanting to feel sorry for him, but how could she when the man had done nothing to earn her sympathy but only her resentment? She frowned with the thought. He'd always got his own way in their relationship. But not anymore. She was her own woman, her own person – he wasn't going to boss her around any longer.

Reaching into her saddlebag, she straightened and took a long swig from her water bottle. Unusually restless in the saddle, she swatted a persistent fly from her face, cursing it for following her all the way from the stables. Her mood still stormy, everything was annoying her, more so than it should. She really needed to take a breath and try to find gratitude in her heart. That would be the only way to get rid of her anger before sitting down to enjoy a barbeque dinner with Riley and Zane. She didn't want anything to ruin the short time they had together before she dropped her bombshells in a few days' time – wanting to give the roiling emotions of the funeral a bit of time to settle first.

So she focused outwardly, breathing and releasing, just as she'd learnt to the one time she'd agreed to go to a meditation class with Renee. Sulphur-crested cockatoos perched high in the gum trees and pink and grey galahs squabbled over the best place to rest on the nearby water tank. The call of the cattle travelled on the wind, as did the sing-song of green tree frogs from the creek. She tried to take comfort in the rhythm of Bundy's stride as they reached the ridgeline and turned back towards home. Taking her cue, he widened his gait and they were soon galloping across the flat; the whistle of the breeze rushing past gave her goosebumps, and the thunder of his hooves echoed in her chest. This was the only time she ever felt truly free, unrestrained and real to her very core. Give her a horse and an open paddock over retail therapy any day – this was a country gal's way to de-stress. She imagined the wind whipping away all her worries, at least for today, and as the seconds ticked by and the sound of Bundy's hooves grew more and more thunderous, her anger and frustration began to ease.

Quickly approaching the stables, she slowed him to a trot and then a walk. Bundy's flanks heaved beneath her as the gelding blew out a rolling snort.

'Thanks, boy. I can always rely on you to make me feel better, can't I?' Her tension stripped away, she patted his wet neck. 'Love ya shitloads, mate.'

Stopping beneath the shade of the stable's awning, she dismounted, removed his bridle and then she gave the horse a hug around his neck. As usual, he lifted his front left leg and curled it over hers, snuggling his head in against her shoulder. A horsey hug if she'd ever had one. He was such a beautiful boy, and she felt blessed he was hers.

With Bundy soon unsaddled and back in his paddock, his head buried in a bucket of chaff drizzled with a bit of molasses for a treat, Emma hoisted the Australian stock saddle from where she'd rested it on the railing of the round yard and carried it to the stables and put it away in its usual spot. Stepping outside, the sound of a vehicle grabbed her attention. Looking up, she watched a dusty old LandCruiser rumble down the drive, a trail of dust flying out behind it. It took her a few moments to recognise the old beast as Zane's grandfather's. She quickly tucked her flannelette shirt into her jeans, wishing to God she'd changed into something a little less bogan-ish.

Slipping her hands in her back pockets, she made her way across the round yard, climbed through the railings, and over to where Zane had pulled up. Catching sight of his handsome, smiling face out of the open car window, she was unable to stop her own grin spreading wider, even though her stomach was a jumble of nerves.

Zane tipped the brim of his hat. 'Howdy there, Firecracker.'

'Casanova,' she said with a cheeky glint in her eyes. 'I see you've scored your pa's old truck.' She patted the bonnet. 'He'd be mighty happy about that after all the years it's been sitting in the shed at Wattle Acres, wasting away.'

'Yeah, he would be.'

'Did you go around and pick it up?' She arched a brow.

'Shit no. It was sitting outside the pub when I went back there to get my stuff, and the key had been shoved under my door. I've dropped the rental back to the drop-off point in town. Apparently they rent it out cheap to backpackers to get it back down to Cairns.'

'Oh, cool. How's it faring on the inside?' She peeked in.

'A spring from the seat's digging me in my butt, and the old girl needs some work, but ...' He tapped the dash, a cloud of dust rising. 'She's all mine and that's what matters.'

'But you're going back to the States, aren't you?'

'I am, and I've already thought about that. I reckon it would be a doozy of a first car for Riley, if I got it restored, don't you reckon?'

'Oh, wow, you'd really do that for her?'

'Of course, she's family.' His gaze traced slowly over Emma as he stepped from the driver's side, leaving fire in its wake.

'I don't know what to say.' She felt her cheeks glow beneath his warm gaze.

'You don't need to say anything,' he said slowly.

Starting a few inches lower than his belt buckle, her gaze traced up over his muscled biceps and to the tattoo on his suntanned forearm. He smelt so good, like leather, saddle soap and sunshine – woodsy, spicy, clean and masculine. She took a deep breath. 'Thank you for being so thoughtful.' She tipped her head to the side. 'Anything else exciting happen at the office?'

'Not really; other than this old girl, I came up empty handed in the inheritance department, but we all knew that was going to happen.'

'That really sucks, Zane. I'm sorry Michael and Peter have always been such arseholes to you.'

'All good, I've just gotta roll with the punches.' His deep masculine chuckle sent a flutter throughout her body. 'Anyways, don't apologise. It's not your fault you married a selfish prick, just like I can't help the fact he's Kay's other son.'

Hands shoved in the pockets of her jeans, Emma dragged the toe of her boot across the dirt, her gaze anywhere but on Zane's. His eyes were way too close to hers and the guilt bearing down on her right now was crushing. 'You check yourself out of the pub?'

'Yup, bag's in the back.'

She braved catching his eyes. 'Good, I'm glad.'

'I hope so.' He moved closer and she licked her suddenly dry lips.

'I am.' She breathed deeply. She felt vulnerable, feminine and desperate to tear every inch of clothing from his magnificence. Ached to melt her tense body into his, skin on skin, lips to lips, heart to heart.

'And you sure Riley's okay with it?'

'Of course, I wouldn't have asked you to stay here otherwise.' She looked to his hands, big and strong, yet always so gentle when they touched her. Shocked with the direction of her thoughts, she swallowed down hard and forced her eyes back to his.

'Good, because I don't want to upset her any more than I did at the wake.' He handed her a bag she recognised from the bakery.

Emma looked inside and then back to him. 'Oh yum, you got me some sourdough.'

'Sure did, and I bought Riley some lamingtons.'

'Oh, thanks, Zane, she'll like that.'

'No worries, it's the least I could do.' Reaching behind him he pulled out a sealed yellow envelope. 'Before I forget, I've been asked to pass this on to you.'

She was suddenly breathless. 'From who?'

'Peter … George asked me to give it to you.'

Staring at the envelope, paralysing fear froze her to the spot. 'What's in it?' Her voice trembled and she could do nothing to stop it as her heart sped out of control.

'I have no idea.' He shook his head, sighing. 'God only knows what he thought he needed to write to you, but there's only one way to find out.' He held the letter in front of her.

'I don't really want to read it right now,' she said softly as she gathered up enough courage to reach out and take it from him. Although light as a feather, it felt as heavy as a boulder in her hand. She was dimly aware of the warm breeze blowing tendrils of hair across her cheek as she considered opening it. But terrified of what was inside, and of Zane seeing it, she stopped herself. Tears blurred her name written in bold black ink across the front. What in the hell did Peter want from her now, after his death? She shivered as icy fingers ran down her spine.

'You okay, Em?' Zane brushed the stray tendrils behind her ears. His voice was calm, soothing, as was his touch.

'Uh-huh.' Emma blinked fast, willing her tears away. Craving to rest her head against his chest, she dared not meet his eyes for fear he could read what was hidden in them.

'Hey, don't let it worry you. There's nothing Peter can say or do that will affect your life now. You've cut all ties to Michael, other than Riley of course, so he has no control over your future.' His hand still resting on her cheek, he took another step forward. 'And if you're thinking it has anything to do with what happened that night at the homestead, when we were teenagers, I really doubt it. Michael played a big part, and Peter wouldn't risk incriminating his favourite son, would he?' Although nobody was within a mile of them, he kept his voice low, hushed. 'Especially in a letter.'

Her racing heart slowed and she felt strangely numb. 'I'd hope not, but seeing as I'm the one that caused it all, who knows what Peter would try to do from the grave, what strings he's still able to pull with the people he was tied in with?' She wrapped her arms around herself, the feeling of Zane's hand still resting on her cheek giving her comfort she didn't deserve. 'He always had it in for me, right from the very start.' She chuckled cynically. 'Part of me wants to walk into the police station and tell them everything about that night. I'm sick of carrying the guilt around every waking day. It's crushing me.'

'You know you can't go and do that, Em. Not that I care what happens to me, but you can't risk anything happening to you. Besides the fact it would kill me if anything happened to you, Riley needs you.'

Unable to speak, she nodded. Silence hung between them.

Both hands now came to cradle her cheeks. He was so close she could see the soft scattering of fine hair peeking out of the top of his shirt. 'No matter what's in that letter, I won't let anyone hurt you, Em, or Riley. You have my word.'

'Thanks, but some things are out of your control, Zane.' She braved a glance up at him. 'And besides, you're going back to the States soon, and there's not a lot you can do from the other side of the world, now, is there?'

He held her gaze. 'Well, seeing as your parents aren't here, until everything settles down, I might have to postpone my flight and stay a little bit longer, just to make sure you and Riley are all good.'

'You'd do that, for Riley and me?'

'Of course.' A smile dangled on the corner of his lips. 'It's not like I've got a wife and kids to run home to now, is it?'

'I'm sorry your marriage didn't work out for you, and I'm sorry I didn't check in to see how you were coping with the divorce.'

'Hey, don't apologise. It's not like we were in contact then, Em.'

'You want to talk about it?'

'Nope.' He shrugged. 'I gave it a shot, it didn't work, and I moved on.'

'Fair enough, I get not wanting to go over and over it.' Emma offered him a soft smile. 'What about the bull-riding circuit? You need your points.'

'You and Riley are more important.'

She drew in a shaky breath, silently thanking the powers that be for making it *his* decision to stay a bit longer. Now she had more time to find the right moment to tell him and Riley, and Michael, everything they deserved to know. 'Thank you, Zane, it means the absolute world, you wanting to stick around a little longer.'

He said nothing, the depth in his sky-blue eyes only intensifying. He looked as if he was going to kiss her, and she was terrified that if he did, she wouldn't be able to stop from showing him just how deeply she felt about him. She'd daydreamed about being naked with him so many times over the years, his kiss would be the only invitation she needed right now to lose herself in him.

The voice of reason mentally slapped her into action. 'What are you doing?' She tilted as far away from him as she possibly could without falling.

Remaining silent and leaving his hands right where they were, Zane brought his boots toe to toe with hers. There was a wayward smile on his lips and a glint in his eyes that wasn't there a moment ago. And lord help her. He. Smelt. So. Damn. Good.

'Zane?' Her heart quickened, her breaths were awkward. Eyes wide, she met his gaze. A hint of amusement was veiled within their blue depths. He was clearly taking great pleasure in making her blush, and by god she was blushing from the tips of her toes all the way to the top of her head. 'Zane, bloody hell, what's got into you?'

He chuckled, deep and throaty. 'Stop freaking out, Em.' He tipped his hat back, as if to see her better.

His air of confidence enveloped her, and she forgot how to speak, how to breathe. Everything about him oozed the kind of masculinity that made her toes curl within her boots.

'You're real cute when you're showing your vulnerable side, you know that, Em?'

Straightening her shoulders, she tossed her head. 'I'm never …
cute.'

'Whatever you say.' He moved in closer still, if that were even
possible, so she could feel his breath on her cheek, could feel the
touch of his jeans against her legs. His gaze fell to her mouth, but
leaning in, he brought his lips to her ear. 'Thanks for inviting me
to stay.' He brushed a kiss over her cheek as he finally dropped
his hands and stepped away.

She reached out and slapped him on the arm, hard. 'You're a
goddamn arsehole sometimes, you know that?'

Wincing, he rubbed it. 'Shit, still got it in you, Firecracker.'
He grinned. 'And just why am I an arsehole?'

She stifled a grin and lifted her chin a little. 'I think you can
figure that one out for yourself, Casanova, don't you?'

He grunted and frowned. 'Is it because I like stirring you so
much?' His dimples deepened with his devilish smile.

'Ding, ding, ding, and we have a winner …' she said playfully,
hands going to her hips. 'I'm going to buy you a big wooden
spoon this Christmas and get *Head Shit Stirrer* written on it.'
Enjoying the banter, she was thankful for the distraction. Zane's
mischievous spirit helped her to ignore the letter now shoved in
her back pocket.

'A personalised wooden spoon, huh? Yes, please, I'd really like
that.' His lips curled into that slow, sexy grin she'd come to love,
way too much. 'And by the way, Miss Emma Kensington, you
rise to the bait every single time.'

'So do you, my friend.' She flashed him a challenging grin.
He gave her a megawatt one back. He was handsome and
charming and funny and caring and protective and … she
needed to stop. Beads of sweat ran down her back and between

her breasts, and she suddenly felt like she was on fire. She had to move, do something, anything but stand here, wanting him as badly as she did. She fanned her face. 'Damn it's hot, I need a drink.'

'Me too.'

'I'm going to grab a beer.'

'You going to offer me one while you're at it?'

She glanced over her shoulder. 'Maybe, if you're lucky.'

Laughing, he shook his head as he followed her across the front lawn and up the steps, Tiny by his side.

The verandah was cool and welcoming beneath the corrugated-iron roof. Emma headed for the beer fridge and plucked two longnecks from the back of the top shelf, where it was the coldest, and twisted off the lids. Grabbing two coolers from the hubcap bowl on top of the fridge, she pushed them on and then passed a beer over to Zane, who was making himself at home in the swing chair with Tiny almost sitting in his lap.

She flopped down beside him and took a long glug. The icy cold beer slid easily down her dry throat. 'Ahhh, just what the doctor ordered.'

'My bloody oath it is … beer always makes everything better.' He smiled. 'You going to open that letter, or what?'

'Maybe later.'

'Why not now?'

'Because I don't want to.' She swallowed, trying to slow her quick, shallow breath. 'Please, Zane, just let me open it in my own time.'

'Okay, sorry, I thought you'd be dying to know what's in it.' Turning his gaze to the paddocks, he took a slow swig from his beer. 'I know I am.'

'Yeah, I get that, and so am I, but not right now.' She tried to smile as she squared her shoulders.

'Is there something in there you don't want me to see?' He smiled, but there was something in his voice she couldn't quite read. Perhaps she was just too worked up.

'What are you on about?' She forced a shrug, feigning indifference but feeling as jittery as a colt. 'I'm not in the right frame of mind right now to read Peter's condescending bullshit, that's all.' She looked away. 'I don't want to give him the chance to ruin our first night together, with Riley.'

'That's a good way to think about it, I suppose.' He regarded her thoughtfully. 'I don't know why, but I have a feeling you're not telling me something.'

'Please, Zane, lay off, would you?' Bitter tears stung her eyes and she blinked quickly. 'I just don't want to read it right now, is that okay with you?' She went to stand, to walk off and calm down, but his hand came to her arm, gently stopping her.

'Righto, but it's clearly rattled you.' His gaze deepened with concern. 'You know you can tell me anything, right?'

'Zane, please, just back off and mind your own business,' she snapped, instantly regretful. She had to recover somehow before there was no turning back. She couldn't give him an opportunity to see the guilt in her eyes. Not yet, not here, not now.

He held up his hands in surrender. 'Okay, all right, I'm sorry.'

'I'm sorry too.' She bit her bottom lip to stop it from trembling. 'I'm just super tired and super grumpy.'

Wrapping his arm around her shoulder, he pulled her into him. 'Truce.'

She nodded against his shoulder. 'Truce.'

CHAPTER

15

Silvery moonlight bounced off the row of herb-filled jars lined up along the window ledge, and the scent of the vanilla candles they'd lit at the dinner table lingered. His chin resting on his paws, Tiny snored from his king-size doona folded up on the floor in the corner of the kitchen. Kat was curled up on top of the deep freeze, in what used to be the potato basket but had eventually become her bed. The last of the dishes now packed in the dishwasher, and the leftover potato bake covered and in the fridge for lunch tomorrow, Emma hung the tea towel back in its place on the oven door and yawned for all of Australia.

'I'm a bit like that too, Mum. I'm going to hit the sack before I fall asleep standing up.' Riley rubbed her eyes and then stretched her arms high. 'And I ate way too much. I'm so full.'

'Tell me about it ...' Zane pointed to his belt. 'I had to loosen this bugger off, and that gig started *before* two helpings of your mum's awesome apple pie and custard.' He grinned towards

Emma. 'You've always been a damn good cook, just like your mum is.'

'Thanks, Zane, but that awesome apple pie was all thanks to the forever reliable Mrs Sara Lee.' Her legs weary, Emma leant against the bench, her soft smile coming from the depths of her heart.

'Well, however it was made, it was super delish,' Zane said, a little too enthusiastically.

'It sure was.' Wrapping her arms around Emma, Riley gave her mum a kiss on the cheek. 'Love you so much, night, Mum.'

'Love you too, sweetheart.' Emma squeezed Riley tight, savouring the scent of her freshly washed hair before letting her go. 'I hope you have a good sleep, and thanks for helping clean up.'

'No worries.' Padding towards Zane, Riley hesitated momentarily before reaching out and giving him a hug too. 'Thanks for a nice night, Uncle Zane. I haven't laughed so much in ages.'

Cuddling her, Zane beamed at Emma over Riley's shoulder. 'I don't reckon I've laughed so much in yonks either, Riley.' He smiled tenderly as she stepped back from him. 'Thanks for the good company and the ripper jokes. Tonight was just what the doctor ordered, for all of us.'

'It sure was. I'll try and come up with a few more knock knocks, and we can have a joke-off again tomorrow maybe?'

'I'm up for the challenge, if you are?'

'Great, you're on!' Riley gave him a broad smile. 'Catch you tomorrow then?'

'Seeing I'm calling the workers' cottage home for now, you most surely will.'

'I'm glad you decided to stay a bit longer,' she said, before disappearing out the doorway.

Zane smiled so wide his dimples were like craters.

With a melting heart, Emma admired the bond that was evidently there – more by blood than either of them knew. Even after all the years apart, it hadn't taken much for them to warm to each other again. 'Thanks for tonight. I think we all needed it after the week we've had.'

'It's been my pleasure, Em. I really enjoyed myself and getting to know Riley again. You always make me feel part of the family, and I appreciate it, from the bottom of my heart.'

Emma edged a little closer to him, her hand coming to his arm. 'You *are* a part of the family, Zane, and always will be, so no need to thank me. You're welcome here, anytime.'

'Well, now you're not married to Michael, I'm not really family, but thanks.' Sighing, he rubbed a hand over the dark stubble on his chin. 'It's nice to feel like I actually belong somewhere, and I'm not just this tumbleweed, rolling wherever the wind blows me, without much of a reason to be anywhere, except to get on the back of a bull.'

Seeing the lonesomeness in Zane's eyes broke Emma's resolve. 'Oh, Zane ...' Biting her lip, she glanced out the window at the full moon hovering in the velvet black sky, surrounded by millions of sparkling stars. 'You've been a bit of a lost soul since your mum passed, haven't you?'

'Yeah, you could say that.' He sounded as if he were a million miles away. 'And getting married, and then divorced, didn't help.' He offered her a sad smile. 'But you know all about that, with what you've just been through with Michael.'

'Yes, I sure do.' Having pulled herself together as much as she could, she dared a glance back at him. 'I'm so sorry I made you feel unwelcome when you were here last. It's just, after what happened the first time we gave in to—'

He cut her off with a shake of his head. 'I totally get it, Em. You were a married woman, and I was overstepping the boundaries, big time, so please don't feel like you have to explain yourself.' Hooking his thumbs through his belt loops, he shrugged. 'Like you said, what's done is done, and regrets aren't going to change anything, so let's just leave the past where it should be. It'll do us no favours, bringing it back up again.'

'Yeah, true.' A smile tugged the corners of her lips. 'I'm glad we're friends again. As much as you can drive me batty sometimes, I've really missed you.'

'I've really missed you too.'

'You have?' Although being playful, she couldn't help but take great pleasure in hearing his words.

'Uh-huh, shitloads.'

'Good, and so you should.' She tossed him a carefree smile, which was anything but.

Their eyes met and something inside her slipped. Heat flickered within the deep blue she was helplessly tumbling into. Something shifted; the walls between them started to crumble. She could feel the ties that bound them tightening, pulling her closer to him. Boundaries disappeared, as did the world around them. She wanted him. All of him. Pressed up against her. Making love to her like only he could. If only ...

Zane cleared his throat. 'Well, I should be off, let you get some sleep.'

Snapping herself out of her lust-fuelled trance, Emma looked at the clock above the stove. It was almost midnight. 'Yeah, I better hit the sack, before I turn into a pumpkin.'

Zane gave her a quick hug and kissed her on the forehead. As nice as it was, it just felt awkward, as if they were pretending to be something they weren't – both of them ignoring all that they could be.

'Night, Em, dream sweet.'

'You too, catch you in the morning.' She smiled as he picked up his boots, tugged them on, and then disappeared into the night.

Finally on her own, the reality of what was upstairs hit her like a slap to the face. Flicking off the kitchen lights, she told Tiny to stay on his rug and then raced up the stairs two at a time, almost tripping over her own feet, twice. Dashing into her bedroom, she closed the door and locked it for good measure, grabbed the envelope from where she'd shoved it under her mattress, and tore at it, hands shaking and her heart in her throat. It was only one page, and handwritten. Her stomach churned and she held her breath as she climbed over to the corner of her bed and began reading.

Emma,

If you're reading this, I'm obviously dead, but I'm certainly not going to lie in my grave and let you make light of that. I know, now I'm no longer around, you'll feel you're free to tell Michael and Zane the truth about Riley, and possibly even want to tell Zane about it being his father you killed that night. Knowing you as I do, you will want to clear your conscience.

I'm warning you, if you go and do such a thing, I have evidence linking you to the murder of Zane's father in my safe, and strict instructions to pass this on to the authorities if you go against my requests. I may be gone for good, but I have eyes and ears everywhere, some of them in the unlikeliest of places. I highly doubt going to jail is on your bucket list now, is it?

 Don't underestimate the power I still hold, or the people left behind who will enforce my wishes if the need arises. You will never be able to get away from me, or out from the shadows I cast over you. If I were you, I'd keep those lips of yours sealed, for everyone's sakes, especially Riley's. Zane is not the kind of man you want as a father for your daughter, if his own father is anything to go by. He doesn't know the meaning of sacrifice, or what it takes to financially support a child. And you'll be no good to Riley from behind bars.

 You take care now,
 Peter

The words blurring, Emma lifted her gaze to where the curtains fluttered in the soft evening breeze. Foreboding enclosed her, and as if a pillow had been pressed down on her face, she struggled to draw a breath. Starved for air, she ran for the open window and gulped in the cool night. Her hand going to her mouth, she muffled a sob, and then another. Soft light spilled from the bedroom window of the cottage. Zane was still awake, and she longed to run over there, to tell him everything, but now she never would.

How foolish of her to have thought, even with Peter now dead, that she was allowed to speak the truth. She would never be free of the manipulating, heartless bastard. She was perpetually trapped in her past. Adrenaline fuelled her fear and anger, and she turned away from the window, from Zane, needing to sit down before she collapsed on the floor. Her back to the wall, she slid down, cradled her knees and cried for all that she'd done, and for the love of her life she would lose because of it; not because he resented her for the truth, but because she needed to draw the bridge from the chasm they'd almost crossed. They could never meet on one side of it, not now. She would never be able to be with him, knowing what she did, and not tell him. Self-control was in order, no matter how hard that was, and if it meant being cool, detached even, then that's what she had to do.

* * *

Daybreak flittered between the slats of the timber blinds and dust particles floated on the rays of sunlight like sparkling jewels. The dawning of a new day rousing Zane, he woke to the chatter of crickets, the laughter of kookaburras and the distant drone of a tractor – just shy of six o'clock and it sounded like Emma was already hard at it. He instantly felt guilty for the small sleep-in – farm life always began before sunup, and usually went well after sundown. He'd slept so well in the comfortable queen-size bed and thanks to the calmness he felt just by being at Serendipity. But he better get up, because if he was going to be here for a few days, he would have to pull his weight. It was a lot for Emma to do on her own, as determined and capable as she was to do it. Her fierce independence was even more of a reason to love her, if he didn't have enough reasons already.

Kicking off the cotton sheet, he stretched his long body to life, unkinking it bit by bit, and then not wanting to allow himself too much time to think about the past couple of days, he bounced out of bed. It was always easier to keep moving – a sure way to distract his thoughts from delving too deeply. Pulling his last pair of clean jeans out of his bag, he made a mental note to put some washing on. While getting dressed, he couldn't help but feel enthusiastic about the day ahead, spent with two beautiful people who meant the absolute world to him. But first things first, he needed his morning coffee to help wake him up, and some brekkie.

Wandering into the modernised open-plan lounge, kitchen and dining area, he recalled the time when he and Mister Kensington had knocked the walls down. He liked the fact not much had changed since he used to crash here when Peter was in one of his dark and stormy moods, which had been quite often after his mum had passed away. If Peter had made it known he hadn't liked him much while she was alive, he'd certainly hit the point home hard once she'd gone. No matter the time of day or night, Emma's parents had always welcomed him in with open arms and made him feel a part of the family – the little two-bedder cottage had been his second home.

Other than the new cream paint being less assaulting on the eyes (the psychedelic orange and green floral wallpaper had been a bit overwhelming), and the addition of a new modular lounge suite scattered with patterned cushions and a flat-pack style six-seater dining table, it still felt the same. The warm vibe of the place complemented the little sign hanging above the stove that read, *Please make yourself at home*. The floorboards beneath his bare feet were timeworn, and the pink and lime bathroom was still in the old retro seventies style. He adored the rustic, mismatched character of the place.

His stomach rumbling, he wandered around the timber bench and pulled the fridge open. As usual, Emma had thought of everything – there was milk, butter, a bowl of bum nuts so fresh they still had a bit of chicken poo on them, a loaf of bread, and some freshly sliced leg ham. As much as he liked the smell of bacon cooking, it had always given him heartburn – he loved that she remembered such trivial things. Slicing the bread, he popped two pieces in the toaster and then helped himself to a slice of ham. Flicking the kettle on, he grabbed a mug and spoon and tossed in two heaped spoons of coffee and sugar, added a splash of milk and then impatiently drummed the bench as he waited for the water to boil and his toast to pop up.

Carrying his version of a toasted ham sandwich in hand, along with his half-drunk cuppa, he shoved open the flyscreen door with his toe and stepped out onto the porch to bear witness to a jaw-dropping scarlet and tangerine sky. The golden wattle trees lining the back fence were blooming, the heady perfume similar to that of caramel popcorn. Sinking into a fold-out camp chair, he breathed in the rain-soaked grass, lemon-scented gums and the unmistakable sweetness of the mangos hanging ripe and plump from the tree near the homestead. The smells brought him back to his childhood, when his world was anything but what it was now. Briefly closing his eyes, he smiled, the aroma of the untainted earth invigorating him beyond what any amount of caffeine could. It felt good, better than good, way too good in fact. Although he'd decided to change his ticket and stay for three weeks, it was going to be a fleeting moment in time here at Serendipity; one he knew he had to appreciate every second of before heading back to the States.

The sun reaching across the porch, it brushed over his face. Squinting into it, he looked to the tops of the far-flung mountains, now aglow as the soft morning sunlight brought the distant line of pine trees into silhouette and made the cattle and horses high up on the ridge appear dreamlike. Raucous native birds were taking their first flights of the day, their wings flapping like mad as they rose into the ever-lightening sky. The old outbuildings scattered around the property were scarred with age and the elements, giving them a charm unsurpassed by any new steel shed or stables. Even the old thunderbox had an appeal about it that a toilet really shouldn't. He smiled from deep within. Everything about being back in the Australian bush gave him a sense of strength and solace. Although the United States was beautiful in its own way, it was no comparison to this vast and picturesque, yet sometimes brutal and unforgiving land he'd once called home. This was the place he felt his authentic self, and nothing would ever change that. It made his heart heavy to know he would never own a piece of it.

Sighing, nostalgia struck him with force – so many happy memories had been made here, with Emma, who he'd considered to be one of his best mates, by his side. The majestic Serendipity sprawled across eighty acres, the property bordering Wattle Acres on one side and the Silvergum National Park on the other. He and Emma had always joked about one day combining the two properties and turning it into a happy farm for creatures both great and small. Now Michael had his hands on Wattle Acres that was never going to happen. And with this in mind, his good mood quickly darkened like a storm rolling in. It was so damn unfair that a man who had no love for the place was now the sole heir to the property Zane had dreamt of one day making his own. With just under two hundred thousand dollars in the bank, and no way to borrow any more – Wattle Acres would be worth a million at least – he had to find a way to accept it, and to let the pent-up anger go, because there was nothing he could do about it. Bitterness would get him nowhere fast.

Sculling the last of his coffee, he stood up. Idle time made for pointless thoughts. The yards around the cottage and the homestead looked like they could do with a tidy up, and a few of the trees should be trimmed back in case there was a tropical cyclone. It was the season for it, and jellyfish, and mosquitos and sandflies and deadly snakes – the list went on and on. Everything in a hot North Queensland summer was out to bite you. He had to do something other than sitting here twiddling his thumbs and cursing Michael's name, so yard work it would be. Wandering back inside, he rinsed his cup and cleaned the crumbs from the bench. Emma had told him to rest up for the day, but that didn't sit well with him, especially while she was out busting her bones. He was an able-bodied man, and he was going to help her. Collecting his hat from the back of the dining chair, he tugged it on and headed out, a man on a mission if there were ever one.

It was already hot as he traipsed across the yard, towards the ride-on mower parked under a lean-to. Finding the key in the ignition, he hopped on and revved it to life. He'd start on the homestead yard first, and then work his way over to the cottage and behind the outbuildings. Then hopefully Riley would be up and about, and he could get started on chain-sawing some of the trees near the homestead to get rid of the branches that could damage the roof in a storm.

The rumble of the four-stroke engine blocking everything else out, his mind went in what felt like a million different directions – from Peter's death, to Michael's self-absorption, to never stepping foot on Wattle Acres again, to his beloved mum, to how sweet Riley was, to the mesmerising look in Emma's eyes last night when he'd been so tempted to try to kiss her. Again. What would she have done if he had? Kissed him back, or slapped him in the face? If he went off the last experience, it would have definitely been the latter. He actually chuckled with the thought.

He was doing figure eights in the backyard of the homestead when Riley caught his eye as she stepped from the verandah, two glasses in hand. Pulling the cutter up, he sped over, killing the engine when he reached her. Dressed in jeans, a pretty button-up top and her cowgirl boots, she was the spitting image of Emma at fifteen.

'Morning, Uncle Zane.' Her smile was as warm as the sun beating down on his back.

'Morning, Riley.' He took the glass of water from her. 'You must have read my mind, thanks.'

'You're very welcome.' She took a sip. 'Are you going to come and watch me at horse sports today?' She seemed a little unsure about asking.

'I'd love to. What time are you and your mum heading off?' Emma had casually mentioned it over dinner but he'd noticed she hadn't invited him. He gathered that must have been because Michael would be there. He could totally understand Emma wanting to keep them as far apart as possible, and he hadn't taken it to heart.

'As soon as Mum gets back from slashing the paddock.' She looked at her watch. 'Which is hopefully within the next half hour or we're going to be late, as per usual.' She huffed and shook her head. 'I still need to load my horse too.'

'Well, I'm more than happy to help you with that.'

'You sure?'

'Yeah, of course, and it'll give your mum a bit more time when she gets home.'

'That'd be great, thanks heaps.'

'No problemo. Just let me go and put this baby back in the shed and I'll come and grab the keys to the Land Rover from you and hook up the float.'

'You rock, Uncle Zane, thank you.'

'Pleasure.' Matching her broad grin, he zoomed over to the shed, parked the mower and was back at the bottom of the steps just as she was wandering out the door, keys in hand.

'Here you are.' She tossed them to him. 'I'll get Boomerang ready.'

'Grooviness.'

'Grooviness?' She smiled. 'Is that some kind of hip word from the eighties or something?'

'Ha, yeah … I'm showing my age, aren't I?'

'Uh-huh.' She giggled. 'But good on you for keeping the dream alive.'

'Thank ya.' He tipped his hat playfully. 'I do my best.'

Twenty minutes later, the trailer was hooked up and Riley was loading her slightly nervy horse. Zane stood back and watched her gently coax Boomerang in, her movements reassuring, as was her voice. He believed you either had horsiness in your blood or you didn't, and just like her mum, Riley had it coursing through her veins. Once the horse was in safe and sound, he stepped up and helped her close the back of the float.

'You know you don't have to come along, if you don't feel like it, hey, Uncle Zane?' Her forehead puckered as she waited for his response.

Placing his sunglasses atop his hat, he held her stare. 'Don't be silly, I'm really looking forward to watching you today.'

'Thank you.' Blinking wet eyes, Riley looked down at her boots, her shoulders slumping. 'I really wish Dad would feel that way too.'

Zane looked at her for a few moments and then shook his head sadly. 'I'm really sorry he's like that, Riley. I wish there was something I could do to make it better for you.'

She shrugged. 'Don't apologise, it's not your fault.'

'It's not your fault either, so don't you go blaming yourself, hey.'

Hands in pockets, she drew in the dirt with the toe of her boot. 'That's what Mum always says.'

Zane couldn't help but notice the similar habit – it was something Emma always did when she was deep in thought, drawing shapes in the dirt with her boot, a stick or her finger. 'Well, you make sure you listen to her, because she's a very wise woman, your mum.'

'Ha, yeah, she is, most of the time.' The drone of the tractor grew louder. Turning, she looked out over the paddocks. 'I try not to blame myself, but it's a bit hard not to sometimes.'

Zane's jaw clenched, as did his heart. At a loss for words, he ached to embrace his niece, to take away the heartache Michael had caused her with his inability to show love. Michael was so much like Peter. 'Is your dad coming along today?'

'Yeah, I think so.' She finally looked back at him. The sparkle that had been in her eyes as she'd loaded her horse was now all but gone. She forced a smile. 'Not that he wants to. Mum just nags him until he finally agrees. He hates horses and hates the fact I love them.' She cleared her throat. 'Even though it hurts when he's not there, it kinda sucks when he is too, because all he does is tell me what I'm doing wrong.' She threw her hands up in the air. 'I can't win with him.'

'Well, I'll make sure I tell you everything you're doing right.' Unable to hold back any longer, he cautiously raised his arms. 'Can I give you a hug?'

Suddenly looking as if she was about to burst into tears, she nodded and half stepped, half fell into him. Her head resting against his chest, her quivers told him she was crying. Unable to speak for fear of crumbling with her, he just rubbed her back, letting her stay within his embrace as long as she needed. The sound of the tractor approaching had her stepping back.

'Please don't tell Mum I'm upset. She'll only worry.' She quickly wiped her face, sniffling. 'She's had enough worrying about me lately.'

'I promise I won't say a word.' Even though it felt wrong, keeping this from Emma, he also didn't want to jeopardise the bond he was building with Riley. She needed a male figure in her life she could depend on, one she could trust, and he would make it so.

Riley smiled. 'Thank you.' She cleared her throat. 'Uncle Zane, would you like to come to my deb ball, too?'

'Oh, choice, Riley, it would be my absolute honour.'

'Choice, hey? I like that one.' She beamed brighter than the sun. 'It'll be nice having you there.'

Pulling up next to the open-sided shed, Emma jumped from the tractor and strode towards them, Tiny loyally at her side. 'Hey, you two.' She flashed them a smile. 'Thanks for helping her load the horse, Zane, gives me enough time to have a quick rinse under the shower now.' She scratched at her arms, which were already red. 'Slashing always makes me itchy.'

'All good, Em.' Zane spotted the red around Riley's eyes, but it was too late to warn her.

'Riley, have you been crying, love?' A true mum with the eyes of a hawk, Emma's smile vanished as she took Riley's hands in hers.

Riley laughed a little nervously. 'No, I just got something in my eye, that's all.'

Still holding her hands, Emma leant back. 'Both eyes?' The look on her face showed that she didn't believe a word.

'Yeah, just a bit of dust.' She tugged her hands free and rubbed them. 'Actually, they really hurt so I might go and wash them out.'

'Okay, love, you go do that.' She waited for Riley to be out of earshot then spun to face Zane. 'What happened?'

Feeling like a deer in headlights, he tried to shrug it off. 'Like she said, got dust in her eyes.'

Emma looked around, the rain last night leaving not a speck of dust on the green lawn. 'Uh-huh, because it's so dusty, right?' Arms folded across her chest, she glared at him. 'Please tell me the truth, Zane.'

'I am.' Unable to look at her any longer, for fear of breaking his promise, he pretended to be engrossed in checking the back of the horse float. 'Riley has asked me along, so I'll see you both down there.' And off he went, his strides long as he all but ran towards the cottage, Emma's eyes burning a hole in his back the entire way. Just as he stepped beneath the coolness of the porch, he heard an almighty huff, and turned to see her stomping across the lawn towards the homestead.

Oh hell, now he was really in the shit.

CHAPTER

16

His mind filled with thoughts, Zane almost missed the turn-off to the Silvergum show grounds. Hitting the brakes, his tyres screeched as he pulled off the highway and began looking for a spot to park. A jumble of horse floats and four-wheel drives, some with horses secured to the bull bars as they waited for their events, and the grandstands dotted with wide-brimmed hats and umbrellas, the place was a hive of activity. The mid-morning sun was already casting long shadows, the heat bringing hordes of flies swarming from their hiding places. Swatting one from his face while cursing the little blighter for finding its way inside the cab of his LandCruiser, Zane pulled up in the shade of a towering silver gum. Killing the ignition, he looked out to where girls pranced around on their stunning-looking mounts in the arena, searching only for Riley. He picked her out right over the other side of the grounds, her face a picture of concentration as Boomerang picked up his feet in a high-stepping walk to be proud of. Jumping out, he shoved the keys in his pocket as he headed in that general direction, hoping to god Emma had got over her huff with him. It would make for a hard day ahead if she hadn't. Although, he couldn't blame her – it was eating him up, not telling her what had gone down with Riley this morning. He felt it was her place to know. Talk about being caught between a rock and a hard place.

Weaving his way through the trailers and vehicles, while watching Riley sitting so naturally in the saddle, he finally spotted Emma's old Land Rover, the horse float still hitched. She appeared from behind it, looking so beautiful that it stole his breath. 'Hey, Em.'

She offered him a frown, but her lips curved ever so slightly. 'Hey there, Casanova.' Their arms brushed as she passed him, the fleeting moment of intimacy sending his heart into a frenzied gallop.

She wasn't over it and was baiting him to bite.

He released a slow breath, his eyes catching the shiny rhinestones curving over the pockets of her Wrangler jeans. 'Can I ask a favour?'

'Yup.' Now sitting on her heels while going through a bucket of tack, she didn't bother looking up. 'Shoot.'

'Can you please stop calling me "Casanova", I bloody well hate it.'

She flinched, but still didn't turn to look at him. 'Well, you were given that nickname because that's exactly what you were. And seeing you at your finest down at the pub that first night, with some backpacker, you're still living up to your reputation in my books.' She dared a glance in his direction. 'But if it bothers you that much, I'll stop.'

'Cheers.' Her words were abrasive, but he could read her body like a book. 'I'd appreciate it.' He could see the stiffness of her shoulders, and the tremble of her hands and lips. She was desperately trying to hide her feelings from him. 'I just don't want to be known as that man anymore, especially not to you.'

'Why's that?'

'Because I'm not that man anymore.' He folded his arms.

She mocked him, standing up and folding her arms too. 'I'd have to see it to believe it.'

Goddam it, she was stubborn when she was pissed off. 'Why can't you just take my word for it?'

'Because actions speak louder than words.' She tucked her hair behind her ear as she faced him, her expression somewhat torn.

He shook his head; the change of atmosphere between them from last night to now was confusing. But then, she'd always been one to say it how it is. 'Far out, I'm sorry.'

'What for.'

'For not telling you that Riley was upset.'

She smiled, shaking her head ever so slightly. 'But I thought she was okay?'

'For god's sake, what do you want from me, Emma?'

'I could ask the same of you, Zane,' she said, with sharp impatience.

Her eyes smouldered, and he almost lost all self-control. 'Righto then, I'll go first. I just want ...' His voice trailed off as he tried to find words other than the ones wanting to roll right off his tongue ... *I just want to carry you into that trailer and have my way with you, and you with me. I want to feel your nails dig into my back, as I send you to places you've never been. And then I never, ever, want to let you go. I want us to be together. Forever.*

Her boot tapped the ground impatiently. 'Go on … I'm all ears.'

'I want for you to be happy, and for Riley to be happy.'

'Well then, you need to be honest with me about her.' Her refusal to look him in the eyes made him uneasy. 'She's my daughter, Zane, and as her mother, it's my right to know if she is upset about something, so I can try and help her.'

'I know, I'm sorry. It's just, she asked me not to tell you, and I didn't want to break her trust, not when she's just started having faith in me. She needs to know she can trust men, or she's going to have a real hard time with guys when she's older.'

'Wow, very deep and insightful, Zane.' The rigidness in her face and body softened. 'Okay, that's a good start … now tell me the rest.'

He heaved a sigh, before rubbing his face with his hands. 'Bloody hell,' he grumbled beneath his breath.

Tipping her head, she sighed. 'I'm sorry, but you of all people know how worried I am about her right now, so keeping things from me isn't going to help, her or me.'

He felt like a traitor, but Emma had a damn good point. 'You promise you won't tell her I told you?'

She made a cross over her chest with her finger. 'You have my word.'

'Okay, all right.' He huffed, more at himself than anything. 'She got upset because I was so excited to come and watch her today.'

Her face wrinkled in confusion. 'That's not something to get so upset about …' She stopped and sucked in a breath. 'Oh, because Michael never really wants to be here.'

'Exactly, and she knows it's only because you force him to come.'

'She does?'

'Yup, afraid so.'

She slowly shook her head. 'But I never do it in front of her, or when she can hear me on the phone.'

'She's a clever girl, Em, and she's old enough to understand what's going on.' He took steps towards her, not wanting their conversation to be overheard. 'We all know Michael, and how bad he is at covering up his dislike of something, or in my case, someone. Riley can see that he doesn't want to be here to support her, and he's only doing it to shut you up ... Sorry to be brash.'

'All good, no need to beat around the bush with me, you know that.' She sucked in a shuddering breath as she began to pace. Back and forward, back and forward. 'Poor Riley, I still see her as my baby, and think I can protect her by hiding things from her, but ...' She tried to smile. 'I can't.'

Stopping her from wearing a ditch into the dirt, Zane wrapped an arm around her shoulder. 'You're only doing what you think is best, but honestly, she's almost sixteen.' He chuckled, desperately trying to make light of the situation so Emma didn't bash herself up over it. 'Do you remember how we thought we could rule the world at that age? No matter how much our parents tried to hide stuff, like my mum with her cancer, we were switched on and knew exactly what was going on.'

Leaning into him, Emma nodded. 'They grow up so quick. One minute you're teaching them the alphabet and singing "Twinkle Twinkle Little Star" to get them to sleep, and the next you're watching them pick dresses out for their deb ball ... all in the blink of an eye.'

'You're the best mum, Em, just remember that, okay?'

'Thank you so much.' Emma wrapped her arms around him and gave him a hug. 'And I'm sorry for being a stroppy bitch. You were only doing what you thought best for Riley, too.'

'I was, and you had every right to be stroppy.'

'Well, now, aren't we looking all cosy?' Michael strode towards them, his chest puffed and his chin up. 'Birds of a feather flock together.'

'Speak of the goddamn devil,' Emma whispered before unravelling her arms and smiling gallantly at Michael. 'About time you showed up.'

'Yeah, yeah, heard it all before.' He gave Zane the evil eye. 'Where's Riley?'

'In the arena.'

Grunting, Michael turned and strode off.

'How did I ever marry that man?'

Zane shrugged. 'He used to be nice, before Mum died and then Peter decided to make him his successor after Michael finished high school.'

'That was a long time ago.'

'Yeah, it was.' Zane tipped his head. 'Come on, let's go annoy Michael some more while we do what he should be doing ... cheering Riley on.'

Emma grinned and clapped her hands. 'Let's.'

Leaning against the railings, with Emma close beside him, they did just that, cheering and clapping as they watched the girls hurdle dazzling horses over a maze of jumps – single bars, cross bars and crisscrossed oxer bars. Pride enveloped Zane as he quietly observed Riley in the saddle, assessing the course while she waited her turn, a tiny smile curling her lips when she focused on the final jump with the added test of water beneath it. Just like her mum, she rose to a challenge – what wasn't there to be proud of with a wonderful girl like her? Michael seriously needed his head read. Zane snuck a glance in his direction, only to catch Michael with his head bowed over his mobile phone. Could the son of a bitch be any less interested in his own daughter? It took every bit of his resolve not to storm over there, grab him by his poncey golf shirt collar, and tell him so.

Emma's applauding pulled his attention back to the centre ring. Riley's turn, she gave Boomerang her cue and they were off. One, two, three strides and they hit the mark, and then with a tug on the reins only noticeable by a trained eye, they were over the rail effortlessly. Zane couldn't help the smile spreading across his face, the sense of pride he felt for his extremely talented niece now immeasurable. Anyone who didn't know the situation would think she was his daughter and Michael was the uncle. His heart warming, the thought both amused and delighted him – if only that were the case. Then Emma would be his wife, his queen, and Riley would be his little princess – and he would treat them so, every single day. And he would be the happiest man alive. He could dream, he supposed.

His gaze following Boomerang and Riley clearing the rails, he admired how they moved graciously from one hurdle to the next. Emma beamed proudly beside him, jumping up and down on the spot each and every time Boomerang's hooves hit the ground. Seeing her so happy made him so very happy. On the eighth jump, Boomerang's back hoof just nicked the rail, and although wobbling, it settled back into the cup and remained put. Zane applauded and caught Michael glaring at him out of the corner of his eye – to hell with the bastard. Riley and Boomerang sailed through the rest of the course, making the crisscrossed oxer bars look like a cinch. Zane knew just how hard they could be. Reaching the end of the course, and clearing the water jump with inches to spare, Riley's smile was as wide as Zane and Emma's as she met their gazes.

Next up was Zane's favourite part of the program, the barrel racing. It took massive skill, countless hours of practice, a steadfast horse, and a firm seat in the saddle, to be good at it – as Kay had been. He had no doubt Riley was going to own every second of the gruelling battle. He looked at her sitting high in the saddle, loping Boomerang in circles out the back of the arena, getting him ready to give it his all. A few girls went before her, one of them knocking over the barrel. Her sad face broke Zane's heart. They all took it so seriously, and rightly so – horse sports were like any other competitive activity.

Their number called, Riley and Boomerang approached the gate. Determination written all over her pretty face, girl and horse stood at the ready, waiting for the cue to chase the clock. Boomerang was a little antsy, his ears back attentively as Riley talked to him. The buzzer went, and they were off like a fired bullet. Sitting low in the saddle, her focus steely, Riley slowed just enough to make the first turn, and like a motorbike hugging a corner she and Boomerang were nice and tight to the barrel. The second turn was a bit wider, but she held the reins at just the right angle to edge Boomerang in a little closer as they came out of the turn. Zane nodded his approval – Riley's cloverleaf pattern was close to perfection. A champion barrel racer in her teenage years, Emma had clearly taught her daughter everything she knew.

'For god's sake, Riley, push him harder!' Michael bellowed.

Zane shot a sideways glare, but it was lost on Michael as he continued to call out, telling Riley to do better, go harder.

'Arsehole,' Emma muttered.

'Damn straight he is.'

Zane could see the stress written all over Riley's face now, Michael's incessant shouting only hampering her ride. She blazed over to the last barrel, but Boomerang stumbled. With his front hoof slipping on the uneven dirt, Riley jerked forwards. Gasps were followed by breaths held, the seconds now feeling like minutes.

'Oh, come on!' Michael barked.

Transfixed, Zane's stomach heaved as he willed her to stay in the saddle. 'Hang in there, darling,' he whispered. 'You can do it.'

And she did, as did Boomerang. Regaining her seat in the saddle while the horse regained his footing, they darted around the final barrel, then all but flew towards the finishing line, a trail of dust in their wake. Boomerang's thundering hooves matched the frenzied pound of Zane's heart as the timer stopped, and Riley finally loosened the reins, giving Boomerang control. Then they blasted through the side gate and out of sight. Zane found himself standing on the bottom railing, fists in the air in triumph as he roared Riley's name, yahooing for all of Australia.

'For Christ's sake, that stumble is going to cost her a few points.' Michael smacked the railing, drawing attention from unamused onlookers. Unruffled, he glared back at them.

Zane looked at the clock. Nineteen seconds, very well done. 'She did her best, Michael, and at the very least she's in one piece.'

'For once, lay off her, would you?' Emma said.

Pressing his phone to his ear, Michael turned his back to her and wandered off in the opposite direction.

Zane tried to catch her eye, but her head was down and the shadow her hat was casting over her pretty face made it damn near impossible. A wave of tension assaulted his muscles. This should be a joyous moment, but as usual, Michael had stolen it from her with his obnoxious attitude. He placed his hand on her back. 'You right, Em?'

'Yup, all good, just calming myself before I head over to Riley … She'll be upset enough without my baggage to go with it.'

She glanced over to where Michael was walking in circles, his brows furrowed. Whoever he was speaking to on the phone was clearly, but unfairly, more important to him than going to congratulate Riley.

'She's right, you know, she'd be much better off without him here, harassing her. All he damn well does is upset her.'

'And you,' Zane added.

'Yeah, and me,' Emma said, as if reminding herself.

'Let's go and tell her what a great job she's done, hey?'

Straightening her shoulders, Emma smiled past the sadness in her eyes. 'Yup, let's do it.'

Zane hated seeing her so rattled, and he gathered Riley was going to be the same, if not worse. With determined steps, he headed over to where she would be, Emma right beside him. He spotted her at the water trough, still in the saddle while Boomerang helped himself to a well-deserved drink. Her shoulders slumped, Riley's expression was the epitome of wretchedness.

'There she is, the barrel-racing champion,' Zane said as brightly as he could.

Riley turned to face them. 'Hey, not likely, but thanks for the vote of confidence.' She twirled Boomerang's mane around her fingers as the angry glint in her eyes softened.

Emma placed her hand on Riley's thigh and looked up at her. 'Whatever the outcome, you did so well out there today, sweetheart.'

Zane tipped his hat. 'My bloody oath you did.'

Riley's gloomy face showed signs of a smile. 'Thanks, I have a very talented partner; he didn't get the name Boomerang for nothing.' The smile finally broke through – the action small, but it warmed Zane's heart.

'Can't give Boomerang all the credit, Riley, you played a big part in that too.' Wanting to take her into his arms so he could hug her hurt away, he shoved his hands in his jeans' pockets instead. 'Nineteen seconds is a brilliant time. You did really well.'

She leant in and gave Boomerang's neck a stroke. 'Yeah, but it wasn't good enough. I don't think I'll be getting a ribbon today.' Her smile all but faded.

'Hey, don't you be so hard on yourself.' Zane's throat almost closed over with emotion. 'When I'm bull riding, I try and focus on the fact I give it my all, and that's all I can expect from myself. Whatever the outcome is, that's the way it's meant to be. I'm just grateful for the ride and the exhilaration it gives me.'

Riley considered this for a few moments and then nodded. 'I like your way of thinking, Uncle Zane.'

Emma smiled in his direction. 'Yeah, me too.'

Zane felt Michael's presence behind him before the man even opened his mouth. The look on Riley's face was one of apprehension. Emma's was stormy – the mother bear protecting her cub.

Stepping past Zane, Michael stopped short of Emma. 'I'm going now, Riley. I've got to get back to the head office in Cairns and catch up on some work.'

'Okay then.' Riley fiddled with the reins. 'Thanks for coming.'

'I'll give you a call during the week.' Michael stepped forward and Riley leant down and gave him a kiss.

'Zane, Emma,' Michael said, his voice terse, as he stepped past them and strode away.

A spark of anger lit in Zane's gut as he watched Michael disappear around the back of a trailer.

Riley's eyes watering, she blinked quickly. 'I'm going to take Boomerang back over to the float and unsaddle him.'

'I'll come and help you, love.' Emma looked to Zane. 'We'll meet you back at home, if you like.'

Zane nodded and then tipped his hat. That was clearly his cue to give them some girly time. 'Chow for now, my brown cows.'

Riley eyed him for a few seconds and then cracked up laughing, enticing Emma into side-splitting laughter too. Zane chuckled, but didn't know what was so damn funny. He held his hands up in question. 'Did I miss something?'

Emma wiped happy tears from her eyes, and Riley sucked in a breath and tried her best to answer. 'Your sayings are so old school they're kinda cool. But far out, they're funny, Uncle Zane.'

'Like I said, I'm a groover from way back.' He grinned playfully. 'The grooviest groover in FNQ, I might add.'

'Nope, more like the grooviest groover that ever lived,' Emma added with a warm smile. 'Come on, love, let's go get Boomerang cooled off, hey?'

'Yup, groovy Mum,' Riley said, her playful smile warming Zane's heart.

As Emma strolled past, she offered him a knee-buckling smile. 'Thank you,' she whispered.

Watching her walk away, heat shot through him like a bullet fired from his heart. Damn, she was beautiful. His eyes on the sway of her hips, he found it hard to look anywhere else. Her sexy, well-worn jeans and silky top added to her allure. She had always made him *very* conscious of being a hot-blooded male, but even more so right this very second. He had to force himself to turn around and put one dusty boot in front of the other, towards his LandCruiser, and towards the place she'd just called *home*. He liked the sound of that very much.

CHAPTER
17

A striking bay mare trotted back and forth, her tail high in the air, and in the adjacent enclosure a proud Arabian pranced along the fence line, his hooves striking the earth with thuds as he showed off to his lady neighbour. This was living, Emma thought with a contented sigh – no hustle and bustle, no traffic fumes, no high-rises, just peace and tranquillity wrapped up in Mother Nature's gloriousness. With the top of her Land Rover down, and her arm resting on the window, the breeze cooled her face as she drove leisurely past the lush paddocks that seemed to stretch on into the never never. Her attention turned to the horses up on the rise; it appeared each of them was enjoying the last of the sun's rays on their backs. She loved this part of the day, when the dusk was hinting its arrival, the day's work was completed, and she could take a few moments to slow down and be grateful for Serendipity's beauty. Having officially owned it for almost a year now, after her parents signed it over to her, she still had to pinch herself – it was a dream come true.

Covered from head to toe in sweat and dust, she felt a sense of accomplishment as she parked under the side awning of the shed. Climbing out with Tiny launching out behind her, she paused to ease out her lower back; the three hours she'd just spent shoeing the agisted horses, one of the mares obstinate and grumpy about being shod, had taken their toll. With Riley staying at Jasmine's place for the night, a warm soak in a magnesium bath with a good glass of red was definitely on the cards. She hadn't pulled anything out for dinner, so it would be something slapped together at the last minute. Cheese and biscuits, or eggs on toast – both dishes her bachelorette's saving grace.

Wandering towards the chook pen, she called her seven girls and Peking, and like the good feathered friends they were, they came running from every direction, clucking as if to let her know they were on their way home, with Peking right beside them. She was just latching the pen door shut when a meow caught her attention. Kat was balancing on top of Boomerang, massaging the horse with her paws. It was a sight that had to be seen to be believed, and had got over ten thousand views when she'd shared it on her Facebook page a few years back. The hype had even caught the attention of *Sunrise* and in a fleeting mention by the host, Kat and Boomerang had had their fifteen seconds of fame. In a world of absolute bliss, Boomerang was leaning against the railings, his back leg resting and his head drooping while Kat worked her magic.

Smiling, Emma ditched the idea of heading straight home for a beer and wandered over to rest against the rustic timber fence of the homestead paddock, her boot up on the bottom rung. In a world of her own, until her mobile chimed from her back pocket. Jumping to attention, she plucked it out. It was a message from Renee.

Hey, Em, just checking in on how it's all going with Zane there? I'm dying to know.

She quickly typed a message back. *Pretty good, why don't you and Jackson come over for a barbeque tonight, and we can yak about it in person?*

She had the makings of a potato and garden salad, and she knew Renee would be more than happy to pick up some snags from the local IGA on the way over.

A reply bubble popped up instantly. *It's a date, gurrrrl. What should I bring?*

Some meat, if you don't mind, and I'll cover the salads.

Done. See you in about an hour.

Thanks. Can't wait, love you Rennie.

Love you, too, Em. Xo

The magnesium bath might have to wait until tomorrow night. Oh well, friends, good times and a couple of drinks would help her all but forget about her aching back. Catching sight of her owner, Kat leapt off Boomerang's back and scuttled towards Emma, rubbing against her leg when she reached her, begging to be loved and fed. Leaning over, Emma scooped her up and cuddled her to her chest, giving Kat a good scratch around the neck and behind the ears. Her eyes rolling shut, Kat purred like a generator while Emma watched Boomerang making a mad dash around the paddock, buck a few times, and then find one of the only patches of dirt to roll onto his back.

'Hey, you bugger, Riley only just groomed you this morning,' she called out, shaking her head.

'Bloody typical, huh.' Zane's voice came from behind, startling her.

She hadn't even heard him pull up. Her heart sped with the thought of being near him. Kat leapt from her arms as Emma turned and glanced over her shoulder, the cheeky smile that claimed her lips completely out of her control. There he was, the man she'd arm wrestled with, cried with, laughed with, made love with just once but could recall every gasp, every shudder; the man she was keeping so much hidden from. His hat was pulled low over his eyes, his face a little grubby from the day's workout fixing some of her fencing. He looked so deliciously good.

'Howdy.' Lifting his sunglasses to the top of his hat, he smiled like butter wouldn't melt in his mouth, but she knew better, way better. He looked her up and down. 'Dirty suits you, Em.'

Although she knew she looked a right state, his compliment fanned the fire already burning deep within her soul. She ached to tell him he looked edible, but held back. 'Ha, yeah, right. I always do my best to dress for the occasion.' As he came closer, she noticed blood on his sleeve. 'Shit, what did you do to yourself?' She stepped forward and carefully grabbed his arm, looking at the deep gash on his forearm.

'Oh, it's nothing. Just got caught up on some barbed wire … all good.'

'Have you had a tetanus shot lately?'

'About a year ago.' He rolled his sleeve back down. 'Don't worry, I'm sure I'll live.'

'I'm a mother, it's in my DNA to worry.' She took a full breath and caught his eyes falling to where her breasts momentarily strained against her shirt.

He quickly looked back to her face, and grinned. 'You've always been a worry wart, Em, motherhood has nothing to do with it.'

'Oi, that's enough with the digs, Mister-I-can't-help-but-overthink-the crap-out-of-everything.'

He mocked offence and then laughed it off. 'I reckon I might have to get you one of those wooden spoons for Christmas too.' He saddled up beside her on the fence. 'You know, the one that reads *Head Shit Stirrer*. Except yours will be *Assistant Shit Stirrer*.'

'Deal.' She turned to give him a grin. He was so tempting – all bad boy on the outside but with a good man's heart. 'I invited Renee and her new man over for a barbeque tonight? Like to join us?'

'Burnt snags smothered in tomato sauce, count me in.' His smile was so big and warm Emma felt its heat flood her body. 'What do you want me to bring?'

'Maybe some beer?'

He nodded. 'I reckon I can do that.'

'And seeing as you're the man of the place at the moment, you can hold fort at the barbeque with Jackson, while us gals make the salads.'

'You bloody ripper.' He rubbed his hands together. 'I love having a pair of tongs in one hand and a beer in the other,' he said. 'When's Riley back from Jasmine's?'

'She's sleeping over there tonight. They've decided to have a Channing Tatum movie marathon in their PJs.'

'That'll do her the world of good.'

'It will. She and Jasmine are like sisters.' She sighed, shaking her head with the memories. 'They met in kindergarten, and were joined at the hip, until they fell out when Riley started hanging around her dickhead ex-boyfriend and his loser mates, but now they've broken up, she and Jasmine are besties again. I'm glad, because Jasmine's a respectable girl, and a good influence on Riley.'

'I'm pleased to hear it. Being a teenager is tough enough without having the wrong kind of people around you.' He tapped the railing and straightened up. 'Right, I better go run through the dip and get scrubbed up for dinner.' He smiled. 'I'm looking forward to a good Aussie barby.'

'Yup, me too.' She gave his back a friendly pat as they headed away from the paddock. 'Thanks for helping out with the fencing today.'

He flashed her a smile. 'Least I can do, considering as I'm staying here. Besides, I'd go nuts sitting around doing nothing all day.'

'You and me both.' She waved him off; the thought of climbing beneath a hot shower made her almost run up the front steps of the homestead.

Two hours later, and the stereo Zane had set up on the back verandah was pumping out one classic country tune after another. Taking a sip from her second margarita, the first one having gone down way too easily, Emma licked the salt from her lips. Shuffling up to the sink, she did a little jiggle beside Renee, who was busy rinsing dishes and popping them into the dishwasher. Renee tapped hips with her, laughing as she tossed a handful of suds her way.

'You sure you don't want to stay for the night? I can make up the spare room.'

Renee threw back the last of her cocktail. 'With the rate we're going with the bevvies, we might have to, hun.' She held up her empty glass. 'I think we better make ourselves another before we head outside.'

'Oh, yeah, girlfriend,' Emma said with a cheeky grin.

In high spirits, and with cocktails made, she and Renee carried the potato and garden salads they'd just whipped up, along with two garlic breads Emma had found buried in her deep freeze, out to the table.

'I truly don't think the two of you tumbling into bed together is a one-off thing, Em.' Renee gestured towards where Zane was flipping the lamb chops over, beer in hand. 'He looks at you like he wants to throw you down on the nearest surface and have his way with you, and to be honest, I don't know how you say no to him. He's one hell of a spunk.'

'I have to say no.' It was such an abrupt response that Renee stopped and stared at her, before sitting down. Emma slumped into the camp chair beside her. 'Between you and me, it's a never-ending struggle. But I can't go there with him, Rennie, and I'm not going to tell him anything after that bloody letter.' Her mind flashed back to their night of passion, all those years ago, and every inch of her tingled.

'About that, my gorgeous friend, do you really believe Peter has proof in his safe?'

'I honestly don't know, but I can't risk going against him and finding out either.' She shrugged. 'I've tried to work out what it would be, but I can't for the life of me come up with anything, maybe other than video footage of it.'

'Yeah, possibly, I wouldn't put it past Peter to have had sneaky security cameras everywhere in his house.'

'Who knows?' She sighed. 'Life at Serendipity has been so great with Zane around, and Riley is the happiest I've seen her in years.' She picked at a thread hanging from her denim shorts. 'I'm going to be sad to see him leave in a couple of weeks.'

'Does he have to go back?'

'That's where his life is. There's nothing keeping him here now I'm not telling him about Riley, and Michael has Wattle Acres.'

'There's you.' Renee looked at her with tenderness.

'He can't have me, and I can't have him.'

Renee chewed her lip and then grinned. 'Have you thought about going over to the homestead, to try to break into the safe?'

Emma's eyes widened. 'No.'

'Well, I think you should.'

'I'm not really up on the whole breaking in thing, Rennie.'

'Google it.'

Emma couldn't help but laugh at the serious expression on Renee's face.

As if she were a five-year-old about to be given a present, Renee bounced up and down in her chair. 'I'm serious.'

'No way am I going to try and break into a safe, but ...' She leant forwards. 'Maybe I could go over and try and work out the combination.'

'Why the hell not, Em? It's worth a bloody try.'

Emma grimaced. 'Well, because I'd be breaking and entering.'

'Kinda sort of not really. You are the dead man's ex daughter-in-law.' She looked to where Zane and Jackson were deep in conversation and dropped her voice even lower. 'I'm sure, if you somehow get caught in the act, you'll be able to talk your way out of it.'

'Yeah, maybe.' Emma's belly pitched and rolled. 'You're a really bad influence sometimes, you know that?'

'Nah, I just encourage you to do what has to be done, that's all.' Renee smiled. 'If it makes you feel better, I'll come with you.'

'No! One of us breaking in there is bad enough,' she said. 'But thank you.'

'Well, if you change your mind, I'll be your partner in crime, but you got this.' Renee offered her a confident smile. 'Whether you want to admit it or not, Zane's your soulmate, Em. And you only get one of them in a lifetime. Anything is worth a shot to try and fix this mess before he gets on that plane.'

As terrified as she was, Emma knew Renee was right. Zane was a gift to her *and* Riley, and she didn't want to give up the fight. She nodded, her heart aching. They could be so good together – all three of them. A family. Like she'd always wanted. All week the pull between them had been growing stronger, the invisible tie that bound them tighter, more binding – delightfully so. To hell with Peter and his threats – she would get to the bottom of it, somehow, some way.

Emma sighed as she threw her hands up in the air. 'Anyway, enough of the heavy stuff, let's just enjoy the night for what it is … wonderful friends, good times and yummy food. Tomorrow's another day, and I can start worrying about it all again then.'

And that they did, all four of them groaning about eating too much at the end of the glorious feast as they stared into the flickering flames of the fire pit. It took a good hour for the food to settle enough for them to consider clearing up, and even then, Emma and Renee were only half-hearted about it.

'Us blokes will help, hey, Zane?' Jackson said.

'No bloody way … that's a woman's domain.' The mischievous glint in Zane's eyes as he dodged a poke in the ribs by Emma had them all in hysterics.

'I think Zane meant, he'd love to.'

'Yup, spot on, Jackson,' Zane said with a chuckle.

'Before we do that, though, lovely ladies, I think we need to boogie some of this food off.' Jackson leant in and kissed Renee on the cheek. Unfolding from his chair, he held out his hand. 'Dance with me, you gorgeous minx!'

'Well, why the hell not?' Renee bounced to her feet and joining him on the front lawn, shook her tooshy in time to the music, both of them laughing and having a wow of a time.

The flames reaching for the star-spangled sky, Zane caught Emma's eyes in the soft glow. 'Looks like fun, you wanna join them?'

She took a few moments, wary of what she might want to do being wrapped in his gloriously masculine arms, but then thought, *What the hell?* 'How could I say no to such a suave invitation?' she said light-heartedly.

'Oh, indeed, and from an equally suave man.' Zane's attempt at an aristocratic accent was terrible, and they both laughed. Grinning cheekily, he took her by the hand and helped her to her feet, twirling her across the grass like the rock-n-roll pro he was.

Moving in time to the music, and to each other, every single one of Emma's nerve-ends fired to quivering life. They spun and twirled, and at one point Zane lifted her up in the air to raucous cheers from Renee and Jackson, her feet hitting the ground gracefully thanks to his skill and hers. And then, after a few songs, the music slowed, Big and Rich's 'Lost in This Moment' sending goosebumps all over her. She went to retreat to the camp chair, but Zane held her round the waist, his eyes begging her to stay.

And so she did.

Dancing arm and arm, barefoot on the grass, within his big strong arms, was the most amazing place she'd been in what felt like forever. Heat sizzled through her as they swayed, the friction of his jeans against her skirt sensual within itself, let alone the way he was subtly undressing her with his gaze. His fingers traced up and down her spine, arousing her beyond words. Shivers ran across her skin, and her feminine roar growled from deep within. She craved his kiss, his naked touch, but no way in hell was she going to let it happen. As much as she wanted to be at one with him, she just couldn't. Why did he have to keep tempting her so?

As if reading her wayward thoughts, Zane's lips quirked into a wicked smile. 'You having a good night, Em?'

'I am,' she said softly. 'I don't want it to be over, but I reckon I'm going to have to call it a night and go to bed soon. I'm absolutely knackered.'

'Me too.' He gestured towards Renee and Jackson, now entwined as they kissed. 'And I don't think they'll be far off bed either … but maybe not so much for sleeping.'

Emma laughed. 'Oh god, if they're staying here, I hope they keep it down.'

'Jackson stopped drinking a while ago, said he told me he likes to wake up in his own bed. So I gather they'll head home.'

She shrugged. 'I get that.'

And Zane had been right. As they helped clean up, Renee announced that she and Jackson were heading home as soon as they'd finished. By the time they'd all said their goodbyes, and Emma and Zane had sat back down for a nightcap, the campfire was dying. Zane grabbed a few logs and strategically placed them over the top. Orange flames celebrated with a wild dance, rising and swirling. Sparks flickered into the blackness, disappearing mid-flight.

'I love fires,' he said as he cosied up beside her, American Wild Honey over ice in hand. 'I could sit and watch one for hours and not get bored.'

'Me too, I love how they're so wild and powerful, yet they can also be so calming and peaceful.' She rested her head on his shoulder, feeling comfortable in doing so. 'I'm sleepy,' she mumbled, as her eyelids slowly closed. And then she drifted to a place only dreams were made of before she could stop herself.

CHAPTER
18

The wind whipping around the cab of the rattly old four-wheel drive, Zane's belly grumbled as he bounced along the dirt track leading from where the main pump drew water from the creek. Noticing when he'd driven past yesterday that it was in need of servicing, he'd taken it upon himself to work on it when he'd woken up at sparrow's fart this morning. He'd been hoping for a sleep-in, but with his body clock still all over the place, it just wasn't going to happen. After tossing and turning, he'd given up trying to go back to sleep and headed out to do something useful. Which wasn't hard. Like any property, be it livestock or produce, just about everywhere he looked, there was something to be fixed, mowed, slashed, fed, tidied or serviced. He once again admired Emma's resilience, doing it all on her own. She was one hell of a strong woman.

Cresting the rise, he fought the urge to look towards Wattle Acres, but like metal to a magnet, he couldn't resist. A sprawling property with a number of outbuildings, generous native gardens, neatly arranged paddocks and two windmills, one at either side of the two hundred and fifty acres, it was hard to miss. He slowed down but refused to pull to a stop – he didn't need to sit and think about losing it. It was easier to have fleeting moments of sorrow, rather than to wallow in the heartache of it all. He could just make out the four-bedroom homestead – the paddocks beyond it, although green, lay deserted; the horses his mother had saved from anywhere and everywhere she could, had been sold off less than a week after she'd passed away. He hated to think of how many of them went to the meatworks because Peter and Michael just wanted to get rid of them. And he'd been helpless to stop it, just as he was helpless to stop Michael selling the place. The fact his mother's ashes were there would be a cross he'd bear for the rest of his days. It made him detest Peter and Michael all the more. Why did men like them always seem to land on their feet? He shook his head. If there was a god, he couldn't even begin to fathom how he worked – mysterious ways for damn sure.

Losing sight of his childhood home, and focusing on the track ahead, Serendipity's homestead and cottage came into view, and a warm sense of belonging washed over him. The corrugated-iron roof flashing in the fierce midday sunshine, he found himself momentarily blinded. So he tugged his hat down a little lower to ward off the glare. His head was feeling a little woozy from the lack of sleep and the amount of alcohol he'd knocked back last night. It had been so late when he'd finally hit the sack, it had tipped over into Sunday. Not wanting to leave Emma's side, his arm had gone dead from the weight of her sleeping on it. He hadn't minded one bit – he loved being able to watch her sleeping so peacefully. With some skilful and gentle manoeuvres, he'd managed to gather her up into his arms without disturbing her too much, and then carried her inside. Trudging up the stairs, he'd fought to keep his breath quiet as he took her into her bedroom and carefully laid her on her bed. Moaning softly, she'd rolled over, her breathing deep and peaceful. Pulling a blanket up and over her, he'd gazed at her for a few moments, at the way her hair fell across her pillow – he would've been able to stand there all night, just admiring her. It had been a struggle to leave and go to his own bed, the pull to climb in beside her and drift off to sleep was strong, but he'd dragged himself away; every step he'd put between them was laborious. How in the hell was he going to go back to the States, feeling like this about her? He may as well rip his beating heart out of his chest right now.

Pulling up in the shade of the old gum, he noticed Emma's Land Rover was gone. He hadn't seen her out and about amongst the paddocks, so maybe she'd ducked into town. Uncurling himself from the cab, he looked up to see Riley crossing the front lawn. She seemed upset, or worried, or both. His heart lurched.

'Hey, Uncle Zane ...' she said a little breathlessly. 'Have you seen Mum?'

'Hey, Riley, no, I haven't. Why's that?'

'Jasmine's mum dropped me home hours ago, and Mum had left me a note saying she'd gone out and would be home around ten. Nothing about where she'd gone, which was strange.' She chewed the inside of her lip.

'Have you tried her mobile?'

'Yup, and it rang from her bedroom.' She rolled her eyes. 'She's hopeless at remembering it half the time.'

Even though Zane was a little freaked out by Riley's concern, he tried to remain a picture of calm. 'Right, well, I can go for a drive, see if I can find her.' He jumped back into the four-wheel drive and revved it to life, a cloud of smoke bellowing out the exhaust as he did. 'You want to come along?'

She thought about it, and then shook her head. 'No, I'll wait here, in case she comes home. Then I can call you and let you know to stop looking.' She fidgeted with the buttons on her shirt. 'I'm probably making a big deal over nothing. It's just not like her to be late without letting me know.' She groaned. 'Now I know how she feels when she can't get a hold of me.'

'I'm sure she's fine.' He tapped his door. 'Back soon, with your mum.'

Riley finally smiled. 'Thanks.'

Deciding to head in the general direction of town first, Zane breathed a sigh of relief when he spotted Emma parked on the side of the long dirt road, at the junction that led to Wattle Acres. The way the Land Rover was parked, facing him, meant she'd come from that direction. Why she'd be going over there in the first place baffled him, but there was only one way to find out – to ask her. He couldn't help but wonder if it had something to do with the letter she'd remained tight-lipped about. Surely she'd have opened it by now.

Hearing him pull up, Emma peered around the corner of the raised bonnet, her expression one of surprise and maybe even a little like she'd been caught red-handed. Or was he imagining that? 'Hey, Em, need a hand?' By the time he reached her, she'd regained a poker face.

'Hey, Zane, nah, I'm all good, thanks. The old girl does this a fair bit.'

Watching her bent over the diesel engine, her gaze intense, his whole body tightened. He wanted her so badly. All of her. Now. And forever. But he also needed to know what she was doing here. 'So, where have you been gallivanting off to this morning?'

'Why's it your business?' She flashed him a fiery look so hot it singed him all the way down to his toes, and then she changed the subject. 'As I said, I don't need a lift, thanks.'

He wanted to ask her why she was acting so guarded, and if she had read the letter from Peter, but bit his tongue. Standing side by side, an awkward silence fell between them.

'Riley asked me to look for you. She was worried.'

'Oh.' He heard her hesitate. 'Yeah, I was meant to be back a while ago, but got side-tracked.' She didn't offer to elaborate.

'You're not usually a side-tracker, Em, that's generally my domain.' He eyed her quizzically. 'Where'd you get side-tracked to?'

'Gee whizz, we're a bit nosey today, aren't we?' Green eyes glared at him, challenged him, *tempted* him.

Zane held his hands up in surrender. 'Sorry, you're right, not my place to ask.'

'Damn straight it isn't.' She finally hinted amusement before looking back at the engine. 'Bugger of a thing keeps overheating. I can usually get her going again, after she's cooled off a bit, but today, she's not bloody budging.'

'You might be needing that lift you knocked back after all, huh?'

'Maybe.' She huffed, her greasy hands going to her hips. 'This is probably going to cost an arm and a leg to fix too.'

'I can help.'

'Fix it?'

'Try to, and if that fails, pay for it to get fixed.'

'I couldn't take your money, Zane, but thanks.' She wiped her hands on a rag and slammed the bonnet shut. 'But I will take up your offer of a lift. I'll come back in an hour or two, see if she starts.'

'Righto.'

He led the way to the passenger door and opened it.

'Thanks.'

'No wuckers.' Resting his hand on her lower back, he heard the sharp intake of her breath and could see the beat of her racing heart against her chest. The passenger seatbelt dodgy, he leant across her, wriggling it free. She looked to him, eyes wide and breath held. If she closed that last inch of space between them, he'd be a goner.

Job done, he stepped back to the ground. She tugged it on, a little defiantly. 'Don't start to think you're my knight in shining armour now, will you? First carrying me to my bed, and now saving me from the side of the road, all in less than twenty-four hours.'

'Trust me, I won't.' Sliding into the driver's seat, he hid a smile.

He felt a desperate need to kiss her – but he'd tried that already and had been put in his place. So he was wary to do it again. Like a startled wild horse, he was sure she'd bolt, and he'd have ruined his already very slim chances of ever making her see he was worth the risk. Her wall was up, way too high for him to climb over just yet. But brick by brick, he would try to pull it down, steady as she goes, so he didn't freak her out. The thing was, he only had a few weeks to give it his best shot.

A chestnut mare raised her head inquisitively as he pulled to a stop back beneath an old gum. The horse stamped a pesky fly as she watched them. Climbing out, Zane unfurled and reached for the heavens.

Riley ran from the homestead as Emma stepped out from her side. 'Oh my god, Mum, I was worried sick. Where have you been?'

'Far out, love, it's broad daylight, and I was out doing stuff and broke down. Why's everyone so worried about where I've been all of a sudden?' Although smiling, Zane could see the tremor in Emma's jaw as she pulled Riley into a hug. 'But thanks for caring so much.' She stepped back. 'Now you know how I feel when I can't get a hold of you, missy.'

'I know, I know.' Riley rolled her eyes. 'That's exactly what I said to Uncle Zane.' She smiled, looking in his direction. 'Hey?'

'You sure did.' He found Emma's behaviour a little strange but decided not to say anything more. Emma would tell him if there was anything she wanted him to know, or worry about, or so he hoped. 'Well, I'm going to grab myself some lunch, and a cold shower. Catch you two a bit later on.'

'Yup, me too.' Emma wrapped her arm around Riley's shoulder and walked towards the homestead. 'Thank for the lift,' she called out.

'All good, anytime.'

* * *

Having had a few hours to gather her wits, Emma couldn't believe her bad luck – first breaking down and then Zane finding her. She knew she'd done a pretty shitty job of trying to act cool, calm and collected, possibly coming across pigheaded and defensive instead, but what else was she meant to do? He couldn't know why she'd dared to go over to Wattle Acres, even though it had been a wasted trip. Her nerves getting the better of her, she'd sat in her Land Rover behind the stables for half an hour, trying to will herself to go inside. Finally, once she'd gathered enough courage to get out of the four-wheel drive and walk to the back door, all the while terrified Michael was going to show up, she'd realised she'd brought the wrong set of keys. A walk around the outside of the homestead, to try to find another way in, had proved fruitless; the place was locked up like a fortress. She'd try again tomorrow, she decided, and this time, there'd be no chickening out. She needed to know what was in that goddamn safe, if anything – there was the possibility that Peter was playing her bluff.

* * *

Her footfalls echoed as she traipsed across the front verandah of the cottage. Knocking three times, she called out, 'Anyone home?' Of course there was, but still a bit shaken, it was the first thing that came to her mind.

'Hang ten, I'm coming.' A few seconds later, Zane came to the door, shirtless, a towel wrapped low on his waist and his hair damp. A trickle of water ran down his chiselled chest, and she ached to lean in and lick it off. Caught up in his manliness, she suddenly forgot how to breathe as her insides steamed up.

'Hey, Em.' He smiled lazily, matching the mood of the Sunday afternoon.

Stepping back a little, to make some space between her and this hunk of spunkiness, she said, 'Hey, there, you. Good shower?'

Tongue-tied she shook her head. What in the hell was she doing, acting like some loved-up fool? She had to fight to focus on his face and not on his washboard abs.

He eyed her with a searing blue gaze. 'Sure was.' Raising his arm, he rested against the doorframe, the muscles in his bicep clenching. 'What's up?'

'Oh ...' She glanced over her shoulder. 'Riley and I were wondering if you'd like to come for that ride? Better late than never, hey?'

He gave her the most brilliant smile. 'Damn straight I would, thanks, Em.' He moved past her, the brush of his arm sending shockwaves through her, and gave Riley a wave. 'Thanks for the invite!' he called out.

Riley grinned and gave him the thumbs up. 'All good, you coming?'

'Is the Pope Catholic?'

She tipped her head, and then shook it, smiling. 'You and your sayings.'

Laughing, he stepped back past Emma. 'I'll just go and put some clothes on. Meet you over at the stables in five.'

'Cool beans, I'll go and start saddling up Dad's old horse for you,' said Emma.

'Hank Williams?'

'The one and only, you remember him?'

Zane smiled. 'How could I forget him? The bugger threw me off a couple of times when your dad and I were breaking him in to the saddle.'

'Oh, that's right, I forgot about that.' She grinned with the memory, and then spun around and walked away. 'Don't rush.'

'Be there in a sec, I want to help you saddle up.'

I'd like to saddle you up, she thought waywardly as she wandered back towards the stables.

*　*　*

Creaking saddles, clinking metal and the rhythmic sounds of the horses' hooves – this was Emma's idea of heaven. They'd been riding for a few hours, the dirt track that meandered in a ribbon now drawing them back out of the national park bordering Serendipity. Trying not to take too much notice of the way Zane's hands slid over his jeans or wiped the beads of sweat from his forehead, or held the reins, or stroked Hank's neck, Emma smiled from deep within her soul. The three of them having fallen into a comfortable silence, and their horses into a steady walk, the soft jingle of harnesses and the clip clop of hooves were the only sounds. Meaningless chatter wasn't needed to pass the time. This vast land rolling out before them had a voice of its own, one that could be heard in the call of the birds, the thump of a bounding kangaroo, and the whisper of the wind. The sigh of the warm breeze stirred the leaves of the towering natives. Dappled light through the branches fell on their path, and the horizon shimmered.

'You're far away.' Zane's husky voice interrupted her thoughts.

Emma looked over at him, a smile curling her lips. 'Oh, sorry, no, I'm very much here, actually.' Her gaze swept their scenic surroundings. 'We couldn't want for a more picturesque place to ride, or live.'

'A big fat ditto to that, Em.' His sleeves rolled up, exposing sun-bronzed, tattooed forearms, Zane tugged the brim of his hat down further, shadowing his handsome face. 'There's something special about this place. The smells and sounds make me feel so at home.'

'I'm glad.' She offered him a warm smile and he returned it.

'Are you two starving, or what?' Riley came up between them. 'I'm about to chew my own arm off I'm that hungry.'

'Yeah, I'm a bit Hank Marvin myself.' Zane grinned.

'Is that old person's lingo for "starved", Uncle Zane?'

He grinned even wider and nodded. 'Yup.'

'Well then, we better get home before we all starve to death, don't you reckon?' She turned to Emma. 'That lamb stew you put on before we left is calling our names, Mum. I can almost smell it from here.'

Emma licked her lips. 'Oh stop, just the thought of it is making my mouth water.' She looked to Zane. 'And yes, before you ask, of course you're invited.'

'You bewdy! Now if that isn't an open invitation to race home, I don't know what is.'

'First one back gets the biggest bowl, and the loser has to do the cleaning up after dinner,' Emma said, her reins at the ready.

'Them's fighting words, Em. You know you're setting yourself up for a thrashing, don't you?' Zane gathered up his reins and grinned.

'Is that so?'

'Oo-roo,' he said, as he and Hank whooshed past her.

'Oi, that's not fair!' Bum glued to the saddle, Emma flicked the reins and took off after him, as thunderous hooves quickly approached from behind.

'I'll see you two losers back there.' Hand over her hat, Riley tore past them both, her face a picture of triumph.

'You little terror,' Emma called after her as she and Zane gave chase.

They reached the stables in record time, all of them breathless. 'You won fair and square, Riley,' Emma called out as she followed Riley into the round yard.

Zane fastened the gate behind them. 'Hot dang, that girl rides like there's no tomorrow.'

'Bloody oath. I'm super proud of her.'

'And so you should be.' Zane dismounted. 'You two go and have showers and I'll put the horses in their paddocks, if you like.'

'You sure?'

'You cooked dinner, so damn straight I'm sure.' He waved them off. 'Go on, you're both making the place look untidy.'

Later, with the pot of stew all but demolished, the cleaning up done, and Riley now in bed with her earphones in, Emma poured them both a nightcap and they headed outside.

Zane nodded towards to the cottage. 'How bout we hang over at my place tonight, change things up a bit?'

Emma changed direction and headed down the steps. 'Sure, why not?' Tiny agreed, and was at the cottage before them, his butt reversed up on one of the camp chairs. Shaking her head, Emma laughed at her lanky, four-legged mate.

A thin sliver of moonlight shone, lighting the verandah as they sat down on the comfortable double-seater cane chair. For a moment, neither of them spoke, but sipped their hot chocolates, laced with whisky, as they stared out at the moon-drenched landscape.

'I'm so tired, as usual,' Emma said softly.

Zane smiled. 'Me too ... comes with being an adult, I reckon.'

'Ha, yeah. You're probably right.'

Sliding his arm across the back of the chair, he massaged her neck, making her even sleepier, and also hungry for him to pick her up and take her to his bed. It would be so easy for her to rest her head on his shoulder, like she had last night, close her eyes, and drift off to another time and place for a while. It wasn't until she jerked herself awake that she realised she'd done just that.

'Oh, I'm sorry,' she said.

Zane chuckled. 'What for?'

'Being such terrible company.'

'You're not terrible company at all, Em.' He gazed at her as if she were the most beautiful woman on earth. 'I love hanging out with you, even when you're sound asleep.' The atmosphere sizzled between them.

Emma suddenly sat up straight, deciding she should go before she did something really stupid.

'Leaving so soon?'

'Yeah, I need to hit the hay,' she said, part of her wishing he'd ask her to stay. 'And I better let you get some sleep.' His shaggy, dark hair begged to be ruffled by her fingers.

He nodded. 'Night then.'

'Night.' She padded down the steps and across the lawn, every single inch of her wanting to turn around, run to him, and never let him go.

CHAPTER

19

Although exhausted when she'd climbed into bed, as soon as her head had hit the pillow Emma's brain had kicked into action. She couldn't sleep, wondering what in the hell Peter had on her, imagining all sorts of things, hardly any of them making any sense. At first light, she slipped her runners on and greeted the rising sun. She needed to clear her head, and what better way to do it than some cardio and fresh air – and this would also be the safest way to go to Wattle Acres, her Land Rover proving yesterday to be too unreliable for her secret mission. There was no way she was going to risk breaking down on that long, dead-end of a road again. And at this time in the morning, it would be very unlikely that Michael would be anywhere near the place, with Cairns being an hour's drive away.

Trying to remain calm and focused, Dolly Parton's 'Silver Threads and Golden Needles' playing from her headphones, Emma slowed her pace to admire the silhouettes of the horses

and cattle backdropped by the pink-hued sky. Sunrises and
sunsets usually captivated her, but today, she didn't have the
luxury of time. Picking up speed again, she headed towards
the hill where she would catch a glimpse of Wattle Acres. Just
the thought of sneaking in there again made beads of sweat
form above her brows and her stomach tighten. If she got
caught, how would she explain herself? She'd just have to ad
lib in the moment. Reaching the crest, she paused, her breath
unusually heavy – her nerves were getting the better of her.
Her gaze locked on Wattle Acres homestead. Strands of loose
hair clung to her sweaty face and she tucked them behind her
ears, her heartbeats frenzied. Jerking the cord lying across her
chest, she freed the headphones, bent over, and tried to catch
her breath, and her nerve.

Not wanting to stay still for too long, for fear of chickening
out, she straightened and pounded the dirt road again, her eyes
fixed on her finishing line – the back door of the homestead. The
key in her pocket felt leaden; the fact she'd kept it all these years
now made perfect sense. So many times she'd gone to throw it
out, but her instincts had told her to hang onto it. Go figure.
Reaching the fence, she made sure to stay in the shadows as she
dashed across the house paddock, through the gate, up the steps
and to the back door. Her hands shook like crazy as she pushed
the key into the lock and quickly slipped inside. Pausing, she
listened for any sounds of life, but other than the ticking of the
grandfather clock, there was none.

Padding down the shadowy hallway, her eyes flicked over
the valuable paintings hanging on the walls. Not one family
photograph was amongst them all – although, with Peter, it
didn't surprise her. Her running shoes were silent on the Persian

rug as she approached his office. As her hand went to take the door handle, men's voices caught her attention. She sucked in a breath, covered her mouth, and stepped back. There hadn't been any cars out front, but why hadn't she checked the garage? Terrified, her instinct was to get the hell out of there, but then curiosity got the better of her. Cautiously, she flattened her back against the wall and pressed her ear in close. Someone was pacing impatiently, his footfalls heavy.

'So, have you found her will yet or the deeds for this place?' Michael's voice was unmistakable.

'I've searched high and low, but nothing. Wherever Kay put it, she's done a damn good job of hiding it.'

Silence fell and footsteps paced once more. Emma picked the other man's nasally voice as Peter's head honcho solicitor – she'd dealt with him a fair bit last year during her divorce, and she knew he was as dirty and shrewd as they came.

'Goddamn it, George, we can't risk it ever being found. The truth about bloody Zane's father being the sole heir to this place has to stay under lock and key, for more reasons than one, as you very well know.'

Emma smothered a gasp. So that's what Zane's father was doing there that night, looking for paperwork to show this place was rightfully his. No wonder Peter was so keen to get rid of the body and demanded she didn't go to the police. All so that he could keep his grimy hands on something that wasn't his to begin with.

'You really need to calm down, Michael, stressing is going to get you nowhere fast.' George's voice was urgent, gruff.

'Sorry, yes, you're right. It's just, not only could it land me in jail, but it would legally show Wattle Acres is Zane's, because he's his deadbeat father's only successor.' Michael huffed. 'It's over my dead body I'm ever going to let that bastard get this place.'

With everything falling into place, Emma's head spun, and the walls felt as if they were closing in on her. She recalled Zane's father down on his knees, feeling around the floor in front of the sink as if he'd dropped something. She'd thought it was a knife, or a gun, but … And then it hit her like a slap to the face. The kickboard below the sink …

'I know it's worrying you, Michael, but there's nothing more I can do, other than tear the place down searching for some paperwork that might not even exist.'

'Oh, I don't doubt for a second that it exists. Mum's will and the deeds were exactly what he would've been here looking for that night it all went down. We're just lucky Emma stumbled in on him, or things could have worked out very differently, for all of us.'

Although frozen to the spot and terrified of being busted in the hallway, Emma felt like barging through the door and punching Michael right where it hurt – the selfish, greedy, son of a bitch.

'Maybe you're right, Michael, who knows? One thing I know for certain, though, is that Peter spent years trying to find where she'd put them, and he came up empty-handed too, so I don't reckon I've got any more of a chance than he did of finding them, and therefore, neither does anyone else.'

'For god's sake, George, as if Dad's death isn't enough for me to deal with right now.'

'I know, but try to take comfort in the fact Peter has covered his tracks, as best he could, of course. There's no reason to not go ahead with the sale of Wattle Acres.'

So he was selling it, although no shock there, Emma thought.

'There's no possible way these fake deeds Peter paid a fortune for will come back to bite me on the arse?'

'Unless the real ones are found, which I really doubt they will be, your arse is safe and sound, Michael.' George chuckled.

'Good, because I've already put an offer of 1.2 million in for a waterfront house in Cairns, and I'm going to be needing the money for it real soon, before someone else snaps it up.' There were more footfalls, followed by a weighty huff. Emma primed herself to run, if need be. 'Just how long are all the legalities going to take?'

'As you of all people know, I have to follow protocol, so we don't raise any red flags. We're a week into the twenty-eight day cooling-off period now, so just three weeks to go.'

Emma breathed a small sigh of relief. At least this gave her some time to try to stop Michael and his shonky deal.

'There's no way to make it go faster?'

'Afraid not, Michael.'

'Even with a substantial bribe.'

'Not when it comes to this.'

'Damn it all to hell.' Michael's voice was becoming louder, his footsteps heavier.

'Look, there's nothing that either of us can do, so just take a deep breath and sit back. The CEO of Zhao Pastoral is keen to get started on the demolition of this place, so they can start building the feedlot before the meddlesome locals of Silvergum have too much time to get up in arms about it all.'

Emma's heart sunk to deeper depths. Demolish the place? Not only would this kill Zane, but it also meant she would have a major corporation as her neighbour, and they obviously didn't give a shit about anyone.

'There's so much at stake, George,' Michael grumbled.

'I know, but everything will work out, you have my word.'

'And they're good for it, the money, I mean?'

'Of course, they're millionaires. I'm not too sure how Emma's going to react, though, when she learns about a feedlot being right next door to her place. The smell alone is going to be hard to cope with, then there's the flies that come with it, and the trucks coming in and out all hours of the day and night.'

'To be honest, I don't give a shit what she thinks, George. It'll be her problem to sort out with the local council – and I'm guessing it's nothing a bit of money passed under the table to the mayor won't fix on Zhao Pastoral's behalf. In the grand scheme of things, she's really got Buckley's of stopping it all unfolding right under her nose.' He laughed sarcastically. 'Excuse the pun.'

Red rage flooded Emma. If she wanted to punch Michael before, she wanted to throttle him with her bare hands now. 'Hate' was a strong word, but she hated him, with every fibre of her being.

George snorted a laugh. 'Very true, when a wad of cash is shoved in the mayor's face, anything is possible, as we know.'

'Damn right. We're lucky he was one of Dad's best mates.'

'Indeed, we are.'

'Thanks for getting this all sorted for me, George. I owe you one.' There was a slap to the back.

'I was your father's confidant for many years, Michael, the keeper of all his secrets, so to speak, and now I'm yours. Of course I have your back, and always will.' He cleared his throat. 'And on that subject, you really shouldn't have pulled that gun out on Zane the other day.'

'Yeah, I know, but he was getting me so damn hot under the collar, the bastard.'

'He might well have been, Michael, but that gun has a history. You don't want to go drawing attention to it.' It was said sternly, almost warningly. 'Why do you still have the bloody thing anyway?'

'There's just something important to me about keeping the weapon that killed Zane's father, even though it was Peter who pulled the trigger.'

Emma choked back a cry. The world slipping out from beneath her feet, she grabbed hold of the wall to stop from slamming to the floor. Bile rose and she swallowed down the need to vomit. All this time, she'd thought it was her fault, had believed Zane's father was dead when she and Zane had been told to go to the bedroom, while Peter and Michael got rid of the body …

'A memento, of sorts.'

'Yes, George, and a reminder of just how far Peter was willing to go to keep this place for me so I could sell it and get ahead in life.' Michael cleared his throat as though emotional. 'Anyway, we better get back to the office to open for the day's business.'

That was Emma's cue to make herself scarce, as quietly as she could. She hightailed it down the hallway, towards Zane's old room – the only place she felt somewhat safe. Her head spun wildly; twice she had to reach out and grab the wall for support, her legs feeling as if they were about to give out beneath her. Blind fury made her tremble and fear swirled in her stomach. Quietly closing the door behind her, she slipped under the bed, taking measured breaths to try to calm her racing pulse. All these years, she'd blamed herself for Zane's father's death, had battled through suffocating pain and guilt. Now she'd discovered that Peter had been the one to end it, while Michael had watched on. Her ex-husband was even more vile than she'd thought. She silently thanked God he wasn't Riley's father. Just how she'd stayed married to such a callous man all those years was beyond her.

Her heart ached for Zane; there was so much he didn't know, and now she was free to tell him. Peter had nothing on her – he'd been blackmailing her all this time for a crime he'd committed. It was no wonder he'd been at the top of his game, being able to lie and cheat so damn easily. She had to make this right, for everyone concerned, and the sooner the better. In three weeks, Wattle Acres would be sold to overseas investors that didn't care about heritage and blood ties, and Zane would miss out on what was rightfully his.

Car doors slammed, followed by the familiar grunt of Michael's Jag starting up. Then she heard the squeal of the garage roller door. The crunch of tyres disappearing was music to her ears, but even so, Emma lay where she was for what seemed like ages, needing to make sure they didn't return for anything they'd forgotten. Then, scrambling out from under the bed, adrenaline flooded her. Racing into the kitchen she dropped to her knees and tried to pull the kickboard out, but she'd lodged it back in so firmly on the day of the funeral that it wasn't moving. Jumping up, she grabbed a knife from the block and used the tip of it to prise the kickboard out of place. After what felt like an hour, but was minutes, she got it to dislodge. Reaching into the darkness, she felt around, stretching her arm as far as she could, dismayed there was nothing. She sat up, staring. Sure it was in there, she wasn't giving up. Lying down, she rolled onto her back and slipped her arm in the opposite way, feeling beneath the cupboard. Right at the back corner, her fingers touched what felt like an envelope. Stifling a cry of joy, she tried to pull it free, but with it taped in place, it was proving difficult. With careful persistence, she finally had it. Sitting up, she stared at it in shock. Ripping the seal open she slid the paperwork out and quickly flicked through. It was Kay's will and the deeds. This was going to change everything.

CHAPTER

20

Needing time to get her head around it all, especially before she told Zane, Emma was glad to see that the spot under the gum tree where he parked his old LandCruiser was empty, and Riley was still sound asleep. Quietly, she went to her bedroom, closed the door, and then rested her forehead against it for a few moments. Everything she'd believed to be true all these years was a lie, a cover-up for Peter and Michael – and she was their scapegoat. How Michael could have kept all this from her, when they'd lived as a married couple, was beyond her comprehension. Fear and shock quickly evolved into red rage. This had gone on way too long – it was time she did the right thing. She had to tell Zane everything she'd just heard. Although, as right as that was, it would be easier said than done.

Sinking to her bed, she placed her phone in her lap and stared at it. Ten numbers. That was all that separated her from the past, and her future. She recited Zane's number, over and over, willing her fingers to move. She had to do this and do it now. Stay calm, ask him to come over, tell him she needed to talk to him. Her stomach clenched into a tight fist as she picked up the phone and pressed one number after the other. Pushing it to her ear she drew in a mammoth breath, every ring like a bomb dropping.

Please go to message bank, please go to message bank.

'Hey, Em.'

'Hey.' Her mouth feeling like it was full of cotton, she couldn't get anything else out.

'I'm just in town, at the post office. You need anything while I'm in here?'

'No, thanks.' She tried to swallow down the nerves.

'I'll be back soon, to give you a hand with the cattle, if you like.'

'Thanks,' she breathed, her voice trembling.

'You don't sound good. Is everything okay?'

'Not really.' She bit back tears.

'What's happened?'

'I'm afraid I can't tell you over the phone.'

'Oh, right, well in that case, I'll be back as soon as I can, okay?'

'Okay, see you soon.' She hung up just as the sobs she'd been fighting off began to fall. She rolled onto her side and pulled her knees to her chest, petrified of what was about to come. This was going to be one of the hardest things she'd ever had to do. First she had to tell Zane about his father, and then tell him he is Riley's father. It all sounded so crazy and felt as if it wasn't really happening to her.

Less than ten minutes later she heard the drone of a diesel engine. Zane must have sped all the way back. Jumping from her bed while wiping at her face, she looked out her window.

He hurried out of the driver's side. His steps were determined, fast, his expression the epitome of concern as he cleared the front steps two at a time. Not wanting to wake Riley, she raced down to meet him at the front door.

'Hey, you must have broken every speed limit to get here this fast.' She tried to smile but failed, miserably.

'Yeah, you could say that.' He sounded worried. 'What's going on, Em? Is Riley okay?'

'Yeah, she's fine.' Moving out beside him, she gestured towards the cottage – she didn't want to be anywhere in hearing range of Riley. 'How about we head over there and grab a spot in the shade to sit.' She didn't wait for him to respond as she strode past him. Zane followed her, and she plonked down on the front steps, placing the envelope in her hand down alongside her.

'What's up?' he said, as he sat next to her.

'So much I don't know where to start.' She felt the blood drain from her face as she caught his anxious gaze. She tried to continue, but the words just wouldn't form in her dry mouth.

'Please, Em, say something, anything. You've got me worried sick.'

She needed to get it out fast, before she really found herself unable to speak. 'The man I found in the homestead kitchen that night, he was ...' Sobs rose and before she knew it, she was unable to get a word past them.

Taking her into his arms, Zane tried his best to soothe her. She felt so wrong, seeking comfort from him right now, yet she couldn't help but melt into his tender embrace.

'He wasn't some thug from the Mafia, he was your father ...' she breathed against his chest.

His body went rigid. His hands going to her shoulders, he pressed her back and looked deep into her eyes. 'What did you just say?'

'He was your father, Zane.'

He shook his head. 'You're not making any sense.'

Her pulse was racing so fast she could barely breathe. 'Kay adopted you when he …' She stammered. 'When he went to jail for killing your mother.'

His face pale, Zane shot to standing and took faltering steps away from her. 'What the hell, Em? Is this some sort of sick joke?'

She shook her head. 'As if I would joke about something like this.'

Looking like he might pass out, he sunk down to the floor and sat on his heels, his hands rubbing his face. 'Who else knows about this?'

She bit her lip.

'Who?' His voice was an angry hiss.

'Michael, and George, and Peter did too.' She tried to clear the lump from her throat. 'And there's more to it.'

Zane stared at her in disbelief.

'When I pushed him and he hit his head, it's not what killed him.' She sucked in a shaky breath. 'Peter shot him when they took him wherever they did afterwards.'

'Peter shot my father?' Zane shook his head. 'But why?'

'Because when Kay passed away, he was the sole heir to Wattle Acres, and Peter didn't want him getting his hands on it.' Emma saw that Zane was looking confused and distraught, so she went on. 'That's what he was doing in the house that night, looking for evidence.'

He just nodded, seemingly unable to speak.

She passed the envelope over. 'I gather he was looking for this.'

Zane snatched it and pulling the paperwork out, unfolded it. 'Mum's will,' he said, his voice shaking, 'and the deeds for Wattle Acres.' He looked back up at Emma. 'But how do you have it?'

'I found it this morning, behind a kickboard in the kitchen at Wattle Acres.'

'Is that why you went over there yesterday, to try to find this?' He waved it towards her.

'Not really, but it just panned out that way.'

'What were you looking for then?' His sharp gaze sliced through her.

'Peter had said, in the letter you brought to me, that he had evidence of what I did that night, in his safe. I wanted to try and open it and see what that evidence was. He said he would use it against me, if he had to. The lying bastard.'

Zane's fierce gaze softened, but only a little. 'Why didn't you tell me?'

Emma sucked in a shaky breath. 'I thought you had enough on your plate.'

'But why would he blackmail you with something like that? He had no reason to?'

Wanting to give Zane time to come to terms with the bombshell she'd just dropped about his father, she wasn't ready to tell him about Riley. So she shrugged. 'I have no idea.'

His expression told her he wasn't buying it. 'How did you know about this then?' He held up the paperwork.

'When I went back there this morning, to try and get into the safe, Michael and George were there. I overheard them talking about that night, and how Peter had pulled the trigger on some gun Michael pulled on you—' She was going to ask Zane when this had happened, but he cut her off.

'Holy shit, so that was the gun used to kill my father?'

Emma nodded. 'Apparently, and they were also talking about some overseas livestock company that's going to buy Wattle Acres and turn it into a feedlot.'

Zane's eyes narrowing, his nostrils flared like a bull about to charge. 'Over my dead body.' His jaw clenched as he stood and began to pace. 'My mother's ashes are there, in those paddocks.'

'I know.' Her words were a mere whisper. Silence hung between them before she found the strength to speak again. 'We're going to have to go to the police with what we know.' She pointed to the paperwork now clasped between his hands, his eyes upon it once more. 'We have to prove your father is dead for you to be in line to inherit Wattle Acres.'

'For Christ's sake, this just gets better and better.' He drew in a deep breath and then huffed it away. 'We can't go to the police until after Riley's deb ball ... she's been counting down the days. I can't let this upset her big night.'

'Yes, I agree. I don't want to ruin it for her with all this.' Emma sniffed back tears.

'Well at least you finally know you weren't the killer.'

'Yes, it is a relief.' She stood and went to comfort him.

Zane shook his head 'Don't.' He stormed towards the steps. 'I think it's best if you just leave me alone. I need some time to get my head around all of this, or I might say something I regret.'

Helpless to stop him, she sunk down into the swing chair and watched him stride across the front lawn. The slam of the cottage door behind him made her jump. 'I'm so sorry,' she whispered, as the heavy tears she'd been fighting back streamed down her cheeks.

And yet, he still didn't know everything.

CHAPTER
21

The small boom box Zane had found in the shed while searching for tools was now on the driver's seat, the car door wide open and the sound up loud. He liked having music playing while he was working – just as long as it was country or seventies rock. It helped him to tune out everything else and stay somewhat sane. And by Christ, he needed to tune out of the mess he was in right now, before he lost his mind.

The classic Highway Men song carrying him away, he got to work fixing the gaping hole in the top paddock's fence. Emma's prized bull was chewing his cud and eyeing him as if he were about to be a victim to his deadly horns. The one-tonne brute wasn't happy Zane had caught him in the act of trying to escape into the scrub; the bull bar of the old LandCruiser came in very handy for a careful nudge. Having been out repairing the fence since dawn, it was pure luck he'd been in the right place at the right time. God help the damn bull if he tried to charge him – he wasn't in the mood for any more bullshit.

One eye on the job and the other on his opponent, Zane cautiously watched the bull take a few steps towards him, then paw the ground and snort. 'Go on then, you cantankerous old bastard, I bloody dare you to try it again,' he called out, shaking his head. It felt good to yell at something, even if the animal really didn't understand a word he was saying.

The fence stretcher now in place, he crimped the two broken pieces of barbed wire together with a splice – three down and now one section to go. Pausing, he wiped the beads of sweat from his forehead. It was stiflingly hot and humid, and although he was covered in dust from head to toe, he was loving every minute of feeling downright dirty and sweaty. A hard day's yakka had never hurt anyone, and it was helping take his mind off the bombshell Emma had dropped in his lap yesterday. So far out of left field, he was still struggling to get his head around it all, and his sleepless night didn't help any. It was going to take time, and plenty of it. He knew the shock of it all would eventually ease – but for now, it felt overwhelmingly raw. He also understood it was his choice whether he held onto the anguish or not. His Aunty Kay would always be his mother; and knowing now that his father had killed his biological mother in cold blood made him glad he never met the bastard. Zane probably would have shot him dead himself, if Peter hadn't, but for very different reasons. Greed would've had nothing to do with it.

He heaved a weary sigh. The whole damn thing was a crazy mess, the stuff movies were made of, and the harsh reality of it was, this was his goddamn life. Go figure. At the very least, he now understood the icy chasm Peter had created between them. Zane never had a hope in hell of making it across. Amidst the madness of it all, things now made perfect sense, and in a bizarre way, it gave him a feeling of peace that Peter hadn't simply hated him for the man he'd become or the career path he'd chosen. It ran way deeper than that. No matter what he'd done, or tried to do, he never would have been good enough in Peter's eyes.

Momentarily losing focus, he winced as he bumped his swollen knuckles against the stake holding the fence in place; his hand was already tender after punching the brick wall of the stables. It was that or Michael's jaw. He was glad he hadn't chosen the latter, needing to do this right if he wanted to rip the rug out from under the immoral man before he had the chance to cover his tracks. Zane wouldn't put it past the dirty mug to try to pull some strings, and he wasn't going to risk giving him a head start. Wattle Acres was rightly his, and he would make it so – the very thought made his heavy heart a little lighter. But first things first; he and Emma needed to go to the police after Riley's big night and tell them everything in a formal statement. Then he needed to find an out-of-town solicitor to take on his case – someone unknown to Michael and Peter, but who had the skills to be ruthless in the courtroom.

Job done, he double-checked that the fence was as bull-proof as possible with a few firm shoves. Groaning as he stood, he wandered towards the LandCruiser and put the tools in the back. Emma's distraught expression as she'd told him everything filled his mind again. He hated seeing her so upset, and knew, deep down, none of this was her fault. He should be rejoicing in the fact she hadn't been the cause of his father's death, and thankful she'd come to him straight away with what she'd heard. If she'd kept it from him, for whatever reason, that would have been a different story. Annoyed at himself for giving her the silent treatment and feeling like a bastard for holding a grudge, he decided to apologise for his reaction, before Riley's deb ball tonight. Bad blood between them was the last thing he wanted.

Packing the last of the tools into the tray, the rumble of Emma's Land Rover grew louder as it climbed the crest. Leaning against the back tray, he watched her drive over to him and climb out, offering her a smile as she did. He could hear the hammer of his heart, caused not only by his need to apologise, but also by how captivating she was. 'Hey, Em.'

Emma matched his smile. 'Hey, you, just thought you might like a bit of lunch.' She passed him a brown paper bag. 'I guessed you probably haven't eaten anything yet.' Her eyes were filled with so much sorrow it split his already broken heart even more.

'Oh, thanks, you didn't have to.' He peeked inside and his mouth instantly watered.

'Homemade corned beef with tomato, onion and pickles on fresh sourdough – just how you like it.' She shoved her hands in the pockets of her denim shorts.

'Sounds like someone after my own heart.' Questioning his poor choice of words, he quickly laughed off his comment. 'Is this your idea of trying to win me over?'

'Maybe, maybe not,' she said a little guardedly. 'See it as a peace offering ...' She shrugged. 'Lame, I know, but I couldn't think of anything else.' She looked down at her feet. 'I'm so sorry I had to be the bearer of bad news, Zane, and I understand you being upset with me.'

'It's not your fault, Em.' He closed the distance and pulled her into his arms. 'I'm sorry I reacted like I did. I was just shocked, that's all.'

'You had every right to be shocked, and mad, and ...' She sniffled against his chest.

'Please don't beat yourself up, I'm not mad at you.'

She glanced up at him. 'So we're good?'

'Damn straight we are.' He hugged her a little tighter.

'Oh, thank god.' She released a heavy breath. 'I know we've got some yucky stuff ahead, like having to go to the police so Wattle Acres can be given to its rightful owner ...'

'Oh, and just who might that be?'

She slapped him on the arm. 'You're a shit stirrer.'

'And I'm getting a wooden spoon at Christmas to prove it.' He chuckled. 'How cool is it that we're going to be neighbours?'

She folded her arms. 'Does this mean you're going to hang around here now?'

'Of course it does.'

'Good.'

'Just good?'

'Hmm ...' She smiled softy. 'How's about great?'

'Great works for me.' He couldn't help but flirt with her; there was just something about being near her that made his heart and soul fire on all cylinders. 'So, tonight's the night then, huh?'

'For what.' She looked shocked, her cheeks suddenly a bright shade of red.

A fair idea of what she was thinking, he bit back a laugh. 'Riley's deb ball.'

'Oh, yeah, I'm going to be a blithering mess when I see her all dressed up, I just know it.'

'I'd say I'll shed a quiet tear, too.'

'You will not.'

He chuckled. 'I reckon I probably will.'

She smiled now, making his heart sing. 'Are you going to be okay, being near Michael tonight?'

'I'll just have to be.'

'You sure you won't snap?'

'Don't worry, I'm not going to do anything to ruin Riley's night.'

She bit her lip and nodded. 'Thanks.'

'Don't mention it.'

Changing the subject, she gestured to the paddock with a nod of her head. 'Ted tried to escape again, did he?'

'Sure did.'

'Bad boy,' she called out, shaking her head as though telling off an unruly child. 'Thanks for stopping him and fixing up his mess.'

'Pleasure.'

She looked at her watch. 'Well, I'll let you get back to it. I need to get home before the hairdresser and beautician arrive. Riley's having an up do and her nails and make-up done, and she wants me to get the works too.' She rolled her eyes. 'Not that I'm one for all the fuss, but I'll do it for her sake, just this once.'

'It'll be nice for you to be pampered. You're gonna knock the socks off all the blokes there tonight, I bet.'

'Oh, stop it,' she said with a laugh.

'True shit.'

'You're such a charmer, Zane.'

'I do my best. Thanks for the sanga.'

'Pleasure.' Sauntering back to her Land Rover, she gave him a wave. 'Catch ya.'

'Oo-roo.' Zane couldn't tear his eyes from her butt. What he'd give to grasp it as he made sweet love to her again.

* * *

Emma bit back a fresh flood of tears as she watched Riley emerge from her room; her turquoise ankle-length dress with the lace bodice was perfect. 'Oh, love, you look ...' She sniffled, wiping an escapee tear. 'Absolutely stunning. The colour brings out your eyes.'

'Stop it, Mum, or you're going to make me cry.'

Not wanting to smudge her mascara, Emma carefully wiped under her eyes with a tissue. 'Sorry, love, I can't help it, I'm a big sook.'

'That makes two of us.' Riley looked her up and down. 'That dress is smoking hot, Mum, I'm so glad you ended up buying it.'

'Thanks, sweetheart, I do love it, but I'm a bit worried what people are going to think of me in it.'

'Why?'

'Well, there's not a lot of it.' Emma tried to peer over her shoulder at the low-cut back. 'And the fact I'm not able to wear a bra feels a little risqué.'

'Just own it, Mum, and to hell with what anyone else thinks. The other mothers will just be jealous that you look so hot and their husbands can't stop gawking at you.'

Emma rolled her eyes and chuckled. 'I wouldn't go that far, but thanks for the vote of confidence.'

'Anytime.' Riley cautiously touched the boho-style twist of hair arranged at the nape of her neck. 'With the amount of bobby pins the hairdresser put in, I reckon I'm going to be finding them for the next two months.'

'I know ...' Emma touched the barrel curls cascading over her left shoulder. 'And don't even get me started on the amount of hairspray she used – the woman almost gassed me to death.'

'Ha-ha, yeah, she did use a lot, huh?' The rumble of a V8 made her stop and listen. 'Sounds like he's here,' Riley said a little nervously.

Emma took her by the hands. 'Deep breaths.' She smiled. 'I thought you didn't like him in that way.'

'I don't.' The look on Riley's face before she spun away and raced down the stairs told Emma she was lying through her teeth.

Quietly rejoicing, she followed Riley out the front door.

'Hi, Ms Kensington.' James Jones blushed from the roots of his copper red hair, all the way through to his freckle-scattered cheeks as he turned his attention to Riley. 'Wow, Riles, you look, amazing.'

'Thank you, and you're looking very handsome in your suit.'

'Cheers.' James beamed from ear to ear. 'I don't scrub up too bad, huh.'

Running in to get her phone from the entrance table, Emma came back out and held it up. 'Can I get a photo before you two go?'

'Oh, Mum, do we have to?'

'Yes, you do.' She smiled. 'You'll thank me, one day in the far-flung future, for making you do such a horrid thing.'

Shuffling in beside each other, James seemed to blush even brighter. Emma quickly took a few shots before Riley all but dragged him down the steps. 'Bye, Mum.'

'Bye, Ms Kensington,' James called over his shoulder.

'Bye,' Emma said. 'See you there, you two.'

'Okay, Mum,' Riley called out as laughter carried across the lawn.

'Did you have to go and get this thing jacked up so high?' Riley said as James opened the door of his beefed-up LandCruiser, and helped her up and in.

Clearly amused, James mumbled something in reply as he closed the door behind her.

'You know I don't understand a damn thing when you start talking truck lingo, right?' Riley called out the window.

Leaning against the verandah rail, Emma waved them off, smiling at their playful banter. They reminded her so much of Zane and her years ago. Young love was so sweet, and they didn't even know it yet. Hopefully, in their case, history wouldn't repeat itself and they'd figure it out before it was too late. The deep rumble of the exhaust echoed across the paddocks and through the house as she stepped back inside. Catching her reflection in the hallway mirror she stopped and stared. Although she'd probably spend most of the night checking and double-checking that not too much of her cleavage was showing, the knee-length silky dress *did* make her feel super sexy. She couldn't help but wonder what Zane was going to think when he saw her. Should she go over to the cottage and invite him to catch a ride with her? She'd been so nervous when she'd gone up to the top paddock to take him his lunch today, she hadn't even thought to ask how he was getting there. It made sense, though, that they went together.

Picking up her clutch-bag and keys from the bowl, she gave the bodice of her dress one final tug to make sure everything was staying put, which it was, for now, and then headed out the front door. Tiny leapt to action and went to barrel over to her, but she quickly and firmly told him to stay put. She didn't want him to come anywhere near her dress as he'd been rolling in something very smelly this afternoon. Skidding to a stop just shy of her, with his tail between his legs, Tiny turned and wandered back to his bed, his head so low to the floor he was almost dragging his bottom lip along it. She laughed and decided that he would be getting a bath tomorrow. Then he could have all the affection he longed for and deserved.

Her heels clip-clopping across the verandah, she caught Zane's heady scent – a mix of spice, leather and testosterone. Looking up, she felt her jaw drop, but then quickly snapped it shut. Black jeans, an electric blue shirt, jacket, and his going-to-town cowboy boots on, he was absolutely, unequivocally, drool worthy. 'Oh wow, you look …' She took a quick breath. 'Very fetching.'

'Why thank ya, Em, and you look …' The tilt of his head and the mischievous smile on his lips let her know he liked what he saw. 'Breathtaking.'

Her cheeks flamed, and she felt like a teenager beneath his blazing blue eyes. 'You want to catch a lift with me, seeing as we're going the same way?'

'I was just about to offer the same thing.'

'Great minds think alike.'

'They most certainly do.' He reached out and brushed a hand down her arm, leaving a trail of heat. 'Put your keys away, I'll drive.'

She hesitated, and then tossed the keys into her bag. 'Okay, thanks.'

Stepping in front of her, he went to open the passenger door, while she observed the play of his back muscles and the tautness of his sleeves around his biceps. He was so damn yummy.

Flinging the door open, he waved his arm in to welcome her.

She walked past him, noticing how she had emphasised the sway of her hips as she did. He made her feel so womanly, it was entrancing, invigorating. 'It's good to see chivalry isn't dead,' she purred.

'Not with me, it's not, Em.' He closed the door and leant on the window. 'I'm old school.'

Oh, how she ached to kiss him, from his desirable lips all the way down to his … stop, she silently screamed as she watched him walk around the front of the four-wheel drive, climb in and then rev it to life.

* * *

So beautiful were the hundreds of hanging snowflakes, fairy lights and wide ribbons of white satin draped from the ceiling that Emma found herself completely enthralled, by them and the fact she was wrapped in the arms of the most handsome and charming man there. In what felt like the blink of an eye, the formalities of the evening were over and she and Zane were arm in arm, dancing beside Riley and James, with Michael giving them the evil eye over the shoulder of his young lover. Not caring what he thought, or the handful of women who were looking at her with envy, and proud of Zane, who had stuck to his word, albeit his hands clenching into fists beneath the table while the three-course meal had been served, she felt on top of the world.

'Riley seems so happy,' Zane whispered in her ear.

Emma looked to where James and Riley were gliding around the dance floor. He looked proud as punch holding Riley in his arms. 'She does, hey.'

Zane's fingers gently stroked the bare skin of her lower back. 'They'd make a cute couple.'

His touch doing insane things to her libido, she ached to tear every inch of clothing from him, right here, right now. 'They would,' she said. 'I've tried to encourage it, but Riley's hell bent on them being just friends.'

'Sounds strangely familiar.' The look on Zane's face spoke a thousand words. 'Speaking of which, let's get out of here,' he said with a cheeky grin.

'Is that your try on a pick-up line?'

'Maybe.'

'Well, in that case …' She moved a little closer to him; the three glasses of red wine she'd enjoyed gave her an edge she normally wouldn't dare let him see. 'I'm ready if you are.'

Allowing him to take her by the hand, they hurried towards the back door of the hall and into the privacy of night. Weaving through parked cars and four-wheel drives, they headed to a dark corner of the paddock and finally reached Zane's LandCruiser parked under a towering gum tree.

Jumping up, she sat on the back tray, her legs swinging to and fro while staring into the starlit sky, feeling soothed, calm … and suddenly rather drunk. 'There's nothing quite like a country night sky, huh?'

'Damn straight, Em.' Zane remained standing, his perfect arse leaning against the tray beside her and his arms crossed over his chest. 'Give me this over a city skyline any day.'

'Ditto,' she said, as a breeze whipped up, sending a scattering of leaves falling from the tree above. Wrapping her arms around herself she shivered. 'Far out, it's cold out here.'

'Here, this will help keep you warm, you tropical-blooded woman.' He chuckled, deep and husky, as he took his jacket off and handed it to her. She wrapped it around her shoulders, still shivering. He took her by the hand. 'Oh, Em, you're shaking like a leaf,' he said against her temple as he pulled her to him. 'Better?'

She nodded. It felt better than better. It felt so right, as if this was exactly where she was supposed to be, and not only for now.

'Good.' He pressed her closer, his touch filling her with warmth.

Looking at him from under her fake lashes, ones she couldn't wait to take off, she offered a small smile, hoping it looked a hell of a lot braver than she felt inside. 'Thanks, Zane.'

'What for?'

'Just being you.' She cleared her throat, the flutters in her belly going into overdrive. Goddamn it, why couldn't she find it in herself to tell him the truth right this very second, and not only about her feelings for him?

'I'm me because of you.' Capturing her gaze, his hand found the small of her back and urged her even closer. His suggestive smile tempted the dimples that made him appear even more wayward and made her want him all the more.

'You're too sweet.' She knew it was wrong of her, but how was she meant to resist a man who had such a kind and loving heart beneath his armour? A heart, she truly believed, only she knew held so much love and passion. With trembling fingers, she reached out and traced his lips, ran them over the dark stubble on his chin. 'I really want to kiss you.' The words left her lips before she'd had time to stop them.

He gave her a slow, considering gaze. 'Ditto.'

Her lips tingled and her heart felt as if it were just about to beat its way out of her chest. Silence hanging between them, she drew in a shuddering breath, and then another.

Zane took her hand and gently kissed the tip of each of her fingers, his eyes never leaving hers.

Her voice of reason was screaming to stop. 'Zane ...'

'Shhhhh …' His breath was a soft caress against her neck as his hands slid up her back. His fingers tangled in her hair and he brought his lips close to hers.

Her willpower all but disappeared. Wrapping her arms around his neck and her legs around his waist, she closed the gap between them. The moment their lips met, time stumbled, stalled and rewound. He silenced her uncertainties by kissing her, hot and heavy, demanding and possessive, stealing her sense of what was right and wrong. It was as mind-blowing as she remembered, maybe even more so. His kiss caressed her soul and set her heart on fire. She returned it passionately – hard and urgent. Moaning against his hungry mouth she felt his breath catch in his chest as she silently begged him to make love to her. But even as he whispered his longing for her against her lips, while his hand slipped beneath her dress and skated up to tease her nipples, she knew she shouldn't be doing this. It wasn't right. It wasn't fair to him. She had to stop. Now. But how was that even possible when he felt so damn good, so damn right? She was in his arms where she was meant to be. But she didn't deserve the pleasure of it, of him. Not now. Not ever.

'Zane, we can't.' Somehow she found the strength to pull away, only barely able to drag her lips from his. It took every bit of willpower to lean back and look into his eyes, his baby-blues burning with a desperate, fiery need that rivalled her own.

'Oh yes we can …' he coaxed, his voice rough with desire. 'You're a single woman now.'

A pang of longing hit her chest. Breathless, she almost tumbled back into him. But if she buckled, she would hate herself even more than she already did by letting it get this far. 'I'm sorry.' Her voice so soft it was almost silent.

Groaning, he pushed away from her, turning his face into the shadows. Not wanting to bear witness to his hurt, she was glad for the small reprieve. She could hear his breath, short and laboured.

'We can't do this again, Zane. It's not right.' Even so, her body still ached for his touch like the desert yearned for rain.

He spun to face her, the hurt in his eyes tearing her to pieces. 'Not right? Are you serious, Em? We're more than just friends, and this isn't about a one-night fling. And as much as you want to deny this, deny us, I know you feel it too.'

Lost for words, she just gazed at him, her mouth open.

He raked his hand through his hair. 'Goddamn it, you don't get it, do you?'

'Get what?'

He stared at her for a long moment. 'Just forget it.' He huffed and shook his head. 'It doesn't matter.'

'If you knew the real me, I have a feeling you might not be so keen.' She jumped from the tray and took a tentative step towards him, went to reach for him. But grabbing her gently by the wrists, he stopped her.

'What do you mean, if I knew the real you?' He eyed her cynically. 'Because I think I'm the only person that walks this earth that knows the *real* you.'

'There is something about me you don't know.'

'What kind of thing?' His voice was stronger now, almost angry as he took a step back from her.

She remained silent.

'For god's sake, Em, we all keep secrets about ourselves, that's only human. I know all I need to know to—' He slammed his mouth shut.

Was he just about to say 'love you'? Her heart pounded with the thought. If she was being completely honest with herself, she could so very easily say it to him too. But that would be selfish of her. She wished she could fill in the blanks for him, tell him about Riley, but not now, not like this. 'I think I better go back inside.'

'You're not going to talk about it?' The pain on his face sliced through her. 'You can't just say something like that and then leave me hanging.'

If she didn't walk away now, she would make rash promises she wouldn't be able to keep. 'Tomorrow, Zane, please, let's talk about it all when we're sober.'

Glaring at her, he shook his head. 'Yeah, righto.'

'I'm going to go back inside. You coming?'

'No, not like this. I don't want Riley to see me angry again,' he said. 'You want me to wait out here for you, to give you a lift home?'

'No, you go, I'll get a lift with James and Riley.' She choked back a sob. 'Are you right to drive?'

'I've only had four beers, and we've been here for almost five hours, so yeah, I'm right.'

'Okay, I'll see you back at Serendipity then.'

Without another word, he turned and strode towards the driver's side, jumped in and slammed the door shut. Emma all but ran back towards the hall, not wanting to watch him drive away. She blinked back hot tears, telling herself over and over that this was Riley's night and she wasn't about to ruin it with her dramas. Later, when she was alone, in bed, she would cry herself to sleep. But for now, she was going to put on a brave face and make sure her daughter enjoyed the night with a happy heart.

CHAPTER
22

Tiny was curled up as much as a sixty-five kilogram dog could be at Emma's feet, and Kat was pacing back and forth on the bench purring as Emma stroked her soft coat. Savouring the last of her extra-strong coffee, she stood at the kitchen window, staring out into the night, towards the cottage. Zane's LandCruiser was parked out front, so she knew he was inside. No lights were on but that didn't mean he was sleeping. Sighing, she pressed the palms of her hands to her eyes, begging her mind to stop torturing her with *what ifs* and *maybes*. Resolutely, she swallowed back the knot of emotion in her throat. She couldn't wait another five hours to talk to him. Grabbing her mobile from the bench, she grimaced as the screen shone to blinding life, and quickly dialled his number before she chickened out, hoping to God he was up pacing the hallways like she was, and not dead to the world.

'Hey.' Zane's voice was husky with sleep, or heartache, she wasn't sure.

'Hey, sorry to wake you.'

'All good, I wasn't asleep anyway. You okay?'

'Not really.' Her heart was drumming and her mouth was parched. 'Can I come over?'

'Right now?'

'Uh-huh.'

'You know it's two in the morning?'

'Yup, sorry, but this can't wait.'

'Okay, door's unlocked.'

'Thanks, see you in a sec.'

Less than a minute later, she was sitting facing him, at the end of his bed, her heart in her throat and her mouth as dry as a desert. She wished she could forget about everything and just climb beneath the sheets and snuggle against his burly, bare chest. She knew, with his arms wrapped tightly around her, it was a marvellous place to be.

'So ...' she said, and then stalled.

'So,' he echoed.

She tried to continue, but simply couldn't.

'I'll go first then.' Propped up on his pillows with his back resting against the wall, the soft lamplight fell across his face, softening his chiselled features. 'I'm really sorry about before, Em. Normally I'm so restrained, but with you ...' He closed his eyes and shook his head, the smile on his face slow and sexy. 'You just make me want to do things I shouldn't, through no fault of your own.'

She shifted restlessly, his searching gaze making her falter. Her breath was trapped in her throat as she wrung her hands together. 'You do crazy things to me, too. It's just, well, I feel like it's wrong of me to let you.' She pulled her knees to her chest and wrapped her arms around them, releasing a long-held sigh to try to calm herself.

'Why would you think that?'

'Because ...' She tried to choke back a sob but failed.

'Em, don't. You know what it does to me when I see you cry.' He reached over and pulled her to him. 'You should know by now that anything you have to tell me, I'll come to terms with, no matter how bad or messed up it is.' He moved back, placed a finger beneath her chin and tipped her face to his. 'I'm just going to say it like it is. I love you, Em. I always have and forever will, no matter what, and nothing's ever going to change that.'

Then, without warning, he captured her lips with his and she surrendered to him in a moment of utter weakness. Desperately wanting to tell him how much she loved him, too, but feeling she wasn't entitled to, she begrudgingly pulled away before the kiss led to so much more. 'Zane ... I—'

He silenced her with a gentle finger to her lips, sending a delicious spark of fire through her. His gaze was hot with promise. 'Not now, whatever it is, I don't want it to take away this moment, because there's been too many of them taken from us in the past. We'll talk in the morning.' Removing the elastic band around her ponytail, her hair spilled over her shoulders and halfway down her back. 'I've always loved it wild and free, like you.'

Before she could respond, or slap some sense into herself, he kissed her again, stealing her breath and her thoughts, drawing her to him, enfolding her in his protective arms. The warmth of his embrace flooded through her like whisky on a cold winter's night. Every inch of her was suddenly alive, electric – *he* was where she belonged. She twined her arms around his neck and threw herself to him recklessly – he was right, to hell with everything else.

In a hot, fevered rush, his fingers skated up her spine and then flicked the silky straps from her shoulders. The black camisole dropped to her waist, revealing her breasts. His gaze was greedy as he drunk her in. Then, as if reading her mind, his hands cupped them and he brought his searing-hot mouth to her nipples, biting, licking and sucking them until she was in an erotic trance, the simultaneous sensation of pain and pleasure mind-blowing. She groaned and moaned, and he muttered something low and raspy in response.

While sending her to dizzying heights, he flipped her over and pinned her down by holding her hands on either side of her head. Her heart pounding wildly, she stared up at the man who owned her heart, and he looked down at her as if she was his world. Fingers laced together, he ran his lips down the side of her neck, biting and kissing along the way, sliding lower and lower. Pausing at her navel, he slipped his fingers under the band of her silky shorts, his hot breath lingering on her skin. She shut her eyes in anticipation as he eased them over her hips and down her legs. Using her feet, she kicked them off just as he brought his mouth to her in teasing, tongue-twirling caresses that had her gripping the sheets and crying out. Wanting to reach the peaks of shivering heights, she arched in to him, but the higher her hips rose from the bed, the more he pulled back, just enough that it was only the tip of his tongue stroking her, circling her, tasting her.

And just when she thought she couldn't take any more, he grabbed her arse and pushed his tongue inside of her, his mouth coming down to take all of her in. She shuddered as she ran her fingers through his hair and pressed him in harder. Teetering on the edge for a few blissful moments, she then went into freefall, unable to breathe as she came harder than she'd ever come before. He groaned as he felt her tremble, quiver and then release, his tongue savouring all of her as she did.

With her sated, for now, he slid back up to kiss her and her hunger roared out of control. Her fingers were clumsy with haste as she tugged his boxers off, enough for him to wriggle free of their constraints. His tongue circled hers in a wild dance of desire as she wrapped her legs around him tight. The hardness of his long, thick erection pressed against her, making her ache for him to be at one with her.

'Please, Zane, I want you inside me.' She was brazenly begging, and she didn't care.

'How much do you want me?' He breathed heavily, his slow smile wickedly sexy as his hand slid between her legs, his fingers skilfully massaging her.

'Bad, really, *really*, bad.'

'Good, that's what I want to hear.'

Taking the tip, he rubbed it up and down, flirtatiously sliding just a little within, making her writhe beneath him. Then, when she cried out for him to take her, inch by glorious inch he slowly slid inside.

Emma gasped for air, then moaned as he pulled all the way out and then crashed back inside her, pausing to kiss her before doing it again and again. She loved the weight of him above her, loved how her mind went blank each and every time, loved the anticipation of him sliding back deep within her, over and over, harder and harder. The way he filled her so perfectly was exquisite. She found it hard to draw a breath. They moved in time together, slowly at first, gradually building to their crescendo – their hips pounding one another's. She felt so safe, so happy, so … deeply, head-over-heels in love. He was magnificent in every single way, so how could she not? She'd never wanted any other man like she wanted him, and never would.

Zane pushed himself even deeper, faster. The heat between them built, and his body tensed, hardened, trembled. She could feel herself starting to climb again, while the sensation that drove her to the edge and back in breathless coils enveloped her. Stars exploded behind her eyelids and fireworks erupted within. Then euphoria claimed them, together, as they tumbled into ecstasy. Panting and moaning, they clung to each other. Spent and gasping, they collapsed, their breathing slowly returning to normal, as they left not an inch between them.

Propped up on his elbows, so he didn't crush her beneath his weight, Zane eventually rolled onto his side, taking Emma with him in his arms. 'Wow, Em, you're one hell of a woman.' His eyes met hers. 'And now I've got you, I don't ever want to let you go.'

Unable to speak for fear of breaking down, Emma kissed his jawline, his neck, his cheek, as his fingers skilfully feathered over her back, enticing goosebumps. He filled a void deep down in her soul, one nobody else had ever been able to fill. Resting her head against his chest, she snuggled into him and closed her eyes. She wanted to savour this moment, to memorise every kiss, touch, stroke and gasp, knowing very well that it may be their last, because come tomorrow, she was going to tell him everything.

* * *

A sliver of light stirred Emma. Bolting upright, she took in her surroundings. The familiarity of the cottage both soothed and concerned her, as did the muscular arm draped over her stomach. She shouldn't be here, naked, in Zane's bed. She pulled the covers up against her neck and sank against the pillow, desperately trying to avoid staring at his deliciously muscled abs leading right down to a very desirable part of his body. It would be so nice to put her head against that big, strong, broad chest of his and tell him everything, including just how much she loved him. But first, she needed to get home and changed, before Riley caught them doing things they shouldn't be.

As if feeling her gaze upon him, Zane stirred and his eyes met hers in sleepy, heavy lidded contemplation. 'Hey there, gorgeous … fancy seeing you here.' A slow and sexy smile dangled from the corners of his oh-so-kissable lips. 'I'm one very lucky man, waking up to such a beautiful sight.' Taking her hand, he entwined her fingers within his.

'Morning.' She offered him a smile, hoping he didn't see her lips trembling.

It was all so intense, so real, so overwhelming, in the light of day. What was she going to tell Riley if she busted her sneaking back into the cottage in her silky pyjamas, looking all dishevelled? Good god, she hoped Riley was still sound asleep. So many scenarios played out in her mind, and her heart hammered in response as her throat tightened. Suddenly she thought she was about to have a full-blown panic attack.

Zane's smile faltered. 'You okay, Em?'

'Yeah, sorry.' She swallowed down hard, shaking her head. 'This is just a little overwhelming, that's all.'

'I hope you mean in a good way.' He sat up, resting on his elbow. 'So what was it you came over here to tell me?'

'Oh, it's not really important right now.' She shrugged, hoping it appeared nonchalant. 'I better get back home before Riley wakes up and wonders where I am.' She dragged in a deep breath, desperately trying to catch it.

'So, even though it was crucial that we talk about it at two this morning, it's not now?' His piercing blue eyes held hers for a long moment before she had to look away, the ache inside her so strong she had to stifle a moan of despair.

'No, it's still very important.' She wished to god she were anywhere but here right now, about to deal a crushing blow to what could've been a romantic, love-filled morning.

'Uh-huh.' The questions in his eyes, and the doubts, were devastating. 'Well then, there's no time like now, so spill, Em.' He glanced in the direction of the main house. 'If Riley wakes up before you go back home, you can just tell her you popped over for a cuppa … she's not going to suspect a thing. It's your guilty mind that's making you believe she will.'

Her guilty mind! He had no idea just how guilt-ridden it was. He was right, though, she had to tell him everything before she walked out the door. Taking another desperate breath, she clung to a very small reed of hope that maybe, just maybe, he'd be so happy about Riley being his daughter he would forgive her for keeping it from him all these years. 'I'm so afraid you're never going to be able to forgive me for what I'm about to tell you.' Tears were spilling down her cheeks and she let them fall. Zane went to comfort her, but she recoiled. 'Please, don't. Trust me, I don't deserve your comfort.'

'I can't believe there's anything more shocking than telling me Peter killed my father.' His words were tense.

'In a way, it will be.' Grabbing her pyjamas from the floor, she climbed out of bed and quickly tugged them on. Shifting from foot to foot, she wrapped her arms around herself. 'I just hope that you can find it in yourself to see the good of it, and not hate me.'

'Try me.' He stepped from the bed, naked before tugging on his boxers.

Now she was standing on one side of the bed they'd made such sweet love in, and he was on the other. The atmosphere was suddenly heavy. Desperately, she tried to find the right words. She knew it was probably best, for both of them, if she didn't beat around the bush. 'Riley's your daughter.' Rigid with tension, she waited for his reaction.

Looking as if he were about to pass out, Zane leant back against the wall and crossed the arms that had given her so much solace over the years. The silence was excruciatingly long, the hurt in his eyes profound. He shook his head as though trying to make sense of it. 'Riley's my daughter?' He said it like he didn't believe it.

'Yes.'

'Does she know?'

'No, of course not. I thought I should tell you first, and then we could maybe tell her together?'

'I can't believe you've kept this from me, and from her.' The look of disappointment in his eyes tore her to shreds. 'How could you?'

She stared at him for a long moment, at the genuine confusion in his eyes. What was she meant to say?

'I'm so sorry. I wanted to tell you, I really did, but Peter threatened me, told me to stay quiet, said he would go to the police and tell them I killed ...' She stuttered to a pause. 'Your father, and make sure I went to jail and never saw Riley again if I spoke a word of it.'

'Peter knew?'

'Yes.'

He shook his head in a daze. 'How?'

'He opened my mail and saw the results of the DNA test.'

'How long ago was this?'

She was terrified of answering but had to. 'At Riley's eighth birthday party.'

Zane looked as if she'd just king hit him in the chest. He shook his head and turned away from her. And then he paced, his expression hardening with each and every weighty step.

'Zane?' Nervous, she chewed her fingernail.

Steely silence met her. All the dreams she'd carefully stored away in her heart were tossed to the wayside. It was so stupid of her to think this was something they might have been able to work through. There'd be no going back from here. Not ever.

'Zane, please say something, anything. Yell at me if you have to.' She took a few hesitant steps towards him. He didn't answer. Just stopped pacing and stood there, silently, staring right through her, his fists clenched at his sides. A muscle in his jaw ticked. His breath was heavy, strained. His handsome face looked as if it were carved from stone, the rage growing in his stormy eyes.

'I've wanted to tell you the truth, so many times, but was terrified of you reacting like this.' She blinked, trying desperately not to let the tears fall.

'Please, just leave.' His words burnt, scorched her already bleeding heart to a crisp.

'Can't we at least talk about this?'

'No,' he boomed. He pointed to the door. 'Please, leave, now.'

The tears she'd done so well keeping at bay slipped and fell down her cheeks. Wrapping her arms around her waist, she turned away from him – wishing he would forgive her, comfort her. Anything but this.

'And, Em …'

She stopped, hopeful.

'Don't tell Riley.'

Nodding, she turned and kept walking, leaving her heart and soul behind, where it belonged, with Zane.

CHAPTER

23

Four weeks later

Zane's mobile buzzed from the dash. Grabbing it, he noted the caller ID before drawing in a deep calming breath. 'Hey, Emma.' It had been the most he'd said to her since the day she'd told him about Riley.

'Hey, yourself.' She cleared her throat. 'I just wanted to congratulate you on your win at court yesterday.'

'Yeah, thanks, it was Kay's will and the recovery of the gun from Peter's office that did it.' His stubborn ego rearing its ugly head, he reminded himself of what Emma had also done to help make it all happen – not that it changed a thing as far as they were concerned. 'Cheers for your affidavit and for taking the stand to back it up.'

'Of course, it's the least I could do. I'm so relieved to know there was nothing in the safe to incriminate me, despite what

Peter had said in his letter. Not that there could have been, but we both know he could do almost anything.'

He silently agreed with her. 'How's Riley coping with it all?'

'Yeah, okay, I suppose. In a way it's helped her to see the man Peter was, and she's come to understand why he and I never saw eye to eye.'

Indicating, he turned towards home. 'Well, that's a good thing.'

'Uh-huh,' Emma said.

Silence fell and then hung.

'Anyway, I'm driving, so I better get off the phone.' Not that it had ever bothered him before, but he needed an out; everything between them was still too raw.

'Yup, okay, but before you go …'

'Yeah?' Oh god he ached to tell her that he loved her, and that he forgave her – but he wasn't ready yet and wasn't sure he ever would be.

'We can't leave everything like this, Zane.' Her tone toughened. 'Regardless of how angry you are with me, and how much you want to pretend I don't exist, Riley deserves to know you're her father. Just remember, she's innocent in all of this.' She sighed. 'I just really hope you want to be a part of her life.'

Zane huffed, disappointed with himself. Emma was right – their grievances had nothing to do with Riley. He was acting like a damn child by wallowing in his anger and disappointment. 'Of course I want her in my life, and I want to be in hers.' And he meant it, from the depths of his heart.

'You do?'

'Yes, of course I do. I love her, and I'm proud as punch I'm her father.' He wanted to tell Emma he was going to get around to doing the right thing – he just needed some time to let it all sink in, but bit his tongue.

'That's so great.' She breathed a sigh of relief. 'I was thinking, if you agreed, that maybe we could camp out for a night and tell her then, away from everything else.'

'If that's what you think is best.'

'I think it's one of the better ways to break it to her, out where she's most at peace, yes.'

'Okay then, when?' He knew he was being short but couldn't help it.

'Tomorrow night, if you're free. We can leave here mid-afternoon.'

'Okay, I'll be over at your place sometime after midday.'

'Great, thanks, Zane.'

'Riley's my daughter, so don't mention it.' It felt strange, saying it out loud, but he liked the sound of it – very much.

'Bye.'

'Catch you tomorrow.'

Tossing the mobile onto the dash, his stomach backflipped as he turned down the familiar dirt road. Not only because they would soon be telling Riley he was her father, but also because this was it, he was going home, and this time it would be for good. Permanency was a foreign feeling for him, and he wasn't sure how it settled within his travelling soul. But he wouldn't want it any other way – especially having Riley as his neighbour now.

Pleased to be free of the stuffy hotel room he'd been living out of for the past four weeks, he pulled his LandCruiser to a stop at the gate of Wattle Acres and then regarded the urn safely belted up against the passenger seat. It had been a fairly easy process to have his biological mother's ashes released from the neighbouring township's crematorium. At Zane's request, the judge who had heard his case ordered Alison Yate's remains to be passed over to him with a crash of his gavel. Just as Kay's ashes were there, as was her spirit, he'd spread Alison's in the same place in Wattle Acres. This was where they belonged. The woman who had carried him and the woman who had raised him. Martin Turner's remains, which had been recovered from the makeshift grave in the Silvergum National Park, could stay where they were now, in a simple plot at the local cemetery. One day, Zane might be ready to visit him.

With shaky hands he pressed the remote to open the gates and rubbed his sweaty hands over his jean-clad thighs. He imagined the sign he was having made for his bull-riding rodeo school hanging above them – and he welled with pride as the flash new gates swung open in wide arcs. He'd decided this level of security was necessary, given how heated Michael was outside of the courthouse. He'd yelled out to anyone who'd listen that he would make Zane pay.

Let him try …

Rattling over a cattle grid, he shifted through the gears, accelerating as he headed up the long, winding dirt drive. As he cleared the top of the rise, he saw the picturesque acreage sprawled out before him, and the magnificent old homestead. He cut the engine, the pounding of his heart growing stronger as he tried to get his head around the fact that all of this was now legally his. It had been a bittersweet victory – having to hear all the sordid details of his father's death while bearing witness to the black-and-white photos of his shallow grave and skeletal remains. The solicitor he'd hired from the big smoke of Sydney had fought hard, but fair, in the courtroom. Michael hadn't had a chance in hell of winning, no matter who he was rubbing shoulders with. The evidence had been overwhelming.

As much as some thought it should, it didn't give Zane an ounce of satisfaction to see Michael stripped of his right to be a lawyer. There was nothing to be gained from being revengeful. And although he never wished to speak to him again, he was relieved Michael wasn't charged as an accessory to a murder Peter had so callously committed, the judge ruling that he, Michael and Emma were young and impressionable at the time. He said they had been brainwashed into believing they had to do what Peter told them to do or pay the price. The judge made it clear that, in his opinion, Peter Wolfe was the devil himself.

Retrieving his bag from the back seat, and the urn from the front, he made his way over to the front door. Slipping the key into the new locks he'd had put in, he smiled as he stepped inside. All Peter's personal belongings long gone, it was a clean slate for him to start a new life. One he had decided he wanted to share with Riley. No matter how much he still loved Emma, he just didn't know if he could ever get past her keeping something so life-altering from him. He wasn't sure if he could ever look at Emma in the same way again. Tomorrow would be the first time they'd been in each other's company, outside of the courtroom, since the morning after making such beautiful, soul-deep love. It would be interesting to see how it all unfolded.

* * *

As the sun sank below the distant mountaintops, a sudden chill filled the night air. The three of them were sitting on a log Zane had dragged into the camp, enjoying the welcoming warmth of the campfire and the sight of the heavens filled with seemingly endless stars. They ate their camp stew in grateful silence, plates precariously balanced on their knees.

Cutting three more pieces of damper, Emma gave one to Riley and then offered Zane a piece. 'Would you like another, to mop up all the yummy juices?'

'Does a bear shit in the woods?'

Riley gave him a slap and laughed through her mouthful of food. 'Uncle Zane, that's gross.'

'Nah, it's not, Riles, it's nature,' he teased.

Emma flashed him a look of sympathy when Riley called him 'uncle'. He smiled back and shrugged gently. Not long now and that would all change. He was just waiting for Emma's first move to break the news to their daughter. The thought both excited and terrified him, for Riley's sake. Thinking about this, he mopped up the stew on his plate, shoved the damper in his mouth, and stood up. Suddenly feeling nervous as all hell, he needed to move. Collecting Emma and Riley's plates, he headed over to the bowl of sudsy water and washed them up, along with the empty cast-iron pot. Placing another log on the dwindling fire, he watched the sparks dance and twirl into the night sky, the glow of it lightening up Riley's pretty face. The blue eyes, the wavy hair, and the way she smiled as she talked to Emma – how could he have not seen the similarities there before?

Stretching her arms in the air, Riley yawned. 'I think I'm going to hit the sack.'

Emma looked to her watch. 'It's only seven-thirty, that's a record for you, love.' She threw Zane a subtle sideways glance.

'Yeah, I know it's super early, but all this fresh air makes a girl tired, I tell ya.'

'Yeah, it does, huh.' Emma gave her a tight hug. 'Night, love, sleep well.'

'Night, Mum.' She padded over to Zane and gave him a hug too. 'Night, Uncle Zane, sleep tight and don't let the bed bugs bite.'

'I'll try not to.' Zane kissed her on the forehead. 'Night, sweetheart.'

With the fear of a snake crawling into her bed, Riley had set up her swag on the back of Zane's LandCruiser. She climbed up and settled in, her soft snores announcing she was fast asleep only minutes later.

'Far out, she really *was* tired,' Zane said with a chuckle.

Emma held her hands up to the fire, twisting them back and forth as she warmed them. 'She's right, though, being out under a blanket of stars does make you feel sleepy.' She yawned. 'It's catching.'

Zane turned to her, his heart reaching for hers. 'I reckon I might hit the sack too, then.'

'Actually, me too.' Emma padded over to her swag.

Stretched out in his swag, gazing up at the Southern Cross and the sweep of the Milky Way, Zane released a pent-up breath. 'We have to tell her soon.'

'I know. Let her have a good night's sleep and we'll tell her first thing in the morning.'

'Promise.'

'You have my word.' She glanced over at him, and the same familiar blaze of heat shot through him. He was never going to be able to get away from what she did to him, and so innocently too.

'Okay, night,' he mumbled, turning so his back was to her.

'Night, Zane,' she whispered.

* * *

Up before first light, Zane boiled the billy over the glow of the campfire just as the sun began its ascent into a pink-hued sky. Stirring and then climbing from her swag, Emma joined him. It was not long after that Riley came over too, a huge smile on her face as she looked to where the new day was breaking in a jaw-dropping sunrise.

'Wow, what a glorious sleep,' she said, raising her hands up high and stretching up on her tippy toes.

'That's good, love.' Emma's voice shook. She patted the log beside her. 'Come, sit. We have something we need to tell you.'

Riley's smile all but disappeared as she walked towards her mum. 'This sounds serious.' She looked to Zane for answers, but with his heart in his throat he remained tight-lipped. She sat, her expression one of deep concern. 'What is it?'

Emma took Riley by the hands and held them tight. Zane shifted from boot to boot, not knowing where to stand or what he should be doing. Taking a deep breath, as if drawing strength from the untainted land around them, he watched Emma and slowly released it.

'Riley, there's no easy way to tell you this.'

'Oh my god, Mum, are you sick? Have you got cancer?'

'No, nothing like that.' She looked to Zane, and then back to Riley. 'Years ago, Zane and I went on a date.'

'You did?' Although her eyes were as wide as saucers, Riley was smirking now.

'Yes, and one thing led to another, and well, Riley, Zane is your father.'

Tearing her hands from Emma's, Riley stood and stepped back. 'What did you just say?'

Zane took a few hesitant steps towards her. 'I'm your dad, Riley.'

She laughed and shoved her hands in her pockets. 'You're kidding, right?'

Emma and Zane both shook their heads.

Her hands moving to cover her gaping mouth, Riley kept shaking her head. She stepped back further, away from them, her eyes filling with tears. Turning, she ran for where she'd tethered Boomerang to the LandCruiser. Tugging herself up, she jumped on bareback and then cued Boomerang into action.

'Riley, please wait,' Emma called after her.

But like a bullet fired, she was gone, Boomerang's thudding hooves disappearing into the thick scrub.

'We have to go after her.' Emma's face was as pale as a ghost.

Hating to see Riley so distraught, Zane wanted nothing more than to comfort her, but he also understood her need to run and get some headspace. That was what he always did when something was too hard to face straight away. 'Do you think that's wise?' He sighed. 'Maybe we should give her time to let it sink in, before we go chasing after her?'

Emma raked a hand through her hair. 'Maybe.'

The silence that fell between them was broken by a single, high-pitched scream.

Fear exploded in Zane's chest. He shook some sense into himself, and racing forwards, began following the hoof tracks. With no other horses, and the track too narrow for his LandCruiser, he'd have to look for her on foot. His boots slipped on wet leaves, and he caught Emma as she stumbled over fallen branches beside him. Blinded by her tears, she struggled down the slippery slope, holding tightly to his hand, her whispers to God, begging for Riley to be okay, tearing his heart to pieces. Thundering hooves approached and Boomerang galloped towards them. Wooing the gelding up and then soothing him, Zane hoisted himself onto his back. Holding out his hand, he then helped Emma up.

He tapped her leg. 'You right to go, Em?'

'Yes, go, please, and hurry.'

Zane enticed Boomerang onwards, his eyes switching from the hoof marks to the thick scrub he was trying to weave through. It seemed to be taking forever, but cresting the ridge, he spotted Riley, lying alongside a huge fallen tree trunk. Although they were still a distance away, he could see she wasn't moving and his heart almost exploded in fear.

'Oh my god, Riley.' Emma's cry was almost primal, her pain unfathomable.

Horrified but refusing to show it, so he remained a pillar of support for Emma, Zane quickly directed Boomerang over to Riley.

Coming to a halt, Zane saw that her face was pale and filled with pain.

'I'm okay, I think I've just broken my leg.' Her brave words contrasted with the tremor in her voice.

Zane felt himself slump and breathe out, as if he'd been holding it for a lifetime. Not a religious man, he still thanked God for answering Emma's prayers.

'Oh, Riley, sweetheart …' Emma cried, as she quickly slid off the horse and crouched at Riley's side.

Zane followed her, overwhelmed with relief as he knelt alongside their daughter. Adrenaline and terror lingered in his body like a bad aftertaste, and he watched Emma lean over and gently pull Riley into her arms, and then weep from the depths of her heart. He didn't want to disturb them, but from the way Riley's leg looked, he knew they had to get her to the hospital as quickly as they could. He knew all too well, with an injury like that, once the shock wore off, immense pain was going to kick in. He wanted his beautiful daughter to have relief from it sooner rather than later.

He gently touched Emma's back, and she let go and sat up, although her hand remained clasped around Riley's. 'I'm going to have to carry you to the LandCruiser, Riley,' he said, brushing hair from her dirt-smudged cheek.

Biting her lip, Riley nodded. 'Okay.'

Very carefully, he scooped her into his arms and cradled her against his chest as he rose.

Riley's pain-filled eyes falling upon his, she wrapped her arms around his neck and then tucked her face into his shoulder. 'It hurts so much.'

'I know, sweetheart. I'm so sorry.' He choked back his emotions – they weren't going to do him any favours.

'I'm the one that should be sorry,' Riley whispered through her tears.

'Why?'

'For running off.' She smiled ever so softly now, her lips trembling. 'And just so you know, I've wished so many times for you to be my dad, and I'm glad it's come true.' She winced and cried out, halting the huge smile she'd just enticed from his heart.

'Shh, rest now. We can talk about it later.' As if he were on the back of a bucking bull, tension rode him hard. He hated knowing it was basically because of Emma and him that Riley was now in pain, both physically and emotionally. He silently vowed he'd do everything in his power to make things right, and to give her the life she so deserved. It was over his dead body he would ever let her suffer again the way she had at the hands of a man who was meant to be her father.

* * *

After dropping Emma and Riley off from the hospital, it was almost midnight when Zane arrived home to Wattle Acres, and yet, as bone-tired as he was, he couldn't fathom sleeping. He was relieved Riley was on the mend, albeit very sore. But all he could think of while he paced the back lawn in his bare feet was how close he'd come to losing her, and just how much he still loved Emma. He longed to tell her so. But should he open that can of worms again? Groaning, he shook his head and looked up at the glimmering country night sky, silently asking for answers. A shooting star zoomed across the velvet black, and if that wasn't a sign, he didn't know what would be.

Oh, for god's sake, who was he kidding? He loved Emma – with every single fibre of his being. He'd kill for her. Die for her. Swim the oceans to be with her. So how could he even consider living right next door and go on pretending to be just friends for the rest of his days? He needed her, all of her. Otherwise, he would die a very lonely man, because he was never going to love another like he loved his little firecracker. No woman would ever come close to what he felt for the beautiful Emma Kensington.

Racing to his four-wheel drive, he revved it to life. Fishtailing down the driveway he found himself at Emma's front door within minutes. Trying it, he was relieved to find it unlocked. He swiftly took the stairs two at a time, his heart in his throat. She met him at her bedroom door, her robe tucked in tight. Bravery filled him as soon as he laid eyes on her. Reaching for her, his fingers tightened around hers.

'You okay?' she said softly; her gaze didn't waver.

'I needed to see you, so I could tell you face to face just how much I love you, Em.' He wiped the tears from her cheeks as she pressed her face into his hand.

'You do?'

He nodded. 'I do.'

'I love you, too, with all my heart and soul.' She relaxed into his arms, her tears soaking through his shirt. He breathed in the scent of her hair, of her. She smelt like passionfruit and sunshine and felt so soft and warm and womanly.

'I thought I'd lost you forever,' she murmured.

He cuddled her in tighter. 'That wasn't ever going to be a possibility.'

'So we're going to get through this?'

'I'll make sure we do.' And he would – nothing and nobody would come between them again.

As she pulled back, he held her cheek against his palm. 'You look exhausted. I really should let you get some rest.'

'No, please, stay with me tonight.' It was straight from her heart; the pull of her hands as she grabbed hold of his shirt was desperate. She dragged him towards the bed and fell back, bringing him with her. 'Make love to me, Zane, please. I need you, all of you.'

'God, you're beautiful, Em.' His heartbeat steadied, as if calmed just by being near her. She was so strong, yet so fragile. Cupping his hand around the nape of her neck, their lips met, clashing in a hot, open-mouthed kiss.

Caught between the desire to comfort her, to protect her, and the desire to make slow, sweet love to her, he wrapped his arms around her, pulling her to his chest. Up until now, wanting her had been a sweet, yet heavy ache. But now it was an intense demand, as if she were his oxygen beneath a deep, infinite sea. Holding her gaze with his, he untied her robe and slipped it from her shoulders, and then, as she watched, undressed himself. Pressing her back onto the bed, he lay atop her, drinking her in as he slowly slid inside her. Her fingernails tracing down his back, she arched her hips into him, her purr of satisfaction music to his ears. And then, he played with her, taking her to the edge and pulling back just in time to make her gasp for breath, for her nails to dig into his back a little harder. Never had he felt like this, not even with her. They'd finally made it to the other side, where nothing stood between them. And it felt even more mind-blowing than he'd ever imagined. She was his world, his life, his reason for living.

EPILOGUE

Twelve months later

Early morning sunshine peeked into the bedroom, sending a soft orange glow across the floorboards. Untangling her arms and legs from Zane's, while being careful not to wake him, Emma slipped out of the tousled bed. She glided across the rug and into the ensuite. Before closing the door, she took one last look at him. Wedged against a pillow, one arm above his head, and the doona in a bundle at his feet – he truly was a sight to behold. With chiselled abs, tattoos and so very well endowed to boot, he was a man worthy of very naughty dreams – dreams that were now her daily reality. Her heart swelled. The bliss of their connection went far beyond the realms of lovemaking – they were old souls, re-joined from one lifetime to the next, she was sure of it.

Each and every time they made love, it felt as if a thousand stars were exploding within her soul. How lucky was she to call him her boyfriend? Slipping into the shower, she turned on the taps, making sure the water was nice and hot before stepping under the stream. She lathered up; the soap's sandalwood scent was both alluring and relaxing. Tipping her head back, she could feel the warm water lengthen her wavy hair to her waist.

Her eyes closed and her thoughts far away, she jumped when strong hands slid around her. Resting her head back, she melted into him, loving the feel of his naked body pressed up against her own. So electric was his touch, that even after a year together, she still went weak at the knees. Turning to face him, he kissed her so softly, so gently, she felt her heart trail away with his lips. He caught her moans with his mouth before sliding down to his knees, his lips coming to meet with her sweetness. She clutched his hair and gasped his name as he skilfully brought her to the brink within minutes, and then tipped her over it, trembling and quivering.

Smiling wickedly, he stood, his hands tangling her wet hair. He captured her gaze with his, his look intensifying and stealing her breath.

A delicate smile curled her lips. 'What is it?'

Reaching up, he plucked a red velvet box from the top of the shower door and, making sure to keep it out of the stream of water, got down on one knee and opened it, revealing a glittering diamond ring.

Her mouth fell open and her hands moved towards it as happy tears stung her eyes.

Zane's baby-blues intensified. 'Emma Kensington, exactly a year ago today, we finally committed to one another, and now, I want to take that a step further. Will you marry me?'

'Oh my god, yes, yes, yes!' She wriggled on the spot, careful not to slip over.

'I gather that's a yes,' he said cheekily.

She shot her hand out and he slipped the ring on, the tremble of his fingers endearing. 'Riley's going to be over the moon.'

'She is, I asked for her permission first.' Grinning from ear to ear, he stood. 'And she was so excited she almost bowled me over with a massive hug.'

'You did, aw, Zane, that's so sweet of you.' She threw her arms around his neck, leapt up and coiled her legs around his waist and feathered kisses all over his lips and cheeks. 'I love you so much.'

'Love you, too, with all I've got.' He met her teary eyes. 'It might have taken us almost half our lives, but we got there, Em.'

'We sure did, my sexy fiancé.' She beamed from the heart.

'Your fiancé, huh, I really like the sound of that.' Zane held her tight as he chuckled, deep and husky. 'And "husband" is going to sound even better.'

ACKNOWLEDGEMENTS

A humungous thank you to each and every one of my incredible team working behind the scenes at Harlequin Headquarters – my fabulous publisher Rachael Donovan, the leader of my cheer squad, for believing in me and always pushing me to dig deeper so I can reach my full potential, my skilful and persistently diligent editors…Bernadette Foley, who I couldn't imagine not having by my side throughout the gruelling process, and Julia Knapman, a shining star throughout the process, my assiduous proofreader, Annabel Adair, the design magicians who've once again produced an extremely captivating cover, and the rest of the inspiring and supportive team who've helped make *Secrets of Silvergum* the very best it can be. I thank my lucky stars to continually be a part of the wonderfully supportive Harlequin family. You all truly are the best!

To my amazing soul lover, best friend, confidant, the best coffee maker in the world, my beautiful and extremely hot husband, Billy. Just when I thought I'd never find the true, deep, respectful love I was yearning for, you sauntered into my life and knocked me right off my feet – ready to catch me, and take me to heights I'd never been to before. To watch you move mountains to be with me and Chloe, packing up your life in California to be here, by our sides, means the absolute world. You're so strong, so kind, so thoughtful, so faithful, so intensely passionate, and I adore how you're happy to wield the vacuum and mop – SO DARN SEXY! The love you shower Chloe and me with, each and every day, so unconditionally, is one I will treasure for the rest of my life. I'm a very proud wife to walk by your side and sometimes hold on for dear life as you take me on some wild voyage! Here's to the many adventures we are yet to have, and to all the days we get to live out our lives, loving one another the way we do! I love you so much baby, always and forever, with all my heart and soul. Xx

To my incredible, gentle, kind-hearted daughter, Chloe Rose. You, my gorgeous girl, are the greatest accomplishment in my life. Just by being the beautiful soul you are, you brighten my every day, and I love how not a day goes by that you don't make a point of telling me how much you love me, how great my cooking is, and how much of a rocking mum I am. You fill me with so much joy, so much pride – you are going to do great things in your life, sweetheart. I just know it. I love watching as you evolve and grow. I will always be beside you, supporting you, loving you, cheering you on. Thank you for everything you do, and all that you make me feel, so simply and so very unconditionally. I love you bazillions, my darling Rose, always and forever. Xx

To my magnificent mum, Gaye, thank you for always being here for me and for Chloe – and just for the record, you're an awesome Nanna too! You're so kind, and so thoughtful, always willing to help out however you can, regardless of how busy or tired you are. Over the past 18 months, our world has been shaken, but we stand strong, together – I know it's been extremely tough on you, and you have stepped up to the plate, pushed through the fear, and the unknown, and have faced leukaemia head on. I'm always amazed by your strength, and treasure how you've taught me to always be true to myself, and to stand proud, as both a mother and a daughter – and now, a wife. Thank you for being my best friend, and for loving me the way you do. I love you, Mum, to the moon and back, and beyond. Xx

To my wise dad, John, you sit back quietly and watch my life floating along, praising me, loving me, guiding me, always allowing me to choose my path, always making sure I know you are there, whenever I need you. I love sitting and chatting with you, about all there is in life – you have a way that calms me, that gives me deep inner strength. Thank you for being a great dad, and a loving grandad. I love you very much. Xx

To my stepdad, Trevor – thank you for always being the positive voice in my ear over the years. No matter what, you've always got a good spin on a situation, and I adore that about you. The optimism you've instilled in me has helped me through so much, and makes me strive to be the very best I can be. Love you lots!

To my awesome sisters, Mia, Karla, and Rochelle – you all touch my life in so many different ways. I feel super blessed to have you all in my and Chloe's life. Love you three heaps! Xx

To my beautiful Soul Sister, and my amazing cheerleader, Fiona Stanford. Our bond was instant, and you have been beside me the entire way, encouraging me, supporting me, caring for me in the amazingly kind-hearted way that you do. I feel very blessed having you in my life. Love you. Xx

To my gorgeous German buddy, inside and out, Katharina (Katie) – I adore how we stay best mates all the way across the oceans. Can you believe it's been 12 years since we first met on the farm! Wow, time flies hey. Love ya cowgirl! Xx

To my darling friend, Rachael Sharaz. Well, what can I say about a human as unique as you – you're a shining light, a beautiful spirit, a person with so much to give those around you, a woman who inspires me to laugh and love with all my heart and soul. I feel extremely blessed to have crossed paths with you. Friends forever, we will be. Love ya! Xx

And lastly, but most essentially of all, a massive, heartfelt cheers to YOU, the reader! I can't thank you enough for grabbing my book and making time to dive into the pages. You give life to my hero and heroine as you tumble into their world and travel through the story with them. I wouldn't be able to do what I do without you. I hope *Secrets of Silvergum* has given you a chance to escape from everyday responsibilities, if only for a little while – to hell with the messy house, the unwashed dishes, the unkempt hair, and the pyjamas you might still be wearing well into the afternoon (maybe refrain from getting out of the car if still in said PJs when you collect the whippersnappers from school – don't want to embarrass the little cherubs!). Never, ever feel guilty for taking time out – in this hectic day and age, we all deserve to put the brakes on and indulge in a little me time. And what better way than with my book! ;) You rock!

Until my next dashing hero sweeps you off your feet, keep smiling and dreaming…life is beautiful.

Mandy xoxo

Are you a huge Mandy Magro fan?

You could win a signed Mandy Magro book pack valued at $300, plus a bottle of wine.

To enter, go to romance.com.au/contest/ mandymagrocompetition/

*Terms and Conditions apply
Competition ends 31 August 2019*

BESTSELLING AUSTRALIAN AUTHOR

MANDY
MAGRO

Novels to take you to the country...

Available in ebook

mira